CYCLORAMA

CYCLORAMA

A NOVEL

ADAM LANGER

BLOOMSBURY PUBLISHING

NEW YORK · LONDON · OXFORD · NEW DELHI · SYDNEY

BLOOMSBURY PUBLISHING
Bloomsbury Publishing Inc.
1385 Broadway, New York, NY 10018, USA

BLOOMSBURY, BLOOMSBURY PUBLISHING, and the Diana logo are
trademarks of Bloomsbury Publishing Plc

First published in the United States 2022

LIBRARY OF CONGRESS CATALOGING-IN-PUBLICATION DATA IS AVAILABLE

ISBN: HB: 978-1-63557-806-5; EBOOK: 978-1-63557-807-2

2 4 6 8 10 9 7 5 3 1

Typeset by Westchester Publishing Services
Printed and bound in the U.S.A.

To find out more about our authors and books visit www.bloomsbury.com and sign up
for our newsletters.

Bloomsbury books may be purchased for business or promotional use. For information
on bulk purchases please contact Macmillan Corporate and Premium Sales Department at
specialmarkets@macmillan.com.

For Beate, Nora, and Solveig
And in memory of my brother, Bradley Garth Langer

CAST OF CHARACTERS

(In Order of Appearance)

Peter Van Daan....FRANKLIN LIGHT/FRANK LICHTENSTEIN

Mr. Dussel.....TYRUS DENSMORE/WILLIAM NICHOLSON

Miep Gies...............................EILEEN MULDOON

Mrs. Frank...............................JUDITH NAGORSKY

Mr. Frank...............................ROBERT RUBICOFF

Mr. Van Daan.........TREY NEWSON, DECLAN SPENGLER

Anne Frank.........CARRIE HOLLINGER, KITTY WEEKES

Mr. Kraler.......................CALVIN BUMBRY DAWES

Mrs. Van Daan...............................FIONA GRENFALL

Margo Frank................AMANDA WEHNER/ASYA LOH

FEATURING

Sammy Doulos, Adam Baldwin, Matt Dillon, Nicol Williamson, Rabbi Jeremy Horvath, Izzy and Beileh Lichtenstein, Ted Lichtenstein, Mary Muldoon, Willa Mae, Mrs. Eustacia Winslow, Coach Pootie Hollings, Estelle Nagorsky, Sanford and Beverly Pinker, the Weird Sisters, Ray Tounslee Jr., Mr. and Mrs. Newson, Will, Keith, and "Fuckin' Stuart" Newson, Kristy, Micki Lanza, Ricky Tate, Mr. and Mrs. Hollinger, Christopher Plummer, James Earl Jones, Todd Merritt, Lloyd Crowder, Da and Mutti Grenfall, Chick Tarshis, Tim Donovan, Mrs. Hargrove, Patricia Roebling, John Falstaff, Old John of Gaunt, Violet Dinh, Lourdes, Hazel and Winnie Nagorsky, Adrian Weekes, Danny Cirillo, Inez, Eleonora Acevedo, Professor Laurence Loh, and Agent Eugene Roche, U.S. Customs.

Direction, Set Design, and Additional Dialogue
by Tyrus Densmore

Stage Management, Props, and Photography: Eileen Muldoon

Lighting and Sound Design: Sammy Doulos

ACT I: 1982

Setting: In and around Chicago and its northern suburbs; New York, NY; Amsterdam.

ACT II: 2016–17

Setting: In and around Chicago and its northern suburbs; New York, NY; Boulder, CO; Washington, D.C.; New Glasgow, Nova Scotia, Canada.

ACT I

Spring 1982

We don't need the Nazis to destroy us; we're destroying ourselves.

—OTTO FRANK, THE DIARY OF ANNE FRANK

Peter Van Daan

For Declan Spengler, everything that wound up happening—to himself, to all of them, to the whole crazy country if you stopped to think about it—started the day he auditioned for the role of Peter Van Daan. It wasn't even supposed to be an audition as much as a formality—one of those annoying motions you had to go through in order to ensure that what was destined to happen would actually wind up happening.

Some things were foregone conclusions. The Cubs would not make the playoffs this year no matter how loudly Declan cheered for them; Burt Lancaster would not win an Oscar for *Atlantic City* no matter how much Declan thought he deserved it; Declan's parents would never get back together no matter how much he might have wanted them to. But a foregone conclusion didn't have to be a tragic one; after all, Declan himself, once he went on the New York theater trip with Ty Densmore, graduated from high school in June, then four years later finished Northwestern with a BA in theater—yes, Declan Spengler—would marry Carrie Hollinger, just as sure as he would be there onstage playing Peter opposite Carrie's Anne Frank.

First, though, if he wanted all that to happen, he had to audition.

The grayish afternoon light was fading behind the nubbly stairwell windows, and the mutters and laughs of nervous auditioning actors grew louder as Declan once again climbed the cracked green lino-leum steps to the Theater Annex of North Shore Magnet High School.

Located in central Evanston and bordered by low-slung factories and warehouses on one side and tidy single-family homes on another, North Shore Magnet, much like Declan himself, was in an in-between sort of place, seemingly on its way to someplace better. Not quite Evanston Township, the massive, sprawling cityscape of a high school one mile away—not quite the moneyed, cosseted enclaves of New Trier or any of the private schools along Green Bay or Sheridan Road—North Shore was equidistant from who Declan was and who he was planning to become. To the southwest was the tiny A-frame that Declan shared with his mom in Lincolnwood, just outside Chicago. Due north was the elegant Tudor home where Carrie lived in Wilmette with her family.

For Declan, though, the Annex had always seemed to be a world apart from all that. On every other floor of North Shore at the end of the day, hallways were cramped and bustling: students gossiping by their lockers; kids in backpacks racing out the door to the bus stop or the Foster Street el, water polo players with hair wet from the showers and pool rushing past clumps of burnouts sauntering to the smoking area for one last cigarette; hotheaded boys squaring off as bloodthirsty crowds chanted "Fight! Fight! Fight!" But up here was only the solitude and safety of a bright, spacious aerie with a pair of classrooms, Ty Densmore's office, and the theater itself.

Declan opened the Annex door. The hallway was pungent with stale smoke, perfume, and Aqua Net hairspray. His outfit was simple: white oxford, new jeans, loafers—not trying too hard, not presuming too much. Not like those freshmen and sophomores who had dressed to audition: dozens of Peter Van Daans in pressed white shirts, ties, knit pants, scuffed black shoes, and newsboy caps; dozens of Anne Franks in plain white blouses, tweed skirts, tights, and dark red lipstick. Franks and Van Daans were doing breathing exercises; Franks and Van Daans were running lines; Franks and Van Daans were practicing European accents.

Declan used to know everyone here, but today, nearly half were strangers. Some skinny, Jewish-looking kid was wearing a medium-blue bike racer's cap with smears of bicycle grease on his yellow MINKY'S BIKE SHOP shirt and faded, saggy jeans. A leggy blonde-haired girl in a white peasant blouse was underlining passages in a book covered in green MARSHALL FIELD'S wrapping paper. Amanda Wehner, hands in the pockets of her red sateen GUARDIAN ANGELS jacket, was sitting between the legs of Rob Rubicoff, who was chuckling over a copy of *Penthouse* he had filched from Tyrus Densmore's desk. Judith Nagorsky—there in her thrift shop scarves and skirts—was doing the splits as she studied her script, pausing only to give the finger to Trey Newson, who informed her that doing the splits was easy, but he bet she couldn't spin around on a dick the way his girlfriend "Kathy Ho-HO-Ho" could, while Eileen Muldoon, who had served as stage manager and company photographer for every play and musical since she had been at North Shore but had never gotten cast in one, laughed so hard that her face turned nearly as red as the ribbed Christmas-gift sweater she was wearing. "You're so sick," Eileen told Trey.

All 275 pounds of Calvin Bumbry Dawes, Afro included, were here too—Calvin paced the hallway, busting jokes about how "a brother such as myself" could never be cast in this play. He slapped Declan five, then attempted an accent that he thought sounded South African and told Declan he would give such a stellar audition that Ty Densmore would have to move the play from Amsterdam to Johannesburg and rename the whole damn thing *The Diary of Aisha Katanga.*

"Splendid idea, mate." Declan smiled broadly, trying to conceal his irritation with the play Mr. Densmore had chosen. *The Diary of Anne Frank* would be Declan's last show at North Shore, and it was a grim play, the story of ten doomed people whose refuge turned out to be their prison. Spring plays were supposed to be comedies or musicals, and if Densmore didn't want to direct one of those, couldn't he at least have chosen something with showier roles instead of this somber ensemble piece about the Holocaust?

Three or four years ago, no one said a word about the Holocaust, but ever since that NBC miniseries that everyone was supposed to watch, it seemed impossible for Declan to escape it. Every time he picked up a magazine, some Nazi war criminal was on the cover; every time he watched the news, there was a story about John Demjanjuk, the alleged "Ivan the Terrible"; the last school assembly he'd attended was about Holocaust awareness; the only field trip he'd taken this year was to the Skokie Library to meet elderly men and women with numbers tattooed on their arms. "Never forget," they all told him. "Never forget." Declan knew this was an awful thing to think and he would never in a million years have said it to Carrie or her family, but he sort of thought the whole point of the Annex was that it should be a place where you could forget about things like the Holocaust.

The door to the audition room opened. The Annex's technical director, Sammy Doulos, now in his fifth year at the high school, walked out in an EMERSON, LAKE & PALMER concert jersey, faded green DARTMOUTH sweatpants, and black shower clogs. He reeked of pot smoke. Sammy flung his hair out of his eyes, then looked down at his clipboard. "Declan Spengler," he said.

Declan nodded gravely. "Thanks, Sam." He could hear the sounds of the hallway fade into silence; his name carried that sort of weight here.

He adjusted the strap of his shoulder bag and strode forward, confident yet gracious and humble—the same way he would handle fame when it came to him. Just a couple of years earlier, he had waited all night down in Chicago at Lake View High School to get cast as an extra in *My Bodyguard*. The most instructive part of the experience hadn't taken place when the camera was rolling; it happened in the downtime when he got to watch how professional actors behaved. Adam Baldwin had been standoffish and rude, but Matt Dillon was totally cool; he even gave Declan useful fashion tips—told him to pop the collars of his polo shirts and grow his hair longer and part it in the middle instead of on the side so he could "get more chicks." Declan liked the idea of dispensing advice like that.

He entered the audition room, and the door shut behind him. So many memories in this room. So much sadness; so much raging glory. The first time Declan had come here, he was still reeling from the worst night of his life. The Sunday before Declan's *Our Town* audition, his father had asked him to carry two suitcases down the driveway to the Mustang—only after Mr. Spengler handed over his house keys had Declan realized his dad was leaving his mom for good. But on that Monday, after Declan read for the part of George, and Ty Densmore squeezed his shoulder and told him he brought "that special vulnerable quality" Ty had been looking for, Declan understood that if he hadn't spent the previous night crying, he wouldn't have nailed his audition. Now he could barely remember the gangly, awkward kid he'd been before Densmore turned him into a star.

As Declan walked to the center of the room, he could imagine his entire high school career converging in this moment: the smell of foundation makeup; the harsh sensation of eyeliner pressed right under your lid; the mounted TV on which Densmore showed videos of Nicol Williamson performing Shakespeare; the window where they watched every other student and teacher leave while they stayed past midnight to get a scene right; the way Densmore would break you down, then build you back up again and tell you exactly what he was doing: "I am breaking you down, Dec, but I will build you back up."

Densmore was sitting behind his desk in his usual black turtleneck and a gray scarf, tall black boots hiked up on the desk. His bald pate gleamed in the glow of the overhead fluorescents. He had a notepad in his lap and he was sucking on the end of a ballpoint pen.

Declan put his bag down on a chair and took his place in front of the desk.

"A bittersweet moment," Densmore said. "Your last audition for me. And the last role you'll play here. Now, tell me which you'd choose."

"I'll be playing Peter," said Declan.

"Who?"

"Peter Van Daan."

Mr. Densmore's face seemed to droop. He stroked his goatee with his pen. "*Peter?* Really?" he asked. "Think for a moment; think very carefully. Peter isn't that much of a role, Dec. He won't showcase your ability to command a stage. He's just such a bland boy: he stutters when Anne flirts with him; he blushes around her. Let's be honest, when it comes down to it, Peter is just an irritating, stuttering, nattering little pussy."

"Not the way I'll play him," Declan said. "And when I'm at Northwestern, I won't get to play lead roles right away; I'll have to get used to being part of an ensemble. Peter will be good practice."

What Declan didn't mention was that he felt certain Densmore would cast Carrie as Anne Frank, and he couldn't stand the idea of any other actor playing her boyfriend. The idea haunted him so much—Trey Newson dancing with Carrie; Rob Rubicoff stealing a kiss from her; Calvin Dawes smothering her—that he had to take the role himself.

"Well, let's see this 'Peter' of yours," Densmore said.

Declan turned his back, closed his eyes, took a deep breath, then spun around and gave Sammy a tight little nod. He was ready.

Densmore read a short introduction to the scene: "*The stage is dark. A cyclorama of Amsterdam at night fades into view. Peter is with Anne in his room. And lights up!*"

Sammy began the dialogue, reading Anne's lines flatly: "I wanna be a journalist or somethin'. I love to write. What do you wanna do?"

Declan peered meekly through imaginary glasses and spoke in a halting middle European accent—not a thick one, just a lilt as he felt himself becoming Peter. "I thought I might go off some*pless*," he said, "*verk* on a farm or *somesing* . . . some job *zhat* doesn't *tekk* much *brenns*."

Densmore kept his face blank, giving away nothing. He never did. And as Declan kept reading, he secretly thanked Densmore for that lack of consideration, for it made him try harder. He could feel Peter's loneliness, his fear of getting too close to Anne, of dying in the war, of becoming a man. His tears flowed as Sammy read Anne's line: "Everyone has friends."

"Not me. I don't *vant enny*." Declan wiped his eyes. "I get along all right *vissout zhem*."

Boom—right on the money. Now Declan's only fear was that he would have no idea how, over the course of the rehearsal process, to delve further into this character. But somehow he would find new depths. It was like when he used to spend his weekend afternoons avoiding his parents' fights by playing *Asteroids* at the Novelty Golf Arcade: just when he thought he couldn't go any further, he'd unlock another realm, just as now, when he read the final line in his scene, he discovered a meaning he hadn't registered before.

"Nine o'clock," Sammy read. "I hafta go. G'night."

"You won't let *zhem* stop you from *comink*?" Declan asked.

Over the dozens of times he had read this line, to himself or when he had Carrie practice it with him, "You won't let them stop you from coming?" had seemed like a simple question: Would Anne come to see him even if her parents told her she couldn't? But there was so much more to it. The question was not just about whether Mr. and Mrs. Frank would allow their daughter to spend time with him; it was about the Nazis outside. Could they be stopped? It was about the world forces that would intervene in their just-blossoming love affair: Could they be stopped? It was about the indefatigability of love and the human spirit.

Declan could feel Carrie near him—could feel himself asking her to assure him that, no, she wouldn't let anyone stop her from coming. Not the Nazis and not Carrie's parents, who always eyed Declan with weary, condescending skepticism, as if their daughter's love for him was something she'd outgrow.

Declan said the final line one more time to give it its full meaning and emphasis. His breaths halted, his voice quavered. "*You won't let them stop you from coming?*"

He dropped his hands to his sides. He took a breath, closed his eyes, then opened them again. Densmore was staring right at him; a smile formed on one side of the man's mouth.

"Well," Densmore said, "*I* won't let them stop you from *cumming*; the question is whether Carrie will."

Sammy erupted in rude laughter—"*Eeh eeh, eeh*"—then mimed masturbating and made sound effects: "*Pfft, pfft, pfft.*"

Densmore winked, then reached across his desk and swatted Declan's ass with his clipboard. "Nice job as per usual, Dec," he said. Declan picked up his bag, lifted the strap over his shoulder, and headed out of the room as Sammy shuffled out to call in the next actor: "Franklin Light." The skinny kid with the bicycle grease on his shirt and jeans walked past Declan and into the audition room.

*

The following day, Declan tried not to be too eager about heading up to the Annex to check the cast list. He had planned to wait until school was over, but something struck him as odd about the way people were talking to him—or, rather, not talking to him. With the exception of *Our Town*, when he had been the only freshman in the show and hadn't known anybody in the Annex, every time he'd been cast, he had learned his role without actually bothering to check the list. Somebody would call him up the night before or he would overhear someone talking in the cafeteria; the afternoon before cast assignments were posted for *Death of a Salesman*, he had passed Mr. Densmore in the hallway, and Densmore, without breaking stride or even making eye contact, had simply mouthed the words "*Loman*. Biff *Loman*."

By now someone from the *North Shore Herald* office should have congratulated him, since the school paper listed casting announcements in its "All Over the Arts" section. At lunch, Calvin was sitting at their usual table with his back to the door and so didn't notice when Declan walked in, then stepped right back out and hightailed it to the Annex.

The classrooms were empty. The door to Densmore's office was shut. The theater door was open; the smell of Sammy Doulos's weed—which seemed to have a half-life equivalent to that of uranium—lingered as always, but there was nothing to see inside save for the empty seats and lighting booth and the sawdust on the stage. Maybe Densmore hadn't posted the list yet.

But no, there it was, tacked to the corkboard in the hallway: a sheet of white paper with THE DIARY OF ANNE FRANK typed at the top; beneath the title, a list of roles and actors playing them.

Declan stopped dead.

He stared at the sheet, trying to keep it in focus. He closed his eyes and reopened them to make sure he hadn't hallucinated. But no matter how many times he reread the list, it did not change. Carrie was Anne Frank; he'd been right about that. But just below her, next to the place where the name Peter Van Daan had been typed, there was a name Declan was fairly certain he had neither seen nor heard before: FRANKLIN LIGHT. Declan had to look all the way to the end of the list to find his own name: DECLAN SPENGLER—MR. DUSSEL.

Mr. Dussel?

No, not the role Declan had chosen and Tyrus had promised. No, not even one of the parent roles that would have given him more lines. No, Mr. Fucking Dussel—the dickish dentist who shared a room with Anne and plotted to oust Peter's cat from the Franks' and Van Daans' hideout.

Declan knocked on Densmore's office door and, when no one answered, tried to open it. Locked. *Mr. Dussel?* What the hell was that supposed to be? Some power game? Payback for some slight? Was Ty pissed at him? Should Declan have laughed when Tyrus made his juvenile *"cumming"* joke? Had he made a mistake by declaring he would play Peter? Should he have said he wanted to play Dussel so Densmore would have cast him in the role he wanted instead?

Declan stood in the Annex hall engaging in two simultaneous mental conversations. In one, he silently accepted the role of Dussel, pretending that nothing was wrong; in the other, he punched Densmore in the solar plexus and told him to take his Mr. Dussel role and shove it up his ass, all the while trying to blink away horrifying visions of Carrie kissing "Franklin Light"—who, in his imagination, looked like Richard Beymer, who had been too old, too white, and too gay for the role of Tony when he played it in the movie of *West Side Story*.

Declan was halfway down the stairs when he heard footsteps and someone whistling. He peered over the railing. Densmore, in a camel hair overcoat, maroon scarf, and black fedora, was mounting the steps carrying a bag of take-out lunch. Declan made as if to run back up and find a place to hide. He stopped himself. *Play it cool, boy*, he thought. *Real cool.*

"How're you doin', Ty?" he asked when he passed Densmore on the landing.

"Very well, Herr Dussel." Densmore smiled provocatively, and clicked his heels together. But Declan would not succumb. You had to seem unaffected, like when you were acting opposite someone who fucked up their lines or made up their own. Even if you felt like grabbing them by the shoulders, shaking them, and screaming, "Can't you just read what's on the page, Rob, you lazy, arrogant piece of shit?" you had to act as if nothing had happened. Or like when your mom's boyfriend was sleeping over and he pissed in the toilet without flushing and left his stubble in the bathroom sink. Even if you wanted to scream at the cuckolding bastard to get out of your house, you smiled, flushed the toilet, cleaned the sink, and moved on. So when Declan kept smiling and uttered an offhanded "See you at four today, Ty," moving on was exactly what he was trying to do.

Densmore furrowed his brow. "Why?" he asked. "What're you doing at four?"

"That's the first cast meeting," said Declan.

"*Riiight.*" Densmore drew the word out. "But that meeting's only for actors playing the Franks and Van Daans; I won't need minor characters and supporting players 'til next week."

It was as if Densmore had found a switch inside of Declan and flipped it. "Minor characters?" he muttered to himself. "Supporting players?" His eyes burned. And instead of all the clever ripostes he would later scold himself for not having thought of, the best he could muster was a weak, whimpering "What did I ever do to you? What do you have against me?"

Densmore cocked his head. "What do you mean, 'what do I have against you'? I actually love you, Declan. But part of loving somebody is doing what's right for them, not what they want you to do for them."

"You specifically said any role I chose."

Densmore began shaking his head before Declan even finished his sentence. "No, no, no, no," he said. "I asked what role you *wanted* to play, but that didn't mean I would cast you in it. Don't be a child. What if you said you wanted to play Anne? Would I have let you play her with falsies and panties in drag? Yes, I wanted to cast you in some role—a parting gift for such a talented actor—but no more than that."

"Well," Declan said, "If I'm so talented, why won't you let me play the role I want?"

Anger flared up in Densmore's eyes. "It's for the good of the show." He grabbed a fistful of Declan's shirt and pulled him close. Declan could smell the coffee on his breath. "I don't know what you think I do here, Declan, but every decision I make is for the good of the show. Get your head out of your ass and think about it: the whole tragedy of Anne's relationship with Peter is about *fucking*." Densmore loved to use the word *fucking*, stared down students and actors whenever he said it, accented it in classroom discussions—how George and Martha in *Who's Afraid of Virginia Woolf?* hadn't fucked in years, and that's why she thought all men were "flops"; how Lady Macbeth's line about "screwing your courage to the sticking place" was all about fucking; how the rain that Starbuck brought at the end of *The Rainmaker* was not rain at all but the ability to fuck Lizzie and "make her cum."

"Think," Densmore said. "In the show, Peter and Anne are in love and want nothing more than to fuck each other's brains out. But they never will because they'll never get to be alone. If I cast those roles with two actors who are already fucking each other, *poof!* There goes your entire tragedy."

Every time Densmore said "fuck," it was as if he were thrusting a blade in Declan's gut, mocking his virginity. "Do you know what?" Declan said, "I don't need this. I have half a mind to quit, and if I do, I won't be the only one."

Declan followed Densmore to the corkboard. "Are you saying you want your name off my list?" Densmore asked.

"Yeah, take it off," said Declan.

Densmore took a pen and struck a line through Declan's name.

"And while you're at it," Declan said, "you can cross Carrie's name off too."

"That would be a shame," Densmore said.

"It will be for you," said Declan. "And I don't give a damn about going with you on your sacred 'New York trip' either, so don't even ask. Find some other peon. When I'm on Broadway, you can buy a ticket and see me there."

Declan hustled down the stairs. He burst onto the first floor just as the tone sounded for sixth period, then stormed through the halls with a determination he hadn't felt since he'd fallen to his knees playing Tony in *West Side Story*, shouting, "Chino! Chino! Come get me too, Chino!"

Declan slalomed through hordes of students dashing for the stairs, shoving each other in front of the boys' bathroom, pleading their cases with teachers and hall monitors: "I didn't push the kid; I just jostled the motherfucker." He scanned the hallways, looking for Carrie's lemon-yellow sweater, her blue jeans, her red bandana. He stood by her locker, vainly waiting for her to appear.

Come get me too, he thought. *Carrie, come get me too.*

When Declan finally caught up to Carrie, last period was over, and she was walking toward the stairs, backpack over both shoulders. He surprised her with a whispered "*Boo!*" and a kiss intended for her cheek that got her earlobe instead. She smiled at him and he took both her hands.

"Where're you going?" he asked.

"The Annex," she said.

Declan adopted an air of befuddlement. "Why would you do that?"

"The cast meeting."

"Yes," Declan said, "I know the cast meeting is now, but why are you going?" He led her through a set of double doors and into a less populated hallway, where he explained the whole Peter Van Daan–Mr. Dussel bait and switch. But Carrie, who had plans to become a pediatrician and no patience for drama department drama, seemed unimpressed. "Why can't you just play Mr. Dussel so we can be in the show together?" she asked.

"But I told him you'd be quitting too," Declan said.

"Why'd you tell him that?"

"Aren't you?"

"Why would I?"

"Solidarity."

Carrie regarded Declan with a pitying expression, one he associated with the way she looked at her family's old dog, Marlene Dietrich, when she had to be carried into the backyard. Carrie said she couldn't drop out; her parents had promised that, if she got cast, they would take her to Amsterdam for spring break so she could see where Anne Frank had lived. She said she knew Declan was angry now, but they would have a great time together. "Besides," she said, "even if I'm supposed to kiss whatever guy's playing Peter, I'll keep my lips closed the whole time."

Declan smiled. Something about Carrie—maybe her innate good-ness, maybe her love for him, maybe the fact that she never seemed to obsess about slights—always calmed him. Okay, he thought, okay, he would play Mr. Dussel after all. "But if I do it," he said with a sly smile, "I'll make sure you eat herring and onions before every rehearsal with a kissing scene."

He draped an arm over Carrie's shoulder. He liked the feeling of having her under his weight, liked walking through these halls as part of a couple. How many times had he watched other couples—making out in the smoking area, holding hands in the cafeteria, pawing each other at YMCA dances—and wondered if he would ever be part of one? He had picked Carrie out of the *West Side Story* chorus and asked if she wanted to join him and some of the rest of the cast at Yesterday's for burgers and cheddar-broccoli soup. The only comparable feeling to hearing her say yes was taking a bow and listening to the audience cheer as they rose to their feet. And later that night when he kissed her before they said goodbye in front of the Tinkertoy factory, he felt as if people were crying "Encore! Encore!" How he loved being in love, and the only thing he regretted was that so few people could understand how he felt. His parents knew nothing of love—his slut of a mother, his drunk loser of a father. He couldn't talk to his friends about love; they just made fun of him or asked about sex or pretended to be happy but were secretly jealous because they had never experienced a love like his. No one understood his love other than musicians, playwrights, poets. Shakespeare understood; so did Leonard Bernstein, and even Frances Goodrich and Albert Hackett when they wrote the attic scene with Anne and Peter that Carrie would perform after she had consumed the herring and onions he'd have her eat beforehand.

Upstairs in the Annex, Declan wasn't sure where to have the conver-sation with Tyrus to say he would consent to play Mr. Dussel. But Densmore was already ceremoniously tacking a new cast list to the cork-board. The list was exactly the same as the previous one with a single exception. Now the actor listed as Mr. Dussel was not Declan; it was Tyrus Densmore.

Declan stood there dazed, unable to speak or keep anything in focus—not Densmore smiling at him, not Carrie calling him, telling him to wait, not Trey asking, "Hey, what's going on, Dec? You all right?"

Declan silently made his way down the stairs. Tyrus Densmore was playing Mr. Dussel and Declan would be playing nobody. *Never forget*, he thought. Yes, here was something else he would never forget.

Mr. Dussel

All right—good work, ladies and gentlemen. Tomorrow we schedule costume fittings and start work on your character diaries. Remember, the more detailed and the more personal, the better grade you'll get. Dazzle me, shock me, titillate me; please do anything but bore me—depending, of course, on how you're using the term *bore*."

The first full-cast read-through was over, and as the cast members of *Anne Frank* exited the classroom, Tyrus Densmore kept his head down, pretending to focus on the sketch of the set he was drawing while he listened to his actors. Amanda Wehner asked if anyone had an extra lighter; no one did. Calvin Dawes asked if anyone wanted to grab some chow at Yesterday's; no one did. Trey Newson, still claiming to have a girlfriend at New Trier named Kathy Ho, said he would head home to "put his ding-dong in his Ho-Ho!" then made twanging "*daou-duh-nuh-daou-daou*" porn movie soundtrack sound effects; Eileen Muldoon said that was so sick; Carrie Hollinger said sorry, Cal, but she had to study for Biology; Rob Rubicoff said that Declan was the one who needed to "bone up on his biology"; Trey sang "*Daou-duh-nuh-daou-daou*"; Eileen said that was so perverted; Rob said he would be taking Amanda to the Parkway to catch a double bill of *Wattstax* and *Monterey Pop*, and hopefully the sound wouldn't be as shitty as it had been the last time; Judith Nagorsky said she would finish her homework at the library, cook dinner for her mother, then sit in the back row of the Skokie Theater and "finger herself" while watching Mariel Hemingway in *Personal Best*; Calvin said he would do the exact same thing but with a fist, not a finger; Trey sang "*Daou-duh-nuh-daou-daou*"; Eileen said that was so gross; all the while Fiona Grenfall pushed PLAY on her Walkman and bopped to the music she was playing, ignoring the lot of them.

Tyrus listened until the voices disappeared behind the doors of the Annex stairwell. Already, alliances were being formed; soon love affairs would blossom and wilt, lifelong friendships would begin or be dashed, all because of Tyrus Densmore.

If you had told Tyrus that casting Franklin Light instead of Declan in the role of Peter Van Daan would wind up changing the lives of every actor in the show, including himself, he would have been amused but hardly surprised. He understood the power he wielded in the Annex, for it was inversely proportional to the power he had over his own life. In the Annex he felt omnipotent, could create or destroy an actor's reputation and self-esteem based on whom he did or didn't cast in a show, on whom he did or didn't take on his annual trip to New York.

It wasn't even necessarily something he did on purpose. He hadn't planned to cast Franklin instead of Declan as Peter, and he certainly hadn't intended to play Mr. Dussel himself. He had only made those decisions in a fit of pique. But now, looking back, his choices made sense. In *Anne Frank*, dire circumstances made even the most good-hearted people suspicious of each other—made them fight over resources, despise the ones they loved. So, for this play to work, he had to create an atmosphere rife with tension and distrust.

However, the moment Tyrus began to descend from the climes of his domain, he could feel power and authority seeping out of him—as if he had just exited the stage, and it was time for him to stop playing a role. He loved the way actors scrambled for his attention and approval like suitors vying for his hand, and he hated how ephemeral their adoration was. After they graduated, they cast him aside like some spurned lover. What did they leave him with after he had changed their lives?

Memories, some framed photographs in the Annex hallway, the occasional letter or Christmas card, and a gnawing feeling of perpetual heartbreak and betrayal. Did a single one of them ever realize all that he had done for them?

Entering the high school's faculty lot, then getting behind the furry steering wheel of his cream-colored Cadillac DeVille (vanity plates: DRCTR 1), he could feel himself once again becoming the man he was outside the Annex: the surly, peevish husband of a society maven, the father of a barely communicative patient at the Chicago-Read Mental Health Center, a supporting player in a bathetic drama that he would have walked out of at intermission, a sad, bitter character—washed up at forty-three.

Driving to the clinic always depressed Tyrus. And the fact that Tom Densmore was sullen, hostile, or utterly blank on the days his dad showed up made Tyrus feel even worse. Whenever he went to visit, he would seek out any sort of distraction on his way, hoping that by the time he arrived the receptionist would tell him, "Sorry, Mr. Densmore, visiting hours are over."

Tyrus was driving along California Avenue through the north side of Chicago. He had just passed Devon Avenue and was sitting behind a slow-moving CTA bus, wondering whether he could find a traffic jam that would delay his arrival at Chicago-Read even further, when he noticed the bus disgorging a familiar-looking passenger lugging a battered yellow bicycle. The kid wore a denim jacket, grimy sneakers, and jeans, and carried a frayed, overstuffed navy-blue backpack that made him hunch over a bit as he loped past Tel Aviv Kosher Pizza and then the Ner Tamid synagogue. Tyrus drove slowly, letting other cars pass as he kept the kid in sight just ahead of him. Then, when he got to Granville Avenue, he sped up, parked his car in the A&P supermarket lot, got out, and walked back the other way until he came face-to-face with the kid.

"Well, hello there, Mr. Light," said Tyrus.

Franklin looked up. "Mr. Densmore," he said.

"You're a bit far afield, aren't you?"

Franklin gave him a look as if to say he didn't understand.

"Don't you live near the high school?" Tyrus asked. "That's what you wrote on your form."

Franklin forced a laugh. "Oh. Yes. Right."

"Whatever bringeth you here?"

"Oh, my dad's parents, Izzy and Beileh, they live around here." Franklin spoke fast. "My dad, he thought he could get them to move to a retirement home, but, man, they're some pretty stubborn coots. So when dad's working late, I come over—you know, take out their trash, do their laundry, fix them some grub, make sure they take their pills, that kinda whatnot."

"Well, isn't that noble of you," Tyrus said.

"Yeah, I guess," said Franklin. "But they're pretty cool cats, Izzy and Beileh, and they have tons of cool stuff at their place. It's like a museum over there—seventy-eight records, old letters in Yiddish. And they tell some pretty fascinating stories too."

"What's so fascinating?"

"Pretty much everything, I guess."

Tyrus opened his eyes wider as if to say, *Tell me more.*

"Well, like the other day I kept asking my grand M about where she grew up, and so she told me about this little village—somewhere in Bessarabia, she said she didn't remember the name. She used to skate on the frozen river and watch baptisms; these Russian Orthodox priests, they would carve crosses in the river, reach in, sprinkle icy water on the babies. It sounds like it's from an Isaac Bashevis Singer short story, except it's actually true."

Franklin looked at his watch. "Whoa," he said, "I'm kinda late. I hope my grand Ps will be okay with just spaghetti and salad. I guess I'll see you at rehearsal tomorrow, Mr. D."

"Why, yes," Tyrus said. "Until then."

The kid skittered past a schoolyard, then turned into an alley. Tyrus got back in his car and followed the path Franklin had taken, but once he got to the alley, he saw no sign of Franklin. Tyrus coasted past garages and fenced-in backyards with dirty and dusty, upturned toys in them. He squinted into lighted back windows and watched Orthodox Jewish families gathering at dining room tables. No Franklin to be seen there either.

Tyrus felt a little like a Peeping Tom and a little like a hired killer as he drove from one alley to the next, observing the lives of people who had no idea he was watching. He relished the image. Save for a handful of aggressive stage-combat performances in college and some Thanksgiving football games where his in-laws criticized him for getting too physical, he couldn't recall having ever actually turned violent. But he liked when others feared he might. He liked the idea that, one day, he might break out of his role and commit some vicious crime and no one would suspect him. Sometimes, on nights when he was out of wine or the wine wasn't helping, he would put himself to sleep imagining crimes he might commit: assassinating Ronald Reagan, holding up a bank, or planting a bomb, then waiting for the police to come, though they never would. He was a beloved teacher with no motive and a respected wife. Who would ever think he was a criminal?

If anyone ever hauled him before a court and forced him to make a confession, he'd blame his crimes on his strict Methodist upbringing in Kansas or the brutal treatment he received at the hands of his fellow soldiers in Korea. He could a tale unfold of marrying for wealth and respectability instead of love, of putting all his aspirations into a son who wouldn't achieve a single one of them, of teaching ungrateful students at a high school where every play he directed felt like an act of unrequited love. But all that would be, at best, half true. When he acted during his younger years, he was cast as leading men, but he always envied the actors who got to play the villain.

Tyrus proceeded south slowly, replaying the conversation he had had with Franklin. Something was off about the kid's story; something in it was a lie—the speech too fast, the details superfluous. Franklin's eyes had shifted as he spoke, as if Tyrus had caught him at something. When Tyrus had first started teaching at North Shore, the school had enrolled riffraff from just about anywhere, but now that its progressive approach had become popular and it admitted kids only from the northern suburbs, the administration had started cracking down on Chicago kids using fake addresses to get in; parents were getting fined thousands of dollars; one had even gone to prison. Tyrus didn't care much about the rules, but he sensed that, if Franklin was attending North Shore illegally, that sort of information could prove useful.

He parked his car across the street from the Hild Library and went straight to the reference section. First he checked the phone books, then the Criss Cross Directories, and confirmed what he had suspected: no Izzy or Beileh Light lived on any of the streets in the neighborhood where he had seen Franklin; and, further, at the address that Franklin had listed on his audition sheet, no one was named Light at all.

*

The next evening after rehearsal, Tyrus followed Franklin as he walked west on Simpson Street. Once again the kid was walking in the opposite direction of where he supposedly lived. Tyrus lowered his passenger-side window and tooted the horn. "Young Mr. Van Daan!" he called.

Franklin shook his head slightly, as if trying to get water out of his ear. "Oh, hey, man—I didn't see you. How's it goin'?"

"No bike today?" Tyrus asked.

"It's busted," said Franklin. "Haven't had a chance to fix it."

"I'll give you a lift."

"Nah, thanks, but you don't need to trouble yourself."

"No trouble at all. Might you be visiting your grandparents again, the venerable Izzy and Beileh Light? Or are you heading home?"

"Just headin' home." Franklin got into the car and told Tyrus his address.

"But that wasn't the way you were walking," Tyrus said.

Franklin was dumbstruck for a moment or two. "Yeah, that's a little bit weird," he said. "Sometimes I get so focused on ideas for things I wanna write, I wind up just going places by instinct. I guess I'm so used to taking the bus to visit my grand Ps, sometimes I find myself there even when I should be somewhere else."

The boy and the teacher talked a while. Tyrus asked if Franklin had prior theater experience; Franklin was vague. He said he'd spent time in "various places" and had performed in "you know, various plays and things." Tyrus wouldn't have heard of any of them, he said; they were school productions, and it had all happened a while ago.

"Hey," said Franklin. "You can just drop me off at the corner. I can walk from here."

Tyrus stopped his car in front of a church. "You're hiding out in the rectory, perchance?" he asked.

Franklin forced a laugh. "No, not here exactly—across the street."

Tyrus nodded, though the building Franklin pointed to seemed nearly as unlikely a location. A nondescript, tan brick mid-rise with a FOR RENT: STUDIOS AND 1-BEDROOM APARTMENTS sign out front, it looked like a cross between a retirement home and a dormitory.

"Home sweet home," Tyrus said.

"Not all that sweet. Long story." Franklin got out of the car. "Hey, thanks for the ride."

"Oh, one quick thing, Van Daan," Tyrus said.

"Yep?"

"We'll be needing to set up that costume fitting for you, sir."

"Sure, no problem, whenever."

"I like doing my fittings in one-on-one sessions. Sometimes actors, particularly young actors, can feel self-conscious when they're being fitted in front of the others."

"Whatever works for you."

"Would you be available, say, Saturday morning, maybe about ten?"

"Yeah, I can do that."

"Good, good. Then let's meet at my house." Tyrus took a scrap of paper from his glove compartment and wrote his address on it. "Will your father or grandparents be driving you?"

"My bike should probably be okay by then," Franklin said.

"Even better. Oh, and remember—you start writing in that character diary," Tyrus called after Franklin. "You seem to keep a lot to yourself, and I'll be looking forward to seeing what you say after you've opened up a bit."

Tyrus drove off but didn't go far. He circled the block, then parked behind another car so he could get a good view of Franklin's building.

He watched Franklin lurk for the better part of a minute until someone opened the front door. Franklin made a show of fumbling with keys, then slipped inside. Clearly the kid didn't actually live here.

*

On Saturday morning, Tyrus was alone. His wife, Susan, had already left with her parents to visit Tom at Chicago-Read, and Tyrus, as was his habit, chose not to join. He loathed spending time at that place and loathed spending time there with his in-laws even more. They never seemed to regard Tom's problems as real, viewed the mania and depression that ran on Tyrus's side of the family as minor complaints that harsh, sensible discipline could cure. They would ask Tom questions like "So, when're you gettin' outta this joint?"; they'd look sourly at the other patients on his hall and tell him he wasn't "like them"; in the cafeteria, they would turn away when he was eating, and when he had one of his fits and the techs came to calm him down, Mr. Chesbro would say it was nothing a belt or a two-by-four couldn't cure. And so, if Tyrus didn't want to do something he would regret or have to pretend to regret—like, say, grabbing both Stanley and Jean Chesbro and throwing them out the window of Tom's room—it was better for Susan to go with them on her own.

Tyrus had finished his second glass of white wine and was relaxing in his study with the Tempo section of the *Tribune* when the doorbell rang. He folded his newspaper and walked in his black socks across the carpet that he and his wife had purchased when they were in Turkey—the last trip they had taken with their son. Franklin was at the door wearing a hooded red AMUNDSEN HIGH SCHOOL sweatshirt and jeans.

"Ahh, young Mr. Van Daan," Tyrus said. "The bike's looking much improved."

Franklin was a little out of breath from the ride. "Can I put it somewhere?" he asked. "I didn't bring a lock."

"Outside is fine. This isn't Chicago where things get stolen. Shoes off, though."

Franklin took off his shoes, then his sweatshirt, draping it on the back of an armchair. Tyrus demonstratively picked up the sweatshirt, removed two bits of lint—one from the chair, one from the carpet—and hung it up in the front hall closet. "Care for something to drink? Water? Juice? Soda? Wine?"

"Wine?" Franklin asked.

"When my wife's parents are in town, I like to start my drinking early."

"Not really thirsty, thanks. How long do you think the fitting will take?"

"Oh, not long, but let's chat a bit first." Tyrus went to the kitchen, opened the refrigerator, pulled out his half-finished bottle of Chardonnay, filled his glass, and fetched another from a cabinet. Frost was on the kitchen window, sparrows had gathered at the bird feeder outside, and there was a light dusting of snow on the driveway. Tyrus sipped his wine, then proffered the second glass to Franklin and raised an eyebrow. Franklin shook his head. Tyrus sighed, put the wine bottle back in the fridge, and led the way into his den, a dimly lit, carpeted room with a big console television, couches, and armchairs. Against one wall was a shelf full of student writing journals hand-labeled with the names of their authors. On another shelf were rows of alphabetized videocassettes, also hand-labeled, of shows, plays, and films taped from television: episodes of *Masterpiece Theatre*, *Mystery!*, and *American Playhouse*, classic movies from the 1940s and '50s. On the walls were framed pen-and-ink sketches of set and costume designs, all signed T. DENSMORE.

Tyrus sat in an armchair, crossed one leg over the other, stretched his arms wide, and, with a broad smile, asked Franklin, "So, why are you attending our hallowed high school illegally?"

Franklin's face paled. He blinked rapidly and stammered like—well, like Peter Van Daan when Anne Frank asked if he had ever been kissed.

Tyrus laughed. "Don't fret. I would never dream of betraying a confidence. But why the charade and the stories? What's so special about our high school that makes you have to lie?"

Franklin looked from side to side but said nothing.

"Come, come, I'm hardly the Gestapo, and I despise snitches of any sort. You needn't tell me anything. Still, how draining an experience it must be to concoct stories, to be forced to decide whom you can and cannot trust."

"Yeah, I dunno," said Franklin. "Are we doing this fitting?"

"Presently." Tyrus left the room, then returned carrying a wicker basket with his sewing supplies. Franklin had been looking at the journals on the shelves, but upon Tyrus's entrance he turned to the videocassettes.

"Finding some favorites?" Tyrus asked.

"I've heard of a lot of them but I haven't seen as many as I'd like," Franklin said.

"Too much time spent taking care of poor Isidore and Beileh?" asked Tyrus.

"Actually, that story isn't made up," Franklin said. "Those are my grand Ps. And I do spend a ton of time with them—chores, cooking, watching movies, all that whatnot. They don't really like watching movies from after 1939, though; that's why I haven't seen a lot of these movies you have."

"Well, those are the best sorts of lies," said Tyrus. "The ones where truths are presented 'in the clever guise of illusion.'" He paused. "That's from *Glass Menagerie*."

"Never seen it either, sorry."

Tyrus smiled grimly. "Blasphemy. Perhaps I can show it to you sometime. I named my son after the narrator of that play; he's a few years older than you. He has some problems but he's getting better—at least, that's what we like to tell ourselves."

Tyrus pulled out a tape measure, a pencil, and a notepad. He measured Franklin's neck, his arms, and his chest, then frowned. He gestured at the untucked flannel shirt Franklin was wearing. "Can you take that damned thing off? It's hard to get proper measurements when actors wear baggy clothes. I should have told you that before."

Franklin unbuttoned the shirt, took it off, and draped it over Tyrus's ottoman.

Tyrus snatched the shirt, folded it, and put it back down.

Franklin stood before Tyrus in his gym socks, beltless blue jeans, and a white T-shirt with a faded yellow Woodstock from the *Peanuts* comics on it. His arms were pale but strong and wiry.

Tyrus remeasured Franklin's chest, then his waist; he crossed out the previous numbers and wrote in new ones. Then he knelt down in front of Franklin. "Well, I seem to be at perfect blowing height, don't I?" he said.

"What?"

Tyrus laughed. "Once you get to know me better, you'll understand my sense of humor." He held the top of the tape measure at Franklin's crotch, then stopped and frowned again. "Do you always wear such baggy trousers?"

"Yeah, my dad and I share clothes a lot and we don't pay much attention to sizes." The more nervous Franklin got, the faster he spoke. "If pants are too long, I just cuff them; if they're too wide, I wear a belt; it's not really a problem."

"Not a problem for fashion, perhaps, but a problem for accurate measurement. Can you take off the pants?"

Franklin made a face. "Is that necessary?" he asked, at which point Tyrus flushed angrily. "Exactly how long do you want this to take?" he asked. "Do you want to make my job even more difficult? I'm already teaching four classes as well as directing a show—something I don't get paid extra for, by the way. I have to design a set and costumes for a cast of ten. Do you think I've never seen a kid in his underwear before? Jesus fucking Christ."

Franklin took off his jeans.

Tyrus took a swig of wine and studied Franklin's legs. Now that Declan was out of the show, Tyrus wondered if Franklin might join him on his New York trip. He normally took upperclassmen, but he could make an exception. He liked taking complicated kids, ones with secrets they trusted he would keep. He introduced them to a new world, made them aware of possibilities they would never have dreamed of, and what he took in return was comparatively trivial. "Do you play sports?" he asked.

"Biking, that's pretty much it. Not a lot of time to do anything else."

A layer of gooseflesh had risen up on Franklin's legs. He would grow up to be a strong, handsome man, and Tyrus hated him a little for that. "Too much time doing chores for poor Isidore and Beileh?" he asked.

Franklin tilted his head one way, then the other. "Those do take up some time."

"Well, then," Tyrus said as he marked down another number, "might you explain why, if Isidore and Beileh Light are so very needy, does no one by that name live on any of the streets where I saw you the other evening? Why does no one by the name Isidore or Beileh Light live anywhere in Chicago or its near north suburbs?"

"Because their last name isn't Light," Franklin said.

Tyrus raised an eyebrow.

"Their name is Lichtenstein. And the truth, if you really want to know—and I hope you don't tell anybody, but whatever; I guess I can't really control that—is that they live with me and my dad in Chicago. Maybe you've heard of my dad? Ted Lichtenstein?"

"The reporter?" Tyrus asked.

"For the *Tribune*, yeah. When my mom was still around, the three of us, we lived over in Budlong Woods—better neighborhood, bigger house, whatever. But after she died—car accident, long story—my pop couldn't keep house and take care of a kid. So we moved in with his folks: Izzy and Beileh. That was pretty much a mess. Every other family on our block worked for the police or fire department, and you can imagine what they thought of my dad's articles. It got pretty gruesome: crank calls, graffiti; they messed with our car. My dad changed my name to Light and got an unlisted number, but that didn't do anything; everybody already knew who we were. My first year at the high school, Amundsen, I could deal with some of the shit—people shoving me, writing 'Lightstein' or 'Lightberg' on my locker, all that kinda whatnot. The really bad part was the messages people left on our phone machine. My dad was used to it and, after a while, I could deal. But my grand M didn't deserve all that abuse, especially after what happened to her during the war."

"Where was she in the war?" Tyrus asked.

"Sobibor," said Franklin. "Anyway, that's why we moved again. And that's why my dad wanted to get me into North Shore. A cousin of ours lives at the place you dropped me off at; we're using his address."

As he knelt on his den carpet, tape measure in hand, sizing up the crotch of Franklin Light, Tyrus remained silent, weighing his next move. Instinctively, he understood that what Franklin was saying was essentially true, just as what he had said during their chance encounter on the north side of Chicago had been essentially false. And although he had gotten to this point more quickly than he had expected, he knew that testing Franklin any further would be foolish. Years of experience had taught him to follow certain unwritten rules: he didn't mess with kids with supportive, happily married parents; he didn't mess with children of lawyers or cops. Now he had another rule to add to his list: he didn't mess with sons of investigative reporters, particularly if their parents had survived the Nazi death camps. Inviting Franklin on the New York trip was now definitely off the table.

The doorbell rang twice. There was a scratching and rattling against the window. Tyrus hurriedly wrote down a final measurement. "Go put your pants back on, Frank," he said.

Tyrus walked to the front door, opened it, and looked out. No one was there. He left the door open a crack, walked back into his house, glimpsed Franklin sitting on the ottoman, putting on his clothes. Tyrus closed the door to the den. He put on a pair of slippers, and walked around the side of the house by the den window. No one was there either, but a car was driving away fast.

Miep Gies

Eileen Muldoon, driving her parents' Chrysler station wagon full of *Anne Frank* props, blew through a stoplight on Green Bay Road as she sped away from Tyrus Densmore's house, trying her best to make sense of what she had just seen. She had rung Tyrus's doorbell; no one had answered. Which was odd, since Tyrus's Cadillac was in the driveway and a bike was propped up against the house. She had gone around to the side, peered through the den windows, and seen— well, what?

Tyrus had seemed to be kneeling, his face close—like, super close—to the waist of a boy wearing white underwear, and not much more than that. The kid didn't look older than fourteen or fifteen; growing up around brothers, she had a lot of familiarity with boys' bodies, though not the bodies she wanted to be familiar with. But before she could see what was actually going on, Tyrus had turned toward the window, and Eileen had run back to her car and jammed on the gas.

Had she actually seen what she thought she'd seen? She'd heard the rumors about "Ty-Ty"; she knew what people said happened on his New York trips. Still, she liked him too much to believe any of that was true. Could her filthy mind have once again misinterpreted something totally innocent?

Lately, to Eileen, sex seemed to be everywhere, so much so that she couldn't help but think that she must have been imagining things. Sex seemed to be in everything being discussed—and in everything not being discussed. It was in the totally gross but pretty hilarious porn mags that Ty-Ty kept around his office. It was in every episode of *Three's Company* and *Bosom Buddies* she watched while she was doing her homework. Sex. Even when she didn't expect it, there it was—in the stories she had to read for English class. It was in the rhythmic motion of "The Rocking Horse Winner," in the dried-up cucumber vines in *Ethan Frome*. It was in every song she couldn't believe they played on WLS and the Loop; it was in that Pointer Sisters song about needing "a man with a slow hand," and it was in "Miracles" by Jefferson Starship, which, one time at breakfast, had her singing, "I had a taste of the real world when I went down on you," until she realized what the lyrics meant, and blushed so much that her mother thought she had a fever.

Halfway home, Eileen resolved to put the whole scene out of her mind, since she could probably never really know what had been going on in Ty-Ty's den. She figured she would wait an hour, drive back, show Ty-Ty the props she had collected, pretend nothing had happened. But then she realized she had something she rarely ever had: an interesting story to tell people. Every rehearsal, she had to hear Trey boast about this or that sex position he'd tried with Kathy Ho ("Gotta stiffen up that Twinkie to get it in that HO-Ho!"); every night she had to watch Declan slobber over Carrie the moment she got out of rehearsal. But no one cared about the stories Eileen told about her brothers' basketball games or the funny things her cousins said when she was babysitting them, which was why she told her stories so quickly: so no one would interrupt them or tell her to get on with it.

She had no particular desire to get Ty-Ty in trouble; she probably liked him more than anyone else in the Annex did. Still, she thought as she pulled into her family's driveway, then walked across the way to the Rubicoffs' house, she couldn't pass up the opportunity to tell a story that made her life seem as interesting as everyone else's.

No one answered the first time she knocked on the door, and she wondered if Rob was watching from a window, waiting to see if she'd leave, or if he'd open the door and pretend he hadn't been hoping to see someone else. *Here she is*, she imagined herself saying. *Just the gal you weren't waiting for!*

Eileen knocked again. This time Willa Mae opened the door. "Willa Mae!" she shouted at the Rubicoffs' cleaning woman, who stood in the doorway wearing a mint-green uniform with a white lace collar. Oh, how she loved Willa Mae. Willa Mae was the absolute best.

"Oh my God, how long has it been since I last saw you?" Eileen asked. "Do you remember me?"

Willa Mae gave a slow nod.

"Do you remember when we all were little and the Rubicoffs used to invite me to their Passover dinner thingie? And that one time you told everyone there was no matzo ball soup left, but you actually set aside two extra bowls for me and Rob? Do you remember that?"

Willa Mae regarded Eileen dubiously through a set of half-glasses that she wore on a chain. "I remember a girl who ate an awful lot of soup," she said.

"That's me!" Eileen grinned. "I'm the soup girl! Is Rob home?"

"I'll go up and check."

"Oh, you don't have to," said Eileen. "I know the way."

"I'll go; you wait right here."

Eileen stood in the hall, admiring how fancy the Rubicoffs' house always seemed even when they weren't expecting visitors—the framed Picasso, Matisse, and Monet exhibit posters; the varnished grand piano; the *New York Times* on the dining room table (CLEVELAND AUTOWORKER SUSPECTED OF NAZI CRIMES ASKS FOR NEW TRIAL)—so different from the clutter and squalor of the home that had been in her family for the last sixty years.

Every so often, she would hear arguing from the Rubicoffs' house: a gruff, raised, male voice—presumably Rob's—yelling, "Drop dead! Fuck you!" But today all she heard was Willa Mae pounding on Rob's door, hollering, "Robert! Robeeeeert! You got a visitor downstairs!" Then some muttering, followed by Willa Mae again: "She's downstairs right now, uh-huh."

A door opened, then closed, and Rob appeared at the top of the stairs in bare feet, blue jeans, and a light-blue dress shirt open all the way to reveal his furry chest.

"Good to see you." He made his way downstairs, then kissed Eileen on both cheeks. "What's goin' on?"

"It is so messed up, I just had to tell someone," she said.

Rob glanced upstairs, then back down.

"Is this an okay time to talk?" Eileen asked.

"Good as any. You want some coffee?"

Eileen didn't drink coffee. "Sure," she said. "Maybe with some cream in it."

Rob turned surly. "We don't have any *cream*," he said, accenting the noun. "In fact, come to think of it, this day has been regrettably devoid of *cream*."

"Well, then maybe just with some sugar."

Rob opened the freezer, took out a bag of coffee beans, opened the lid to the computerized coffeemaker, and pressed some buttons on it. There was a brief grinding sound, then a thin stream of dark liquid filled the coffeepot. Rob lazily scratched his chest. "Everything all right?"

Mr. Densmore often called Rob ugly, and Eileen supposed that was true: he had a serious case of acne; a big nose that her father and brothers consistently pointed out he had inherited from his dad; a perpetual smirk that made otherwise peaceful people say they wanted to haul off and hit him. At the same time, his arrogance, which suggested he found himself hot even though he wasn't, sort of made him hot anyway. Looking around the kitchen, trying to focus on something aside from Rob's chest, Eileen thought it probably wouldn't be a bad idea to expand her definition of hotness to include conventionally ugly guys, giving herself a wider range of possibilities. Objectively speaking, all but one of the guys in Journey were pretty gross looking, but she would have jumped the bones of any of them.

Rob poured two mugs of coffee and handed one to Eileen. He didn't tell her where the sugar was and she didn't ask. Eileen took a sip and then, because it was so vile, pantomimed taking another. She put the mug down and warmed her hands with it as she recounted the morning's events: how no one had answered Ty-Ty's door, how Ty-Ty had been kneeling at a boy's waist, how Ty-Ty had looked up appearing nervous and guilty.

Rob considered the story analytically, like the trial attorney and politician he was intending to become. "This kid, how old was he?" he asked.

"Maybe fourteen or fifteen."

"Did you recognize him?"

"I didn't see his face."

"And what about the state of the kid's underwear?" asked Rob. "Did his penis seem flaccid? Or was it in a visibly turgid state?"

"What?" Eileen asked.

Rob explained.

"God, I wasn't looking *that* closely," said Eileen.

"Did you have the impression that Mr. Densmore was preparing to perform fellatio?"

"Perform what?"

Rob explained.

"Whoa, whoa, whoa," said Eileen.

Rob opined that he had always suspected Mr. Densmore of being a "liberal perv" with the sexual predilections of John Wayne Gacy, but Eileen's story didn't provide sufficient evidence. "I'd need to know more," he said.

"That's why I came here," said Eileen. "I'm driving back to Ty-Ty's house to deliver the props. Wanna come with?"

"Under normal circumstances, absolutely. But I'm a little indisposed right now."

Eileen didn't ask what he meant. The explanation asserted itself moments later when Amanda Wehner entered the front hallway and crept toward the Rubicoffs' front door as if she didn't want Rob to notice her leaving. Had she been upstairs all this while? Had she spent the night? The little tramp probably had. Although Eileen tried not to judge people, she found it hard not to judge Amanda: Amanda, with her little dancer's body and her pert little boobs and her stupid GUARDIAN ANGELS jacket; Amanda, with her negativity and her arrogant eye rolls and her beaded change purse where she kept her dime bags, her pipes, her joints, her lighter, and—who knew?—probably her disgusting lubricated rubbers and the penicillin she needed after using them; Amanda, who had been cast as Margo Frank only because she was cute and slutty, not because she had talent; Amanda, who was so tiny that Eileen always felt enormous, buxom, and matronly around her, even though she knew she was none of those things. Still, she did wish that when people in the Annex compared one another to celebrities—Fiona Grenfall to Bo Derek; Judith Nagorsky to Faye Dunaway; Rob to James Coburn; Trey to Simon Le Bon; Calvin to Flip Wilson; Amanda to Pat Benatar—they could come up with something more flattering than to tell Eileen she looked like a young Julia Child.

"Amanda!" Rob called out. "Care to join us in the kitchen? Eileen's here with a good story, and there's coffee if you want it." He walked to the fridge and took out a carton of half-and-half, which Eileen regarded enviously. "Black or with cream?" he asked Amanda.

Amanda gave a half wave, said, "Hey, Eileen," then told Rob, "No, I gotta get goin'."

"Come on, stay awhile," Rob said. "You and I haven't finished our conversation."

"Well, yeah, actually, we kind of have," said Amanda.

"I don't think so," Rob said. "Where'll you be later?"

"Dance class, then maybe at a movie with my dad."

"And after that?"

"Sleeping."

"You know"—Rob adopted a serious tone—"I meant what I said before."

"Yeah, I get it," Amanda said icily. "Bye."

She walked out, at which point Rob chuckled philosophically and rubbed his chest. "Well," he said, "I guess I have a little more time than I thought. Why don't we swing by Densmore's place? Maybe we can find him fellating someone or hiding them in his crawl space."

Eileen drove with the radio on—she had been listening to WLS, which was playing a totally awesome REO Speedwagon song ("Keep on Loving You")—but after Rob asked if he had to listen to this whiny shit, she let him change the station to WXRT, where Echo & the Bunnymen were singing "Do It Clean," which was pretty pornographic if you thought about it.

"I was kinda surprised to see Amanda at your place on a Saturday morning," Eileen said.

"That's not particularly surprising," said Rob. "What will be surprising is if she's there next Saturday morning."

Eileen adopted a concerned expression. "Are you guys having problems?" she asked.

"I'm not, but apparently she is," he said. "Ahh, who gives a shit: six months from now I'll be on the campus of a ridiculous liberal arts institution, and Amanda will be in Colorado, and it's not like I was planning to be faithful to her—not that I've been faithful to begin with."

"What were you two arguing about?" Eileen asked.

"The usual predictable horseshit," said Rob.

"What happened?

" 'What *happened*?' Exactly what I said would happen when Densmore was being his usual sick, twisted, manipulative self, casting me and Amanda as dad and daughter. I told Amanda the only way to act around a manipulative asshole is to refuse to let him manipulate you. I thought she agreed, but today—what do you know?—just as I fucking predicted. I try to put the moves on her. I start taking off her belt, and she shoves my hand away. 'That stays where it is,' she says."

"Oh, wow," said Eileen. "That's harsh."

"Exactly," said Rob. "So I try again, and she pulls the same bullshit, and when I ask her what's up, she says she feels weird because she's playing Margo Frank and I'm playing Mr. Frank, and maybe we should just cool it 'til the show's over. It's fuckin' bogus."

"Totally bogus," said Eileen.

Rob turned to Eileen, seeking counsel and assurance. "You wouldn't do that, would you? You wouldn't fuck up a real relationship because of a fictional one, would you?"

"Of course not."

"That's what I thought. Because you're cool. You wouldn't just up and blue-ball a guy you'd been dating because of some horseshit theater thing, would you?"

"I wouldn't."

"Your boyfriend's a lucky guy. What's his name?"

"Uh, Tim Donovan."

"Where's he at? Loyola?"

"He is, yeah."

Rob laughed. "Those Catholic boys can be pretty repressed," he said.

Eileen rolled her eyes and feigned hard-won knowledge. "Tell me about it," she said.

*

Tyrus's Cadillac was still parked in front of the Densmore house when they arrived, but the bicycle was gone. Eileen rang the bell. Tyrus opened the door and smiled. "Ahh," he said. "It's the Jewish pimp and his Irish whore. Come on in."

Eileen giggled and lugged her duffel bags into the study, feeling as if she had already transformed into Miep Gies. She loved Miep; actually, come to think of it, she kind of *was* Miep. She could have just seen herself in Amsterdam, bringing food to the Franks and Van Daans. If Nazis ever came to town, it would be totally fun to hide a family or two. In fact, the whole concept of doing it—hiding, say, the Rubicoffs—would seriously liven things up and serve as proof of her all-around awesomeness; maybe, if it really happened, she could even make Rob her sex slave. Just kidding.

Eileen displayed each prop while Tyrus made impressed or satisfied sounds and suggestive remarks. "Here's the Hanukkah scarf," Eileen said.

Tyrus stroked it delicately. "My, my, pretty, pretty, pretty," he said.

"And here're the potatoes you wanted," Eileen said.

Tyrus focused on her chest. "Those are some nice, firm taters you got there, Muldoon."

Eileen handed him a walking stick. "This is Mr. Frank's cane he uses at the beginning and end of the show," she said.

Tyrus eyed it as if he were selecting a pool cue. "A fine, firm staff, and appropriately erect," he said. Eileen produced a menorah and two boxes of candles; Tyrus opened a box, removed a candle, and tried inserting it into a holder. "Hmm, I believe these might require lube," he said.

Meanwhile, Rob studied Densmore's notebooks, the framed posters, and the alphabetized videocassettes. He began to take down one of the notebooks.

"Ah, ah, ah!" said Densmore. "Permission, Mr. Rubicoff. Always ask for permission."

"May I have permission?" Rob asked.

"You may not," said Densmore.

"I'll bring all this to the Annex on Monday," Eileen said, stuffing the props back in her duffel bags. "And what are you doing with the rest of your Saturday?"

"Enjoying the peace and quiet until my in-laws return and make my life a living hell," said Densmore.

Eileen smiled sadly. "Families are hard. I hope you can have some fun this weekend too, though."

"I believe I have already had the highlight of my Saturday," Densmore said.

"What might you be referring to?" asked Rob. "Have you been alone all morning? Or have you had some company?"

Densmore's nostrils flared. "Did anyone ever tell you that you have an ugly nose, Mr. Rubicoff? It suits your ugly, nosy personality."

"Someone needs to do something about that guy," Rob said when he and Eileen were back in the car, driving home.

"What do you mean, 'do something'?" Eileen asked.

"We should talk it over with Mrs. Winslow on Monday."

*

Eustacia Winslow—instructor of English and journalism, faculty adviser of the *North Shore Herald*—was the only high school teacher whom Rob deemed worthy of respect, the only instructor to whose name Rob appended a title. To Rob, "Ty-Ty" was simply "Densmore"; his French teacher was "DuPree"; calculus was taught by "Sweat Stain Stepaniak"; and his PE teacher was "that pathetic, drunk motherfucker."

Mrs. Winslow, a former editor of the *Chicago Defender* who started teaching at North Shore after she retired from journalism, seemed to be the only teacher who was there because she felt a calling, not because something better hadn't worked out. Eileen was terrified of her and still remembered the harsh way the teacher had dismissed her portfolio when she had applied to be the *Herald*'s sports photographer. "Photography is an art and a skill that needs to be mastered, Ms. Muldoon," Mrs. Winslow had said. "It's no place for amateurs who want to ogle boys in locker rooms; if that's what interests you, I'm sure there's a place for you on the yearbook."

Mrs. Winslow was hefting a sealed cardboard box into her office, but when she saw Rob and Eileen, she stopped, put down the box, and eyed the two of them as if their visit portended trouble. "To what do I owe this peculiar pleasure?" she asked.

"We'd like to approach you with a hypothetical story," said Rob.

"Every story is hypothetical before it is written, Mr. Rubicoff," Mrs. Winslow said. "Especially since whatever you think a story might be is rarely the one it becomes." She took off her glasses and put them on her desk atop a paper that had a C– underlined three times on it in red. "And what might this hypothetical story be?"

"Well," Rob began, "let's say that a certain high school instructor has taken certain sexual liberties with certain students under his supervision." He detailed the events Eileen had reported to him, adding embellishments and terms such as "possibly engaging in fellatio" and "in a visibly turgid state."

When Rob was done, Mrs. Winslow asked, "Might this 'hypothetical individual' be on staff here?"

"He might be," Rob said.

"And," Mrs. Winslow asked, "might the initials of this individual be *T.D.*?"

"Hypothetically, they might," said Rob.

Mrs. Winslow shook her head, a blend of disgust and resignation. "The bastard's still at it, is he?"

"You've heard stories like this?" Rob asked.

"Every year since I got here," said Mrs. Winslow. "There's always some rumor: someone saw him at the opera with a student; someone heard something happened when he gave a kid a ride home. He takes kids with him to New York and Lord only knows what happens there. Every faculty party, he shows up reeking of gin, insulting people's husbands, flirting with their wives, making a general ass of himself. Everybody talks about him after he leaves, but no one actually does anything. They laugh it off—'Oh, that's just Tyrus being Tyrus.'"

"So," Rob said, "you're saying there's a story there."

"I have no doubt that there is," Mrs. Winslow said. "But I guarantee you one thing."

"Which is?"

"No one will ever print it."

"Why's that?"

"Because no one will ever go on record, Mr. Rubicoff," Mrs. Winslow said, "and when no one goes on record, there's no story, only innuendo. Innuendo without proper sourcing is a minefield for *lit-i-ga-tion*"—she stretched the word out. "Someday, someone might get that story, but by then I'll be dead and Tyrus Densmore will be an old man."

"Well," Rob said to Eileen after they left Winslow's office, "then we'll just have to catch the bastard in flagrante."

"Is that like fellatio?" Eileen asked.

"More or less." Rob led her by the hand to a stairwell, still empty this early in the day. "Would you care to find out?"

Eileen felt heat rush to her cheeks. "Maybe," she said.

Mrs. Frank

Probably Judith Nagorsky shouldn't have been so flippant. Probably if she had any inkling of the foul plans Rob and Eileen had started to concoct and what the pair of them would wind up doing that year and with the rest of their lives, she could have tried to figure out a way to stop them. But she was in a piss-poor mood and had no time for anyone else's shit, particularly Rob's. So the moment he came skulking around the craptacular Annex vending machines after rehearsal, playing deadline reporter with Eileen in tow and asking if Judith had ever seen Mr. Densmore "engaging in improper behavior," she wasn't sure whether to laugh out loud or beat the shit out of Rob's stupid, presumptuous, scheming ass.

"Improper behavior?" she asked, smacking the pop machine, vainly hoping to get her quarters back. Was he kidding? What year did Rob think he was living in? She had seen just about every member of the high school faculty "engage in improper behavior." Coach Greg Lerner, who invited girls over for hot tub parties with members of the Chicago Sting soccer team and yelled "Call me after ya graduate!" when he drove past cheerleading practice, engaged in "improper behavior." So did her French teacher, Monsieur Charles DuPree, when he leapt on his desk, performed stripteases to "Michèle" by Gérard Lenorman, and asked students to shout out the French words for the items of clothing he was whipping off—"*La chemise!*" When Coach Pootie Hollings swigged Wild Turkey out of a paper bag and sang Rick James in a falsetto while purportedly teaching swimming class, he was also "engaging in improper behavior."

And if Rob and Eileen really wanted to get into it—which of course they didn't, though, why the fuck not, she would—her whole family was guilty of engaging in "improper behavior." To wit: Dr. Herb Nagorsky, who had ditched his wife (whom he had probably met when she had been his patient) and moved in with his thirty-three-year-old girlfriend (whom he had met when she had been his secretary) and her towheaded son; and Judith's own mother, Estelle Nagorsky, who had put her fist through her bedroom window and chased Herb down Oakton Street while she was buck naked. Every one of them had "engaged in improper behavior." And further, Judith told Rob, every time he opened his putrid yap, he was "engaging in improper behavior" too.

"So I take this to mean you won't be able to help us out with this," Rob said.

"Yuh-huh," said Judith.

God, she thought, she was so done with all this petty high school drama shit: the juvenile theater exercises, pretending to be trees, animals, machines—"*Boop!*" "*Beep!*" "*Boop!*" "*Beep!*"; the clapping, slapping concentration games; the eternal boring gossip about whom Mr. Densmore would take on his vaunted "New York trip," when everyone knew it was always the best-looking boy with the most fucked-up home life. The Annex was soul-destroying, acting alongside people, half of whom were in it for the attention, not the art; trying to stay in her own circle of concentration when Trey, high on coke, booze, or just his own immaturity, turned every one of Mr. Van Daan's lines into some dumb sex joke—"Anne, did you see my *pipe?*"; playing the wife of Rob, who would be the first to crank up the Zyklon-B if a real war broke out. Had it not been for the importance of the play they were performing, she would have blown off the whole thing and picked up as many shifts as she could at the Hollywood Diner, because it was already hard to imagine how she would afford four years at the Goodman Theater School without having to rely on the whims of her father, who never gave her a straight answer as to whether he'd actually pay.

On her way out of the school, she practically knocked over Declan, who was standing in the damp cold. "Carrie comin' down soon?" he asked.

"How the fuck would I know that, Spengler?" Judith said as she headed for the athletic field en route to the el. "I'm not her travel agent, her social secretary, or her wife."

Judith had been waiting for a train for nearly five minutes when Fiona strode onto the platform in a belted safari jacket and a beige cap that split the difference between hairnet and snood. She was listening to her Walkman and carrying a thick book wrapped in red Christmas paper.

Fiona peered over the platform, searching vainly for a train, then ducked into the shelter where Judith was sitting. She lit a cigarette, took a drag, and blew out a thick gust. "Hey there," Fiona said. "Northbound, are you?"

"Yep," said Judith.

"Smashing. Normally I walk home, but after that rehearsal, well, I'm pretty well knackered, aren't I?" She proffered her pack of cigarettes. "Care for a fag?"

This was probably the most unscripted dialogue Judith had heard the girl speak since *Anne Frank* rehearsals had begun. Fiona spent most of her offstage time reading wrapped books, listening to music, and either ignoring or actually not hearing when Rob and Eileen joked that Densmore had cast Fiona solely because the script called for someone with "great legs."

Judith took a cigarette. Fiona lit it with a Zippo; she had taken her headphones off, and Judith could hear screaming, whiny treble, and propulsive drumming. "What on earth are you listening to?" Judith asked.

"The New Christs." Fiona handed the Walkman to Judith. The music was louder and more aggressive than the Joni Mitchell and Marianne

Faithfull tunes Judith tended to cry herself to sleep with. She made a face and handed back the headphones.

"Yeah, it's a little rough, isn't it?" Fiona said. "But sometimes one needs to listen to music like that to drown out everything else around you. Donnell turned me on to them—my brother. He's pretty much a half-wit and a fuck-up, isn't he? But he has decent taste in music."

"The New Christs," Judith said. "They're British?"

"Australian."

"You're Australian?"

"No, British," Fiona said. "Also Canadian, South African, German, Hong Kongese, and just about anything else you can imagine."

"Military brat?" Judith asked.

"Diplomat's bitch."

On the train, Judith sat beside Fiona, who read her wrapped book; it seemed to be an advanced chemistry text, filled with numbers and symbols that looked like hieroglyphics to Judith, but Fiona whipped through it as if it were an Agatha Christie thriller.

"Is that homework?" Judith asked.

"'Tisn't. But science and maths at school, well, they're pretty much shit, aren't they? And one has to do one's best to keep one's mind alive."

"And the wrapping paper—uh, why?"

"Because impertinent buggers tend to make annoying, patronizing remarks when they see a bird reading something intellectual, don't they?"

Judith briefly reran the entirety of the conversation they had just had, trying to determine if she'd said anything that could have been misinterpreted—or interpreted all too accurately. When she had first seen Fiona, she had associated the girl with the vacuous Breck shampoo and Serta mattress models she resembled, and when she had first heard Fiona's accent, Judith thought she sounded like an upper-class twat on a BBC period drama.

"Have I said anything annoying or patronizing?" Judith asked.

"Oh, no, of course not. You're aces," said Fiona. "What you said to that vile Robert Rubicoff git, it was bloody heroic, wasn't it?"

"I was just saying what I felt," said Judith.

"That's what I mean."

The train proceeded north. Out the window, Judith could see the roof of Beth Shalom, where she had attended Hebrew school and Rabbi Jeremy Horvath had arranged for her Bat Mitzvah to coincide with a Torah portion in which Judah mistakes his daughter-in-law for a prostitute because, according to the rabbi, she was the only one in his class who could handle such mature material.

They got off the train at Central Street and made their way downstairs. Judith said she was headed west and asked if Fiona was going the same way.

"Alas, not." Fiona jutted her head in the direction of Lake Michigan.

"Don't tell me you live in one of those lavish lakefront mansions," Judith said.

"Yes and no," said Fiona. "The house where we're staying—well, yes, it's quite posh. It's not ours, though. We're just living in it for a year or so amid someone else's rubbish. We had to get out of England so fast, we didn't really have time to arrange a proper place to stay."

"Sounds like some serious drama must've been playing out in England," Judith said.

"Yes," said Fiona. "I believe you might refer to it as 'improper behavior.'"

At street level, there was a station diner called Granny's Kitchen, a dive of a place with a grill, a counter, and wobbly barstools. Fiona suggested they wait there for a while to "have a cuppa and a wee chat" and see if the rain would let up. They sat there drinking coffees and watching the traffic through rain-spattered windows as Fiona told Judith why she had left England. Apparently, her classics teacher, "Lloyd," had become "a trifle obsessed" with her, she said—complimented her essays about Aeschylus and Euripides, invited her out for coffee and films, took her to shows at the Tate Gallery, exhibits at the British Museum, "that sort of rot." She said she had liked the attention for a while; boys in her form were predominantly "wankers," "poofs," "wankers ashamed they were poofs," or "poofs blissfully unaware that poofs could still be wankers." But, after the first time she had "shagged" Lloyd, he had gotten all "barmy"—called her all the time, sent her love notes, chocolates, flowers. When he took to sleeping in his car in her driveway, Fiona's parents had seen only two choices: call bloody Scotland Yard or move across the ocean and hope Lloyd would find another poor girl to terrorize—failing to understand that America had telephones and a postal service too.

"Sounds like a lot for you to deal with," said Judith.

"Sounds like rather more for Lloyd's wife," Fiona said. "For me, it's just a bit of a bugger."

Judith laughed. "Can I just say, I know this might be annoying or patronizing, but I kind of love listening to you—all the 'flats' and 'wankers' and 'buggers.'"

"That's funny," Fiona said. "No one I know really talks quite this way back in England; I guess moving all the time and never having a permanent home is forcing me to create some identity for myself, isn't it?"

They had another cigarette under the viaduct. The rain showed no signs of letting up; it just came down harder. "Maybe we could hang out sometime," Fiona said. "You could come over; we'd have a glass of wine or two, watch a film. I believe you're the one person in *Anne Frank* I can actually talk to."

It was just a simple statement, but it brought tears to Judith's eyes—the tears she could never summon in rehearsal when she was playing Mrs. Frank opposite Rob. How lovely Fiona's invitation sounded in comparison to her real life: the stiff, formal dinners with her father, stepbrother, and evil stepmother in their posh Central Street condo; the guilt she felt when she thought of her mother alone in her tatty Skokie tenement.

Fiona wrote down her phone number on the back of a receipt and Judith stuffed it in a pocket of her jacket. She would have liked to stay with Fiona longer—would have liked, more than anything, to spend the evening in her posh mansion, drinking fab wine and blasting the New Christs while Fiona spoke in her preposterous accent. But the alimony and child support checks were waiting for her at her dad's condo, and her mother was waiting for her at home. So she let Fiona kiss her cheek, told her "Thanks for the fag" but she had to "bugger off" now. "How about Saturday?" she asked.

"That would be smashing," said Fiona.

*

When Judith arrived at her father and Lorna Jessy's condo and found the place empty and the dining room table set for one, as if Alfred Hitchcock were staging the homecoming of Miss Lonelyhearts, Judith wasn't sure whether to feel pissed or relieved that her father had excluded her once again. A note—purportedly from her dad but written in his wife's juvenile scrawl—explained that he had forgotten he had scheduled a dinner at his club downtown. Paper-clipped to the note were the alimony and child support checks, twenty dollars for a cab ride home, and a pair of tickets to *Kabuki Macbeth* at the Wisdom Bridge Theatre; Judith's dad said that he and Lorna had plans to see Georg Solti conduct the Chicago Symphony on the same night, and besides, the *Macbeth* play sounded like the weird sort of thing Judith might enjoy more than he would.

If Judith had half the inner fortitude her classmates assumed she did, she would have torn up the note, the checks, the cash, and the tickets, and hurled the dinner Lorna had made down the disposal. But she and her mother actually needed the money, and if she returned every theater and concert ticket her father slipped her, she would never see any shows. And as for the pasta primavera and chilled tomato soup, the only time Judith had a decent meal was when Lorna prepared it, so she ate everything, even though it made her feel just as queasy as the theater tickets she was taking.

She cleaned her dishes, left an embarrassingly obsequious thank-you note, and, on her way out, paused in the doorway of what could have been her bedroom had she decided to live with her father: pink sheets and a matching lace canopy; a spotless mirror over an empty dresser; framed on a wall, a picture she had drawn when she was a child—a stick figure girl holding hands with a stick figure mom and dad. The room seemed so achingly lonely without anyone in it that Judith couldn't help but wish for a moment that she lived there instead of in Skokie with her mother. But Judith knew her dad too well to feel too much longing in this bedroom that did and didn't belong to her. Had she actually told her father she wanted to abandon her mom and live with him, she would have been, at best, relegated to a couch in the living room. Just as the only time Judith's father slipped her extra cash was when she didn't ask for it. She wouldn't spend that twenty he had left her on a taxi, though; she'd use it to buy dinner when she saw Fiona on Saturday, and meanwhile she'd take the train back south, then ride the bus to the home she referred to as Depressive Manor.

*

Depressive Manor was an oppressively warm and dank five-story apartment building located above the Hollywood Diner in downtown Skokie. The diner served any sort of meal at all hours it was open, but for some unidentifiable reason its dark, carpeted stairwell seemed to preserve an eternal odor of boiled cabbage and beef stew, neither of which was actually on the menu. Judith couldn't say for sure if the bleak establishment and the dwellings above it attracted depressives or turned people into them; she didn't even know which was true for herself or her mom.

She stomped up the stairs, jingled her keys, slowly opened each lock, then threw open the door, slammed it behind her, and turned on the hallway light before yelling "Ma, I'm here!" The intent was not so much to dramatically announce her arrival as it was to give her mother time to stop whatever she might have been doing—vegetating in bed, watching shitty TV shows, snarfing crap out of the fridge, hurling in the bathroom—and let her pretend she hadn't been doing any of those things. Mr. Densmore had certainly made the right choice when he cast Judith as Edith Frank, vainly trying to comfort a daughter who kept pushing her away, but that wasn't the way it was supposed to work for her in real life, was it? At seventeen, shouldn't she have been the one who still got to play the child?

"*Ma?*"

Whenever Judith came home, she felt like a detective gathering evidence of what her mother had done with her day. When Judith would ask how her mother was, Estelle Nagorsky would say she was "just fine, thank you" and had spent the day doing "chores," but Judith would invariably find some stray detail that told a truer, more troubling story: crumpled Oreo cookie boxes stuffed in the bottom of the trash; an empty mouthwash container that had been full in the morning; and, one time, a stuffed toilet with cigarettes and a pair of condoms floating around in it, all of which Judith had extracted with a ladle and plopped into the trash. She had asked no questions.

"*Hey, Ma?*"

Judith tried to sublimate all the thoughts that assailed her whenever she didn't know where her mother was: Where were the first aid kits? Would the CPR she'd learned in Health Ed actually work? She cased the apartment, looking for a note like the one Lorna had forged for her father: *Went out to run errands. Be back soon; Went to throw myself onto the Edens Expressway. Be back never.* Judith wrenched open the rear kitchen door: still misting out there; the back steps were creaky and wet. She walked down in her socks and noted that her mom's Cutlass was parked in its space. What was it doing there if her mom wasn't home? She cupped her hands to look through the driver's-side window. No one inside. No telltale smell of exhaust.

Judith took her socks off, balled them up, and walked back upstairs barefoot—both terrified and oddly exhilarated by the possibility that her mother might have disappeared for good. She imagined living alone there until autumn, when she would move into an apartment closer to college. She could invite friends over for dinners or parties as opposed to having them drop her off in front of the building, fearful of which Mom they would encounter at home: the antisocial catatonic one; her jittery, manic counterpart; or the terrifying personification of rage.

Judith reentered the apartment. Her mother was standing in the front hallway, shaking out a black umbrella.

"Ma, where were you?"

Estelle Nagorsky took off her raincoat and hung it on a hook by the front door. "Where was I?" Her tone was nonchalant, vaguely sarcastic. "I was out having dinner."

"Wasn't I supposed to be home so I could make you dinner?"

Estelle went into the kitchen, twisted a burner on the stove, and lit a cigarette. "I suppose," she said. "But since you were eating with your father, it didn't make sense to wait."

"I was worried," Judith said.

Estelle smoked. "Why?"

Judith's mind cycled through all the obvious responses: *Because, as far as I know, you've spent the last three months inside; Because I thought you might be dead.* She settled on "No reason."

"Hey," she asked her mother. "Do you have plans Friday night? Wanna go see a play?"

"Do I strike you as someone who has plans?" Estelle Nagorsky asked.

*

The day she had tickets for *Kabuki Macbeth*, Judith got home from *Anne Frank* rehearsal at seven. Depressive Manor was as depressing as it always was, but her apartment less so, it seemed. The shades were up. There was classical music on the radio, and the place smelled like perfume that called forth distant memories. It was the same Chanel "Russia Leather" her mother had worn to symphony concerts, musicals, and downtown restaurants before the divorce.

Mrs. Nagorsky stepped into the hallway, all in black—a tight leotard top, a short leather skirt, and hose. (Her mother never wore "tights," only "hose.") The only bit of color was the slash of bloodred lipstick. The effect was not so much slutty as an imitation of sluttishness, the sort of clichéd outfit an inexperienced actress might wear to audition to play a streetwalker in *Sweet Charity*. Judith had opinions about the outfit because it was the one her mother had purchased for her from Crawford's for her sixteenth birthday; Judith had rejected it, saying that if she wanted to act like a whore, she would, but she saw no need to dress like one.

"You look great, Ma," Judith said.

As Judith drove east to Wisdom Bridge, she listened to her mother prattle on about her memories of the theater: the time Avon Long winked at her at the curtain call of *Porgy and Bess*; the time she had seen *Hair* and only the fat actors got naked, while all the "good-lookers" wore T-shirts and shorts; the time she walked out on *A Raisin in the Sun* because she thought Lorraine Hansberry "had a chip on her shoulder."

Judith parked on Custer Street and walked arm in arm with her mom. Nearby, a group of boys about Judith's age were practicing kung fu kicks on a dented mailbox.

"That your mother?" one of the kids asked Judith. He had long, skinny legs and his face looked as though it were frozen in a permanent masque of laughter.

Judith pulled her mother along. "C'mon, Ma."

"Hey, can I date your mother?" the kid shouted. "She's lookin' fine as hell." His friends laughed.

"Lovely neighborhood you're taking me to," said Mrs. Nagorsky.

Judith spoke through clenched teeth. "Ma, shut up; let's just go."

When Judith and her mother entered the theater, a couple in their fifties stood to let them into their row. The man was wearing a navy-blue sport jacket, tan slacks, and a white shirt with a plain red tie. The woman wore a forest-green pantsuit and a cream-colored blouse, a string of gobstopper-sized pearls around her neck. The couple grinned at Judith and her mother.

"Where's the doctor tonight?" the man asked.

"Pardon me?" asked Judith.

"Dr. Nagorsky," the man said. "Are you the daughter?"

"Oh, she has to be the daughter," the woman said. "Herb talks about you all the time—his daughter the actress. What's your name? Julie?"

"Judith," said Judith.

"That's right," the woman said. "I knew it started with a *J*."

Judith answered the couple's questions with "Mm-hms" and "Uh-huhs" while her mother fiddled with her hands as if she were Lady Kabuki Macbeth, trying to rub away evidence of her ex-husband's new life.

They were Sanford and Beverly Pinker. They lived in St. Joseph, Michigan, but kept a studio apartment on Chicago's Gold Coast where they stayed on weekends, now that their kids were out of the house. He'd worked for thirty years in the engineering department of the Whirlpool Corporation. They had a son who attended the University of Chicago business school and a daughter engaged to a "fella" who worked in "site location" for Burger King.

Mrs. Nagorsky rubbed her hands. "I'm uncomfortable; I just feel so uncomfortable," she said. "When did they say the show would be over?"

"It'll be over when it's over." Judith tried to refocus her mother's attention. "Look at the set design, Ma. So minimalistic; just shoji screens and ikebana plants. Isn't it lovely?"

Mrs. Nagorsky shifted her head rapidly with tight little movements as if she were a paranoid bird. "What time does it let out?" she asked. "What time did they say?"

"It's right about to start," Judith said.

Mrs. Nagorsky made for the aisle.

"Ma, where're you going?"

Mrs. Nagorsky waved off her daughter. "Stay, stay; I'll be right back." She walked toward the exit, both hands clutching her purse.

Judith sat and waited. All the seats in the theater were occupied save for the one between her and Mrs. Pinker. The doors closed. A gong sounded. The house lights dimmed. Judith climbed over the Pinkers as three women wearing black kimonos and white masks appeared center stage. The moment one asked, "When shall we three meet again?" Judith was out the door.

At the corner of Howard and Custer, the same teenagers who had been kicking the mailbox were taking turns trying to balance atop a trashcan they had turned on its side.

"That lady was buggin'," the skinny kid said. "She was B-U-G-G-I-N! *Buggin'!*"

Buggin'. A more polite word than the one Judith would have chosen, but she knew who they were talking about, and it was an apt enough description of her mother. *Buggin'*. Probably, if she could see herself in a mirror, she'd look like she was buggin' too.

Judith walked down the block, then stopped. *Shit*. Where she'd parked the car was an empty, sedan-sized space. Of course the car was gone; of course Estelle Nagorsky was physically incapable of allowing her daughter to have a normal evening.

There was a pay phone in the parking lot of Big Rick's Adult Books. Judith kicked aside some gravel and broken beer bottle glass scattered in front of the phone. She shoved coins into the slot and dialed her home number. She let it ring. No answer. She called again. Same thing. She reached into the inside pocket of her jacket and took out the paper with Fiona's phone number on it. When Fiona answered, Judith said, "Thank God."

A quarter of an hour later, Fiona pulled up in front of Wisdom Bridge in a maroon Triumph Stag blasting Graham Parker—"Temporary Beauty." Judith got in the car and the girls embraced.

"Oh my God, you're a lifesaver," said Judith. "How are you?"

"Top hole," Fiona said. "What about you?"

"Bottom hole," said Judith. "Is that a phrase people use?"

"I wouldn't know," Fiona said. "But it sounds good; perhaps I'll try it."

"I don't mean to be such a bother, but I think my mom might've done something stupid to herself. And by 'stupid' I mean even stupider than usual."

"No bother at all. Where to?"

"Is it okay if we go to my apartment? Do you have anyplace you need to be?"

"Not a place in the world, love."

When they got to the Hollywood Diner, Judith directed Fiona into the lot behind it. She found herself both heartened and dismayed to see her mother's car already here. Part of her had been morbidly looking forward to an evening spent with Fiona, cruising from police stations to emergency rooms, showing old pictures of her mom (because she didn't have any new ones) and asking if anyone had seen this woman. She had entertained vaguely romantic visions of holding hands with Fiona and walking futilely alongside canals and the lakefront, then of sobbing in the Grenfalls' living room and telling them she guessed she would have to live with her dad and stepmom. The Grenfalls would pour her a glass of sherry and say things like "ta," "cheerio," and "jolly good" and tell her certainly not, Judith could stay with them as long as she liked.

"Be right back," Judith told Fiona.

"Do you want me to come upstairs with you, love?"

"Lord, no." Judith could only imagine the conversation if Fiona entered Depressive Manor: "What is that grotty odor, Judith?" "Why, which odor do you mean, Fiona: the Listerine or the caramel scent of Roach Motels?" She climbed the back steps fast, hoping speed would overwhelm her gnawing sense of dread.

Lights were on in the kitchen, bathroom, and living room.

"Ma?"

Estelle Nagorsky was on the living room couch. Her hose-clad feet were up on the magazine table. She looked quite pleased with herself as she smoked a cigarette, flicked ash into the tray she held in her palm, and watched shit on TV.

"Ma, what the fuck?"

Mrs. Nagorsky put the ashtray down. "You're early," she said. "How'd you get home?"

"How I got here is immaterial. What is material is that you busted out of the show like a fugitive from a fricking chain gang and I had to chase you down to make sure you were all right. Are you?"

Mrs. Nagorsky regarded her daughter as if she were a construction project going on outside that was interrupting her important television viewing. "Of course I'm all right. What time is it?"

"Eight forty," Judith said. "What the fuck difference does that make?"

"They told me the show let out at ten thirty."

"Yeah, so?"

"So I had at least another hour before I had to go pick you up."

"Oh, that was your plan? That would've been nice to know."

"Well," said Mrs. Nagorsky, "do you know what else would've been nice to know? That you got those tickets from Herb and we would be sitting with his two friends."

"I had no idea who those two twats were," Judith said. "Why do you have to do this every single time? Why do you have to make everything about you? Why can't you ever prioritize my needs over your own?"

"About me? I never ask you a thing. All I want is to be left alone to read my books and watch my shows. It wasn't my idea to see some Oriental *Macbeth*. And why can't people just do plays the way they were written instead of jazzing them up the whole time? If they want to jazz them up, let them write their own play."

"Ma, you are *buggin'*." Judith felt triumphant when she uttered that last sentence, but by the time she got back to Fiona's car, her hands were shaking. "What a nightmare," she said.

"Got something for you." Fiona reached into the back seat, produced a bottle of white wine, and poured Judith a mug of it. "That'll put some hair on your chest, love," she said.

Judith took a sip, then licked her lips. She knew nothing about wine save for what she sometimes smelled on her mother's breath or what she saw poured into goblets at her father and wicked stepmother's condo, all of which she felt predisposed to despise. Whatever this was, though, she felt as though she innately understood it. "Shit," she said. "This is really good."

"Yeah, it's not tosh, is it?" Fiona said.

"No. Definitely not *tosh*. Are you having some?"

"Not while I'm driving, love. Maybe after *Kabuki Macbeth*."

They got back to Wisdom Bridge near the end of the first intermission and found their seats just as Sanford and Beverly Pinker were returning from the lobby. Mr. Pinker looked at Fiona, then at Judith. "Your mother's looks have improved," he said.

For the next hour and a half, Judith stared, immobile, chin cupped in her hands as she watched the play. In that brief time the rest of the world fell away: her father's cold indifference, her mother's madness, Ty Densmore's mediocrity, Rob Rubicoff's bullshit about "improper behavior," the world that murdered the Franks and Van Daans. Instead, Judith found herself completely immersed in this Japanese Scotland of the imagination—its costumes, its makeup, its atmosphere, its language. She wanted so badly to do this herself, to create a world so much more lovely than the one she lived in, to create something that could make her and everyone around her see that hope and beauty were still out there somewhere. The moment after the final blackout, she rose to her feet, threw her hands out in front of her, and clapped, clapped, clapped.

When the applause died down and the houselights went up, Fiona whispered to Judith, "So tomorrow, then?"

"Tomorrow, then, what?" asked Judith.

"Tomorrow, shall we come back to see it from the beginning?"

And that idea was so perfect and so unexpected that Judith hugged her friend and said yes, *yes!* She put her arm in Fiona's and they went to the box office, where Fiona purchased two Saturday night tickets on her charge card. "Don't fret about the cost," Fiona said. "Mutti and Da believe in subsidizing cultural education, and I'm sure they'll be happy I finally found a friend."

"Is it hard for you to find friends?" Judith asked as the two of them walked out of the theater.

"Harder than you might expect," Fiona said. "It's a bit of a bugger, really."

The same teens were still on the corner; they were passing around a joint. "Evenin', my ladies," the lanky, grinning kid fond of the term *buggin'* said. "Can I ask y'all a question?"

"Yes, love?" Fiona asked.

"Uh, yeah," the kid said. "I was just wondering if you two fine ladies were lookin' for a night on the town or whether you were of the lesbian persuasion."

Judith was about to let loose with a torrent of expletives, but Fiona spoke first. "That sort of question's a bit beneath you, isn't it?" she said.

A couple of the other kids laughed. "*Dah-yumn!*" the lanky kid said.

"Look," Fiona said. "If my friend and I are lesbians, that's really no business of yours. And if we're not, well, then, you just ruined your chance for a 'night on the town,' now, didn't you? Come on, then, doesn't a handsome young man have anything better to do than drink soda, smoke reefer, and harass young women?"

"Well," the kid said, "it ain't as if anyone's gonna buy us beers."

"Such a sad story," Fiona said. "Fine young men with no one to buy them beer. I'll tell you what: If we buy you that beer, will you refrain from this ungentlemanly behavior?"

The kid moved his face close to Fiona's. "You're serious?"

"Do I look like I'm joking . . . ?" Fiona prompted the kid for his name.

"Ray," he said.

"Do I look like I'm joking, Raymond?"

"Damn!" a couple of the kids chorused.

Fiona shook his hand. "Fiona. It's good to meet you, Raymond."

"You're not seriously buying those rude dipshits beer, are you?" Judith asked en route to the liquor store.

"It is my opinion," Fiona said, "that rude boys turn out to be a good deal gentler than polite ones." She took Judith's hand and imitated Otto Frank: "Anyway, it's the only decent thing to do. Come on, then."

The boys were at the mailbox, and Ray was perched atop it, when Fiona and Judith returned with a six-pack of Watney's. Somehow, Fiona had managed to bewitch the guy at the liquor store the same way she seemed to bewitch everyone else; he hadn't even carded her.

"You gonna drink some with us?" Ray asked.

Fiona feigned contemplation. "It's rather a shame, isn't it?" she said. "If you'd been a bit more polite, it could have been a possibility. As it stands, my friend Judith and I may just have to return to our house and have our torrid lesbian sex all on our own."

"*Dah-yumn!*"

"But I tell you what, Raymond . . ." Fiona raised her eyebrows.

"Tounslee." Ray spelled it for her.

"You're in the phone book?"

"My dad. Raymond Tounslee Sr. Yeah."

"I tell you what, Raymond Tounslee," Fiona said. "If you ditch a few of your friends, I may just ring you up." She put her arm in Judith's. "Back to my place, then, my lovely, torrid lesbian friend?"

"Smashing," said Judith.

⁂

The front door of Fiona's Posh Palace opened onto a vast, dark hall that had the aspect of a ballroom. Dangling from above, a glass teardrop chandelier. A red-carpeted stairway spiraled up to the second floor. Judith could imagine herself making a grand entrance here: slinking down the stairs in a sleek crimson gown and matching sequined gloves; drunkenly sliding down the banister face-first.

Fiona's mutti and da were in the living room watching a black-and-white movie with subtitles. The girls went to the kitchen, where Fiona snatched a wheel of cheese, half a loaf of bread, and a pair of knives. "Be a dear and fetch two wineglasses from the cupboard," she said, then led Judith upstairs to her immaculate bedroom, where she selected Elvis Costello's *Get Happy!!* from a shelf of records. She put it on the turntable, arranged the snacks on the floor, and poured two glasses of wine.

Judith sat cross-legged, her back against Fiona's bed, fearful she might soil anything she touched. People actually lived like this, she thought— without fretting over whether their mothers would kill themselves or if their fathers would boot them off the family dole. People could afford mansions with red-carpeted spiral stairways, multiple bedrooms and bathrooms, shelves of books that didn't come from the library or the used section at Chandler's. What would it be like to live this way: an actress not above the Hollywood Diner but off in the Hollywood Hills, Jacuzzi out back, fig trees out front, Meryl Streep down the street, Mariel Hemingway stopping by to borrow a cup of sugar and a dildo.

"Opportunity, opportunity—this is your big opportunity," Elvis Costello was singing. Fiona swayed to the music. "What're you thinking about?" she asked.

Judith's cheeks flushed.

"What?" asked Fiona.

"That torrid, lesbian sex you mentioned," Judith said.

Fiona threw her head back and let loose with a throaty laugh. "Well, what of it?"

"I don't know," Judith said. "It was just funny."

"Was it?" asked Fiona. "Are you that way?"

"A torrid lesbian?"

Fiona refilled Judith's wine glass, then her own. "Mmm," she said.

Judith took a sip. "What about you?"

Fiona sighed. "Part of me wishes I was. It would make matters a good deal simpler, wouldn't it? Trouble is, I like blokes too much."

"One can like both," Judith said.

"One can," said Fiona. "But, sadly, I don't. Is that how you are? Do you like both?"

"Lately, I feel like I don't like either," Judith said.

Fiona clinked Judith's glass. "Been there," she said.

On Fiona's nightstand there was a small lamp with a white plastic shade that had shapes cut out of it. Fiona turned on the lamp, turned off the overhead. She twirled the shade and the two girls sat in the dimness watching illuminated stars, crescents, and dots travel across the walls and onto each other's faces.

The phone rang and Fiona swallowed. "Well, there it is," she said. "Every night like clockwork. At least one thing in this world is still reliable."

"What're you talking about?" Judith asked before she remembered. "Ohhh, is it him? That guy you mentioned?"

"Quite," said Fiona. "Lloyd."

"Just let it ring; don't answer."

"But if I don't, then Da will, and his reaction will be so violently out of proportion, I'll wind up feeling sorry for Lloyd."

The phone rang again. Fiona made as if to grab it. Judith held on to her hand. "What happens when you answer?" she asked.

"Nothing too awful," Fiona said. "Mostly he tells me how much he misses me, asks me if I'll forgive him, when I'll be coming home, if he can come visit. Usually I just put the phone on the bed and let him talk until he wears himself out."

"That's horrible," Judith said.

"Sad, really," said Fiona.

"No, horrible." The phone kept ringing. Judith grabbed it.

"What do you think you're doing?" Fiona asked.

"Watch." Judith spoke into the phone, affecting an English accent: "'Ello!" she said. Fiona reached for the phone, but Judith twisted out of the way. "'Ello, 'oo is it, then?"

"Is this Fiona?" Lloyd asked.

"'Fraid not," said Judith. "You must've got me mixed up with some other bird."

"May I speak to her, please?"

"Of all the impertinence," Judith said. "Do you know what bloody time it is?"

"Late, I'd imagine," said Lloyd.

"Well, you're bloody right about that, aren't you? What sort of manners are those—calling up birds in the middle of the night?"

"Can you put Fiona on the phone, please?"

"Of course I will not," said Judith. "Fiona's a bit busy at the moment, isn't she?"

"Doing what?"

"Well, if you really care to know, she's right in the middle of some 'torrid lesbian sex.' Now, why don't you go back to your wife and children and stop messing about with young birds who simply aren't fond of men?"

"Christ almighty." Lloyd hung up.

There was a brief silence. "Is he still on the line?" Fiona asked.

"He's not."

Glowing crescents and stars danced upon Fiona's face, then swirled away. Fiona remained silent for a while. Then she laughed. "You are a vicious one, aren't you? My Lord, Judith, what will I say the next time he calls?"

"Maybe he won't."

"Oh, I doubt that," Fiona said. "No, I don't believe I'm rid of the bugger yet."

Mr. Frank

The overnight run-through of *Anne Frank* was scheduled to begin at seven P.M. on a Friday. Rob got to the school early bearing a backpack containing his Otto Frank costume, toiletries, and a strip of condoms—just in case. The parking lot had a RESERVED FOR FACULTY AND STAFF ONLY sign on it, but Rob parked there anyway, knowing that only kids with shitty cars got towed.

What always impressed him when he walked through the school during off-hours was how inconsequential everything in it seemed. Here was the cafeteria where he stood up to free-lunch kids who tried to bully him into buying their "meal tickets" ("No, I don't got a *dollah* for you, man"). All the chairs were up on the tables now; black trash bags cinched with twist ties were lined up along a wall. In the middle of the hallway was Vice Principal Berniece Roche's sagging black leather armchair, where she would sit with a timer and sheaves of late passes and detention slips. The chair was big, but the authority it represented seemed absurdly small.

Rob looked in on this room then that one, recalling this particular seat where he had argued that interring Japanese Americans during World War II had been necessary, or that one where he had challenged the idea of canonizing *The Great Gatsby*, since the character of Meyer

Wolfsheim was anti-Semitic. All those devil's advocate arguments he'd made seemed petty and stupid now—serious topics wasted on unserious people. Of late, Rob's dad had been on his case for staying out too late and studying too little. "Keeping up with studying is what gets you places," Mr. Rubicoff said.

"Studying the way I do got me into Carleton," Rob told his father. "Studying the way you did got you into U of I."

Rob had been hoping to update Mrs. Winslow on the progress of his investigation of Ty Densmore. Which was, unfortunately, no progress at all. His classmates were all pussies: hardly anybody wanted to say anything, and the few who did said he couldn't use their names. Nearly everyone in the *Anne Frank* cast agreed Densmore was an asshole, but when he asked them specific questions, they all clammed up, afraid Densmore might find out. Rob wouldn't give up, though. He didn't like the way Densmore had messed up his relationship with Amanda, didn't appreciate how Densmore had mocked his nose and called him an ugly Jewish pimp.

Mrs. Winslow was already gone, though. The doors to her classroom and the *North Shore Herald* office were open and the floors were wet. Rob paused at the glass case of journalism trophies, one of which he'd won for an opinion piece about why America should make English its official language. He wandered inside the office and took note of two big sealed cardboard boxes next to Winslow's desk. The return address printed on each box was STATE EDUCATIONAL TESTING SERVICE. Each box was stamped ADVANCED PLACEMENT ENGLISH.

When he got to the Annex, it smelled even nastier than it usually did. The stench of weed, sweat, and hair spray had been replaced by something redolent of two-day-old hot lunch. Sammy was hammering a platform into place while Eileen crouched down with her camera, taking pictures of the set for the yearbook.

"Hey, sexy," Rob said, poking her ass. "You don't have to point it at me for me to check it out."

Eileen whipped around in mock horror. "Hey, ugly!" She tried to swat Rob in the thigh but missed by a few inches.

"What the hell?" said Rob. "You don't just go around smacking guys in the dong."

"How was I supposed to know I smacked you there?" Eileen asked.

"Because how could you not? It's a pretty big target," said Rob.

"Is that what Amanda tells you?"

"Amanda hasn't been providing much oral communication lately," said Rob. "That's the problem."

"Poor you," Eileen said. "How're you dealing with your physical needs?"

"Mostly in the shower, thinking of you," said Rob.

Eileen laughed. "Gross."

"All guys are gross," said Rob. "I'm just more honest about it."

More actors began walking in, Fiona and Judith, hand in hand, giggling and whispering like the lesbians they seemed to want others to think they were. Something was sexy about the two of them together, Rob mused. They probably thought he was an asshole, but he didn't mind. Whenever someone regarded him as an asshole, he felt understood.

Carrie entered the theater fast, probably trying to get away as quickly as possible from Declan, who was growing more pathetically possessive with each passing day. Franklin came in shortly thereafter, wheeling his bike, then setting it against a wall in the aisle before he sat beside Carrie. Rob didn't mind Frank; he was probably some left-wing socialist type, but at least he wasn't all up in your face about it like some people he knew. Calvin and Trey walked in next, the two of them trading Elton John's and Kiki Dee's lines as they sang "Don't Go Breaking My Heart." It was depressing—how gleeful they always acted in the Annex, how aimless and lost when Rob saw them anywhere else.

Amanda was last to appear, sporting the GUARDIAN ANGELS jacket she wore to patrol subways on weekends, which had always struck Rob as laughable—as if any thug would look at all five foot one and ninety-eight pounds of her and stop committing armed robbery.

"What's up, Amanda?" Rob asked, and then, when she didn't answer, added testily, "Fine. Ignore me."

Eileen put the lens cap back on her camera and sat down in the audience next to Rob. He fingered the white frog-patterned turtleneck she was wearing underneath her gray sweater. "Why do you always wear these turtlenecks?" he asked. "Trying to hide the hickeys Timmy Donovan gives you?"

Eileen laughed. "Do they still show?"

Rob inspected her neck. "Nah, that altar boy's probably pretty uptight. The hickeys I give last a long time." He leaned in as if to give her one and bit her shirt.

"Stop." Eileen pushed him away but without much conviction. There was something intriguingly malleable about her; he wondered exactly how much he could get her to do for him and where, if anywhere, she would draw the line. "Hey," he asked, "wanna do a little job for me? It's only a little bit dangerous."

"What sort of 'job' do you have in mind?"

Rob told Eileen that he had seen boxes of AP English exams in Mrs. Winslow's office. Densmore hadn't shown up yet, the school was empty, and it would be easy to go into the office, slit open a box, take out an exam, and seal the box back up.

Rob made a pastime of doing this sort of thing, suggesting crimes other people could commit: "There's that dude who was talkin' smack about you; maybe you should give him a piece of your mind," he'd say. Or: "There's that girl you like; she seems pretty wasted right now."

"Why would I steal a test?" Eileen asked. "I don't even take AP."

"Well, if I get an answer sheet, I could fill it in, copy it, and we could sell it," said Rob.

Eileen covered her mouth with horror and delight. "How much do you think we'd get?"

"Forty bucks a pop, maybe fifty. It'd be easy for you; you won't run into anybody, and even if you do, everyone knows you as a stage manager chick. Everyone expects you to be walking around with a box knife and tape."

Eileen's forehead furrowed. She hemmed and hawed.

"You get fifty percent," he said.

"What the hell; I'll do it."

Eileen bounded off, and Rob surveyed the scene, a world of people he'd soon surpass: Amanda sneaking something into her bag, ignoring

Rob, pretending she hadn't seen him biting Eileen's shirt; Fiona and Judith trading sips from a Thirsty 32-Ouncer soda container that probably didn't contain soda; Carrie and Franklin sitting side by side, scribbling in their character diaries; Trey dancing and singing Heaven 17; Calvin attempting impromptu comedy routines to see whom he could offend— "Now, if Hitler had started tryin' to round up brothers 'stead o' Jews, the whole story woulda turned out a little different," he said.

Sammy Doulos was sitting on a paint-spattered metal stool before his consoles in the lighting booth. He had his headphones on and was pantomime drumming to the Yes tune he was listening to—"Round-about," his favorite. Sammy had an elaborate pantomime drum kit: kick snare, multiple sets of cymbals, a gong, chimes he could run his fingers across. If you paid close attention, you could see him pantomiming a cape.

Rob shouted: "Sambo!"

Sammy turned toward Rob, nodding to the same tempo he'd been beating out. A smile formed eerily upon his face as if he were a ventriloquist's dummy about to take on an evil life of his own. He put the headphones down, gave Rob a big handshake, pulled him in for a hug, and spoke in his late-night deejay's basso profundo: "*Rooooooobbbbbbbbbb*," he said.

"*Saaaaaaaaam*," said Rob.

Sam laughed—"*Eeh, eeh, eeh! Big Rooooobbbbbbb!*"

"I got a business proposal for you," Rob said.

Sammy pumped the air in front of his crotch—"*Pfft, pfft, pfft.*" He shut off his music. "Lay it on me," he said.

*

When Eileen returned, she was grinning and carrying a rolled-up test booklet. She waved it at Rob as if she'd just captured the enemy's flag.

"Well," said Mr. Densmore as he walked down the aisle, carrying a stack of foil-wrapped food containers, "you certainly look like you either just committed a crime or turned a trick."

Eileen beamed at Densmore. "Maybe both," she said.

Tyrus put the containers down on the Franks' dining room table, then left the auditorium and returned with a heavy, beat-up cardboard box that he dropped on the stage with a thump and a clang. He clapped his hands twice as if performing a flamenco dance. "Eyes up here, people," he said. "This will be a different sort of rehearsal. It will last all night and on into the morning, but this is no slumber party. Something has been missing from this show, and it is the same thing that has been missing from every *Anne Frank* I have ever seen—the overpowering stench of reality. The actors are always too clean, their surroundings too pristine. It's like people can't bring themselves to show how bleak the Franks' and Van Daans' lives really were.

"Imagine how it must really have been," he said. "Two years of never going outside; of seeing the same people every hour of every day and beginning to *hate* them; two years of everyone knowing if you're pissing or shitting or fucking—and if you make the wrong noise at the wrong time, you will die.

"It must have been like being locked inside a tragedy. Like performing the same roles over and over, wanting to escape those roles, yet what other roles could you possibly play? Every emotion is magnified, every thought. Tonight, you are prisoners like them. We will run through the script. Then we'll do it again. And again. You will sleep here. If you have to go to the bathroom, you will hold it until morning. And if you can't"—he ripped open the dented cardboard box and grabbed an armful of thrift shop cookware—"here are your chamber pots."

"You must be joking," Judith said.

"Do I look like I'm in the mood for jokes, Ms. Nagorsky?" Densmore took one pot and kicked it across the floor into the Franks' bedroom, another into the Van Daans', the third into the room Mr. Dussel shared with Anne.

"Yo, Mr. D!" Calvin called out. "How come I gotta sleep in the same room with these Jews when my character ain't even Jewish and he spends his nights at home in his own bed?"

"Empathy, Mr. Dawes," said Densmore. "You are playing an empathetic character."

"And what about dinner?" Calvin asked. "Didn't you say you'd get us fed?"

Densmore uncovered the trays on the dining room table, and the theater was suffused with a sour odor of overcooked greens and burnt potatoes. "This is your dinner." He gestured to the trays as if to a skeleton in a crypt.

Trey peeked at the black-and-green-gray contents of the trays and dry-heaved. "How can you do this? You know I'm diabetic," he said. "I can't eat any of this."

Densmore fished in his pocket and handed Trey some coins, then spoke with unusual gentleness: "That's fine, Trey, I understand. Go get yourself whatever you need from the vending machines." He turned to the rest of his cast. "As for the rest of you, *bon appétit!* Fifteen minutes 'til places; get your costumes on."

*

That night Densmore said less than he usually did in rehearsal; he didn't criticize inconsistent accents or missed lines, didn't tell Rob to "show a little more emotion, damn it" or Judith to "show a little less." He seemed most interested in wearing the actors down until he had erased the separation between them and the characters they were playing.

During lulls in the action, Carrie would venture up to Franklin's room to practice their dancing and kissing scene. Each time they did, she would move closer, hold him tighter.

"You still have a boyfriend, don't you?" Franklin asked her.

"I do, but Anne doesn't," she said.

Trey was getting paler and more jittery, which not even a toke off of Amanda's one-hitter seemed to help. Meanwhile, Rob spent the scenes in which he didn't have dialogue either in bed or on the living room couch, methodically completing the AP test. He answered rudimentary vocabulary questions and, in the short-answer section, analyzed passages from stories, all of which he'd read in Mrs. Winslow's class. He knew that the line in "Hills Like White Elephants" about how "they just let the air in" referred to an abortion and that the answer to the question about Richard Connell's "The Most Dangerous Game" was "Both A and B" because the story's themes were "Man vs. Man" and "Man vs. Nature." The "extended essay" question, which counted for half the test score, was even easier: "Pick a quotation from a favorite story, book, or play. Explain why that quote exemplifies the themes of that work of literature."

In the last moments of the final run-through, Carrie and Franklin made as if to kiss, then froze in place at the sounds of marching German soldiers playing over the PA. Densmore raised his hands over his head, then brought them down slowly. "And . . . *blackout!*" he said. "Run-throughs are over for the night, but rehearsal is not done. For the next seven hours, there will be absolute silence."

"I cannot do this," said Trey. "I told you—my blood sugar. I will pass out."

"Trey, you're free to go until morning," Densmore said, again with uncharacteristic kindness. "Everybody else stays."

Trey grabbed his backpack and hurried toward the exit.

"Can we have a break first?" Judith asked.

"No breaks," said Densmore.

"What if we need to use the loo?" Fiona asked.

"You know where the chamber pots are."

"What if we see a 275-pound Black man in the theater. Can we call the cops?" asked Calvin.

"Enough!"

Fiona and Judith shared a blanket on the floor of the theater, so Rob got the Franks' bed for himself. He lay amid the silence and darkness and the smell of overcooked cabbage, contemplating all the literary quotations he could use to answer the essay question. He thought of the time he had played Mitch in *A Streetcar Named Desire* and Judith, playing Blanche DuBois, had cried out that she had always depended on the kindness of strangers. He thought of a William Faulkner passage that Mrs. Winslow made them analyze—"My mother is a fish." He thought of Densmore's favorite line in *The Sound of Music*: "What's the matter with all you gloomy pussies?"

And as he lay on his cot in the dark, he thought more about Densmore, a man he loathed yet couldn't help admiring. He never would aspire to the small life Densmore led, but he did like the power the man wielded. For none of these people onstage needed to stay for this torture, yet they all were still here. Densmore had told them to be quiet, and they were. He said none of them could leave to use the bathroom, and in the silence he could hear fluid filling a pot. If you could act like Densmore in the real world, there was no telling what you could accomplish. Densmore had a vision of how he wanted his play to be, and he didn't give a shit what he had to make people do in order to see it through. If you were certain where you wanted to go, people would follow you and help you get there. Some would follow because they loved you, some because they were afraid, some just because they had nowhere to go and any plan was better than none. He smirked as he thought of the time he had played Laertes in *Hamlet*—"That a man may smile and smile and be a villain."

Rob started to write down that line, and as he did, he became aware of the sound of someone shifting about in bed, then soft footsteps on the stage. He tried to detect where the sounds were coming from but couldn't see anything. He heard socks sliding across the carpet. A shadowed figure approached one of the theater's Exit signs. A rear door of the theater opened quickly, then shut, letting in only a brief haze of light before the space returned to darkness.

Rob put down his pen. "Hey, Muldoon," he called out. "You got your flashlight on you?"

Eileen turned it on and covered the beam with her hand. Her fingers glowed pink.

"C'mere." Rob took the flashlight, made some space for Eileen beside him, and she slipped under the covers.

Rob liked the idea of seducing girls who weren't conventionally attractive. How bored he had been with Amanda, who thought showing her hot body to anyone was doing them a favor. He resented that his parents decried superficiality; yet, if either of them had been fat or poor, neither would have married the other. His brother, pursuing his independent roll-your-own-major program at Reed, was always mouthing off about women's rights, yet whenever he sent home pictures of himself, he always had his arm around some hot blonde babe.

With one hand Rob rubbed Eileen's thigh; with the other he pointed her flashlight at Mr. Dussel's bed. "It's empty."

Eileen put her palm over the light. "So?"

"Densmore's gone," Rob said. "Trey's bed's empty too."

"Trey's diabetic," Eileen said. "He went home."

Rob snorted. "I never heard him say anything about diabetes before. Why's he the only kid Densmore isn't an asshole to? You remember when you went over to Densmore's place and you saw him kneeling in front of some kid? You think it could've been Trey?"

Eileen slipped her hand up the back of Rob's shirt. "Could've been."

Rob pulled back Eileen's collar and flicked her skin with his tongue. "Come on," he said. "Bring your camera."

"Where're we going?"

Rob pulled her up and kissed her lightly on the lips. "Come on."

The Annex hall was dark, but there was a strip of light at the bottom of Densmore's office door. Rob put his ear to the door. He heard a muffled voice inside—agitated, almost frantic—but he couldn't make out words. "Do you hear anything?" he asked.

Eileen listened. "Someone's talking, but it's all garbled," she said.

"The voice I heard sounded excited," said Rob. "Did you hear anyone excited?"

"Like *that kind* of excited?" Eileen asked.

"Possibly."

Densmore opened his door, holding a phone with the mouthpiece pressed to his chest. He looked exhausted. "If you have a question to ask, why don't you just come out with it?" he said.

Eileen stammered, "We were worried about Trey; we wanted to see if he was all right."

"Trey is fine," Densmore said. "I told him he could go home. You know that. Now, is there anything else you want to ask while I'm on the phone with my wife and we try to figure out how my son got out of his room and threw himself in front of a van at the clinic tonight?"

"Oh my God," Eileen said. "Is Tom okay?"

"Don't pretend like you give a shit," said Densmore. "You're not good enough actors. Get back to your places, both of you."

The stench in the theater was stronger when Rob and Eileen returned to Mr. Frank's bed, Rob stewing over what Densmore had said: "You're not good enough actors." He didn't know what pissed him off more, the fact that Densmore had insulted him or that he regarded him and Eileen as equal parts of a pair. As Eileen stroked Rob's chest, flicking his nipple with the cold, hard rings she wore, he wondered if she realized that what she was doing was more annoying than arousing. He didn't understand his peers' propensity to seek out virgins; the practice smacked of a lack of self-confidence. But Rob let her continue, knowing that if he really wanted to ruin Densmore, having Eileen by his side could be advantageous.

Helping Eileen take off her blouse and unfastening her bra strap, he asked what her "boy from Boyola" would think about all this.

Eileen pressed her chest to Rob's and laughed. "Don't worry about Timmy," she said. "I'll handle him."

*

The AP English exam was held in the cafeteria. With $350 cash stuffed in a pocket, $100 of which he would give to Eileen because fifty-fifty didn't seem fair, given how much work he had put in, Rob watched the other students shuffling in. He wondered which ones had paid Sammy for the answer sheet.

Mrs. Winslow eyed her pocket watch, then moved about the room, placing test booklets on each desk, greeting students in an ironic tone as if they were already guilty of something. "Ms. Wehner; Mr. Newson; Mr. Dawes; Ms. Nagorsky; Mr. Rubicoff."

Once the exam began, Rob filled out the answers slowly and carefully; he didn't want to seem as if he had copied someone's sheet, so he made sure to get some things wrong. He defined *officious* as *official sounding*; he confused *oxymoron* with *tautology*. And although he grinned when he saw Trey confidently writing about how a man could smile and smile and still be a villain, Rob didn't use that quote. Instead, he thought about Densmore. And then he looked over to Amanda, who probably was deluded enough to think she could still use him for free weed and concert tickets once *Anne Frank* was over. He watched her filling out her exam, and as he did, a plan began to take shape. Mr. Frank was right, Rob thought as he began writing a quotation on his exam sheet: "There are no walls, there are no bolts, no locks that anyone can put on your mind."

Mr. Van Daan

The morning after the AP English test, the word was already out in the halls of the high school: Mr. Densmore was looking for Trey. Wherever he went, the news seemed to follow him. Before the first bell rang, Vice Principal Roche said, "Hey there, T. You know Mr. Densmore's looking for you?" When Trey went out to the smoking area—not to smoke, cigarettes were gross; just to see if Sammy was there and could sell him some weed or tell him where he could buy some coke—Sammy pointed a thick finger at him, said, "*Trrrrrreeeeeey*," then "Hey, get up to the Annex when you can, dude; Ty's lookin' for you." At lunch, Calvin said, "T.D.'s tryin' to catch himself some V.D., son."

"What?" Trey asked.

"Densmore's looking for Mr. Van Daan," said Calvin.

"Do you know what he wants?"

"I do not," Calvin said. "But if Mr. D's involved, chances are that dick sucking is on the menu."

Trey was so filled with dread that he had to leave English midway through and run for the bathroom, where he shat water and mucus. The way he saw it, there could be only two reasons why Densmore wanted to see him: either Densmore was going to kick him out of the show because somehow he had figured out that he had lied about being diabetic, or Densmore had found out he had cheated on his AP exam and was going to have him expelled.

Trey had been tempting fate for so long that he knew eventually it would come back to bite him in the ass: *The Sun Also Rises* test he had studied for using CliffsNotes he'd shoplifted; the PSATs that he'd paid Rob to take for him; the trig tests Carrie let him copy.

Sometimes he wished that someone would finally catch him and he could end the charade and make his family believe him when he said he wasn't as smart as they thought, and didn't belong in any of the classes he was getting As in. When would it stop? Could he lie his way into Harvard? Could he cheat all the way through med school and get the degree his mom and dad had been talking about ever since he'd improbably aced the placement test that got him into North Shore? Could he lie for his whole career, dispensing medicine and recommending treatments he'd copied off other doctors' diagnoses? He imagined explaining himself at Saint Peter's gate: "But don't you see? I got sent to the wrong place. That bit about smiling and still being a villain? I copied it off a paper some burnout sold me."

After the final school bell, Trey motored through the hallway, accepting soul handshakes, "What's up, Newts," and "My man, Trey-Treys"—none of which he deserved either. Those were really for his brothers, whose reputations at the high school had preceded him: Will had quarterbacked the football team; Keith had gone to State in wrestling; Fuckin' Stuart, so named for his favorite verb, adverb, and adjective, had been undefeated in schoolyard brawls. Trey's brothers had treated him brutally, but everyone in the school knew that if they ever messed with Trey, they were as good as dead. When Mr. Densmore first cast Trey in a show, he said it was in spite of his brothers' reputations, not because of them, but now it looked like all that special treatment might be over.

"Come in, Trey. Shut the door, sit down."

Mr. Densmore's desk looked newly clean. It was free of cigarette ash and pornography; nothing was on it save for a rose in a thin clear vase, a handful of trophies Tyrus had won in his high school acting days, and a copy of the *New York Times* opened to the theater listings.

Trey mentally calculated how fast he could run from the office to the bathroom.

"Feeling all right?" Densmore asked.

"Fine, I guess," said Trey. "You?"

"Oh, fine as far as it goes. But I've been so focused on the show and what's happening with my son—we have to move him again; it has been one nightmare after the other—the semester seems to be getting away from me. Spring break's almost here. Have you made plans?"

"Not really, I'll just be hanging out doing the usual stuff. What about you?"

"New York, as always," Densmore said.

"Oh, right, the famous New York trip." Trey flashed his palms like Roy Scheider playing Bob Fosse in *All That Jazz*. "Showtime!" he said.

"So," said Densmore. "What do you think?"

"About?" Trey felt his pulse in his throat. He did not want to let himself believe Densmore was about to ask what he seemed like he might be asking. And yet, who else would Densmore take to New York? Declan had been the obvious choice, but he and Densmore had been fighting and he wasn't in the show. Judith would have made sense, but Trey didn't know if Densmore took girls, and anyway, she and Densmore hated each other. Densmore and Rob couldn't stand each other either: at Yesterday's, Rob was always asking for dirt that could help him "take Densmore down." Eileen got along with Densmore better than anybody, but casting her in *Anne Frank* had been favor enough. Densmore had cast Calvin in most Annex shows, but for the New York trip Densmore seemed to favor athletic leading man or chorus boy types, and, no offense, Calvin didn't really meet those descriptions. Trey had heard the rumors about the trip: that Densmore's wife was always supposed to come but never showed up; that Densmore got kids drunk and took them to peep shows and porn shops. But right now he didn't care about any of it; he just wanted to go.

Densmore pulled some brochures out of his drawer and laid them on the desk. "We'll stay four nights," he said. "We'll see the new Lanford Wilson play, we'll see *Agnes of God*, *Othello* with Christopher Plummer and James Earl Jones. You'll have your own room, of course; Susan and I will have the other."

"You're asking me to come with?" Trey asked.

"I am," said Densmore. "It's quite an opportunity and quite an honor." He listed some former students who had accompanied him to New York: a director currently studying for a master's at Yale; a member of the original cast of *A Chorus Line*; Kirk Massie, who had just gotten cast on *General Hospital*; Todd Merritt, who had started out as an assistant to Joe Papp at the Public Theater and was now a hotshot producer.

Densmore spoke of other tourist attractions in New York. But although they sounded fine, what mattered most to Trey was that New York was eight hundred miles from home. New York sounded like wondrous, dangerous freedom, a place where he could be who he was and not who he was pretending to be. Which was the thing he liked most about the Annex too: when the door to the theater closed and there was no light from outside, just the beams shining down upon the stage, he could feel he was most himself—even, perhaps especially, when he was pretending to be someone else. For Trey, one of the hardest parts of playing Mr. Van Daan was trying to remember he was hiding because his life was in danger. Because, when he didn't stop to think about Nazis and the Holocaust and six million Jews, the idea of being holed up forever in Amsterdam sounded so much cozier than his life in Glencoe, where he felt he had to hide himself from his family every single minute he was with them.

Mr. Densmore gave Trey the brochures and a parental permission slip. "Will your parents be okay with you going?" he asked.

"Sure, of course, why wouldn't they be?" said Trey.

*

Trey entered his house right as his mother was putting dinner on the table: gray lamb chops topped with dollops of green mint jelly; rice pilaf with flecks of mushroom in it; a hunk of iceberg lettuce dressed with creamy garlic dressing. Mr. Newson, president of Newson Demolition, was at the head of the table, hands on his armrests, listening to John Cody on WBBM. Mr. Newson liked listening to the news and arguing with it, liked having opinions; the fact that he had started off on Throop

Street as a stock boy in his dad's hardware store and wound up as head of one of the two biggest demolition companies in Illinois made him feel as though his opinions mattered more than other people's. "Why're they talking about extraditin' that guy Demyanjook?" he asked, intentionally mispronouncing the name. "Sentence the bastard to death right here in America, or in Israel; they don't screw around there."

Whenever Trey arrived home, he became virtually unrecognizable to himself. Gone were the filthy jokes and the impromptu New Wave songs and porn-movie sound effects; he behaved politely and formally in the manner of the Ivy League boy his parents insisted he would become. He filled goblets with ice water, and after he and his parents held hands and said grace, he handed his father the permission slip and asked him to sign it.

Mr. Newson took a pen from the pocket of his golf shirt and uncapped it.

"It's the trip I was telling you about," Trey said.

Mr. Newson squinted at the document and made a vague motion. His wife fetched him his reading glasses. "What kind of school trip starts on a Friday but doesn't end until Tuesday?" he asked.

"The New York trip, like I said," Trey told him.

"New York?" Mr. Newson looked at his wife. "Have you heard anything about this?"

Thao Newson shook her head.

Trey affected exasperation. "It's one of the highest honors you can win at the school. We'll see the UN, the Empire State Building, the Met Museum."

"And where'll you be staying?" Mr. Newson asked.

"The Statler Hilton, like it says."

"Who's payin'?"

"It's a school trip," Trey said. "Every year Mr. Densmore takes his top student."

"So just the two of you? Just you and Mr. Drama Teacher for four nights in a hotel in New York?"

"Of course not; I'll have my own room. Mr. Densmore'll be in the other with his wife."

"His *wife*? He has a *wife*?"

"Yes, Dad. Also a son."

Trey had long known that his family suspected he might be gay, though no one ever specifically asked if he was. He knew this suspicion was the unstated motivation behind the questions he fielded about who he would take to this or that dance, behind his dad's rage whenever a relative bought Trey a paint set or a Broadway record for his birthday, whenever Trey wore a pink polo shirt or played his Flock of Seagulls or INXS albums. And he knew it was why, on his fourteenth birthday, the worst birthday of his life, his brothers had dragged him to an acrid strip club in Lakeview. They had gone to a back room and tied him to a chair while a stripper named Cookie bopped his face with her boobs, then unzipped his pants and kept spitting in an ice cube and sucking it out, all the while his brothers laughed hysterically, tucked bills into her G-string, and shouted, "More ice cube tricks!" Until Trey, trying to free himself, fell to the ground, still tied to the chair, and Cookie said, "I think that's about all the time you paid for, guys."

Probably he was gay. He knew he was in theory, but the specifics made him want to retch. Imagining guys naked grossed him out; seeing them naked was even worse—so much so that, after swimming class, he avoided the showers altogether and put his pants on over his wet bathing trunks. And as far as sex was concerned, that anal stuff was just too repulsive to contemplate. Calvin had once said that there were people into "anal sex" and people into "banal sex," which was when you "do it with a tree." Maybe he just wasn't into sex—anal, banal, or otherwise. He felt attracted only to ill-fated movie stars of both sexes: Sal Mineo, Montgomery Clift, Jean Seberg. And even then his erotic fantasies, such as they were, never really got past the point of dance routines.

What pissed Trey off most about the fact that his father seemed ready to crumple up the New York permission slip was that his parents cared so much about how others saw him while remaining completely blind to the life he actually led. They worried about how it would look for him to go to New York with Densmore but had no clue how often he drove his mother's Audi wasted, hurling beer cans and pipes out the window whenever he saw a cop. They had no idea about the allowance money he spent on tests and essays. On the occasions when he passed out at cast parties and Carrie or Amanda brought him home, the only thing that seemed to matter to his parents was that he was with a girl. He hadn't understood why his mom and dad let him act in shows at the Annex until he realized it was because he always played characters who had girlfriends or wives.

"Nothin' doing," Mr. Newson said. "You and Mr. Drama Teacher in a hotel in New York? Nothin' doing."

"Jesus." Tears came fast to Trey's eyes. "Did you listen to anything I said? Mrs. Densmore is coming too; so are other people."

"Who else?" asked Mr. Newson.

"My girlfriend," Trey said.

"Whose girlfriend?" asked Mr. Newson.

"Mine," said Trey. "I was going to bring her over on Sunday so you could meet her, but apparently you don't care."

"Wait, which girlfriend? What's her name?"

"Oh, don't act like you're all interested now." Trey slid his plate off the table, tossed its contents into the trash, and stomped upstairs to his room, where he blasted the Go-Go's and danced furiously until he was interrupted by a knock on the door.

Mrs. Newson stood in the hallway, one hand cupping the other. She looked contrite. "Is it too late?" she asked.

"Is what too late?" asked Trey.

"This girl. Inviting her to dinner."

Trey flopped down on his bed, grabbed a pillow, and hugged it. "I guess I could ask," he said.

"Your father and I talked about it. We know we have been harsh. We would like to meet this girl."

Yeah, Trey thought, he wanted to meet her too.

*

"Why would you even want to go?" Judith asked after rehearsal when half the cast had gathered at a table at Yesterday's. "Seriously, Trey, if you have such a stiffy for New York, your parents would take you, wouldn't they?"

"But that's the problem: it would be with my parents," said Trey.

"Better than with Tyrus," said Judith.

"No," said Trey. "Worse, so much worse. I don't want to get into it; I just really need to go."

"He does," said Rob. "He does need to go." He turned to Trey. "You'll go and you'll take detailed notes—everything Densmore says, everything he does. Reconnaissance. We need to gather as much evidence as we can."

"But my parents won't let me go if I don't have a girlfriend," said Trey. "They only said yes because I told them I was bringing a girlfriend."

"Bring Kathy Ho-Ho," said Rob. "Your folks like her, right?"

Trey didn't know if Rob was making fun of him or if he actually thought Kathy Ho existed. "Kathy's out of the picture," said Trey. "Forget her; I need to find someone else. She doesn't need to be my girlfriend forever, just at Sunday dinner so my parents'll get off my ass."

Calvin looked around the table. "No takers?" he asked. "Hell, I'll do it if no else is woman enough. Get me a dress, a wig, a pair of size fourteen double-E high heels, and twenty bucks, and I'll be your girlfriend all through Sunday dinner, Trey. Gimme a hundred bucks and a bottle of Ronrico and we can start talking extras and fringe benefits."

"This is serious," said Trey.

"I *am* serious," Calvin said. "I can seriously use the cash. What's the matter? Don't your folks like brown people?"

"No, actually, they don't," said Trey. "They don't like brown people or Jews or homosexuals or any people other than white people and maybe Vietnamese people. It's seriously fucked-up; that's why I've gotta get outta there." He turned to Eileen. "Come on. How about it?"

"Me?" Eileen asked.

"You'd be perfect," said Trey. "You like talking to people's parents, you go to church. You can talk to my dad and my brothers about football."

Eileen put her arm in Rob's. "I wish I could, Trey-Trey," she said. "I'm just involved with too many people already."

"But someone has to step up," said Rob. "We need to know what actually happens on these trips, what kind of shit Densmore's into; otherwise, it's all just rumor and innuendo." He fixed his gaze across the table. "Nagorsky?"

Judith gave him the finger.

"Well, really, why not?" Trey said to Judith. "You're the best actress here—no offense to anyone else. You can play a fifty-year-old mom in Amsterdam; you could play my girlfriend. How hard could that be?"

"I met your parents that one time; they hated me." Judith imitated Mr. Newson: "'Did you enjoy *Masada*? Do you get gifts all eight nights of Hanukkah? Do you listen to Barbra Streisand and Neil Diamond? That's real music.'"

Trey looked desperately at the people around the table, then at random waitresses. He seemed on the verge of tears. "Really?" he said. "No one can help? Really?"

"So," Fiona interjected, "how old is this bird supposed to be, anyway?"

"Which bird?" Trey asked.

"The bird you're supposedly having it off with so your parents don't think you're a nancy boy," said Fiona.

"It doesn't even matter," Trey said.

"Is it that important to you?" asked Fiona. "To travel to New York with that grotty little man?"

"It is," Trey said, "and if you ever meet my parents, you'll get it. Every second I spend with them, I feel like I'm gasping for air."

"Is there some reason why you've asked everyone except me?" asked Fiona.

"Well, yeah: because you are fucking intimidating," Trey said.

"Intimidating?" Fiona asked. "Am I?"

"A bit," Judith said.

"Of course you are," said Trey. "You're gorgeous, you speak eight zillion languages. How would my parents believe I was dating you?"

Fiona lit a cigarette and took a drag.

Trey watched her. And as he considered why his parents would never believe Fiona was his girlfriend, he realized something: no, Fiona would never date the Trey he really was, the one who paid for exams and copied test papers and shat water whenever he was nervous and fantasized about James Dean in *East of Eden*. But the Trey his parents wanted him to be would have a girlfriend exactly like her.

"Just tell me when and where," Fiona said.

Judith grabbed Fiona's arm. "You're not seriously considering doing this."

Fiona shrugged. "Why not, love? It's the only decent thing to do."

*

Trey didn't call Fiona before the Sunday dinner. He feared that if they spoke on the phone, she would find some reason to cancel. But the moment he pulled into her turnaround, she was heading down her steps in a trench coat and a pink Borsalino that matched the umbrella she was twirling.

"Lovely car," she said. "Nice and sporty, isn't it? A good way to pick up a bird and make an impression." She turned on the radio and fiddled with the knob, settling on a college station at the left end of the dial that was playing Black Flag. She turned it up; Trey turned it back down. "That's not the music my girlfriend would listen to," he said.

"Righto." Fiona twisted the station dial all the way to the right where WGCI was playing Grandmaster Flash and the Furious Five.

"Not that either," said Trey.

"Christ," said Fiona, "what sort of bird do you think I am? Am I supposed to be listening to operas and symphonies and shite of that nature?"

"Exactly," said Trey. " 'Shite of that nature.' Can't you just be quiet and polite for a few hours? Then you can go back to being who you are, whoever that is."

Fiona folded her arms. "If you insist. I haven't the slightest idea why you want this trip so badly. If you were my brother, I'd tell you to sod it. But I shall do my best."

Trey sighed, and mouthed "Thank you." As he stopped at a traffic light, he watched Fiona flicking ash out the window. He imagined that, to anyone driving by, they would look like a beautiful couple.

*

The beautiful couple were among the last to arrive at the house. The Newsons had brought the tents and the picnic tables out of the garage. Apparently, they had invited everybody—the biggest crowd to gather here since Trey's confirmation, which had been pretty much ruined when his brothers had taken turns shoving each other into the pool while they were still wearing their suits and their father had bellowed that if they didn't knock it off, he'd throw a lawn mower into the deep end and electrocute the lot of them.

There was a green tarp over the pool tonight—too early in the year for swimming. Guests were on the lawn, drinking beer and snacking on the chips and Roquefort dip that Mrs. Newson had arranged in bowls on picnic tables topped with red-and-white-checkered table-cloths. Music blared from the speakers: Mr. Newson's favorite, Frank Sinatra. The men wore blazers and ties; the women wore pantsuits—as if no one had changed after church.

Trey and Fiona walked hand in hand along the house's curved side path until they reached the lawn. His brothers were here—two with girlfriends, one with a pal from high school; so were Trey's aunt Ming and his uncle Wayne and their three kids. Mr. Newson's brother, Billy-Boy, who wasn't really his brother but had been his best friend in the service, was here with his second wife and her two sons. There were neighbors, high school buddies, colleagues from Newson Demolition. Mr. Newson was working the grill. "Two burgers up. Who wants 'em?" he shouted. "Someone better get on these dogs; they're ready to go."

Trey and Fiona circulated, distributing handshakes and hugs like they had just returned from a honeymoon. Trey's brother Fuckin' Stuart—who, now that he was in his senior year at Lake Forest College, came in only about one weekend per month—was in the company of yet another new girlfriend whom he seemed to be auditioning for the role of wife. Kristy was a speech language pathology student who had worked as a Honey Bear cheerleader for the Chicago Bears. Fiona told Kristy that she loved her handbag and asked where she had gotten it, and Kristy told her that the Bears' quarterback, Bob Avellini, had given it to her. Fiona said it was "smashing," at which point Fuckin' Stuart wondered aloud how "smashing" the gift would be after he had smashed the thing in Avellini's fuckin' face. He told Fiona he liked her accent and asked where she was from, and she said London. He asked her which part and she told him Mayfair, but he didn't know where that was, so he asked if anybody in her family played rugby and she said no, all those men rolling around in the mud—it really seemed just like ritualized homosexuality, didn't it? She said she had no problem with men wanting to bugger each other, but why didn't they just do it instead of pretending they were really doing something else? Trey pinched Fiona hard—"Jesus," he said—but Fuckin' Stuart cracked up. "Fiona is fuckin' awesome, man," he told Trey. "Where the fuck'd you find her?"

"Walking the streets in Piccadilly," Fiona said.

Will Newson was up from Champaign-Urbana with Micki Lanza, the girl he'd been dating for the past year and a half; he'd met her at a frat party. Will and Micki were holding plastic plates and feeding each other forkfuls of side dishes. Trey introduced Fiona to Will and Micki, and Will, who seemed to want to impress Micki with his newfound maturity, complimented Fiona on her accent. He asked where she was from and, when she said London, then Mayfair, he asked what she thought about the war in the Falklands. Fiona said war was just phallic role-play; the only thing countries cared about was who had the bigger gun between their legs. Trey gasped, but Will cupped Trey on the shoulder and said Fiona was a "keeper." "You better make sure not to let this one go, bro," he said.

Keith Newson hadn't brought a date to the party; he had brought Ricky Tate. Keith was managing D.B. Kaplan's, a deli in Water Tower Place, and living in an apartment near Wrigley Field with Ricky; all the Newsons said Ricky was a bad influence on Keith, even though whenever cops pulled over Ricky and Keith, they always held Keith but let Ricky go.

"Whoa there," Keith said as Trey tried to swerve Fiona away from him. "Aren't me and Rick gonna at least get an introduction?"

Keith told Fiona she had an awesome accent and asked where she was from. She said London, then Mayfair, and since neither Keith nor Ricky knew where that was, Ricky asked for her opinion of the Rolling Stones. Fiona said they were "a pack of vile little gits" who "ponced about onstage as if they were having a wank."

Keith laughed and asked why such a "classy English broad" would hang around a "lowlife" like his brother.

"Because Trey is bloody good in the sack," Fiona said. "Isn't that why you and Ricky are together? Or are you just good pals?"

"Aww, man," Keith said, laughing, "Lemme shake this girl's hand."

Trey, who had already almost had three heart attacks, left Fiona to fend for herself while he went back into the house, ostensibly to use the john. Instead, he went up to his bedroom, closed the door, and looked from his window down to the backyard. Fiona was hugging his mother and shaking hands with guests, and for the first time Trey sensed this actually might turn out all right. Although he had never felt as attracted to any girl as he did toward, say, John Garfield, he did like Fiona, or at least whoever she was pretending to be, who seemed to perfectly complement the person *he* was pretending to be. He was halfway toward a thought of asking Fiona if she might want to date for real when his stomach started gurgling. His father was heading toward Fiona—greasy towel over a shoulder, burger flipper in one hand.

Trey ran to the bathroom, then downstairs, and found his dad by the grill, quizzing Fiona about her accent. Mr. Newson told Fiona his grandfather had come over from England but he'd never had any desire to go there; why travel somewhere his ancestors had wanted to leave? Although he averred that sometime he would like to fly over Europe to look down and see the places America had bombed. He asked what Fiona's parents did and she said they worked in the diplomatic corps. Mr. Newson asked if she'd ever thought of being a model, and she said, "Sure, could do," but since she was planning to be a climatologist or an aerospace engineer, she wasn't sure she'd have the time to "strut about in her knickers in front of a whole lot of tossers."

Mr. Newson chuckled, then walked Fiona and Trey toward an unoccupied table. "I wanna talk to this girl about something," he said, then asked Fiona. "What do you think about all this New York jazz?"

Trey bit his lower lip so hard, he actually tasted blood.

"Well, New York isn't London, is it?" Fiona said. "But it's about the best you Yanks can do."

"That's not what I'm driving at," said Mr. Newson. "I mean, what do you think of this trip with that teacher? A grown man payin' for a coupla kids to stay with him in New York? Doesn't it sound a little peculiar?"

Fiona appeared to give the matter some thought. "Yes, that notion crossed my mind as well," she said. "But Mr. Densmore—he's just a harmless little creep, and I didn't much like the hotel he reserved for us; quite a dump, really. So Trey and I will be staying uptown at the Sherry-Netherland, where we can have a spot of privacy, if you know what I mean. To tell you the truth, if all goes how I'm planning it, I doubt we'll be seeing much of Mr. Densmore at all."

Mr. Newson looked Fiona up and down, then smiled. He put a big paw on Fiona's shoulder.

"This one's okay," he told Trey. "I wasn't crazy about the others you've brought around, but this one's okay. I hope you two have a good time in New York. Send us a postcard." He took the parental permission slip out of his pocket and signed it, and as he did, he sang along with Frank Sinatra: "Fly me to the moon."

*

Later that night, Trey stalled his car in Fiona's turnaround. He turned down the stereo and pulled up the windows. "I don't know how I can thank you," he said. "I know this all started as kind of a favor and a joke, but maybe it wouldn't be the worst idea."

"What wouldn't?" asked Fiona.

"You coming to New York," said Trey. "My dad could pay your way, and we could stay together at the Hilton or that place you said." Images sparkled before him: ordering room service with Fiona; seeing musicals and plays with her; the two of them walking into restaurants and getting the same deferential looks they got in his family's backyard.

"I wouldn't want to break up your party with Mr. Densmore," said Fiona. "And besides, I don't believe I've been invited."

"*I'm* inviting you." Trey grasped her hands. "Maybe this sounds like a line, but it's almost like you saved my life. We could do it again next week, only it wouldn't be pretend." He pressed his lips to hers, but after he tried to put a tongue between them, her body stiffened and he felt her pull back like a dummy in an auto crash test.

"That does sound lovely," Fiona said. "But I don't think my boyfriend would approve."

"Boyfriend?" asked Trey. "Who?"

"He's from Chicago," Fiona said. "His name's Ray."

"Really. Is it serious?"

"We've been only going out a fortnight or so, but I certainly hope it'll turn serious. I do like this bloke quite a lot. You'll meet him sometime. After rehearsal, I'll bring him 'round."

Trey sighed. "Well, you do deserve to be dating a good bloke, Fiona," he said.

"And you deserve a good bloke too." Fiona opened the car door. "It's been a pleasure. And I do hope it all works out for you in New York."

Anne Frank

For Carrie, the worst part of Mr. Densmore's announcement was that she had to pretend she was thrilled. She had to sit there smiling and clapping like everyone else as if this were the best thing that could have happened when she knew it would just make everything worse.

"No doubt you've heard the news," Densmore said. His cast sat in the front two rows of the theater while he paced the stage. "Charles 'Trey' Newson III is no longer a part of our company. It pains me to say it. And yet, it is the truth, and therefore it must be said. Trey has transferred to Lake Forest, and the less said about all that, the better."

The theater was quiet—palpably so. Of course, everyone already knew about the AP exam question Trey and seven other students had copied, all eight of them making the exact same mistake in the *Hamlet* quote they had chosen, none of them admitting to Eustacia Winslow how they had procured their exams in advance. But hearing Mr. Densmore confirm Trey's fate out loud lent a new sense of finality.

Calvin broke the silence. "Yo, sign me up," he said. "Double role for Calvin. Mr. Kraler *and* Mr. Van Daan. Like Tony Randall in *7 Faces of Dr. Lao*. Only with actual talent. I know all those lines. Plus, we can save tall cash on greens and taters and we can spend that on beer."

Mr. Densmore chuckled. "No," he said. "I'm perfectly happy with you as Mr. Kraler, Cal. Anyway, we already have our new Mr. Van Daan." He clapped three times. "Mr. Van Daan!" he called. "Paging Mr. Van Daan!"

Declan jogged in from the aisle, already costumed in a heavy corduroy suit and a dark brown cap. The cast burst into applause.

Declan tipped his cap to the actors and bounded up onstage like an injured star quarterback unexpectedly returning to the field after half-time, ready to lead his team to a come-from-behind victory. He shook hands with Densmore. He embraced Calvin with a knowing chuckle. He hugged Judith, Rob, Eileen, and Amanda. He introduced himself warmly to Fiona, coolly to Franklin. Then he got down on one knee in front of Carrie and hugged her close, his head in her stomach.

"I only found out this morning," he said. "I wanted to surprise you—probably the hardest secret I've ever had to keep. Why aren't you saying anything?"

"I guess I just feel bad for Trey," said Carrie.

"That's because you're a good person," Declan said. "But he wasn't really right for the role anyway." He jumped up, clapped his hands, and hollered, "Let's do this; all right, let's do this. We do not have much time."

And Carrie couldn't help feeling a little like the Franks and Van Daans had when Mr. Dussel arrived at the Annex. no one could argue with his being here; all the same, it had been better when he wasn't.

"Places for act one, people," Mr. Densmore said.

Even in this first rehearsal, Declan brought a new professionalism to the show. He was hard on the other actors, harder on himself: before Mr. Densmore would tell them to redo a scene, Declan was already moving back and saying, "Come on, people, we need to get this"—slapping his hands thrice—"*right* this time." Watching him rehearse, Carrie saw exactly why she had fallen in love with him during *West Side Story* when he'd gaze at her instead of the actress playing Maria while singing "One Hand, One Heart." It seemed stupid and naïve now, but she had felt flattered that Declan had chosen her: she loved watching Gene Kelly musicals with him at his house; eating ice-cream cones at the Bunny Hutch and making out at the picnic tables; cuddling in a sleeping bag in his backyard, listening to show tunes and operas while they watched the stars and Declan planned their future.

Lately, though, just about everything that had endeared Declan to her had become annoying, and the more annoyed she appeared, the more insecure and annoying he became: he'd nod vacantly whenever she discussed her own dreams of becoming a doctor, then wait for a pause so he could shift the conversation back to himself; he'd cockily dismiss any of her plans that didn't directly involve him; he'd look wounded whenever she told him she wouldn't have time to act with him once she got to college because she would be premed, then he'd tell her that Northwestern's premed program was the best in the country, and keep staring at her until she agreed. She didn't know what was more aggravating: the fact that Declan had become so self-involved and insecure, or that those were the exact words her father had used to describe him.

Declan made her feel so claustrophobic that she felt drawn to Peter Van Daan—both the character and the actor playing him. Usually, during her kissing scene with Franklin, she just gave him a brisk, dry peck. But tonight, even though it wasn't in the script, she pushed herself into the kiss. She held him tight, opening his lips with hers, closing her eyes as he closed his, imagining how much Anne needed to escape this suffocating apartment in the arms of someone she loved, imagining how much she herself needed to escape this suffocating theater in the arms of someone she didn't feel required to love.

Only when Mr. Densmore shouted "I said 'Blackout!'" did Carrie realize that she and Franklin had been kissing for a good half minute and that some of the other actors were clapping and whooping. Declan clapped along with them, smiling grandiosely, as if to assert that the kiss represented good acting, which he approved of. Densmore held up his thumbs. "Good job, lovers," he said. "I'm giving that scene 'two big thumbs-up.'"

"Watch where you put those thumbs," Calvin said.

During the break, Carrie went to the vending machines; then, Diet Rite in hand, feeling uncharacteristically bold, she paused in the doorway of the theater classroom where Franklin stood alone, gazing out the window up at the sky. A bright amber exterior light illuminated his face. He started when he saw Carrie was looking at him.

"That scene felt good tonight," Franklin said. "You were really good in it."

"Yeah. You too." Carrie reached into her LeSportsac bag and pulled out a pen. She took his hand and wrote her phone number on the back of it.

"What's this for?" he asked.

"Just in case you want to call and do something sometime," she said.

"Like rehearse the scene more?" asked Franklin.

"Or whatever," she said. "Like maybe this weekend?"

Franklin stammered. "I could do Sunday after I'm done at the bike shop," he said.

"Sunday's bad," said Carrie. "I'm going with my family to Amsterdam. Saturday?"

"I'll be home with my grand Ps all day," he said. "You could come, but it might be kinda boring."

"It doesn't sound boring to me," Carrie said. "What's the address?"

Franklin didn't say anything.

"What's the matter?" Carrie asked.

"If I tell you, could you not tell anyone else where it is?"

"Of course," said Carrie. "Why? Is it some big secret?"

"Kinda," Franklin said. He dictated his address.

"In Chicago?" asked Carrie.

Franklin nodded.

"That's cool. I won't tell anyone." Carrie scooted fast out of the room.

When Carrie returned to the theater, Declan was sitting on the edge of the stage next to Mr. Densmore, who had his arm around him. "You know, Dec," he said, "there's a film you might enjoy; you can come over to my house to watch it anytime."

"What film?" Declan asked.

"*Baby Doll*," said Densmore. "It's terrific. Twisted but terrific. Tennessee Williams wrote it, so of course it's twisted and terrific. Karl Malden plays this poor sap of a husband. He keeps his wife in a crib and calls her

'Baby Doll.' He wants to consummate the marriage, but Baby Doll keeps putting him off. Then one night, before Malden can fuck her, she just up and fucks Eli Wallach. You really have to see it, Dec; you could learn a lot from that story."

The previous evening, after rehearsal, Carrie had gone out to Yesterday's with the other actors, but tonight, when Declan said he'd come with, Carrie said she had to study for a test, so Declan asked if she could give him a ride home. When they got to his house, she kept her car in neutral; Declan shifted it into park. "I'm really proud of you," he said.

Carrie made a face: "Proud? Why?" She found it weird when people said they were proud of her. Her parents never said it—her father because he thought his pride was something she already understood, her mom because pride wasn't something she ever expressed.

"It's obvious how hard you've worked on this show, on Anne," Declan said. "It's a real talent to make the audience believe you're attracted to someone you aren't attracted to. For a moment—it's funny—I actually thought you were really into that Franklin kid."

"Well, Anne's really into Peter," Carrie said.

"That's what I mean," said Declan. "When you were onstage, I almost forgot you were Carrie and I started thinking you were Anne. You were so convincing."

"Oh. Great." Carrie let him kiss her, acted as though she were into it, because, apparently, she was good at that. But when he started to reach under her sweater, she pushed his arm away. "I don't want to do that in front of your house," she said.

"It's not like anyone's home," Declan said.

"Even so."

"Then come inside."

"I have to study."

"Then this weekend. Let's go all out—drinks at Ambria on Saturday night, then Orchestra Hall; they're doing Dvořák, the 'New World' Symphony. And afterward we could pick up dinner somewhere and eat it by the planetarium in your car, maybe in the back seat."

"That sounds sweet," Carrie said. "But I'm flying to Amsterdam Saturday."

"Isn't that Sunday?"

"No, Saturday." The lie came easily to Carrie's lips—as easily as pretending she was Anne kissing Peter.

*

Driving alone to meet Franklin on Saturday felt like an adventure; going to Chicago always did. The city wasn't foreign to Carrie: she was here at least once a week, even more during the summers. Chicago was where her father's ad agency was, right on Michigan Avenue, with a view of the boulevard. Chicago was where her mom volunteered as a public school "music docent," wheeling her cart of musical instruments and LPs to elementary schools in neighborhoods that Carrie only glimpsed from the back seat when she drove downtown with her family to museums, plays, or concerts—the neighborhoods where Declan urged her to ride through red lights because he said that traffic signals didn't apply to white people here.

Carrie never drove to Chicago by herself, though, and the city she was passing looked different than the one she usually saw. The sky was the color of steel, and a light rain was falling. Western Avenue looked almost dangerous: there was a pizza place with a misspelled "Happy Birthday" message on its sign; dented cars were waiting in line for gas at the Standard station; an old man in a stained white undershirt was wheeling a shopping cart full of Old Milwaukee out of the Armanetti liquor store. But after Pratt Boulevard the neighborhood shifted again.

The houses here were smaller and grouped more closely together than the ones in Wilmette, and there were more people on the sidewalks. A woman wearing a sari was shoving a tricycle into the trunk of a car; a boy in a gray hooded sweatshirt was dribbling a basketball and practicing layups in a narrow driveway. Orthodox families were walking to or from shul—men and boys in black suits, hats, and tzitzit; women in raincoats worn over dresses; an old lady with a clear plastic babushka.

Carrie parked in front of a brick apartment building on Washtenaw Avenue. She thought she had the address right, but every building looked the same, so it was hard to say for sure. Walking into the vestibule didn't provide much guidance; there were names beside all the buzzers—STRIMLING, GALAVIZ, WELLER, O'HARA, MOSS, MONDELLO—but next to the 3B buzzer no name was listed, only a shallow gray rectangular indentation where the name was supposed to be. Carrie walked outside again to double-check the address. She came back in and was about to press the buzzer when Franklin galloped downstairs to open the door for her. He was wearing his denim jacket and his hair was a mess.

"Cool, you made it," he said, his gaze stopping at her wet hair. "Is it raining?"

"A little."

"I'll get some umbrellas. You wanna come up real quick?"

"Are we going somewhere?'

"Yeah, sorry." Franklin led the way up two flights of stairs upholstered in worn beige carpet. "This day's nuts," he said. "My dad was supposed to get my grand Ps their medicine, but he's been stuck on work calls, and my grand M, she started complaining the weather's bad for my grand D's circulation and whatnot. I'm like, 'Lemme just go to the drugstore for you.' You don't mind coming with?"

"No, of course not. Are they okay?"

"They're totally fine," said Franklin.

There were two doors on the third floor. One was marked 3A and the other didn't have a number. Franklin opened the door to the unmarked apartment, then called out: "It's raining; I just came back for umbrellas!" The radio was on, tuned to news on WBBM; top stories were still John Demjanjuk and the Falklands. At a small table in the kitchen, Franklin's grandmother ladled soup into a bowl, then carried it slowly to the table where Franklin's granddad—in a short-sleeve yellow shirt with a white undershirt underneath—was sitting. In the front room, Franklin's father held a phone to his ear with one hand and used his other hand to furiously rub his mop of gray hair. "We never said 'off the record'!" he was shouting. "You can't stop in the middle, then say what you just said was 'off the record.' That's not the way the game is played."

Franklin yelled over the tumult, "Dad, Grandma, Grandpa, this is Carrie; Carrie, these are my grandparents, my dad." Franklin's father raised his hand over his head and offered a greeting midway between a wave and a salute. His grandmother waved cheerfully. His grandfather glowered. "You get those prescriptions filled yet?" he asked.

"I'm getting them, I'm getting them, I only left fifteen seconds ago and I just said I was getting umbrellas." Franklin grabbed two from the hallway coatrack, gave one to Carrie, and kept the other for himself. "Back in a flash!" he shouted, and Carrie followed him downstairs.

"We can take my car if you need to get the medicine quicker," Carrie said.

"They have plenty," said Franklin. "They just get anxious when they're down to a couple days' worth. Do you mind if we walk? It's a Saturday, so I don't like being in a car."

"Are you Orthodox or something?" asked Carrie.

"No, but a lot of the neighbors are, and driving past them on Saturdays when they're not supposed to drive feels disrespectful." Big drops of rain were falling on the lawns, pooling in the potholes of the alley they were crossing. "I'm just sorry you're here on such a dull, dreary day," he said.

"That's okay. So what's the deal with the big, secretive location, anyway?"

Franklin squinted. "You mean the Chicago thing?"

"No, I get that, but I mean no name on the buzzer, no number on the apartment door."

"Oh, yeah—a mixture of Old World and New World paranoia," Franklin said. "My grand M, she's afraid of Nazis; my grand P, he's afraid of pogroms; and my dad, he's an investigative reporter and he's working on this story for the *Trib* about police brutality and he's worried about payback from the cops. But it's not like keeping the name off the buzzer is gonna help. The Nazis are too old to chase us, there are no more Cossacks, and the police, if they're looking for my dad, they know how to find him."

Along their way, Franklin greeted neighbors. A woman in a salmon-colored suit with white piping asked how his grandparents were and he said fine, thanks. "That's the *rebbetzen*—you know, the rabbi's wife," he told Carrie. "She escaped Berlin with her family right after Kristallnacht and lived out the war in this tiny Jewish community in Shanghai."

The boy Carrie had seen playing basketball in a driveway was still practicing layups in the rain. "What's up, Frankie?" the kid called out.

"Not much, Reuben," Franklin called back. "That's Reuben Samuelson," Franklin told Carrie. "He dropped out of Mather a couple years back and he's running a snow shoveling and lawn mowing business with his dad. When it's cold and there aren't any sidewalks to shovel, all he does is shoot hoops, do a bong, then go back to sleep, but he's a good guy." At Devon Avenue, Franklin pointed out the bike shop where he worked. "One of the guys there, he's a real interesting cat," he said. "He was a paratrooper in the war, and when he came back he was so shell-shocked, he couldn't get on a plane again. He couldn't even ride in a car or a bus. That's why he likes bikes so much."

A tall, slim kid loped by carrying a plastic bag from General Camera. "How's it goin', Muley?" said Franklin.

"Pretty good, Frank," the kid said.

"That's Muley Wills," said Franklin. "Good guy. He was on a show on NPR for a while."

Carrie thought of her Wilmette neighbors—the Primers next door, the Mazers across the street, Mr. Sucherman at the corner. She didn't know much about them save for their names and occupations: a psychologist and his wife; a pair of jewelry salespeople; a retired judge. Was she rude? Or pathologically incurious? Were their stories less interesting? Or was everyone on her block so busy getting in and out of cars that no one had time to learn anyone else's stories? "How did you find all this out?" she asked Franklin.

"From my dad, in a way," he said. "You know who he is? Ted Lichtenstein?"

"I think I've seen his name in the paper."

"Yeah, well, what he says is, if you're interested enough in what people have to say, eventually you get to know their story."

They kept walking—past a kosher supermarket with faded newspaper advertisements in English, Russian, and Hebrew in its window; a photo studio with a display of framed family photographs, most of which looked like they had been taken in eastern Europe at the turn of the century; an Israeli restaurant; an Indian pizza place; a dingy little record store called It's Here with life-size cardboard stand-up figures of Grace Slick and Peter Frampton.

"This place, it's amazing," Carrie said.

"I guess," said Franklin. "But that's the thing about places you see every day: pretty soon you don't appreciate how amazing they are, and then it's too late. It's the same with people." For a moment he looked far away.

"Do you mean someone specific?" asked Carrie.

"Oh, I guess I do." They walked past a kosher bakery—shuttered until Sunday. "We're having a nice conversation," Franklin said. "I don't want to be morbid."

"That's okay," said Carrie. "I like morbid." This wasn't remotely true, and it sounded dumb, but Franklin didn't seem to notice or care.

"Well"—he took a breath—"if you really wanna know, I was kinda thinking about my mom, which I only do about eight zillion times a day. Right after she died, I figured there'd be a day when I wouldn't think about her all the time, but so far it hasn't really worked out like that."

"I'm sorry," Carrie said. "How long ago did she—"

"About three years ago now."

"I'm so sorry." Carrie thought of her own life; the grandparents who were gone had died before she was born, and everyone else she was close to was still alive. The only person she knew who had died was a girl who had had a fatal asthma attack in the summer between first and second grade, but that had seemed so surreal that she had never really processed it as a death: the girl was there in June; come September, she was gone. It didn't seem all that different than if she had moved out of town. Carrie took Franklin's hand as they crossed Richmond Street. "I can't imagine," she said.

"Yeah, it's pretty tough," said Franklin. "I'm not over it. I'm sure I never will be. There's something ironic about it, though, her dying the way she did. After all she went through: loses her family in the camps, comes to America by herself, gets married, loses her first husband—Korea. Then she settles down in Chicago with my dad, has a kid, starts going to school to become a nurse, and BAM! Car accident. It's like her luck just ran out."

"Oh my God," Carrie said.

"Yep. Morning, she drops me off at school; three hours later, my dad's pulling me out." He forced a laugh. "I'm sorry," he said. "You come over, we go to get medicine, and I tell you the uplifting story of how my mom died."

"I wish I knew you then," Carrie said. "I would've liked to help."

"Better you didn't," he said. "I was pretty messed up. I smoked so much pot, it was like I was on a permanent high."

"When you were twelve?"

"Yeah, I guess hearing you say that makes it sound kinda insane, but it seemed normal then. I don't do it too much anymore, but it helped."

"What changed?" asked Carrie.

"It'll sound corny," said Franklin.

"What?"

"A movie. I was with my grand Ps, and they were watching *Here Comes Mr. Jordan*. It's like *Heaven Can Wait* or whatever, about these angels who come back to life in other people's bodies. I'm not religious. Are you religious?"

"I mean a little, like Hebrew school and whatever, but not really."

"I'd like to be, but religion never really made sense to me. When I saw my mom at the hospital, I figured that's pretty much it. But then I thought, 'What if it isn't? What about the one in a billion chance that my mom's up there watching? What if she sees me blowing off home-work, smoking a bowl before and after school?' So I decided I'd live my life as if she were really there, watching. That's one of the lousy parts of having a dead parent they don't tell you about: when they're alive, you pretty much know when they're watching you; when they're dead, they're with you all the time."

"Well, if she's watching us now, I hope she's happy." Carrie waved at the gray sky. "Hi, Mrs. Light."

Franklin looked up at the sky too. "Yeah, hi, Ma," he said.

They picked up the medicine from Rosen's Pharmacy, along with a Robert Stone paperback that Franklin said he wanted to read and a copy of the *Tomorrow*, a free alternative weekly. Then, at the Russian delicatessen next door, Franklin bought a big jar of borscht and two small jars of herring with onions. Carrie laughed. "Are you joking?" she asked.

"No, why?"

"Herring and onions?"

"Yeah. My grand Ps, they sure do like their Old World foods. Whenever you ask them about where they came from, they don't wanna talk about it; you have to keep bugging them before they tell you anything. But if you ask what food they want, it's borscht or herring or kreplach soup all the frickin' time. Why's that funny?"

"I probably shouldn't tell you," said Carrie. "When Declan found out you were playing Peter and he wasn't, he said he wanted me to eat herring and onions before our kissing scene."

"Why would he want you to do that?" Franklin asked.

"Oh, just because—" Carrie didn't finish the sentence. "Never mind. Maybe it isn't funny. Declan just gets weird sometimes. I'm sorry I brought him up."

By the time they got back to the apartment, the rain had let up. Franklin's grandparents were on the couch in the living room watching the news, and his dad was still on the phone.

They occupied the time before dinner in the building's basement laundry room, then up in Franklin's room, where Carrie watched Franklin fold his father's and grandparents' clothes. His room was small, cluttered; every surface—desk, dresser, night table—was full of books and papers.

"I've never seen anyone our age with so many books," Carrie said.

"I bet you have just as many," said Franklin.

"Yeah, true," Carrie said. "But no one else I know."

On the desk there was a typewriter, an old, pale green IBM Selectric the shade of government file drawers; beside it, haphazard stacks of onionskin typing paper, one with STORIES scrawled in black marker across the top page; the others were marked POEMS and DOODLES and ROUGHAGE. Carrie made as if to pick up a page, then stopped. "Sorry, I'm nosy," she said.

"It's okay," said Franklin. "You can look. It might not be any good, but I'm not private about it."

She took a sheet from the STORIES stack; it was one long block of text, a sentence that seemed to go on forever. "You have something against punctuation?" she asked.

"That's when I was getting high way too much and I was going through my Beat phase," said Franklin. "I was reading Kerouac, Burroughs, Ginsberg—you know, those cats—and I thought, if I wanted to be like them, I should write like them. It was kind of a habit, writing like the people I was reading. One time I was reading *Ordinary People* and I wrote this story kind of like it. My dad read it and made me see a shrink because he thought I was suicidal."

"Were you?"

"No, just sad." Franklin piled underwear in a mustard-colored laundry hamper.

"So," said Carrie, "that's what you want to do? Write like your dad?"

"Yeah. But also not like him. My dad, you know, he's rooted: one place, one job. I respect the hell out of that, but I couldn't live that way. I want to be a foreign correspondent, something like that. I want to write novels that take place wherever I'm living. Maybe someday I'll settle down, but there are so many different places to live, different lives you can try out. That's one thing I learned from my mom: nothing's permanent. If you can accept that—and that's a pretty fricking hard thing to do—you start seeing the world isn't as small as you think. It's like *Anne Frank*: you think about those people who could never leave their annex, then you realize how free you really are, and you can't take that for granted."

Maybe she was tired, maybe she felt relieved that she wasn't with Declan, maybe she felt Mrs. Light looking down at her. Or maybe she was thinking too hard about the life Franklin was describing—the freedom of it, the adventure—and wondering whether she could ever live that way. Whatever the reason, tears filled her eyes; they skidded down her cheeks and she shuddered. Franklin put his arm around her and she cried into his shirt. "I'm sorry," she said. "I don't even know why I'm crying."

"That's how it always works," Franklin said, sighing. "I tell people my story, and they start to cry."

Franklin wiped Carrie's tears with something soft, but when she saw what it was, she laughed. "You're wiping my tears with a sock?"

Franklin laughed too. "That's all I have." He walked to his bookshelf and took down a paperback: *The Baron in the Trees*, by Italo Calvino. "This one's my favorite lately," he said. "Whenever I get sad, even thinking about it makes me happy. You can borrow it if you want, and when you're done, you can bring it back and tell me what you think."

"What's it about?" asked Carrie.

"A boy who climbs up into the trees and never comes down."

When Franklin and Carrie got back to the living room, Franklin's dad was off the phone and had gone into his bedroom to write. Carrie could hear clacking on a typewriter behind the closed door. Franklin's grandparents were sitting on the plastic-covered couch. A sketch of John Demjanjuk sitting in a courtroom was on TV. Yes, he had lied about who he was so he could come to America, but he had never been a Nazi prison guard; they had confused him with someone else, he said.

"Grand M," Franklin asked his grandmother. "Do you recognize that man in the drawing? Could you identify him? They say he was at the camp where you were."

Franklin's grandmother squinted, then shrugged. "They were all dogs, every one of them," she said. "Who could tell them apart? Who knows whether he was or wasn't? That was years ago, and everybody looks old now; how can I recognize him when I barely recognize myself in the mirror? Go on, Frankeleh, change the channel. Maybe there's a movie or a comedy program we can watch."

*

On Saturday nights Franklin's family ate takeout, so he and Carrie went to pick up dinner. The sun was down and the Orthodox neighbors were all getting into their cars, and Franklin said it would be okay to drive. "Where're we going?" Carrie asked once they were in the car.

"Yen Ching, for Chinese," said Franklin.

"I thought you said they only liked Old World food," said Carrie.

"For Jews, Chinese counts as Old World food."

In the restaurant, the food wasn't ready yet, so they waited on the lobby's red vinyl couch, eating mints from the big glass bowl by the register. "I think I figured it out," Carrie said.

"What?"

"Why I was crying."

"Why?"

"It's that I miss this so much."

"Miss what?"

"Having a friend. I used to be best friends with Amanda when we were little; now we barely talk to each other, and when we do, we don't have anything to say. Declan—we've been boyfriend and girlfriend so long, pretending like we're adults, it's like I forgot what having a friend even means."

"Oh, that's cool," Franklin said. He seemed like he wanted to say something else, but he just let out a deep breath.

"That came out wrong," said Carrie. "I mean it's just nice to have someone you can be yourself around, who lets you be who you are, and you don't have to worry they'll tell you you're doing it wrong."

Their eyes met.

"Takeout order for Light," the woman at the register called out. "Two orders spring roll, two orders vegetable dumplings, one crab Rangoon, one hot-and-spicy bean curd, one garlic chicken, one Mongolian beef, two hot-and-sour soups, three egg drop soups."

During dinner, Carrie hoped she might learn more about Franklin's grandparents' histories or about the article Franklin's dad was working on, but those topics didn't come up. Isidore and Beileh said they'd be going out of town for the summer but didn't know where: in winter, they went to Hot Springs, Arkansas, but you couldn't go in summer because temperatures got up to 110 degrees, and why pay to shvitz when you could do it at home for free? Meanwhile, Ted Lichtenstein kept getting up from the table, walking to the drawn blinds, peeping out, then rubbing his head with his palm before he returned to the table, only to get up again a minute later.

"What's out the window?" Carrie asked.

Franklin laughed. "My dad always thinks someone's casing our place," he said.

Ted Lichtenstein looked ticked off. "That's because cops do case our place," he said. "You don't think it's true? You don't think cops want to intimidate me after what I've written? That's exactly how CPD operates: they're the goddamn Gestapo, no different. They want you to know they're always watching."

"Okay, dad," Franklin said, but Mr. Lichtenstein kept going: "When my tires got slashed, but everyone else's were fine, you think that was just random?" he asked. "Do you really think your mom died because of faulty brakes when I had just had them checked?"

"Dad!" Franklin looked demonstratively over to Carrie, then back.

Mr. Lichtenstein took a breath, let it out. He sat back down. He spooned some sweet-and-sour and mustard sauces onto his plate, swirled them together with a chunk of spring roll, and took a bite. "I'm sorry," he told Carrie. "I'm not some kind of conspiracy nut. It's just the more you look into the way things work in this country, the more you realize some conspiracies are real. Everyone's for sale; everyone's cutting some deal." He went back to the blinds and looked out. "Jesus," he said. "I should just go down, knock on the guy's window, ask him up for coffee."

Franklin puckered his lips and made an exasperated noise. "So some guy's in a car outside. There's ten apartments in this building; he could be waiting for anybody. How do you know it's you specifically?"

"Because I know what an undercover car looks like," Mr. Lichtenstein said. "You wanna take a look for yourself, smart guy? Learn something, maybe?" He used his thumb and index finger to make a space between two of the blind's slats. "Right down there."

Franklin got up; Carrie followed. Mr. Lichtenstein was pointing down at a green Pontiac Catalina. "That car?" Franklin asked.

"Yeah, that car."

Carrie squinted, then gasped. "Oh my Lord," she said.

"What's the matter?" asked Franklin.

"That's Declan. He's in his mom's car," she said.

She felt angry. Then scared. Then angry that she felt scared. Then guilty. Then angry she felt guilty. She walked to the front door.

"I'm really sorry," said Carrie. "I'll go down but I'll come right back up."

"You want me to come with?" asked Franklin.

"I can do this on my own." Carrie steeled herself for the argument that was sure to come. Declan would say she'd lied when she told him she was leaving for Amsterdam on Saturday; she would admit he was right but tell him the reason she had lied was because she knew if she had told him she had already made plans with Franklin, he would have gotten angry, and he didn't have a right to feel that way. She would tell him nothing was permanent and that she wouldn't be going to Northwestern the following year unless that was the best school she got into, and that seemed unlikely. She would say she still loved him, although maybe she wouldn't, because she was beginning to wonder if she really did. She liked the idea of every happiness being permanent and she hated the idea of abandoning Declan the same way his dad had abandoned him, but Franklin was right, nothing was forever, and odds were that she and Declan wouldn't stay together. People just didn't marry boyfriends they had when they were sixteen; this wasn't the 1950s.

The temperature had dropped outside, and Carrie had left her jacket upstairs. She walked briskly toward Declan's car with certainty of purpose and confidence in her rectitude. She watched her breath in the mist; it glowed a pinkish orange in the streetlights. But as soon as she got to the car, Declan peeled out and laid on the gas. On his stereo as he sped off she could hear an aria from Handel's *Xerxes* that he had played for her before: "As You Betray Me."

When she got back upstairs, Franklin asked if she needed to go home.

"Probably, but I don't really feel like it," she said.

"How 'bout I ride with you?" said Franklin.

"That'd be great, but how would you get home?"

"We can just throw my bike in the trunk."

Carrie felt paranoid that Declan would be following them, so as Franklin sat in the passenger seat, he directed her on a dark, convoluted route, taking alleys just about the whole way until they crossed the Chicago border into Evanston and she knew where she wanted to go.

Carrie alternated between complaining about Declan and apologizing for talking about him so much.

"Am I wrong or is he out of line?" she asked.

"I don't really know Declan," Franklin said. "Criticizing the guy would feel weird, but I don't want to defend him either. I think my motives would be suspect either way. The only thing that matters is whether you're happy or not."

"Are you really that selfless?" Carrie asked.

"Not at all," said Franklin. "Totally self-interested. If you're happy around me, that's good news. Are you happy right now?"

"Yeah, I think I am," Carrie said.

When she saw the Beth Shalom synagogue, she signaled a turn. She parked her car in the lot, got out, and walked nonchalantly to the back door as if stopping there was something they had already discussed. When she turned around, she noticed Franklin was still waiting by the car.

"Come on," she said. "It's okay."

"What are we doing at this place?" asked Franklin.

"I don't want to go home yet," said Carrie. "And I kinda wanted to be somewhere where I knew Declan wouldn't follow us. I tutor kids after school here and the rabbi's cool. He gives me the keys so I can lock up when he's not around. I pretty much feel safer here than anywhere."

At home, Carrie was a little afraid of the dark and usually fell asleep reading with a night-light on. But she'd been coming to Beth Shalom for so long that she felt no fear as she held Franklin's hand and led him past the dark classrooms, the utility closets, the music room, and the sanctuary where the only illumination was the flickering glow of the Eternal Light. A cement stairway led down to a dimly lit recreation room where there was a Ping-Pong table, air hockey, and an old gray couch that smelled like one of her grandmother's sweaters.

Carrie led him to the lumpy couch, and as they sat, she found herself speaking more rapidly than she usually did; although she prided herself on making sure everything she said was well thought out, right now she wasn't really sure what she was saying or why. She began to say something about Declan, then said she didn't want to talk about him. Then she said something about her little sister and how guilty she felt about going to college and leaving her behind, but she knew that sounded ridiculous. She started to tell Franklin how hard it was to please her mother, then stopped, realizing she'd been rambling.

"Is there something you want to talk about?" she asked Franklin.

"Not especially," Franklin said. He leaned in closer to her.

They kissed in the darkness. There was something different about the way Franklin kissed. It was like one of those mirror games she had played in Mr. Densmore's Theater Basics class where, if you were doing it right, you didn't know who was following whom—hand touching hand, mouths open, then closed, lips upon lips, tongue touching tongue, a hand upon her breast, and she didn't know whether he had placed it there or if she had guided his hand.

Franklin took his hand away. "Are you worried about Declan?" Carrie asked.

"No," said Franklin. "I'm not as empathetic as I act. It's just that, when we do more than kiss, I want it to happen on a night when it's just about me and you, and we're not still kinda wondering if some guy is watching or following."

When she was so tired she could barely keep her eyes open, Carrie lay back with her head in Franklin's lap and sighed. "Do you ever think about what would have happened to them?" she asked. It was dark enough that it seemed as if she were posing the question to herself as much as to Franklin.

"Who?" he asked.

"Anne and Peter," she said. "Like, if they lived through the war, then saw each other again, would they have stayed together forever?"

Franklin took a long, uncertain breath.

"What?"

"I kinda doubt it," Franklin said. "The time they spent together, it was too intense. If they got back together, all they'd be able to think about is what they'd survived."

Something sounded so sad about what Franklin said, yet there was the ring of truth to it. She knew nothing of what it was like to endure terror or even hardship; what Franklin and his family had already experienced was beyond her understanding. She was playing Anne Frank, but couldn't begin to fathom what Anne had felt once she no longer had a diary to write in and she understood that all hope was lost.

"Well," she said, "I guess the point is that we can never know."

*

When Carrie arrived back at her house late that night, all the lights were off save for the one on the front porch and one in the living room. Her father was stuffing a garment bag into a suitcase. "I'm gonna head up to bed," Carrie told him. "I'll pack in the morning first thing." She walked toward the stairs, but her dad called out to her.

"Just one sec, Carrie," he said. "I want you to listen to this." He went into the kitchen. On the counter, a red light was blinking on the answering machine. "I've played this a couple of times, and I have to say I find it a little troubling."

He pressed PLAY. There was a long pause and then a crackling. "Did you have a good time tonight? I hope somebody did," a voice said. "Oh, and if you want to call to say you're sorry, don't bother. We are through." Then there was a click.

"That's Declan, isn't it?" asked Mr. Hollinger.

Carrie bit her lower lip. "Yeah."

"Is there anything I can do? Is everything all right?"

"It's fine, Dad," said Carrie. "I can handle it; it's not a big deal." She waited for him to say that he had warned her about Declan, but he didn't need to. He just gave her one of his sympathetic frowns, and that was enough. Carrie looked up at the ceiling. She took a breath and let it out. And then she smiled and winked as if Mrs. Light were watching.

*

On her first days in Amsterdam, when she still felt the jet lag and hadn't yet gotten accustomed to the fact that all the dramas of the past weeks were more than an ocean away, Carrie found herself picturing this trip alternately with Declan and Franklin and imagining how each would behave. Wherever they went, Declan would make a big show of grabbing her hand, putting his arm around her, and setting up time-lapse photographs so he could have "romantic" pictures of them kissing wherever they went. With Franklin, they would go so many places and see so many things that, when they returned to their room in the Grand Hotel Amrâth, they would realize they hadn't taken any pictures at all.

But by the time the Hollingers had been in Amsterdam for a few days, Carrie no longer cared to think too much about how things would be different if she were here with this or that boy. Instead, she started to appreciate that she was here with her family and not with either; soon enough, she would be going off to college, and there might not be many more trips like this left.

She adored Amsterdam: the clean streets; the old architecture; the bakeries with pastries so much more delicious than anything she had ever tasted in America. She loved watching schoolkids on bicycles and families riding in little boxy cars with smiling headlights. She liked walking into bookstores and seeing stacks of novels with titles she had to work hard to decipher; liked passing newsstands with folded-up copies of the *Herald Tribune* on spinning wire racks—DEMJANJUK'S LAWYERS FIGHT EXTRADITION. It was hard to believe that, less than forty years ago, a war had been going on here, that she would have had to wear a yellow star, that she wouldn't have been allowed to even ride a bicycle or walk the streets at night.

Inside the Anne Frank House, she had trouble getting a sense of perspective, what with all the flag-hoisting tour leaders herding their groups. Wherever Carrie stood, someone's head was in her way or people were brushing past her, asking her to excuse them in any number of languages. She was struck by both the immensity and smallness of the place: how easy it would be to get lost in all the rooms, stairwells, and corridors; how horrifying to imagine spending the rest of your life there. Here was the kitchen where they prepared old potatoes and greens; here was the tiny bathroom they couldn't use during the day; here was the room Anne shared with Mr. Dussel and copies of the movie magazines she read; here was the room where she danced with Peter.

One room was empty except for a giant screen showing a short movie of Anne on a loop: Anne smiling; Anne waving out a window. The screen was high enough that, despite the crowd, Carrie could watch it without anyone in her way. She studied those brief seconds of film, imagining Anne alive, smiling and waving at the girl below her who was playing her on a stage in a town she'd never heard of, smiling and waving at all the girls who had played Anne, who had read her story, who had imagined what it might have been like to be her.

Franklin had told her about living his life as if his mother could still see him, hoping she was happy with what she saw. Of course, Anne herself would have better things to look upon than a spoiled sixteen-year-old American girl who had all the freedom in the world, parents and a sister who loved her, money to go to college wherever she pleased, a boy she was through with, a boy with whom she hoped she was just beginning. And yet, Carrie thought, maybe that wouldn't be the worst way to live—as if Anne were watching her—savoring every moment, every freedom. She stared into the black eyes of the black-and-white girl. Yes, if Anne was watching, she would try to become the person Anne would want her to be.

Mr. Kraler

The morning Calvin Bumbry Dawes arrived at Mr. Densmore's house to start the "New York Trip," the door was already half open. Declan was inside, talking with Densmore, and he sounded pissed. Probably about the trip, Calvin guessed. Probably Declan thought he should have been the one going. Declan could be a loyal friend, but only when he didn't view you as competition. If Calvin ever dropped eighty pounds, got a race-change operation, and started putting the moves on Carrie, Declan would talk shit about him the same way he did about everyone else. Fine, Calvin thought, let that polo-shirt-wearing, part-his-hair-down-the-middle honky fend off the New York ass fuckery, and Calvin could stay home, watch movies on WGN, and raid his mom and stepdad's liquor cabinet.

"He is *illegal*. He is here among us *illegally*," Declan told Densmore, seemingly unaware that Calvin was standing there, suitcase in hand. Declan had the same studious, concerned expression on his face as he had in *Twelve Angry Men* when he had played righteous Juror Eight and Calvin had played (who the fuck else?) "the Accused."

Calvin considered going back outside but, damn, it was cold, so he entered, clearing his throat loudly before trying to break the ice with an impromptu Shakespeare riff: "When shall we three meet again? / When the ass fucking is done, when the condom starts to run." Densmore thrust a hand in the air to cut Calvin off.

"He's '*illegal*'?" Densmore asked, imitating Declan. "You sound like a Nazi. Who's 'illegal'? People are not '*illegal*.'"

"Franklin Light," Declan said. "He's going to North Shore but he lives in Chicago. That's illegal."

"So?" Densmore asked. "So what?"

"So," said Declan, "when the school finds out, he'll be expelled and we'll have no Peter. We need to find a new Peter."

"And how will the school find out?" Densmore asked.

"They just will," said Declan.

"And how did you find out?"

Declan spoke more calmly, as if he had rehearsed this part of his speech. "I was driving through Jewish neighborhoods," he said. "To get a feel for Mr. Van Daan's background. And I saw him—Franklin—going into his apartment."

"Bullshit." Mr. Densmore made a circle-wipe gesture with his palm, then clenched his fist—the same gesture he made when he was directing Sammy Doulos to cut the sound or the lights. "I believe *you're* the one who needs to find a new 'Peter,' because it sounds as though someone has lopped off yours. I don't like snitches and I don't like creeps stalking old girlfriends, then lying about it to my face. Yes, I am aware of Franklin's 'situation,' but apparently you are not. Franklin lives in an apartment in Evanston but he has grandparents in Chicago. They are *Holocaust survivors*, Declan; his grandmother survived *Sobibor*, Declan. So unless you want to stop playing Mr. Van Daan and start preparing to play a Gestapo informant, I suggest you mind your own business. Now, Calvin and I have to catch a taxi, so why don't we forget this conversation ever took place, and you can go home and do what you should have been doing in the first place—namely, working on your fucking lines."

Declan walked out without a word to Calvin, who looked up from the old character diary he was snooping through. "Does this mean I don't get to play Mr. V.D., Mr. D?" he asked.

*

In the taxi to O'Hare, Mr. Densmore behaved with smooth, authoritarian professionalism, like a pompous maître d' in a mid-season replacement sitcom. He gave Calvin a xeroxed itinerary; arrival and departure times; check-in and check-out dates; appointments with former students ("drinks with Todd Merritt at Joe Allen"). There were lists of museum exhibits, restaurants, and shows, including a new musical whose title seemed all too apt—*Is There Life after High School?*

"Your wife still meeting us in the Big Apple, Mr. D?" Calvin asked.

"She is not," said Densmore. "There are complications: our son; it's a long, sad story. It's hard for both of us to go out of town at the same time."

Calvin had been expecting this sort of BS answer, but that didn't make hearing it any more comforting.

The idea of this trip—of actually being chosen to go after Mr. Newson had bought Trey out of a suspension and into fancy-schmancy Lake Forest Academy—seemed so improbable to Calvin that he found himself narrating the journey in his mind like Rod Serling introducing a *Twilight Zone* episode: *Meet Calvin Bumbry Dawes, getting on a plane for the first time since he flew to Mississippi for his great-grandma's funeral . . . This is Calvin Bumbry Dawes, an eighteen-year-old man flying above the clouds, bound for New York Titty . . . Consider the case of Calvin Bumbry Dawes, looking out his window at the Statue of Fucking Liberty . . . Here is Calvin Bumbry Dawes, standing beside Tyrus Densmore in the taxi line at LaGuardia Airport . . . Entertain the vision of Calvin Bumbry Dawes riding through the Lincoln Tunnel . . . Imagine, if you will, Calvin Dawes wheeling his suitcase into a land of shadow and substance, also known as his hotel room in the Statler Hilton.*

What impressed Calvin about New York was neither its size nor its density but the myriad possibilities that size and density seemed to offer. Back home, he could never see anybody else's life and imagine living it: Declan would go to Northwestern and study acting, but Calvin wouldn't; Carrie would be a pediatrician, but Calvin wouldn't do that; Rob would be a shyster lawyer or politician; Sammy would be the kingpin of a multimillion-dollar drug empire; Trey's dad would buy him into Harvard. But Calvin wouldn't do any of that. And since there didn't seem to be any realistic examples of what he might do in the world, he couldn't imagine living in that world for very long. Whenever anyone asked what he would do with his life, he would laugh and say he was "most likely to die at twenty-seven," but it wasn't really a joke.

In New York, though, every person he saw out of his hotel room window seemed to represent a possible future. He could be that businessman in a gray pin-stripe suit crossing the street; that wisecracking car hiker standing in the loading zone in front of the hotel; that fucked-up-looking dude on the corner selling chestnuts out of a hand truck.

He had about an hour to himself before he had to meet Densmore downstairs to go to pre-show dinner, and Calvin spent that time luxuriating in the shower and singing whatever New York songs came to mind: "Across 110th Street"; "J'ai Rêvé New York"; "Walk on the Wild Side"—"And all the colored boys go *doo-duh-doo-duh-doo-doo-da-da-doo-duh-doo-duh-doo.*"

Calvin got out of the shower, then walked back into his room and stood buck naked, dripping onto the carpet: *Meet Calvin Bumbry Dawes, a young man who at this very moment is shaking his hips, wagging his dick, and singing "New York State of Mind" at the passersby on Seventh Avenue . . . Consider Calvin Bumbry Dawes, an ordinary if somewhat beefy young man, smiling at the kids on the street pointing up to his window and laughing their asses off . . . This is Calvin Bumbry Dawes, giving those kids a big thumbs-up and laughing right along with them because no one knows who the fuck he is, he could be anybody, just some crazy naked-ass dude dancing in his hotel room, wishing he could live the rest of his life like this.*

A sudden wave of darkness crashed over Calvin, the kind that made him feel as if someone had reached into his brain and violently twisted a dimmer. For a moment, he couldn't help but think how cruel Densmore was, showing him a future he wanted but could never have. Ten years from now, if he lived that long, he'd be working the shake machine at Jack in the Box, boasting to the guy who worked the fries: "I know it's hard to believe, but one time not that long ago I stood naked in a hotel room, imitating Rod Serling and flashing Seventh Avenue."

Near the TV, there was a small refrigerator. Inside were candy bars, bags of nuts, cans of soda, and little bottles of scotch, vodka, and rum. He grabbed a fistful of bottles.

This is Calvin Bumbry Dawes, swigging rum on his hotel bed, he thought. Then: *This is Calvin Bumbry Dawes, mixing that rum with a three-dollar Coke because straight Ronrico is some nasty-ass shit, and who gives a fuck— Mr. D is paying.*

He downed the rest of his drink, put on a red-and-blue-checked sport coat and a pair of white slacks, took a swig of Listerine from the little plastic bottle in the bathroom, looked at the ingredients, confirmed there was alcohol in it, took another swig, then swallowed.

Calvin and Densmore had dinner at Raoul's, a candlelit restaurant downtown where Densmore ordered for both of them: a bottle of wine, steak frites for two, a green salad to share.

"That's the same thing I order at Ponderosa only you get your choice of salad—coleslaw or three-bean," Calvin said.

"Actually, this was what Hemingway used to eat on the Boulevard Saint-Germain," Densmore said. "And the wine"—he filled Calvin's glass—"it's from the same region as the first glass of wine I had when I moved to New York."

"You lived here?"

"For a short time, yes."

"Why didn't you stay?"

Densmore peered into his wine glass as if hoping to find an answer there. "It can be a hard life here," he said, "the wrong place if you want things like a family and a house. I never really wanted to settle here— just to prove to myself I could make it. So, after I got cast in my first show, *Teahouse of the August Moon*, I left. All this pursuit of stardom and renown, it's so"—he twirled a finger in the air describing a trail of smoke—"ephemeral."

"Man," Calvin said, "if I got cast in a show here, I'd never go back. I'd call my mom, tell her to ship out all my shit. Maybe I'd come back on Christmas, but that'd be it."

Densmore poured more wine. The more he drank, the more philosophical he became; the more Calvin drank, the harder it was to focus, not only on what Densmore was saying but on anything around him. He didn't know how he'd possibly stay awake through *Othello*. He understood Densmore was trying to get him drunk, but at the same time there didn't seem to be any more logical way to deal with the fact that his teacher was trying to get him wasted than by drinking his ass off.

"One time," Densmore said, "I came here to visit an old student of mine: Todd Merritt; you'll meet him tonight. He was working for Joe Papp at the Public and he was begging, pleading with me to audition. They were doing *Much Ado*. 'Audition for Joe,' Todd said. 'You can have any role you want.' And I sat Todd down and I told him, 'Never in a million years. I have a wife and a son and a life and a job I'm happy with.'"

"So you told him no?" Calvin asked.

"And, to this day, he doesn't understand; to this day he thinks I was either a liar or a fool." Densmore smiled. "Which do you think I am, Cal? Or are you too drunk to even answer?"

"It takes more than a half bottle of wine to get a man of my girth drunk," Calvin said.

Mr. Densmore raised an eyebrow. "What sort of girth are you referring to?" he asked.

Calvin finished his third glass.

The New York trip seemed to be going exactly the way people always said it would—the absence of Densmore's wife, the abundance of alcohol—and yet, it didn't seem quite real. Of course it was happening, but at the same time it couldn't be, not in a way that you could take totally seriously. He wondered if having told so many jokes in the Annex had actually been doing Densmore a favor. Whenever Calvin had made fun of Densmore, people laughed, then moved on to the next topic as if the fact that you could laugh about something took it out of the realm of reality. If you could make the worst things funny, they couldn't be that bad. Densmore liked jokes too. Jokes were a good way to talk about something while acting like you weren't really talking about it.

They didn't have time for dessert. On Prince Street, Mr. Densmore put one arm around Calvin and hailed a taxi. "This can be the best city in America if you're right for it," he said. "You can be anyone you want here, Calvin, so there's a place for people like you. Next time I bring one of my students, maybe you'll be the one we're visiting."

From the back of the taxi, Calvin looked out at the blurry city—which, given all the booze he'd had, looked like a time-lapse photo of a cityscape, all streaks of colored light. "People like you," Densmore had said. Which people were those? Everybody knew that Densmore liked taking fucked-up kids to New York. Was he as fucked-up as the others? He felt Mr. Densmore's hand on his back, guiding him out of the cab toward the Winter Garden Theatre.

Othello proved to be one of the most blissful times Calvin had ever spent at a show. The seats were plush. It was dark. There was an empty seat to his left. Not only could he use the armrest, he could actually put his arm over it and loll his head on the back of that seat. The stentorian timbre of James Earl Jones's voice offered a lulling sound bed, like the bass on a really good hi-fi. If not for the one "Shhh!" from a man sitting in front of him, Calvin might have snored the whole way through. He awoke seconds before the end, right when Jones thrust his sword between Christopher Plummer's legs and smote his uncircumcis'd dong thus.

"What'd you think?" Densmore asked after it was over.

"I liked that part at the end where Darth Vader cut off Captain von Trapp's nuts," said Calvin.

They walked along Eighth Avenue. Calvin was just about sober now as he listened to Mr. Densmore criticizing Christopher Plummer, who, he said, played Iago "like a mincing queer," and fending off Times Square prostitutes: "Sorry, sorry; no syphilis, please; we're British"; "No, thank you; I'm married and he's underage." They turned a corner, and Densmore led the way into Joe Allen, where he stopped at the bar and flung open his arms. "Mr. Merritt!" he shouted and Todd Merritt jogged toward them, hair bouncing.

Todd Merritt was a flamer. No doubt there were more charitable words to describe the man, but that was the first one that came to Calvin's mind. Despite the fact that Calvin had spent nearly four years in the Annex with other boys wearing makeup, tunics, and jazz pants stuffed with strategically placed socks, never mind that Calvin had once sucked off Trey Newson on Lighthouse Beach, leave aside the fact that when he'd had sex in the balcony of the Varsity Theater during *Jabberwocky*, Calvin had fantasized that his partner was Sugar Ray Leonard and not Amanda Wehner, Calvin could not say with certainty that he had ever encountered someone who was indisputably homosexual. Yes, some people seemed gay and many probably were, but there was always some disclaimer. People were described as "a little sweet" or "kind of funny but I don't know." Mr. Breechen, who taught sophomore English, assigned *Women in Love* and *Deliverance*, and asked his students to compare and contrast the nude wrestling and ass-raping scenes in the movie adaptations, always arrived at school events in the company of his "lady friend"; Mr. Densmore left copies of *Hung Jury* and *Dong Patrol* around his office, but he had a son, he was married, and he had just called Christopher Plummer "queer." Even that time when Trey had asked Calvin for a blow job, he had insisted that Calvin pretend to be a girl. Sometimes Calvin had a hard time making sense of his own sexual proclivities. Whenever anyone asked, he'd say, "I'm an opportunist."

With Todd, there was no such ambiguity. "Ahhh, the New York trip!" he shouted, and embraced Densmore, then Calvin. He wore a billowy lilac-colored shirt opened three buttons, a pair of roomy white *Pirates of Penzance* pants secured with a macramé belt, and clogs. He had a big Harpo head of blond curls, wore a slew of gaudy rings, and laughed loudly and throatily as if everything in the world were one long, lewd joke—*huhuhuhuhuhuhuh!*

They sat at the bar, where Todd ordered Pimm's Cups for the three of them, and Todd and Densmore gossiped about shows and actors. Todd told a story of how he had once visited the set of the film *Moment to Moment* and walked into a trailer and found John Travolta standing there wearing only a towel—"And I said, 'Mr. Travolta, do you mind if I take that?' *Huhuhuhuhuhuhuh!*" Densmore described the *Othello* he and Calvin had just seen, exaggerating Christopher Plummer's mannerisms while Todd cackled, clapped his hands, and said, "Oh my God, that sounds *awful!*"

"Are you an actor?" Calvin asked.

"I tried," said Todd. "My first and only role was in the chorus of *Applause*. Even Lauren Bacall saw how bad I was. Could you imagine? The worst actress with the worst singing voice calling me out. Do you know what she told me? 'You're lucky you're easy on the eyes, because you're sure not easy on the ears, boy.'"

"So what do you do?"

"I produce," said Todd. "It's what you do when you can't act but you want to be rich and hang out with actors."

"Hot stud actors," Densmore corrected.

"*Huhuhuhuhuhuhuhuh!*" Todd turned to Calvin. "And what will you be doing after you graduate, young man?"

"Oh, I dunno," said Calvin. "Model for Bigsby & Kruthers's big and tall store, maybe? Suck dicks for beer money? Get a sitcom where they pay you by the pound?"

"Where're you going to college?"

"Haven't quite figured that out yet."

"Who's your agent?"

"Haven't figured that out yet either."

"Do you even have a headshot?"

"I do not."

Todd looked at Densmore, concerned. "Might I borrow Calvin tomorrow morning? Just for a few hours? I might be able to help him."

Densmore took a long breath. "We were going to see the Rodin at the Met, but I suppose I can go myself and catch up with Calvin afterward."

"I'll send a car around to the hotel," Todd told Calvin. "Where're you staying? Statler Hilton?"

"Where else?" Densmore asked.

"Ahhh, memories," said Todd. "So my driver will take you to my office. I'll have a photographer waiting. After the photos, we'll go through my agents list and make some calls."

Calvin eyed the men suspiciously. "Why would you do that?" he asked. "We've never met. You've never seen me act in anything."

"Because you're on the New York trip," said Todd. "Whoever Tyrus takes is sure to be an amazing talent. I'm the only exception, but now I make more money than the talented ones, so I guess it all worked out."

Densmore got up to use the bathroom. "I'll leave the two of you to make your little plans," he said.

Todd sipped his drink, paused, then leaned in close to Calvin. "Is he gone?" he asked.

"What?"

"Is he gone?"

"Yeah," Calvin said. "The dude's in the john. What's up?"

Todd spoke quickly and in a softer voice. "Listen: Don't let him into your room tonight. If he knocks on the door anytime, don't answer."

"What?"

"When you go back to the hotel, don't go up to the room at the same time he does. And when you get to your room, lock the door and put the chain on it."

"Are you joking?" Calvin asked.

"I wish I was," said Todd.

"What happens if I let Mr. D in my room?"

"The sickest thing? I don't even know," Todd said. "All I know is what happened to me when I went with him to New York. In a way, it was the most important trip of my life. Not the best, just the most important. I was really messed up back then; you don't even want to know the shit I was into. I can only remember half of it, and that half's enough. I was so sick—like, seriously sick, like big *C*—cancer sick. Just imagine being seventeen and thinking you might die any day. And Tyrus—I thought he was great; I really did. He took me to restaurants, we saw shows, we hit the bars, we had cocktails—banana daiquiris, which were uh-*mazing*. But the thing is, and I'm sure you've seen this already, there are two Tyruses. He can have a true generosity of spirit; I've seen him do lovely things for people. But there's a darkness in his soul, and it comes out after he's been drinking. Is he back yet?"

"All clear."

"Anyway," Todd said, "we'd been at the theater, and afterward we went to Sardi's. We were having a great time, but when we got back to the hotel, everything changed."

"What happened?"

"We go upstairs, and I'm thinking, 'Okay, that's it for the night.' I open the door to my room; he walks in right after me. He takes off his coat, his jacket, his shoes. He gets into my bed. I'm like, 'What's going on?' But I'm already so drunk. And he's like, 'What? Do you think I'm trying to have my way with you?' The last thing I remember is him laughing and the room spinning. And when I get up—worst hangover of my life—Tyrus, he's all dressed. I'm like, 'I can't remember anything. What happened?' And he goes, 'What happened? What do *you* think happened? I *ravished* you.' Then he laughed."

"Jesus, what'd you do?"

"I laughed too. I pretended it was all a joke. And to this day, even after getting healthy, even after a decade of therapy, even after one shitty relationship after another, I can't figure it out. I blacked out, and whatever happened, it's just one dark space. And, you know, I think that's what Tyrus really wants. I'm sure he wants sex, but the thing he's really after is control. That's half the reason I came out to meet you tonight: when I went on the New York trip, we met all these people, but no one offered to help."

"What's the other half reason?" Calvin asked.

"Because Tyrus knows talent. Whoever he likes is someone worth watching. But that's his tragedy too: Recognizing talent is the only talent he has. I remember Joe Papp was casting *Much Ado*. Tyrus called me, pleaded with me to get him an audition. He was so bored: his wife was a nag, his kid was out of control. He was like, 'I'd do anything to get out.' So I get him an audition and, oh, God, it was embarrassing. His accent was bad, his line readings were pretentious, he was so mannered. A minute in, Joe Papp walks out; he's like, 'Why are you wasting my time on some amateur reading Benedick like he's got a broomstick up his ass?'"

"So," Calvin asked, "then you weren't serious about the car picking me up in the morning?"

"Oh, I was dead serious," said Todd. "We New York trippers have to stick together." Calvin looked past Todd; he saw Densmore approaching.

"Is he coming?" Todd asked.

Calvin nodded.

"Say something to me and I'll pretend it's really funny."

Calvin assayed an impersonation of Densmore auditioning for *Much Ado*: "I am loved of all ladies, only you excepted," he said. "Now, wilt thou help me get this broomstick out of my ass, motherfucker?"

"*Huhuhuhuhuhuhuhuhuh.*"

"Talking about me again?" asked Densmore.

"And what else is there to talk about?" Todd asked.

"What has he been saying?"

"He said you're white on the outside, but inside you've got a black soul," said Calvin. They all laughed at that, but when Densmore said he'd buy the next round of drinks, Calvin said he'd just have a Coke. Densmore looked at him, then Todd, as if he suspected they were conspiring against him, but he didn't ask.

After they left, Densmore seemed in a hurry to get back to the hotel. He crossed streets against the light. "Come on, keep up," he said. "Chop-chop."

Outside the hotel was a pay phone. Calvin stopped in front of it while Densmore looked at Calvin with an impatient scowl; he hunched his shoulders and turned up his hands in a *What the fuck're you doing?* gesture.

"I just remembered I haven't called my ma yet," said Calvin.

"I believe our hotel is equipped with telephones," Densmore said.

"I know that. But something about being outside in New York at night, it's such a cool feeling. My ma, she's never been here; I want her to hear what it sounds like." He picked up the phone. "I'd like to make a collect call," he told the operator. "Calvin Dawes."

Densmore lit a cigarette.

"Mama," Calvin said. "It's me. Yeah. It's great. You wouldn't believe this place—you've gotta see it. It is seriously *on time*. Yeah, I'm with Mr. D, and guess who we saw onstage. C'mon, guess. Okay, James Earl Jones. I'm not lying. As Othello, can you believe it? Yeah, I don't even know if he was good or not; being so close to him just blew my mind. No, no autograph, sorry. Maybe from Geraldine Page tomorrow. You don't know who that is? Serious? Aw, she's great too." He held the phone away from his ear. "Can you hear that, Mama? That's what New York City sounds like. Taxicabs and drunks and people everywhere talking, going places, yukking it up. When I get famous, I'm gonna take you here. How've you been doing?"

Densmore looked at his watch, then went inside the hotel, apparently unaware that Calvin was talking to a dial tone, that no one had answered when Calvin had placed the call, that ever since his mother had remarried and had a child with her second husband, she seemed to regard

Calvin as a lost cause. Calvin was dead tired, but he didn't want to risk going in and meeting up with Densmore. He wasn't sure he trusted Todd either; yet, even the possibility that Todd might have been telling the truth filled him with an unusual sense of hope: maybe his life wasn't over just yet; maybe he could live past twenty-seven, or at least past eighteen.

Once he had run out of things to say to his imaginary mother, he crept into the Hilton lobby: no sign of Densmore. His room was eight floors up. Still, he took the stairs, stopping on a landing to catch his breath before lumbering up the rest of the way. He opened the door at the top of the stairs, made sure the hallway was empty—*Don't let him into your room tonight. If he knocks on the door anytime, don't answer.*

Calvin took off his shoes, then booked it down the hall faster than he had ever run, even in Pootie Hollings's gym class, where he had done the hundred-yard dash in 12.5 seconds and Hollings had checked his stopwatch and said, "Twelve-point-five? Your ass is too big to get a twelve-point-five; run it again." He opened his door fast, closed it behind him, locked and chained it.

He turned on the TV: on-screen, John Demjanjuk in court, some old man who'd murdered thousands or maybe he hadn't but either way his life was done. He switched the channel to a late-night comedy show called *Fridays*. Huey Lewis and the News were singing a song called "Workin' for a Livin'" even though it looked like none of them ever had. He turned the volume up, got into bed—*This is Calvin Bumbry Dawes in his New York hotel room, listening to some pasty-ass white boys*—but he felt too sober to relax; every time he heard a sound, he wondered if Densmore was lurking in front of his door. *Here's Calvin Dawes going to the fridge for more hooch.*

He took two bottles of rum and a can of Coke, mixed them in a wax cup he found by the sink. He lay back in bed, sipped his drink, and watched *Fridays* fade into *SCTV Network 90*. Maybe he would get on a show like that someday, he thought, then tried to stop thinking about that, because imagining something good was the surest way to jinx it. He'd spent so long living without hope that allowing himself to imagine anything good seemed dangerous.

Midway through *SCTV*, he fell asleep.

He awoke to the sound of someone trying his door, then lightly rapping on it. What time it was, he didn't know. The TV was still on—some movie with Bob Hope playing a detective; who the fuck thought that was a good idea? More rapping on the door. His immediate instinct was to see who was there, but he stopped. He went to the window, looked out. It must have been late, because even New York seemed asleep. No one on the sidewalks; empty taxis sped by, dispersing the steam that rose from the sewers.

The knocking grew louder. At first it sounded like knuckles on the door, then a fist. "Calvin, are you there?" Calvin's throat felt so dry. All he wanted was a glass of water, but he didn't want Densmore to hear him go to the bathroom and turn on the sink. He drank the rest of his flat rum and Coke, then got back into bed. "Cal, are you awake? Calvin? Open up, damn it."

Calvin covered his ears with his hands. "Cal, I can hear the TV on in there. I said open up." Densmore jiggled the doorknob. Calvin lay on his stomach, pillows over his head. It was so hot, so stuffy, but he didn't move. What would he do if Densmore broke in? He imagined himself snoring as loud as he could, drool dripping out of his mouth, pretending he'd OD'd.

The knocking and the low, ominous chatter persisted. It kept Calvin awake the whole night, it seemed. And yet, he must have slept. For when he opened his eyes and got out from under the covers, he saw daylight through the drapes. He looked out his window: people everywhere, cars stuck in traffic, construction workers lined up in front of a coffee truck.

Another knock on the door. "Oh, Jesus Christ." Calvin threw open his suitcase, grabbed the first clothes he could find: boxers, white slacks, a black-and-orange paisley shirt and tan loafers. He opened the door.

A slim young man in a maroon blazer with gold buttons was standing before him. "Mr. Dawes? Mr. Merritt's car is downstairs. They want to know how long you'll be." Calvin probably should have showered or washed his face or at least looked at himself in the mirror, but he just grabbed his wallet and his room key. "Heading down right now," he said.

Densmore was in the lobby, seated in an armchair, scowling as he read the *Times*. Calvin pretended he didn't see him and walked into the shockingly clear and bright Manhattan morning, and as he did, he couldn't stop cracking up. He felt as though he had wandered into some Hollywood rags-to-riches comedy: standing by the curb next to an open car door was a uniformed chauffeur. Todd Merritt had sent a limo-fucking-zine.

Calvin ambled toward the car feeling that, no matter what happened with Mr. Densmore and *Anne Frank* or anything else, none of it would matter, because that was all in the past and ahead of him was only blue sky and possibility. *Meet Calvin Bumbry Dawes*, he thought, *whose new life has just begun*.

Mrs. Van Daan

O n opening night, it all went to hell. No surprise there. Everything and everyone Fiona came into contact with tended to go to hell. But she had been so distracted by everyone else's dramas—Judith checking her mother into Skokie Valley Hospital; Declan giving Franklin and Carrie the silent treatment; Mr. Densmore polluting the atmosphere with his foul moods; Eileen and Rob plotting some filthy evil; Amanda wandering about in a pot smoke haze; Trey leaving her messages, asking if she could come over to his house "just one more time"—it hadn't occurred to Fiona that everything could go to hell for her specifically. At least not until ten minutes before showtime.

The actors were in costume backstage. Declan was doing facial exercises, smiling, puckering, smiling, puckering; Judith was shaking out her hands; Franklin and Carrie were practicing their kiss; Amanda was doing ballet stretches.

Eileen was peeping through a gap in the curtains and excitedly pointing at someone in the audience. "Oh my God, guys, he is such a fox," she was saying. "He looks like one of those men on the Irish Spring ads. That is such a hot dad. Who has such a hot dad?"

Judith said she didn't know; neither did Rob.

"Fiona-yona," Eileen said, "do you know that man?"

Fiona had been sitting at the top of the emergency exit steps, her back against the fire door. She took off her headphones, got up, and walked to the curtain.

"Right in the front row with the flowers," Eileen said. "He is so hot, I am just dripping. You know who he is?"

"Good God." Fiona took a breath. It all looked like some nightmare Hieronymus Bosch had drawn just for her, didn't it? Or a scene from a Patricia Highsmith thriller, one where a murderer unwittingly sits beside his next victim, neither yet knowing the role each will play in the other's life.

Mutti and Da were out there, dressed as if for some dour embassy event. Trey was in the front row, sitting with his parents and brothers, bearing a garish bouquet. Apparently, he hadn't told them that he and Fiona were no longer a couple, which would be tough to explain to Ray, who was looking quite dapper in his white shirt and skinny black tie.

And there, right where Eileen had been pointing, was Lloyd Crowder in his heavy white fisherman's sweater and pleated pants, his black hair combed back, his beard trimmed—Lloyd Crowder who'd taught her about Euripides and Aeschylus, who'd taken her to exhibits at the Tate and shows at the National, who'd brought her back to his house when his wife and daughters were in Rome; Lloyd Crowder, whom she thought would be an amusing fling after all the immature, drug-addled musicians and poets she'd fancied but who turned out to be needier than any boy her age.

Still, he did look sort of lovely sitting there, one leg crossed over the other, two hands cupping a knee as he studied the xeroxed yellow sheet that passed for a program, not noticing or registering Fiona's mutti and da, who apparently hadn't noticed or registered him, while none of them took any note of Ray Tounslee Jr. or the Newsons. Everyone was so unsuspecting. Like dear old London before the Blitz. Like the Franks and Van Daans before the knock on the Annex door.

"Yes," Fiona said, "I do know that man."

"Lucky!" said Eileen.

"Places!" Mr. Densmore whispered loudly. "*Places!*"

Sammy started the sound cues: a siren; soldiers marching; children singing a jump rope song. The lights went down. And in the blackness Fiona wished she could just stop time. Why did it have to hurtle forward? Why couldn't she just stay backstage forever or at least until she'd figured out what to do? But then there was that loud, braying, mechanical hum—the lights blasting on, the cyclorama fading into view, followed by the last cough of someone in the audience before Rob, his hair dyed gray, entered, propelling himself forward with his cane. Eileen took Rob's arm and spoke the first line: "*This way, Mr. Frank.*"

Fiona would have liked the play to go on as long as possible, but of course the first act went faster than ever. She would have liked to spend her time onstage avoiding contemplation of what would happen after the show. And yet, at every moment, her mind seemed to be in two places: she was showing off her legs and flirting with Mr. Frank, and she was wondering how she would steer Lloyd away from her parents, the Newsons, and Ray; when she sobbed over her ruined fur coat, she was shedding tears not only for Mrs. Van Daan's lost status in Amsterdam but for the dreadfully uncomfortable position Lloyd was putting her in. Maybe everyone led a minimum of two simultaneous lives, just like the characters in the play, she thought—all those conversations, arguments, and rituals to distract themselves from their most paralyzing fears.

At the close of Act I, Judith lit the Hanukkah candles, and the families gathered at the dining room table to sing. The stage was dark enough that all Fiona could really see was the candlelight on the other actors' faces as they joined in one desperate plea—"One for each night, they will shed a sweet light to remind us of days long ago"—but then Judith blew out the candles, the stage went black for intermission, and everybody followed the glow tape back to reality.

In the greenroom, the girls checked their makeup and costumes in the mirrors, adjusted pantyhose, applied blush, spritzed Aqua Net. Declan dotted his mustache with spirit gum to make sure it stayed in place. Franklin and Carrie ran Peter's and Anne's lines, or maybe their own lines—it was hard to say anymore. But the moment Fiona sat beside Judith and asked if she could "bum a fag," everyone had free advice.

There was something so American about that—a squadron of emotional imperialists involving themselves in other people's problems to avoid facing their own.

"I could scare that bugger off again," Judith said, imitating Fiona's accent. "'I've an appointment to wank off Fiona, so why don't you just sod off?'"

"Let me take him off your hands," said Eileen. "I'm sure I could find something I could do with him, *hahahahahahahaha.*"

"Hey, Fiona, if you need to get high, just ask." Amanda mimed a joint.

But Fiona was not used to having anyone else solve her problems. For the first seventeen years of her life, she had been the one who solved other people's problems. When her parents couldn't talk with her older brother without yelling or threatening to institutionalize him, she'd convinced Donnell to see a psychiatrist; at her boarding school, whenever her phone rang in the middle of the night, it was either her stoned brother or one of her parents pleading with her to talk sense into him: "Fiona, please, you're the only one he'll talk to." Whenever some horrible war or conflagration was threatening to break out, she had always been the one telling her classmates they could come home with her.

"You don't think Lloyd could be dangerous, do you?" Judith asked Fiona.

"Dangerous? Of course not; the poor sod loves me."

"Those are usually the most dangerous of all," Judith said.

Densmore poked his head into the dressing room. "Five minutes, Miss Lenska!" he said with a grin, imitating an ad for Alberto VO5 hair spray.

"Pretty soon that guy won't be smiling so much," said Rob.

"*Hahahahahahaha,*" said Eileen.

Fiona went to the loo and checked herself in the bathroom mirror, where she was only moderately horrified to note how much she looked like a tart and, at the same time, how closely she resembled her mother. She followed the rest of the cast backstage; the houselights flicked on then off and she looked out at the audience. "*Holy shite,*" she whispered.

She had imagined the scene before her would be much as it had been at the beginning of Act I, but it wasn't, no more than life had remained the same for the Franks and Van Daans. A year and a half had passed, and the place was in total disarray.

Out in the auditorium, Fiona's da was stabbing a finger at Lloyd, his bald head crimson, his voice spluttering like the engine of an old MG on its way to the shop. Trey, pale and jittery, still clutching his flowers, was engaging his family in conversation to distract them while that horrid Keith Newson and his pal Ricky elbowed each other and glared at Mr. Grenfall and Lloyd.

"*Places!*"

The houselights dimmed, the Dutch National Anthem crescendoed, and Carrie's recorded voice played through the speakers: "*Another new year has begun and we find ourselves still in our hiding place.*"

If Act I had proceeded in relative haste, Act II seemed like one long, inexorable march toward doom. In Act I, Fiona had felt all the emotions of her personal predicament informing Mrs. Van Daan's dialogue; throughout Act II, she thought that just about everyone there, whether onstage or in the audience, was an insufferable wanker, herself most of all.

As the play neared its finale, she walked offstage to the sound of marching German bootsteps while Carrie's voice-over told the rest of the story, and Mr. Frank, Mr. Kraler, and Miep Gies surveyed the wreckage the war had wreaked upon all their lives. "*In spite of everything,*" Carrie said, "*I still believe that people are really good at heart.*"

Rob closed Anne's diary. He leaned on his cane and stared blankly into the middle distance.

Backstage, Mr. Densmore raised one hand, then bent it slowly forward, mimicking the fading of the lights: "And fade to . . . *blackout!*" he whispered.

Applause crackled through the auditorium; the actors returned to the stage for the curtain call—Calvin first, Carrie last, Fiona between Declan and Franklin; they raised their hands high, brought them low, then saluted the lighting booth, where Sammy gave them a thumbs-up and a big stoner grin. Eileen hugged Rob, Carrie grasped Franklin's hand, and on the way offstage Calvin beat his fists against a wall and led an impromptu Sly and the Family Stone chant—"*Boo-chuk-a-luka-luka-boo-chuk-a-luka-luka-boo-chuka-luka-luka-BOO!*"—as if they had just won a game.

While the rest of the cast was changing in the dressing rooms, Fiona, still in her costume, walked back through the theater, excusing and pardoning her way past the bouquet-clutching throngs until she found Mutti entering the hallway.

Mrs. Grenfall kissed her daughter on the cheek, then wiped away the lipstick with a hankie. "The show," she said, "was most excellent." She made a ring of her thumb and index finger.

"Ta, thanks, but where the bloody hell's Da?"

Mrs. Grenfall looked about warily.

"Where?" Fiona asked.

"We did warn that dreadful man to stay away from you," said Mrs. Grenfall.

"Where did Da go?"

"To get the police."

"Bloody hell, Mutti." Fiona sped into the auditorium—just about empty now. Lloyd was still in his seat, bouquet of roses in his lap, a flash of color against his white and gray ensemble. "Fiona, darling." He stood and tried to throw his arms around her. She ducked. "For fuck's sake, you know how to make a bloody entrance, don't you?" she said. "Couldn't you have given me some warning before just materializing like Mary bloody Poppins?"

"But you would have told me not to come," said Lloyd.

"Correct," Fiona said.

He reached out to touch her cheek. "And I wouldn't have had the chance to see your lovely face."

"Sod off," Fiona said. "What were you and my da going on about?"

"We were having an amicable conversation," said Lloyd.

"Like hell you were," said Fiona. "He's called the bloody police."

"Let him. I told him to go right ahead," said Lloyd. "No crimes have been committed. I'll tell that to the police or to anyone else."

"Would you just get out?" Fiona said. "Go back to your wife and family while you still can."

"I won't," said Lloyd. "I can't. I have no wife, no family. That's why I'm here. You were right. I can't lead two lives. I had to choose, and so I've chosen." He leaned in to kiss her.

"Oh, no, you will not." Fiona grabbed Lloyd's hand hard and dragged him onstage, where Sammy was resetting furniture and props for the next day's show. Near the curtain ropes and pulley were the rickety metal emergency exit steps; above them, the door that led to the fire escape outside.

The escape's landing was littered with cigarette butts, guitar picks, and a couple of crumpled condom wrappers. From there you could see the cars in the lot crawling toward the exit: families heading out for celebratory dinners; kids walking to Yesterday's or the beach. The damp, misty breeze held the promise of summer, but all Fiona could think of was how trapped she felt up there with Lloyd gazing at her moonily as if she were in a frame on a wall of the bloody Tate Gallery. Was it awful to think that the freest she had felt all night was onstage awaiting the Nazis? Probably.

"The view's lovely up here," Lloyd said.

"There's nothing lovely about it," said Fiona. "It's factories, houses, parking lots, and gas stations."

"It's your being here that makes all of it lovely."

"Christ." Fiona rolled her eyes. "Here's what you'll do. When the lot's clear, you'll go down and find your way back to wherever you came from."

"But I don't want to keep any more secrets," said Lloyd. "I want to speak to your mother and father directly with you beside me."

"You will not," said Fiona. "Do you not know who my father is? Go on."

"You're coming with me?"

"I certainly am not; I'm still in my bloody costume, aren't I?"

"Then meet me." Lloyd told her he had a room downtown at the Drake. "Let's spend the night together, please, and in the morning I'll tell you all I've planned. When can you meet me?"

Fiona looked down at the parking lot, briefly entertaining the notion that the rest of the evening would become a whole lot simpler if Lloyd tripped on the steps and fell down to the asphalt. She checked Lloyd's watch: just past ten thirty. "Midnight," she said.

"That's too late," said Lloyd.

"Midnight," Fiona said again.

"All right." Lloyd handed a room key to Fiona, pressed his lips lightly to hers. She kissed him back—partly because she knew if she didn't, he would stay until he'd gotten his kiss, and partly because he was a good kisser. It was one of the things she had liked about him: he was romantic, gentlemanly; he knew things, spoke like characters in films, and it certainly didn't hurt that he bore a slight resemblance to Jeremy Irons in *Brideshead Revisited*, eight hours of monotonous wankery made tolerable only by imagining Irons and Anthony Andrews giving each other a toss.

"Midnight?" Lloyd asked. "You'll meet me?"

"Yes."

"Because if you're only saying it to get rid of me . . ."

"Of course I'm saying it to get rid of you—that's why we're on a fucking fire escape, Lloyd—but I'm not a bloody liar. The Drake—midnight."

"Fiona." Lloyd spoke sharply. "I have left my wife. I have left my family. The only life I have now is with you. If there's no life for me with you, I don't know what I'll do."

"Leave off with the little suicide hints," Fiona said. "They are ugly and egotistical, and not in the least bit enticing. I will meet you if you leave now."

"All right." Lloyd began descending the fire escape, then stopped. "I do love you, Fee," he said.

"Fuck off." Lloyd smiled as if what Fiona had meant to say was *I love you too*.

Fiona walked back into the theater, down the steps, out onto the stage where Sammy was pushing a broom and blasting Rush's "Spirit of Radio" from the auditorium speakers, then into the Annex hallway, where everyone had dispersed save for Eileen's family.

"We're all waiting for Eileen Muldoon," Mrs. Muldoon said. "Have you seen her?"

"I haven't." Fiona pushed open the door to the dressing room, then flicked on the light. "*Christ.*" Miep Gies was on the floor, one boob out of her dress as she furiously yanked Mr. Frank's dong. Fiona swooped up her clothes, exited the room, and breezed past the Muldoons. "She'll be out in a jiffy," she said. "These costumes take a bit of time."

On the lawn adjacent to the high school parking lot, a small crowd had gathered: flower-toting parents and grandparents; faculty and administrators debating whether to head home or hit the Chicago bars; students hoping to glom an invitation to some party that had to be happening somewhere. The Newsons were there—some of them, anyway: Mr. Newson in a tight, dark sport coat, Mrs. Newson in a floral print dress, Keith Newson in a just-out-of-the-box blue oxford shirt, accompanied by his pal Ricky, who hadn't gotten the semiformal dress memo and was wearing a black I ATE THE WORM tequila T-shirt. Trey was already sporting his new school's colors: a black sweater with an orange Lake Forest Academy insignia on it.

"I said she wouldn't be here," Trey told his father, speaking even faster than he usually did. "They all go to Yesterday's on opening night."

Mr. Newson shrugged. "It's a nice night," he said. "We can wait a little longer. And we're not the only ones here; people must be waiting for something."

Ray Tounslee Jr. was leaning against a lamppost, holding a single red rose. Mr. Newson sidled over to him. "Young man," he said. "You were at the show, right?"

Ray responded warily. "Uh-huh."

"You know somebody in it?"

"Yeah," said Ray. "Friend of mine."

"And you're still waiting for him?"

"Her."

Keith and Ricky sauntered behind Mr. Newson. They had a sixth sense for trouble, and a talent for starting some if no one else did.

"Hell of a story, wasn't it?" Mr. Newson asked Ray.

"Which story?"

"The war." Mr. Newson told Ray he felt proud that the U.S. had saved Europe from the Nazis. He mentioned that some of his buddies had been in Normandy on D-Day, and they'd said that the "colored soldiers" there fought just as hard as anybody else. They were hard-working people, most of them; he knew that from his business and from watching sports. He offered his hand and said his name was Chuck Newson. "You know that name? Newson?" he asked.

Ray shook his head.

"That's okay," Mr. Newson said. "There's still plenty of people who don't. What's your name, son?"

"I'm Ray."

Trey walked fast toward his father. "Come on, Dad; this is lame, waiting like this. Let's head out."

Mr. Newson pretended not to hear. "Who did you say you're waiting for?" he asked Ray.

"My lady," said Ray.

"Aww, that's swell," said Mr. Newson. "Every young man should have a young lady." He thumbed back to Trey. "My son's here to see his young lady, you're here for your young lady. Which lady are you here to see, Ray?"

"Mrs. Van DAMN!" Ray said.

Mr. Newson frowned. "That's her name?"

"The character, yeah. In the play."

"Van Daan?"

"Yeah."

"You mean the big girl—black hair, husky voice?"

"Nuh-uh," said Ray. "Blonde hair, blue eyes."

Mr. Newson looked at Keith and Ricky, then back at Ray. "Anne Frank's sister?" he asked, holding his flat hand at waist level to indicate someone short.

"Nope," said Ray.

"Blonde hair, you said?"

"That's the one."

"Tall girl? Long legs? Like real long? Talks with an accent? English?"

"Oh, yeah, you know it."

"What's her name again? The real name, not the one in the show?"

"FIE-o-na," Ray said.

Mr. Newson laughed mirthlessly. "That's a little bit funny. We're here to see the same girl." He motioned to Trey. "Could you explain why this guy"—he jutted his chin in Ray's direction—"says he's here to see his girlfriend and she's Fiona too?"

"Fiona has tons of friends," Trey said. "She's very sociable. Can we just go?"

"I don't know about any of that," said Mr. Newson. "The way this fella here is talking, it doesn't sound like he's talking about any regular sort of friend. Right, Ray?"

Keith and Ricky flanked Mr. Newson as if they were members of some dictator's personal security contingent.

"Nope, not a regular friend," said Ray. "Fiona, she's my lady."

"You hear that?" Mr. Newson asked Trey.

"It doesn't matter," Trey said.

"Maybe it doesn't, maybe it does," said Mr. Newson. "What're you gonna do about it? That's what matters."

"Who cares?" Trey said. "It's just some guy talking."

Keith got up in his brother's face. "It's some guy talkin' about your woman, Trey."

Ray watched Trey backing away from his brother, then burst out laughing. He tried to suppress the laugh but he couldn't help himself. He beat his fist into his palm and stamped his foot. "Trey? You're Trey?"

"What's so funny about that?" Keith asked.

Ray laughed until he started coughing. "Aww, shit," he said, sputtering, "Aww shit!" He held up his hands in mock surrender and backed away. "That's all right," he said. "I get it. I won't inconvenience 'Trey' and his 'woman.'"

Keith advanced toward Ray. "So who're you waiting for, for real?"

"Don't worry about it, man," said Ray.

"I'm not 'worried' about it," said Keith. "I'm just asking. Who?"

"Keith, come on," Trey said.

Ricky placed his palm firmly on Trey's chest as if to say this was a discussion between men, and Trey didn't qualify.

"Ray can speak for himself, can't you, Ray?" said Keith.

Ray didn't say anything.

"Yeah," Keith said. "I knew this *brutha* was full of shit. Thinkin' he could get himself a hot-lookin' white chick." He gestured with the back of a hand as if flicking away dust.

Ray flinched. "Which 'hot-lookin' white chick' you got in mind?" he asked. "You talkin' about the one who pretended to be Trey's girl-friend so you guys wouldn't find out he's a little sweet, so he could go to New York and get his ass plowed by his drama teacher?"

"Motherfucker!" Trey shrieked. His eyes looked wild.

"Whu-HO!" Ricky said.

Fiona was leaving the school at her normal pace, but when she saw Trey charging at Ray, she took off her shoes and dashed in her stockings toward the boys. "For the love of Christ!"

Ray swung at Trey, but Ricky grabbed Ray's arms and Keith held him around the waist. "Free-shot time," Ricky yelled. "Come on, Trey, take your shot."

"Let him go, you fucking Neanderthals!" Fiona yelled, but Mr. Newson blocked her path. "This isn't the place for you, honey," he said.

Keith and Ricky pinned Ray's arms behind him, and he struggled to break free. "Come on, do it, Trey, have at him," Keith said. "This guy's a strong fucker and we can't hold him all night."

Fiona pushed past Mr. Newson. Trey raised a fist, but Fiona grabbed him hard by the arm.

"If you lay a hand on him," Fiona told Trey, "I will fucking pulverize you."

Trey shouted through tears: "Yeah, you and everybody else."

Ray wrested himself from Keith and Ricky's grip. "Get away from him, Fiona. I'm serious, now; I ain't playing." He lunged for Keith, pushed him down hard on the lawn. Ricky pulled Ray off. "You want a piece of this?" Ray asked. He swung hard at Ricky, hit him in the jaw.

"Christ, stop!" said Fiona.

Ray stepped into a shaft of light. He threw another punch at Ricky; kicked away from Keith, who was lunging for his shoe. He struck a boxing pose and moved in on Trey, backing him up on the lawn. "What the fuck you gonna do about it, Flock o' Seagulls boy?" Ray asked. "What're you gonna do? Come on, you tough now?"

Fiona dropped her voice down an octave. "*Raymond.*" Keith got up from the lawn but he had turned quiet; so had Ricky.

"How many of y'all?" asked Ray. "How many gonna fight me for telling the truth? Give it up, how many?"

"*Raymond,*" Fiona said again.

"I am so fuckin' sick of this shit, man," Ray said up in Trey's face. "Being the quiet guy, staying outta trouble, letting people do shit to me, not getting to do shit back. 'Turn the other cheek,' 'Be the better man.' Fuck that."

"Raymond!" Fiona shouted.

Bright light flickered in Ray's eyes. "Stop!" a man's voice called out. "Stop it; let go!"

Ray yanked Trey by the shirt then threw him down hard. "How's that feel, boy?" Ray asked. "You want some more?"

"Hold it. Now," the voice said.

Light beamed on Ray's white shirt. Ray caught his breath. He coughed, cleared his throat, and spat as Fiona looked purposefully toward the light and the voice.

"Aww, shit," Ray said. A police car had pulled onto the lawn, highway lights on. A uniformed officer was holding a thick Maglite and shining it at Ray. Fiona's father was walking behind the officers.

Ray took off across the lawn. He ran past Simpson Street toward the factories on Ashland Avenue. An auto testing track was there; at the end of it, a fence. Beyond the fence, a dark, rocky path led down to the canal.

"I said hold it!" The officer—a beefy white guy, pockmarked face, brush mustache, maybe about fifty, but still fast as hell—sprinted across Emerson Street: "Stop, hold it right there; you don't wanna make it worse."

"But he's done nothing!" Fiona said.

The officer gained on Ray as he neared the testing track.

Behind Fiona, Mr. Grenfall and the officers were approaching the Newsons, and Trey was heading the other way fast. Fiona ran past Peacock's ice-cream factory, shouting into the wind. "Stop! Listen!"

Ray made for the fence. "*Damn!*" He tripped over a crack in the sidewalk, seemed to keep running even as he fell, one hand stretching forward, the fence just out of reach.

The officer pounced on Ray, brought him to the ground, provided his own soundtrack. "Bam, motherfucker!" he shouted. "BAM!" He kneed Ray in the back, grabbed his hands, cuffed him, then yanked him to his feet. "*Come on.*" He shoved Ray back toward a waiting squad car.

"He was only defending himself," Fiona said. Her stockings were torn and she could feel the cold asphalt on her feet. "They all ganged up on him, didn't they?"

Ray kept his head down, muttering to himself as the officer pushed him into the back of the car.

"I'll help you out of this," Fiona said to Ray. "It was all my da's fault, wasn't it?"

The officer shut the car door and got in front.

The others were still on the lawn, Keith, Ricky, and Mr. Newson talking to the police as if they were all old friends. Probably they were. Only Trey was gone, but no one was asking where he was.

Mr. Grenfall rubbed his temples with his thumbs. As he walked toward Fiona, looking as if he wanted to initiate some grievous father-daughter chat, she felt suffused by loathing. No doubt he loved her and had been acting out of love, but so what? She couldn't help but see that everything happening tonight had been caused by love or what people had mistaken for it. If Lloyd hadn't loved her, if her father hadn't loved her, if Trey hadn't loved himself when he was around her, if she hadn't loved the way she felt when she was around Ray, none of this would have happened. Better to always keep a distance, she thought. Don't ever get too close; if anyone ever does, tell them to run for their life.

Ray was in the back seat of the squad car, head down. Fiona tapped on the window. He didn't look up.

*

The police station was smoky, and everyone and everything in it looked green or gray. On the walls were creased, faded photos in cheap frames: officers who had either retired or died in the line of duty. The man behind the front desk was eating from a bag of chips and staring at a small, crackling mounted TV broadcasting a baseball game.

"Raymond Tounslee Jr.," Fiona said. "Is there someplace I can post bail for him or whatever it is you call it?"

"We're not at that point." The man kept eating his chips. "When we get to that point, we'll let you know."

Fiona sat on a bench and tried to read a newspaper someone had left behind but couldn't focus on it. Every so often an officer would emerge to get something from a vending machine, pour himself coffee, or leave the building with a gym bag. One tried to chat her up, but when she said she had just turned seventeen and asked what the age of consent was here in the colonies, he told her to have a nice night.

She stepped out for a smoke and looked out into quiet, peaceful downtown Evanston. The shuttered storefronts and the swaying trees, only a few buds on them, took on the configuration of a memory. She thought back to Zimbabwe, to Hong Kong, to Ottawa, to London: how quickly the time had passed when she had lived there; how unreal it seemed that she had lived in any of those places. A year from now, this time would seem just as distant. Like a role she had performed in a play. She tried to view this as consolation.

When Ray finally emerged, carrying some folded sheets of flimsy yellow paper, Fiona almost didn't recognize him. He scuffed along, hands in his pockets, eyes focused on his shoes. It took him a second to register the fact that Fiona was calling his name, and when he looked up, he barely acknowledged her—just a terse nod and a scratchy "Hey." He didn't slow his pace to let her catch up. The wind was picking up;

branches swayed and a dented white Styrofoam McDonald's container somersaulted off the sidewalk and onto the street.

"Need a lift home?" Fiona asked.

Ray didn't answer.

"Well, I'll give you one, won't I?" Fiona took his hand, grasped it firmly; he didn't return the pressure. They got into her car and she drove south.

"What did those bastards charge you with?" she asked.

"Assault or something, whatever."

"Do you have a lawyer?"

"Nope."

"A court date?"

"Probably I got it written down somewhere."

"Do you want to go someplace to chat?"

"Naw, I'm beat. Just gonna go home and crash."

"I'm so sorry for all this; it's all my fault, really."

Ray said nothing. Apparently he agreed with her.

Fiona stalled her car on Juneway Terrace in front of Ray's house; Ray had told her never to come to this block alone after dark, and if she ever did, to stay in the car with the doors locked. Tonight he didn't tell her anything.

"I'll make Da get you a lawyer," Fiona said. "He has contacts all up his arse. They'll defend you from these bloody ridiculous charges; they'll sue the Newsons and the police. There might even be a bit of money in it by the time it all gets sorted out."

Ray just shook his head and laughed.

"What're you laughing at?" Fiona asked.

"You have no idea how this works," said Ray. "Some things you just can't fix, no matter how much money you have, no matter who your pops is. Sometimes things happen and there's nothing you can do about them."

Ray got out of the car. "You got a good heart, Fiona," he said. "You take care of yourself, and I'll take care of me." He slammed the door and didn't look back.

Fiona looked at her clock: nearly three in the morning. *Some things you just can't fix*, Ray had said. Yet that was how she had lived her whole life, wasn't it? Fixing things, pretending. Like Mrs. Bloody Van Daan, making believe her marriage wasn't a sham and that her husband wasn't hoarding food and that a stupid bloody fur coat was worth worrying about when the fucking Nazis were waiting outside. All her life she'd made excuses for people: her brother, her family, poor, pathetic Lloyd. Oh, Jesus, God—*Lloyd*: What time had she said she would meet him? She took her foot off the brake.

Driving south to the Drake hotel, Fiona didn't catch a single light, just glided along Sheridan Road, then Lake Shore Drive, and found a parking space right on Michigan Avenue in front of Stuart Brent Books. Displayed in the window was a stack of copies of *Sophie's Choice*: THIS MONTH'S TOP SELLER.

The Drake had the aspect of faded luxury: a nearly empty seafood restaurant, just a few drunks and old-timers at the bar, a shuttered florist, a barbershop. A bloodred carpet led up to the lobby. At the front desk, a man in a dark suit appeared to have nodded off. She had planned a story if he tried to question her on the way up to Lloyd's room, so he wouldn't waylay her as if she were some Piccadilly tart, but he didn't stir, and the elevator operator didn't say a word to her.

Fiona knocked lightly on Lloyd's door. Nobody responded. She took out the key Lloyd had given her, turned it in the lock.

Flickering light illuminated the gray walls, a mirror, and an open window. "Lloyd?" Fiona felt for a light switch and flicked it on. "Oh, bloody hell." The bed was made as if no one had slept in it. No luggage. The bathroom door was open, but the shower and sink were dry and all the towels were arranged neatly on the racks and shelves.

On top of a lacquered wooden dresser, a circle of lit candles flickered in foggy tea glasses. The lights were reflected in the mirror behind them; leaning against that mirror, a photograph with charred edges. Fiona recognized the picture: it was one of her and Lloyd. Or it had been. A hole had been burned through Lloyd's face. Now there was only a headless body in tan slacks and a blue blazer, a hand on her shoulder.

The photograph looked like a memorial offering. The sight chilled her, but she felt more afraid for Lloyd than for herself. She went to the open window and looked down. The hotel's black canopy strained against the breeze; there was no sign that anyone had fallen or jumped. And when she went back downstairs and outside, no one was on the sidewalk beyond that canopy, no one walking, no one splayed on the pavement. All she could hear was the traffic and the lake.

Fiona briefly considered going back into the hotel and asking if Lloyd had checked out; she considered asking the police if anyone had reported a man missing from the Drake. Instead, she drove home still thinking in spite of herself how she might fix things.

The party, she thought, settling on the first idea that gave her hope. God, she needed that party to take her and everyone else's minds off their troubles. There would be drinks and dancing and maybe afterward a walk down to the rocks and the lake to watch the sunrise. Somehow, she thought, a party could make everything better.

Margo Frank

Amanda was on her way to the high school after teaching her last dance class at the Gus Giordano studio. She was walking from alley to alley so her young students wouldn't see her smoking and have their idyllic image of her ruined, when a car slowed down alongside her.

"Margo F.," Rob called out from the window of his father's Mercedes. "Lemme give you a ride."

Amanda kept walking in and out of the shadows cast by the fire escapes at the back of the old Tinkertoy factory.

"Come on," Rob said. "Just one more show; it's time to negotiate some détente."

"That's all right; I'm good."

"Yo, I got something to talk to you about, and I'm pretty sure you'll find it appealing." He had taken off his sunglasses and was smiling with uncharacteristic sweetness. Probably Amanda should have seen a sign in that. If she had known this would wind up being Amanda Wehner's last night on Earth, would she have done anything differently? Doubtful. She sighed and got in the car.

Rob was playing his usual pretentious bullshit on his tape deck: Sun Ra. He never seemed to actually listen to music as much as use it to make other people feel stupid. "You comin' to Fiona's party tonight?" he asked.

"I don't know. If my dad comes to the show, I might wind up doing something with him."

But of course Amanda's dad wouldn't come. As of eleven in the morning, when she left for the dance studio, he was still crashed out on the living room couch after having returned at four from banging Tammy or Jeannie or Lexie or Barbie or whichever twenty-three-year-old wait-ress, hostess, or manager he had picked up at one of his restaurants, all of which he had named after Led Zeppelin songs, e.g., Whole Lotta Lox; Stairway to Hummus; the Bagel of Evermore.

"I was scoping out Fiona's place. It's pretty decent; you should come," Rob said. "And you should come with me."

"Oh, should I, now?" asked Amanda.

"Yeah. You should."

"And why's that?"

"'Cause before the bash, we're gonna make a pit stop at Dave Blumberg's place in Skokie to pick up a little bit of the old *yayo.*"

"A little bit of the what?"

"*Cocaína.*"

"For real?" Amanda asked.

"Most definitely," said Rob. "Most definitely for real."

At the Annex, before the house opened, Mr. Densmore gave notes to the cast. The man's temper seemed to be getting worse each night, because of something about his son, rumor had it, or because of some-thing that had or hadn't happened with Calvin in New York, and on this night he seemed less interested in motivating his actors than in simply humiliating them. Fiona needed to stop gaping at the audience like some slack-jawed yokel, he said; there was a fourth wall, and unless Mrs. Van Daan had supernatural powers, she couldn't see through it; Miep Gies had to stop looking like she had just had an orgasm and start looking like she was about to have a baby. Mr. Van Daan was supposed to seem frustrated and afraid, *Declan,* but only because the Nazis were coming, not because his ex-girlfriend was "fucking some young, hot stud."

"Oh, and Anne." Carrie looked up, puzzled: all through high school, she had been exempt from these tirades. "Yes, you, Miss Hollinger." Densmore lasered his eyes at Carrie and made breast-squeezing gestures. "You need to wear an undershirt and a thicker brassiere or stuff something in it," he said. "I don't know if it's cold in your room or if you're just happy to see Peter, but nobody needs to see Anne's nipples on the rise."

Amanda's face ignited. Mocking her or Rob or Declan was fine, but she couldn't fathom the cruelty of anyone speaking that way to Carrie. When she and Carrie had been in elementary school in Wilmette and lived next door to each other, the two of them were inseparable: they ran through each other's sprinklers, played hide-and-seek in the summer, board games in the winter. But after the divorce and the move, she didn't see Carrie anymore. And when the two of them had run into each other at *West Side Story* auditions, Amanda felt awkward, as if fourteen-year-old Carrie was the same sweet, optimistic girl she'd known, while fifteen-year-old Amanda was already past her prime. During the entirety of *West Side Story* rehearsals, the only words she'd mustered in Carrie's presence were "Hey," "What's up," "Cool," and "If you want, I can pick you up a pair of tights from Capezio." Even so, Amanda felt protective of her, as if Carrie were still the younger sister she'd always wanted but never had, as if Carrie represented something she wished she'd hung on to but lost years ago.

"Leave her alone, you fucking asshole," she told Densmore. "What is wrong with you? Get some fucking therapy."

Eileen gasped.

Calvin laughed.

Rob stifled a snicker.

Judith, Fiona, and Franklin burst into applause while Amanda sat, waiting for Densmore to—what? Kick her out of the show? Smack her in the face?

Instead, he looked her up and down as if weighing his options, then laughed. "Well, at least we know which of you would have stood up to the Nazis," he said. "Okay, places, people. Places!" When Amanda and Carrie found themselves in the Franks' apartment, checking their props,

Carrie caught her eye and said, "Thanks," but Amanda just shrugged. "No big deal," she muttered. "You'd do it for me."

"I'd like to think so," said Carrie. "Maybe the next time he talks like that to you, I will."

"Or someone else," Amanda said. "I'm used to it."

*

There was a different energy to the show this night. The more they performed this play, the more Amanda disliked just about all the other actors save for Carrie; if she had to perform it for a year, maybe she'd get a sense of what it would have been like to be the Franks and Van Daans. Or maybe that was just Amanda's cynicism, the characteristic that had probably led Densmore to cast her as Margo, whose last line in the play was one Amanda could relate to all too well: "Sometimes I wish the end would come," Margo said. "Then at least we'd know where we were."

These days that phrase summed up Amanda's life philosophy. It was the same sort of feeling that had led her to date guys like Rob, whose main attribute was his ability to procure good drugs and concert tickets; it was the feeling that led her to patrol the el in her GUARDIAN ANGELS jacket, primed to use the self-defense techniques she was sure would never do any good if some Vice Lord pulled a knife; and it was the same feeling that had led her to say yes to Rob when he asked if she wanted to drive with him and Eileen to Skokie to get some coke.

In the final moments of the play—before the sounds of the SS marchers—Carrie spoke the line that made just about everyone in the audience choke up: "*In spite of everything, I still believe that people are really good at heart.*" Amanda could hear the gasps and sobs. But the more she considered those words, the colder they left her. That was what Anne said before she was taken away, before her mother and sister died. Anne's words weren't the point of the play; Margo's were: "Sometimes I wish the end would come; then at least we'd know where we were."

At the curtain call, Amanda was the only actor who didn't bow. Acknowledging applause for playing people who'd been murdered by

Nazis seemed stupid and shameful. She didn't even step forward, didn't look out to the audience to see if her dad had shown up; she knew he hadn't. She just stood frozen, waiting for the end to come so she would finally know where she was.

*

Rob's car smelled a little like sweat, a little like old spunk, a little like lemon-scented air freshener, and a lot like Eileen's baby powder and L'Air du Temps perfume. Amanda sat in front while Eileen rode in back as they drove to Skokie with Rob blasting Herbie Hancock's "Magic Number." Eileen bopped along, playing air bass and imitating the music—*"Bayaouuh-baou-buh-baouu-baou-buh-baouu-baou-buh-baoubuhbaouh."*

Amanda wondered how the two of them could seem so cheerful, why the play hadn't affected them more. Had either Rob or Eileen ever seen death up close? Had they ever experienced anything like she had when she was nine and had let herself into her grandmother Asya's apartment as usual, then saw Baba Asya lying on her kitchen floor by the refrigerator that must have been open for hours, maybe even days, because it smelled like spoiled milk and everything in it was warm? She couldn't get in touch with either her mom or dad, so she called 911 and sat there shivering until the paramedics showed up and one gave her a blanket. He asked if she wanted to go to a different room or wait in the ambulance. "She'll still be dead those places too," Amanda had said.

"So," Amanda asked Rob, "what's up with this alleged cocaine?"

"Next stop on our itinerary." Rob drove with one hand on the wheel and the other out the window, slapping the side of his car while Eileen gnawed a piece of beef jerky and made suggestive remarks: "Oooh, this jerky is so good—so stiff, thick, meaty, *hahahahahahahaha.*"

Skokie was a strange place. Whenever people talked about it or mentioned it on the news, it seemed peaceful, geriatric—a village of old, retired Jews who had survived the Holocaust and, just a few years earlier, had stood up when the Nazis wanted to march downtown, then ate smoked fish and lox at Sam & Hy's or Barnum and Bagel. But every memory Amanda had of this town was exceedingly fucked-up: smoking hash in the storeroom every afternoon when she was working one summer at Just Pants; sneaking a flask into *Scanners* at the Old Orchard and vomiting in the women's room before the movie was half over; jerking off and getting jerked off by some guy she had met waiting in line for Styx tickets at Record City.

And, invariably, although pot was easy to get from Sammy, whenever anyone wanted something actually good, they wound up at the house of some random Jewish kid dealing out of his mobbed-up parents' house.

Rob left the keys in the ignition and the radio on; it was now tuned to "Blues Breakers" on WXRT. Junior Wells was singing "Ships on the Ocean."

"Back in a minute with the *'fine Colombian,'* " Rob said.

"You need money?" Amanda asked.

"Nah," said Rob. "There's other ways to pay me back."

"*Hahahahahahahaha,*" said Eileen.

Amanda had little to say to Eileen, but it didn't really matter; Amanda knew well the odd equalizing effect drugs had, forcing you into awkward social situations with people you had nothing in common with except for the product you were buying and consuming.

"Ever done coke before?" Eileen asked.

"Just twice, but I kinda loved it," said Amanda. "What about you?"

"Too scared," said Eileen. "But I love cutting it up and dividing it into those cute little lines. Same thing with pot. I don't really do it, but packing it into bongs or rolling it up in joints is so fun. You excited about Fiona's party?"

Amanda shrugged. "Yeah, I guess. What about you?"

"Oh, yeah, baby," said Eileen. "It's gonna be one to remember."

*

Fiona's house was packed. Burnouts in jeans and concert jerseys had wandered over from the beach, apparently guided by the sound of Prince thumping out of Bang & Olufsen speakers. "*Con-tro-versy!*" Polo-shirted Northwestern frat guys had slowed their cars at the sight of the illuminated mansion and felt drawn by the promise of free hooch and underage tail. "*Con-tro-versy!*" Seniors from North Shore who were generally unseen outside the cafeteria, the gym, and the smoking area, and routinely called Annex actors "dykes" and "fags," had nevertheless sat through two acts of *Anne Frank* to secure their invitation. "*Con-tro-versy!*" Punks wearing ironic Chicago Police Department jackets patrolled the premises, scoffing at the sellout assholes among them. "*Con-tro-versy!*" Sammy Doulos worked the turntable, well aware that if you wanted a party to rock, you had to put your King Crimson and Procol Harum records away for the night and get people up and dancing. "*Con-tro-versy!*" A delegation of Black kids, members of a church social club called Fly Girls 'n' Fellas, were dressed nattily in white shirts and blouses and dark pants or skirts to make sure no one mistook them for gangbangers; they were clapping and line dancing to "*Con-tro-versy!*" Mr. and Mrs. Grenfall's friends sipped cocktails, munched hors d'oeuvres, and joked about politics in the kitchen, apparently oblivious to the pot smoke and the booze. "*Con-tro-versy!*" The entire *Anne Frank* cast was here save for Calvin, who had told Fiona he feared drinking too much, choking on his vomit, and never making it to New York; and the first Mr. Van Daan, aka Trey, who had made only a brief appearance, leaving shortly after Fiona told him he had a lot of nerve showing up after all the trouble he'd caused on opening night; he'd mumbled a "Sorry" that couldn't be heard over all the "*Con-tro-versy!*"

Declan was at the piano, playing and singing show tunes, putting everything he had into "Hey, Look Me Over," every so often shifting his eyes to see if Carrie and Franklin were still holding hands out on the lawn, then surveying the scene for mousy underclass girls he could wow into submission. When he had first asked Carrie out, he didn't realize that he would wind up dating an equal; he wouldn't make that mistake again.

Fiona, barefoot, already pretty trashed, in a short, black-and-white zigzag-striped dress, was at the punch bowl, ladling pink fluid into crystal glassware. Off to one side of the main staircase, in a dimly lit room, Judith was on the phone with her mother: "No, I won't be able to 'pop by the hospital' at least until morning," she was saying. "No, they said you have to stay at least one more night"; "Yes, I've been drinking"; "No, not nearly enough!" She slammed down the phone, exhaled dramatically, then flipped both of her middle fingers and moved them in a quick up-and-down motion that suggested the aggressive milking of a cow. She grabbed two glasses of punch from Fiona, poured one into the other, and glugged it like Gatorade.

Underneath a teardrop chandelier, the head of the dining room table was occupied by Tyrus Densmore, who swirled whiskey in a snifter as smoke rose from the cigar in his ashtray. He was playing poker with a group of half a dozen boys, all of whom had auditioned unsuccessfully for *Anne Frank*, all of whom were hoping that next year, since Declan, Rob, Judith, Calvin, and Amanda would be gone, they would have a better chance of getting cast in a play and being chosen for the "New York trip." The deck was a set of *Playboy* Playmate cards with pictures of centerfold models on them, and the pot at the center of the table consisted not of money but wrapped condoms. Densmore laid his cards down. "I've got a nine-inch cock and two smooth balls; what've you got?" he asked.

Rob guided Amanda through the crowd, grasping her forearm or nudging her along by the elbow, but he had the coke, so she didn't object. Parties weren't really her thing; if not for the blow Rob had promised and the fact that nothing awaited her at home except for *The Stand*, the Stephen King novel she'd been reading, she wouldn't have come. She didn't even like to dance at parties, because she was good at it, so when she did, people just assumed she was showing off or trying to draw attention to herself. Thank God no other member of her graduating class would be going to Colorado College. She would study philosophy and choreography there, she would grow her own weed or maybe she wouldn't even smoke at all, and, if she dated anyone, it would be someone completely different from anyone she'd ever been with, maybe some bespectacled physics major who didn't even party.

"Where's that blow?" Amanda asked.

"All in good time." Rob stopped at the base of the grand staircase. Eileen danced over to them, holding two glasses of punch, singing along with Prince—"I Wanna Be Your Lover." She handed the first glass to Rob, the other to Amanda. "This is the stuff—drink up!" she said, and danced away.

Rob downed his drink, then Amanda downed hers. As the sound from the party seemed to fade into one continuous rumble, she followed him upstairs, ignoring the foreboding feeling she'd had this entire evening, wishing the end would come, so then at least she'd know where she was.

The hallway of the Grenfalls' second floor seemed to have more doors than any house was supposed to and a carpeted hallway longer than any Amanda had ever seen outside of a museum. Most of the doors were closed, but one was open, and a narrow beam of light emanated from it.

"Kinda seems like you've been here before," said Amanda.

"Nah," said Rob. "I just have a feel for the place." He led her toward the light.

As Rob opened the door, Amanda felt unsteady—maybe because of the punch, although she hadn't had all that much, just a glass. Maybe because she hadn't really eaten anything since a couple of bananas after her last dance class. Rob pushed the door open, waited for Amanda to come in, then closed it. "Well, what might we do in here?" he asked.

The room was tidy, but coldly so—like one of the furnished condos Amanda and her father had toured shortly after her mother had moved to San Jose with her twenty-six-year-old boyfriend, and her dad had said he just wanted a place where he could move in on day one and never worry about decorating. There was a bed with white sheets and a tan comforter, a small bedside table with a lamp on it, two closed doors that presumably led to a closet and a bathroom. There was a tall, antique wooden dresser, but Amanda would have bet money nothing was inside, not even a Bible. The room swayed; light-colored dots seemed to speckle the white walls.

"How're you feeling?" Rob asked.

"Just a little light-headed," said Amanda. "You have the coke?"

"Right here." Rob slapped his jeans pocket. He untucked her shirt, put his hand on her stomach, then pushed his lips against hers. She wasn't particularly into it, but she also wasn't sufficiently not into it to strenuously object. The good and bad thing about Rob was that he never pretended there was anything more to sex other than what he wanted out of it.

Rob pressed Amanda down on the bed and the room seemed to spin; the dots on the wall looked thicker and darker, and Amanda was growing less aware of her surroundings, so much so that she had the sense that reality was something available to her only sporadically, appearing in bursts she was watching from a distance. Here was Rob unbuttoning her blouse, and then there was nothing; here he was, unsnapping her pants and yanking them down, then nothing again. A toilet flushed, a door opened, somebody whispered something, somebody snorted and laughed. Then the next thing Amanda felt conscious of was being naked and alone on the bed in the pitch-dark room. She felt an urge to get up and leave, but her head was too heavy. The room was cold, but she couldn't muster the strength to pull the covers over her. She was conscious enough to understand something was happening to her, not conscious enough to know exactly what.

Downstairs in the ballroom, Fiona was at the piano, and Judith was leaning against it with a cocktail like a vamp in some 1940s movie, belting out "In the Air Tonight" as if the louder she sang, the easier it would be to block out everything else. Carrie and Franklin had moved inside and were sitting cross-legged on the carpet in the study, playing Trivial Pursuit while a solemn figure loomed in the doorway.

"What do you want, Declan?" Carrie asked.

"We need to talk about us," said Declan.

"There is no more 'us,'" Carrie said. "You broke up with me over the phone, remember?"

"I didn't mean it forever," said Declan.

"But I did," said Carrie, and Declan walked out fast so she couldn't see him crying.

Tucking his shirt into his pants, Rob approached the poker table where Densmore—now with the largest pile of wrapped condoms in front of him—was holding his cigar, dealing cards, and regaling the young actors at the table with a story of a night he claimed to have spent with Tennessee Williams: "You know, his original title for *Streetcar* was *The Poker Night*, which was an apt description of our night together; all the man did was poke." Densmore turned to Rob. "Shall we deal you in?"

Rob picked up a card, and frowned at the centerfold model on it. "No, actually I'm past the age of getting off by looking at airbrushed T and A, and I'd think you would be too," he said.

Densmore puffed on his cigar. "You talk a pretty big game for someone whose only partner this evening seems to be his right hand."

Rob laughed throatily, the sort of laugh he imagined he'd give someday in Washington, D.C., when he was conducting backroom deals and sending dumb schmucks off to war.

"You've got me pegged wrong," said Rob. "Can the two of us go somewhere to talk?"

Densmore nodded. "I'll be back for the rubber match," he told the other players. "Nobody touch my stash."

Rob and Mr. Densmore found their way into a dim sitting room with a low daybed and a screened-in porch. Rob took a cigarette out of his shirt pocket, lit it, and smoked. "Do you know what would be cool?" he asked.

"No," Densmore replied, repeating Rob's words in a mocking tone. "'What would be *cool*?'"

"Well, pretty soon, I'll be at Carleton," Rob said. "But I'll be back for breaks, and the idea of hanging around these same kids, doing the same things we've been doing for years, that sounds pretty beat."

"'Beat'?"

"Old." Rob said he didn't think he'd ever live in Chicago—right now, he had his eyes on D.C. and New York—but whenever he came home, he wanted to go to blues clubs and wine bars, see live jazz. "A year from now, if you see me still going to Yesterday's for foot-long hot dogs, do me a favor and shoot me dead. I was thinking maybe you and me could hang out sometime."

"You and I?" Densmore asked.

"I bet we have more in common than you think. We could see plays, hear jazz at Gold Star Sardine, maybe even pick up some women."

Densmore chuckled. "I'm a married man."

"All the more reason." Rob looked around to make sure no one was eavesdropping. He spoke confidentially yet openly, like a man who has discovered someone who shares his secret vice. "I think you and I have similar tastes," he told Densmore. "We like the ones who are a little rough around the edges; the ones you can't corrupt because they've already been corrupted."

Densmore raised an eyebrow, then nodded.

"Can I let you in on a secret?" Rob asked.

"Please do."

"Upstairs in a bedroom—third door on the right—there's a girl lying in bed and she's pretty far gone, like she doesn't even know where she is right now. I came in with her. I think you know who I mean. Someone could have a real good time with her—a lot better than you can have with any airbrushed pussy on the back of a playing card."

Densmore exhaled sharply. "You know, you are a truly despicable individual," he said, then paused. "I imagine you have a great future in front of you."

"I learned from the best," said Rob.

"Third door on the right?" Densmore offered his hand to Rob and quoted Humphrey Bogart in *Casablanca*: "Louie," he said, "I think this is the beginning of a beautiful friendship." He walked toward the staircase.

Rob took Densmore's place at the head of the card table and laughed to himself.

"What's so funny?" a boy asked.

"Come Monday morning, I imagine there'll be a pretty interesting story on Eustacia Winslow's desk, one that nobody's had the balls to tell before." Rob grabbed the *Playboy* cards, shuffled them, then, with one swoop of his arm, cleared the condoms off the table and onto the floor.

"Fuck these rubbers," he said. "Get your wallets out; we're playing for money."

Densmore walked toward the staircase, but when he was out of Rob's line of sight, he stopped, chuckled, then turned the other way and made for the doors that led to the Grenfalls' backyard.

Just about everyone outside had arranged themselves in couples or clumps. Couples were making out on the lawn or under the trees; couples were sharing beers to acquire the courage that would turn them into the couples that made out on the lawn or under the trees. Meanwhile, clumps sat in circles, passing around joints and wondering aloud whether the half-moon above them was the same half-moon everywhere on Earth or whether it was in different phases in different time zones; clumps were dancing sloppily to Kool and the Gang; clumps were discussing the play they'd just seen and asking if anyone here would have the guts to fight if a Fourth Reich ever emerged. Sometimes, pairs broke off from clumps and made out like couples—sometimes, couples argued then joined the nearest clump—but no one out here was truly alone.

Except Declan.

Declan sat by himself on the lawn against the trunk of a bare syca-more tree, staring hatefully straight ahead as if trying to sear a hole through every kissing couple and dancing clump, burn everything in sight, burn the house where Carrie and Franklin were playing Trivial Pursuit and not giving a damn whether he lived or died.

"Is this patch of grass *occupado*?" Tyrus Densmore asked, his voice soft.

Declan looked up as Densmore crouched before him, and his face flushed with rage. "You sick, twisted bastard," he said. "What are you even doing at a high school party? That's pathetic. You're an adult. What's wrong with you? You're just a fucking loser—like Amanda said. You and your mind games. You fucked everything up, my whole life. If it weren't for you . . ."

"Yes?" Densmore's tone shifted as if Declan's insults were making him rethink the reason he had initiated this conversation. "Yes, Declan? If it weren't for me, what?"

"If it weren't for you, Carrie wouldn't've met Franklin, I would've played Peter Van Daan, Carrie would've gone to Northwestern, we would've gotten married, moved to New York when I got my first Broadway role . . ." He sobbed; Densmore put his arms around him.

"Easy," Densmore said softly. "*Easy.* She isn't worth it; no girl is. Better you learn that now than when you have a career and kids and you can't get out so easily."

"I don't want to get out; that's the point. You don't get it."

Tyrus grabbed him by the wrists. "I do get it," he said. "More than you. You don't think I know what it's like to want to fuck someone, then have them slam the door on you and shut you out even after all you've done for them?"

"Stop it," Declan said.

"It doesn't have to be that way for you, though, Dec," said Densmore. "You're young. You're good-looking. I'll be here for the rest of my life, I know that, showing up at parties where I don't belong, listening to people I love call me a loser. You're right about that. But you know why I've been so hard on you, don't you? You know the real reason why I didn't cast you in the role you wanted. You know all that, don't you?"

"No, why?"

"Because it made you an even greater actor than you already were. It's what I always tell you: when you come back after I break you down, you're that much stronger. Did you see all those girls watching when you were singing at the piano?"

"I didn't," said Declan.

"I did," Densmore said. "There were dozens."

"Dozens of what?"

"Girls," Densmore said. "Looking at you. You have a gift, Declan. A power. You know you have it, but you're going to have to learn how to harness it, control it. You were always a great actor, but now you're more than that; you've become a great performer. You know what the difference is?"

Declan shook his head.

"Acting is about convincing the audience you're the character you're playing. Performing is about getting the audience to want to fuck you.

You don't think that half the girls here want you more than Carrie ever did?"

Declan didn't look angry anymore. He was staring up at Densmore, rapt. For a bit more time, Densmore still had power over him, and now was one of his last chances to use it; all he had to do was tell Declan what he wanted to believe about himself. "Let me tell you a secret, Dec," he said.

"What?"

"Upstairs, there's someone who wants you right now. She's waiting for you. In bed. Everyone here knows she's waiting for you. Everyone except you."

"Who?" Declan asked.

"I think you know." Tyrus told Declan to go up to the second floor and find the third door on the right. He reached into a pocket and pulled out a pair of condoms, then pressed them into Declan's hand and closed Declan's fingers over them. "Go on," he said. "Now don't say I don't love you. Someday, when you're on Broadway or off in Hollywood or wherever you wind up, I hope you still remember all I've done for you." He patted Declan on the shoulder. Then Tyrus walked through the couples and clumps toward his car.

*

Upstairs, Amanda was regaining awareness of her surroundings. Slowly. There were still blank spaces in between sensations, yet those spaces seemed to be getting shorter; she no longer had to remind herself exactly where she was and how she had gotten here. Her head still felt heavy but now she could lift it. A bit. She understood she was naked, and didn't have to remind herself who had undressed her. The scent of baby powder and L'Air du Temps perfume lingered. Something was moving, shifting its weight, beyond a wall or closed door. Bass thumped through the floor, getting louder when a door opened, muffled after it closed. A hand touched her legs, her stomach, her breasts.

"It's me," someone said.

"God, where were you?" she mumbled.

"Downstairs." But it wasn't Rob's voice, and the way this person touched her didn't feel like Rob either: too tentative, then suddenly too assertive. A hand squeezed her breast hard, manipulated her nipple. She squirmed. She felt a hand on her knee; it moved upward. "Shhh," the voice said. Her body tensed. She grunted as she lifted one of her legs. The person leaning over her, breathing heavily, smelling of lawn and smoke, seemed to take this as an invitation. He moved his hand up her thigh. "Mmmm," he said.

Amanda remembered the self-defense drills she and Chick Tarshis had practiced in the dank gymnasium of the Broadway Armory for Guardian Angels training: *First the groin, then the face*, she thought.

A door opened. A flash of light blasted the room before it returned to darkness. Then another flash. A camera. Film advancing. *Click flash click flash.* She felt the hand between her legs, a stiff penis on her knee. *First the groin, then the face.* She gripped the hand hard, then reached for the groin, grabbed a fistful of dick and balls. Another moan, this one morphing almost instantly from pleasure to pain. She slammed her foot into the guy's balls, swung her fist right for the face, kicked and swung again. She heard a cry but she kept punching and kicking. She punched for Rob who had brought her up here, stripped her naked, and left her. She kicked and punched for whichever motherfucker had taken Rob's place. She kicked and punched for Ty Densmore, who had made a safe place dark and dangerous. She kicked for her mother who had left her, for her father, who always left her alone. She punched for the world that had left her grandmother to die by herself. She kicked for the world that had abandoned the Franks, the Van Daans. She imagined each kick and punch taking her one step farther away— from this room, this house, this town. She kicked and punched so hard that she barely even registered the sounds of someone screaming in pain. More bursts of light, more camera clicks—bright, then dark; bright, then dark until all she could see was the greenish imprint of a silhouette hovering over her body. Then something hit the carpet, the door to the bedroom opened, light from the hall streamed in, someone ran out and slammed the door, and the room returned to darkness until the door opened once again, and two girls ran toward her—Judith and Fiona.

"Jesus fucking Christ," Judith said.

Fiona flicked on a light. "What the bloody hell's going on?"

Amanda pulled the covers around her and sat up, for the first time fully conscious of how cold the room was, how heavy her head felt. Sprawled out on the carpet—pants undone, underwear down, one leg underneath him, the other leg sticking straight out—was Declan. He was cupping his nose with his hands; his face was scratched, his fingers were smeared with blood, and he was rocking back and forth. "Oh, man," he kept saying. "Ohhh, man."

Fiona approached Amanda. "Are you all right?"

Judith stood over Declan. "What the fuck did you think you were doing?"

Declan's voice echoed in his cupped hands. "Tyrus said."

Judith cut him off. "'Tyrus said'? Nobody gives a shit what that bastard said."

"Can I get you something?" Fiona asked Amanda. "Some water? Are you hurt?"

Amanda could hear both girls talking—Fiona trying to comfort her; Judith calling Declan a pervert, a rapist. She could hear Declan sniveling, apologizing. But to Amanda it all sounded as though it were taking place somewhere far away.

"I'm all right, yeah," she said. "I don't need any water, no—no, I can get home on my own. I'll call my dad; he'll pick me up—no, you don't need to wait with me for him—please, just leave me alone."

At a certain point she stopped listening to anything anyone was saying. She couldn't find her underwear, so she just put on her jeans without them. The bra was on the bed, but it didn't seem worth bothering with, so she pulled on her top, then her socks and shoes. She felt faint as she stood but tried her best to make it seem as if she were all right so no one would try to make her stay any longer. In the bathroom she rubbed her face and splashed water on it, but it still looked pale and her eyeliner was smeared.

Downstairs, people were dancing, people were breaking shit, people were playing poker, Trivial Pursuit; arguments were breaking out between old friends; enemies were hugging each other like lifelong pals; grown-ups were laughing, swirling drinks. Couples were flopped in each other's arms on couches; someone was down on her hands and knees, trying to wipe a stain out of the living room rug. Eileen was dancing with a beer bottle, camera bouncing against her hip.

On the lawn, Amanda heard Carrie call her name, asking if she was okay, if she needed anything, but she didn't stop. She walked down the driveway and out toward Sheridan Road. She didn't know what time it was, although all the streetlights were flashing yellow instead of shining red or green, so it was past midnight, probably long past. Her dad would have told her she was stupid to walk alone this late, still half-drunk on whatever Rob and Eileen had slipped her, but to her, danger had always been something that happened inside houses, not outside them. She took a quick glance back at the Grenfall mansion looming dark behind her, just a few lights burning in its windows, like some cursed, secret annex that she felt lucky to escape.

The quick way home would have been to stay on Sheridan; instead, once she had walked south awhile, she found a hole in a wooden fence big enough to climb through and went to the beach. She took off her shoes and walked barefoot through the cold, wet sand, listened to the rush and fizz of the spring waves, kept her eyes fixed on the Chicago skyline ahead. She walked past Lee Street, where Sammy used to sell her weed out of a hot dog truck, past the patch of sand where she and her mom used to go on summer afternoons. Her mom would bring a portable tape deck and play Cat Stevens and Stephen Stills; she'd eye guys in tight swimsuits and say, "Go swim, Amanda. Not now, Amanda. Go swim."

Amanda paused at the water's edge. She could walk in, she thought, fill her pockets with rocks and sand and let the lake do its work. But that wasn't what she wanted; she wouldn't mind if Amanda drowned, but *she* wasn't done with her life. She would call herself Asya now, like her grandmother. After she went to college in Colorado, she would never come back. And everything that had happened—Eileen and Rob tricking her, drugging her; Declan on top of her—would be something that had happened to someone else. She climbed back through the fence, then walked all the way home.

No one was there, of course. The clock on the kitchen wall said two forty-five. She went to the hall closet, took out her GUARDIAN ANGELS jacket, and put it on. She took the elevator down to the lobby, then walked out, bound for the South Boulevard train station, and when she got there, she stood awhile alone on the platform, then boarded an empty car.

The idea of being a Guardian Angel, Amanda's partner, Chick Tarshis, had told her, was not to break up fights or subdue anyone. There were no handcuffs, no guns. You weren't there to stop crimes; you were there to provide comfort and security to the passengers who weren't criminals. The self-defense techniques were designed to save her, not anybody else; if there was real trouble, you found a phone and called the cops. And you never worked alone.

Trains came less frequently this late, but when they did, they seemed to move more quickly. Doors opened at empty stations. The few people who got on kept to themselves: hospital workers finishing shifts or starting them; construction crews in jumpsuits sleeping off the rest of the night before they had to start work; a three card monte player, drunk or pretending to be, looking for someone to scam. At Belmont Avenue a punk girl got on, hair gelled and spiked. She snorted at Amanda, drew a cross on her fogged-up window, then x-ed it out.

You weren't supposed to cross between cars, but nobody said anything when Amanda did, not even the cops who got on shortly after the train descended into the tunnel with a shriek and a flickering of pale yellow dome lights. "How're you doin', 'Angel'?" one cop said with a laugh.

The train rose again into the city night. She had never ridden the el this far south. A couple of teenage guys laughed—maybe at her, maybe not. She paid them no mind. Everybody just looked tired.

Everybody just looked beat-up. Everybody just looked like they were waiting for the end to come so at least they'd know where they were.

She took the el until it stopped at Englewood, then got out and waited for a northbound train. When it finally came, she boarded it, and sat with her feet up on the side of the car. The sky outside was fading from pitch-black into gray—still too early for more than a few people to get on at any stop: a handyman at Jeffery Boulevard; a gaunt old man in a stained rugby shirt at Forty-Seventh; a stooped woman in a pale blue uniform, carrying a metal pail stuffed full of rags and detergent. No one seemed to need saving.

She watched Chicago blur by, drab and indifferent: Fullerton Avenue, Belmont, Addison; the bleachers of Wrigley Field; the headstones and mausoleums of Graceland Cemetery; the Aragon Ballroom; the Bryn Mawr Theatre, the Granada—all the places she hoped would soon be distant memories, if she had to remember them at all.

At Morse Avenue, she saw the sign for the Ashkenaz Deli. She and her mom used to go there after the beach: her mom would have two black coffees and a cigarette; Amanda would get an apple sweet roll, a glass of milk, and, if her mother was in an especially good mood, which wasn't often, a Joyva bar—raspberry gel covered with chocolate.

No one was waiting at Morse when the train pulled in . . . well, just about no one, but the man standing there didn't look like he wanted to get on. He was at the far end of the platform, past where the trains stopped. He had a trimmed black beard with flecks of gray in it, and he wore a black overcoat and polished black shoes. Behind him, he had left a tan leather suitcase as if wherever he was going, he wasn't taking it with him.

Amanda got off the train. The man's eyes glinted with the reflection of the train's lights. He took a small step toward the tracks, his shoulders sagging slightly, then swaying. He stared at the third rail.

"Hey," Amanda said softly, and when he didn't react, she asked, "Where're you headed?"

The man kept looking at the tracks. He spat out a laugh, then repeated Amanda's question as if it were part of an internal monologue, something he was asking himself: "Yes, where am I headed?"

"Would you mind stepping back a bit?" Amanda asked. "You're making me nervous." Always try to engage, Chick Tarshis had taught her: Talk to them the way you'd talk to a friend. "Hey, buddy," Chick always said to people in trouble. "Hey, pal."

"I'm making you nervous?" the man asked Amanda.

"Uh-huh."

"Nervous I might . . ."

Say the word, Amanda remembered, *saying the word takes away its power.* "Jump, yeah. Is that the plan? Jumping?"

"Well, there isn't much of a plan anymore. There was one, and now there's not, and that's—" He turned to her as if to finish the sentence, then stopped. "Margo Frank," he said.

"I'm sorry?"

"We learn so much more about your sister than we do about you, and yet, with what happens in your silences, I imagine one could have filled a dozen diaries."

"You saw the play."

The man nodded.

"You're someone's father?" Amanda asked.

"A friend," said the man. "Former friend, I imagine you'd say." He made a quick dusting gesture at his torso, as if to ask Amanda what her jacket meant. "Who're you supposed to be now?"

"A Guardian Angel," Amanda said.

The man chuckled. "Is that so?"

"Are you still thinking of doing it? Jumping?"

"There don't seem to be any preferable alternatives. Can you think of any?"

"Coffee, I guess," said Amanda.

"Can't stand the stuff."

"Tea?"

"Is there a place in this city where one can find a decent cup of tea?"

"We could try if you step away from the tracks."

"How could I say no to my guardian angel?" The man offered his hand. "My name's Lloyd."

"I'm Asya."

The sky was purplish gray now, fading into periwinkle. The Ashkenaz Deli was just opening for business, and Lloyd and Asya sat at the counter. Lloyd ordered tea—Lipton; it came in a creased bag. Asya had coffee and an apple sweet roll, which was much sweeter than she remembered. They talked for a long while; well, mostly Asya listened and Lloyd talked—about his wife and his children, whom he might never get to see again; about Fiona and how she'd played him for a fool, even though she'd been perfectly right to do so; about how he'd like to start his whole life over someplace where no one knew him. He had two tickets back to London, but it looked like he'd only be using one of them.

Asya liked listening to Lloyd: he made her feel strong in a way she rarely felt except when she was alone; after all, she may have saved his life. And listening to him helped to keep the insistent memories at bay: the smell of baby powder and L'Air du Temps; the camera flashes; Declan over her, then writhing and bleeding on the floor.

After the check came and Asya paid for the two of them, she said it was time for her to start heading home, at which point Lloyd said he didn't have anyplace to go; his flight wasn't leaving until the evening. There was a pull-out couch in her father's living room, she said, and she was sure her dad wouldn't mind if he slept there. She expected Lloyd to say he didn't want to cause any trouble, but he just walked with her along Sheridan Road. Newspaper deliverymen were hauling out bound editions of the Sunday papers, dropping them in front of drugstores, restaurants, barbershops, the 7-Eleven, and the White Hen Pantry. ACCUSED NAZI LOSES APPEAL, read the headline of the Sun-Times.

No, Asya thought, in spite of everything, she still didn't believe that people were good at heart. But if you were lucky enough to find one or two who were, then you might have a shot, and as long as she lived, she would try her best to be one of them.

"You wouldn't be interested in a free ticket to London, would you?" Lloyd asked with a self-deprecating laugh.

Asya smiled. She liked the idea of a long plane ride to somewhere she'd never been before, but only if the seat next to hers was empty.

"No," she said. "No, I'm good."

ACT II

November 2016 and beyond

Never again is what you swore the time before.

—DEPECHE MODE, "POLICY OF TRUTH"

Miep Gies

She was voting for Trump.

That's how it all started, really; that's how everything came rocketing back: she was voting for Trump. She wasn't exactly sure why, she wasn't political, she couldn't even remember when she last voted, but just saying it to herself felt good, like she was finally going to take control of her life: "I'm voting for Trump." It was one of those things you said in private, something that made you realize you had more power than people thought you did—like giving someone the finger when they couldn't see you doing it; like cursing at another driver in traffic when your windows were up. It was like singing swear words during the "Hallelujah Chorus"; like pissing in a clogged hotel shower and knowing you wouldn't be the illegal immigrant who'd have to clean it up. "Fuck you, I'm voting for Trump."

All through this dazzling autumn, she had been repeating the phrase to herself. In her mind, she'd said it just the day before to her mother's home care worker, Ruby Gonzalez, who had arrived late for her last day of work; Ruby Gonzalez, whom Eileen could get deported with just one call to Homeland Security, even though she wouldn't, because word might get back to one of Ruby's ten dozen MS-13 siblings, who would hunt Eileen down and behead her with a machete. *Fuck you, Ruby*, she thought. *You're gonna get shipped back to Mexico or wherever you came from, 'cause I'm voting for Trump.* She said it under her breath to the Indian call service workers who refused to waive their insane fees even though she had never paid her Discover Card bill late before. "Fat chance you're ever getting an American visa, *saheeb*; I'm voting for Trump." She said it to the late Tim Donovan, who, almost a year ago now, had had the gall to drop dead of a heart attack right in the executive offices of U-Stuff-It Storage Solutions before the two of them had gotten married. And, oh my God, how badly did she want to say it to Tim's widow, Carla, and her vengeful twins, Dave and Dori, who had fired her less than a month after their father had died. Fuck them all, she thought, she was voting for Trump.

Eileen might have also said it to her mother, who at this very moment was dawdling in the upstairs bathroom, putting on makeup for her trip to Wheeling Estates Elder Care, where she would be staying supposedly temporarily, but Mary Muldoon had already cast her vote by early ballot. Mom was voting for Trump too.

"Mother!" Eileen called from the bottom of the stairs. "We're supposed to be there by noon."

"With all the money they charge, they can wait a little longer," Mrs. Muldoon called back.

Eileen checked the burners on the stove; made sure the pilot lights were lit; opened and shut cabinet doors—knowing that the moment she stopped moving and fiddling, she would have to face the gravity of what she was about to do. How many decades had Mary Muldoon lived in this house? How many dinner parties had she hosted, how many neighbors had she outlived, how many times had she watered the grass or retrieved the mail or shouted at some motorcycle-riding boy to knock it off, people were trying to sleep? Still, Eileen knew what she was doing was right, even if her "Bernie or Bust" brothers—who came in town only for Christmas, when they stayed in hotels with their families— wouldn't think so. She loved her brothers, but fuck them too; she was voting for Trump.

Mrs. Muldoon slid down the stairs on her bottom, a small, sturdy overnight bag in her lap.

"Mother!" Eileen stopped herself before she could say the bag was too small. She had explained the situation in the exact same words at least a dozen times, but such were the difficulties of dealing with an eighty-five-year-old woman with memory loss: no matter how often you had the same conversation, you had to have it again. It was like *Groundhog Day*, but there was no way to break free—well, only one way, and Eileen didn't like to think about that one. So, fine: Let Mary Muldoon take the tiny suitcase with only enough clothes for two or three nights; the crucial thing was getting her out of this house and into the car, driving to Wheeling, checking her in. Then Eileen could finally come back here and breathe. She could shower, stomp around the house in a towel or nothing at all, give the mailman and FedEx guy the shock of their lives. And then she could get the house ready for Danny Cirillo from Century 21, who was super-cute. She knew other real estate agents had more experience, but if someone was going to get the commission off the sale of the house, let it be the guy who looked like a hotter, younger Mitt Romney.

Was Eileen being cruel? Taking her mother out of her house without even letting her know this would probably be the last time she'd ever see it? Without letting her say goodbye to her neighbors, her plants, or the bed she had shared with her husband for nearly forty years? Maybe, but what were Eileen's options? Mary Muldoon couldn't take care of the house on her own, she could barely climb stairs, she hadn't gone down to her basement for years, she washed her laundry every night in the sink and hung it to dry on the shower rod. Eileen had watched her mother's savings and investments dwindle. And if Hillary won and the stock market went bust, that could wipe out everything her mother had.

"C'mon, Mom, let's go. We're already late."

As Eileen drove her mother west, she couldn't quite get used to the idea that anything had changed in the neighborhood where she'd grown up. Of course, she knew it wasn't the same, had been reminded of this fact every other Sunday when she and Tim had driven in from Lake Zurich for dinner at her mother's house and Mrs. Muldoon reported the neighborhood gossip: how Mrs. Winslow's husband had died and she had sold her house and was now living in a condo downtown; how the Rubicoffs had moved to Maine and broken off contact with their youngest son, Rob; how someone had seen Fiona or Calvin on television or Judith at the farmer's market or read some snoozy article Franklin had written; how Mr. Densmore had shown up at a church social and didn't look a day over sixty-five—a shame about his wife and son, though. Yes, Eileen knew all that, but still, every time she drove this route, she couldn't escape the sensation that everyone she had known must still be here. Could it really be true that, if she turned on Lake Avenue, she wouldn't find Carrie Hollinger riding her bike or raking the leaves? When she saw a girl, maybe fifteen or sixteen, smoking as she waited for a bus, was it really impossible for that kid to be Amanda?

So many things were gone now—and she ached for the lost world they symbolized, the one that existed before she had walked into her first interview at U-Stuff-It and told Tim Donovan, "In high school, I pretended I was dating a guy who had the same name as you," and he said, "Shut the door." No more Howard Johnson's—site of the senior prom, where she'd slow-danced with Rob to "Open Arms" and Rob had whispered that the title should have been "Open Legs," which was totally sick but also totally true. Gone was the Houlihan's where she had worked as a server and hostess for the better part of a decade before she'd answered that fateful "Executive Assistant Needed" want ad in the *Trib*.

Traffic court, where her father's attorney had gotten her DWI charge thrown out during her first summer back from Carbondale, was still here. And so were the Harms Woods stables, where she'd had her eleventh, twelfth, and thirteenth birthday parties. But all the people she'd known there were gone. Even Hackney's, her dad's favorite restaurant, where he always ordered the chopped steak sandwich with green peppers and onions, had burned down. Which somehow made her even sadder than the fact that her father was dead. Now there were Indian restaurants in these strip malls; there were Arabic and Korean groceries; half the guys who worked at these Jiffy Lubes and tire stores didn't speak

English. And all that was fine; she didn't object to their being here—it was just that whoever had been here first should take priority. Wasn't that how America was supposed to work?

The people she'd known, the ones she imagined populating this route, the ones who hadn't died of cancer or drug overdoses or AIDS, had left. They were off doing important things. They had families, kids in high school and college, downtown jobs, mansions, condos, summer houses. They ran companies, medical practices. Billy Wadley, a twerpy little kid from her U.S. history class, who made fart sounds when Ms. Jarrett turned her back, then pointed at Eileen and mimed waving away fumes, was now routinely quoted as the "architect of Obamacare," which kind of made sense, given how much of a shit show "Obummercare" was.

As for herself, though, and the life she had led before Tim had died and she moved back in with her mother, it seemed as if it had all been erased. Precious little evidence existed of anything that had happened: no kids (Tim hadn't wanted any more); no late husband (Tim's wife had been sick and he couldn't divorce her and leave her without health insurance); no job (that was over just days after Tim died); no house (that had never been hers); no money (or not much anyway); no friends, at least none she could talk to about any of this (none who wouldn't secretly blame her for all the years she'd wasted).

But today was Election Day; today was payback time.

*

Wheeling Estates was located on the site of what had once been a drive-in movie theater. Except for the pair of ambulances stationed outside the main building and the nurse's aide leading a man on a walker past the automatic doors, little distinguished this assisted living facility from any other upscale suburban condo complex in a gated community. Life here actually seemed more cheerful than the one Mrs. Muldoon had been leading in Evanston. Here there were movie nights, book groups, political debates, a piano lounge where high tea was served, an art gallery that displayed residents' sculptures and watercolors.

"See, Mom?" Eileen said. "It's just like a hotel."

"A hotel they never let you out of," said Mrs. Muldoon.

At the check-in area, three women in navy-blue suits stood behind a long, narrow, lacquered mahogany counter and tapped on laptops. A Black woman—or "woman of color," as Eileen guessed she should have thought ("Fuck that, I'm voting for Trump")—waved Eileen and her mother forward.

"Mary Muldoon here for check-in," Eileen told the woman, Mrs. Hargrove. She laid the paperwork atop the desk: approved application documents, consent forms, rental agreements.

"I already have those." Mrs. Hargrove gently pushed the papers aside, then typed some more.

Eileen looked at the lobby. Old men and women, some in wheelchairs, one with an oxygen tank, sat at tables arranged around an ornate fountain while some swarthy immigrant waiter in a white tuxedo shirt, black slacks, and a cummerbund poured coffee and tea. Back when her father had been alive, he called all busboys "Sanchez." "I'm not Sanchez," one told him. "Sanchez quit last week; I'm Dominguez." "You're all Sanchez to me," her dad said, and the busboy laughed. These days, no one had any sense of humor.

"Looks a little like the Palm Court at the Drake here, doesn't it?" Eileen asked her mother.

Mrs. Muldoon kept watching Mrs. Hargrove's fingers as they typed. On the TV screen mounted above the check-in desk, Hillary Clinton was shaking hands with voters in Chautauqua, New York, fake smile gleaming as she peacocked about in her cream-colored suit, which looked exactly like something Tim's widow, a card-carrying member of Pantsuit Nation, would wear.

Mrs. Hargrove picked up a phone. "Mrs. Mary Muldoon here for check-in," she said. She listened a while before hanging up. Then she turned to Eileen's mother. "Would you mind coming with me for our intake interview?" she asked.

"Sure," said Eileen. "Whatever you need."

Mrs. Hargrove held up a hand. "Just mom," she said.

"There's no problem, is there?" Eileen asked.

"No problem," said Mrs. Hargrove. "Just a few i's to dot, t's to cross."

"I'm not sure that's the best idea," said Eileen. "Mom gets confused real easily, and it's good when I'm there to translate."

"All the same; this is how we do things." Mrs. Hargrove turned to Eileen's mother. "Mrs. Muldoon, would it be all right if you came with me so I can make sure you'll be comfortable with us?"

"As all right as anything is," Mrs. Muldoon said.

"It'll be okay, Mom." Eileen sat down at an empty table as far away as possible from anyone else, as if old age were a disease she might catch. On the TV, Donald Trump was in Grand Rapids, Michigan, saying something about "draining the swamp." She wished someone would drain *her* swamp, if you knew what she meant—wasn't sure if she could remember the last time anyone had drained it. Trump wasn't as sexy as he had once been. Still, if the occasion arose, she would totally let him grab her pussy. That line had been funny when Trump had said it; she didn't know why people acted all offended by it, then told her she had to vote for the wife of the guy who had shoved his cigar up an intern's snatch, gooped on her dress, and called himself a feminist.

Eileen watched the TV, imagining the time an hour or so from now, when she would return to the house and start putting things in the alley or boxing them up for Goodwill: dresses and skirts Mary Muldoon hadn't worn in ages; her father's suits that her mother had never been able to throw out; her brothers' old Schwinn bikes they always said would be worth something but were going for only fifty bucks on eBay. She figured she would make enough off the sale of the house to pay for about ten years at Wheeling Estates, put a down payment on a condo, and support herself for a year or two while she looked for work.

She had to get a job, had to network; she had to meet people, had to live her life, had to start a new one. What did she have to show for all the time she and Tim had been together other than a few suitcases' worth of clothes, some jewelry she hoped she wouldn't have to hock, and a lot of bad memories that crowded out all the good ones? She couldn't be expected to care for an eighty-five-year-old woman who had never really wanted her help and never seemed to like her much anyway.

"Ms. Muldoon?"

Mrs. Hargrove took a seat across from Eileen. She folded her hands on top of a folder. "I've had a good talk with Mom," she said.

"I hope she's doing okay with all this," Eileen said.

"She is a strong woman," said Hargrove. "You both are."

"I'm just glad she's in a place where she'll be taken care of," Eileen said.

Hargrove pulled out a clipped stack of papers and enumerated Mrs. Muldoon's conditions: the hypertension; the arthritis in the hips and knees; the blackouts and mini-strokes. "We'll get her meds straightened out, put her on a good diet, physical therapy. Then, after two weeks or so, she should be ready," said Hargrove.

"Ready for what?" Eileen asked.

"Home."

"Sure," Eileen said. "It'll probably take a couple weeks for her to feel like this is home."

"Not home here," Hargrove said. "Her home. Where she belongs."

Eileen forced a smile, then said the same thing Christopher Walken did before he blew Dennis Hopper away in *True Romance*, one of her favorite movies: "*Come again?*"

"Ms. Muldoon, we do not keep people here against their will."

"It's not against anyone's will."

"Does your mother understand how long you intend to have her stay here?"

"Well," said Eileen, "it's hard to tell what she does or doesn't know. I'm always repeating things. Ask her what time it is, the date, who's running for president, nine times out of ten, she'll give you a different answer."

"She said she voted for Trump," Hargrove said. "I hope we won't need to get into all this, but Illinois's elder abuse laws, they're very strong. And if I see any irregularity in an incoming resident, I have to report it."

"Excuse me?" Eileen asked. "*Elder abuse?* What are you even talking about? Do you have any idea how nice I am to that woman and how she treats me? Even when she asks the same question or tells the same story?

Do you know how often I go to Walgreens for her Depends? To fill her prescriptions? Do you know how many places I visited before I chose this one so she wouldn't have to live in some urine-soaked dump?" She was reminded of something Trey had said to her after he flunked out of dental school and his dad had cut off his trust fund and the two of them were working the same shift at Houlihan's. Trey was telling some hilarious, X-rated story, and one of the other waiters said he should take an AIDS test. "Why would I?" Trey asked. "It's not like I'd change my behavior." Eileen didn't get what Trey meant then, but she kind of did now. Why was Mrs. Hargrove saying her mother couldn't stay here; she knew Eileen would just find another place.

"Okay." Eileen stared at the woman staring at her, feeling as if anything she might say would only make her look worse, and she couldn't afford to have Mrs. Hargrove call the next facility Eileen contacted and tell them the same lies. "Okay, two weeks. Great."

Mrs. Hargrove offered her hand and Eileen shook it, wishing she had something gross on her hand to wipe off on it.

"Do you want to see Mom?" asked Mrs. Hargrove.

"That's okay. I'll be seeing her soon enough." Eileen took one last look at the Wheeling Estates inmates, their hands trembling as they sipped tea and coffee. She wondered if she would wind up somewhere like this. Well, no, probably not. How would she afford it? And which imaginary child of hers would support her and make the arrangements? Would she live on her mother's savings until nothing was left? She would be the one who'd wind up in the urine-soaked dump, feebly trying to remember the best days of her life and wondering if she had ever had any.

Eileen had driven slowly to Wheeling, but she sped back the whole way, knowing she now had only a short amount of time before her mom would come home. First thing: she had to tell Danny she couldn't sell the house yet. "Siri, call Danny Cirillo at Century 21," she said.

The call went straight to voice mail. "Hey, handsome with the tight little buns," said Eileen. "I've got some interesting news for you, but the phone is so impersonal and your office is so business-y. Why don't you just bring your hot little bod to my house and I'll give you all the raunchy deets. I'll be home in about fifteen minutes, so if you wanna stop by for a nooner, my day is wide-open. And I mean *wide-open.*" She ended the call and couldn't stop cracking up. She couldn't believe she had said all that; just imagine the look on poor Danny's face when he heard.

When Eileen got back home, she left the front door *wide-open,* stripped off her clothes, dumped them on the floor, went up to the shower, turned it on as hot as it went, then soaped herself up and sang "Round and Round" by Ratt at the top of her lungs.

Eileen was halfway through a medley of 1980s hair band tunes when she heard the doorbell. "No way," she thought. She shut off the water and shouted down. "It's open!" Then, after two more short rings, "Keep your pants on!"

She rushed downstairs naked, thinking that if she had been this liberated growing up, she would have had a better childhood, would have wound up having normal relationships with guys instead of random furtive fucks before falling for yet another boss sleazing on her at an office. No offense to Tim—he'd been a good man for a while—but if she'd married someone her age, without all Tim's baggage, she'd probably be living in her own house and taking her kids to school and soccer practice instead of running sopping wet down the stairs of her mother's house to meet Danny Cirillo.

"I'm coming, I'm coming," Eileen said. She stood in the doorway. "Oh *shit.*"

Standing before her was a canvasser wearing khaki slacks, a navy-blue I'M WITH HER hoodie, and a Hillary Clinton ballcap. The girl looked so perfect that Eileen felt ill: white, probably Jewish, straight teeth, straight dirty-blonde hair; she looked a little like Carrie Hollinger—*Dr.* Carrie Hollinger who had just won North Shore High's alumni award for leaving a lucrative hospital job to found Casa Segura, a clinic for freeloaders who wanted to work in America but didn't even pay taxes; Dr. Carrie Hollinger who cared more about treating immigrants than decent, hardworking people who'd lived their whole lives in this country. The girl was carrying a sheaf of flyers. "I'm here with the Clinton campaign," she began, then stopped, now fully registering the image of a naked, wet Eileen.

"Fuck you! I'm voting for Trump!" Eileen slammed the door.

*

The voting line at the Evanston Civic Center went halfway down the block, and Eileen loathed everyone in it: overdressed Blacks who'd be voting for Hillary; slim white hippies with ponytails and family money who'd be voting for Hillary; professorial women with dangly earrings they'd bought at some crafts fair; muscular union thugs with paint-spattered pants and boots who looked like they'd been bused in by the Teamsters; church ladies in bad pantsuits; effeminate men wearing BabyBjörns and pushing strollers beside their resting-bitch-faced spouses; Mexicans who spoke too little English; schoolteachers who spoke too much of it.

For the first time in her life, Eileen felt that voting would mean something. Not to the country—to herself. Going into that booth and punching that circle next to Trump's name meant she was done being mistreated, ignored, mocked, excluded. She inched her way along the line, feeling stronger each time she got closer to the front of it. She felt like she was about to key someone's car or TP their house or hide in a closet, then take flash photos of a clueless loser trying to get up on some conceited slut.

She could have just punched the hole for a straight Republican ticket, but she wanted the moment to last, so she worked from the bottom up, poking holes next to Republicans unless they had foreign-sounding names, in which case she left the space blank. Each time she voted was like kicking an enemy in the throat. *Bam!* That was for Carla Donovan for never divorcing her husband. *Biff-Baff!* Those were for Dave and Dori, who would run their late father's company into the ground. *Ka-Pow!* That was for Mrs. Hargrove and her smug, accusatory looks. *Slam-Bam!* That was for that little "I'm with Her" bitch who had seen her naked. *Buh-buh-buh-buh-boom!* She scrolled up the list, remembering professors who had failed her, siblings who had abandoned her, credit card companies that had overcharged her,

Mexicans and Muslims who would take the jobs she wanted and work for half the pay while getting free medical care, courtesy of Dr. Carrie Hollinger.

When she reached the top of the ballot, she raised her stylus high on its chain as if it were a dagger. She took a breath, held it in for a moment. Then she let loose with a big cough. Anyone who heard might have thought she was choking as she stabbed the stylus into the ballot, spluttering, "Fuck you, I'm voting for Trump! Fuck you, I'm voting for Trump!"

She walked back to her car, thinking she should celebrate by treating herself to some deliciously gross meal before she got back to the rest of her life. Maybe something she hadn't eaten in years; maybe one of those triple cheeseburgers with bacon she used to buy at Wendy's on the way home from getting hammered on Long Island iced teas at Bootleggers with friends from college before every one of them got married and stopped returning her calls.

Eileen unzipped her purse, got out her phone, and was about to ask Siri to find the nearest Wendy's when she noticed a slim man in black boots, a long black leather duster, and a broad-brimmed black hat. The man was striding toward the civic center, toting a walking stick.

"Ty-Ty!" Eileen gasped and threw her arms around Ty Densmore. Oh, how she adored Ty—always had. She could barely believe that one time Rob had gotten her to betray him. But that was so long ago, and Ty-Ty had been too smart to fall for Rob's schemes, which made her love him even more. He was the only teacher who had given her As every year. He didn't even make her do her final project senior year; all he'd asked was for her to bring him the pictures she'd taken at Fiona's party, and after she'd done it, he'd smiled and said, "All is forgiven."

"Well," Tyrus said, "if it isn't the Irish lass."

Eileen laughed and tried to hide the tears she felt coming fast, for she understood why he was calling her "lass." Over the past decades, whenever she had run into Tyrus, he still greeted her with "Well, if it isn't the Irish whore." Even Tim, who didn't care for jokes, thought that was funny. But now that Tyrus was calling her a lass, it meant he saw she no longer was one. It meant he felt sorry for her. It meant she looked old.

"You look terrific," Eileen said. Old age suited him. She couldn't believe that, when he'd directed her in *Anne Frank*, he'd been nearly a decade younger than she was now. Her eyes lingered on the walking stick he was carrying.

"A prop," he said. "I'm rehearsing for a new role. I'll be playing an old man."

Eileen laughed. "You're not that convincing yet."

"Give it time." Tyrus cast a suggestive glance down at Eileen's I VOTED sticker. "So you've done the dirty deed, have you?" he said.

"I have."

"And who did you vote for? The cunt grabber or the cunt?"

Eileen could imagine few secrets she would keep from Ty-Ty, but she feared that if she told the truth, he'd make fun of her. "What about you?" she asked.

"Oh, what difference does it make?" Tyrus said. "I'm cursed. Every candidate I vote for loses: Eugene McCarthy, Edmund Muskie, John Anderson, Ross Perot, Ralph Nader."

By now Eileen had all but conceded the fact that Danny Cirillo wouldn't show up at her house—that he had either erased her message or was playing it for his co-workers and wife, who were all laughing like hell. "Do you want to grab coffee after you're done?" Eileen asked.

*

They met at a Starbucks. Eileen, trying to sound sunny, told Tyrus that her mom was "still living in the same house" and "still goin' great guns at eighty-five" and, now that Eileen was all but through with mourning Tim, she was excited to get back on the job market.

"I envy you," Densmore said. "You have no idea what the future will bring, whereas I know all too well."

"You don't for sure," said Eileen.

"Of course I do," Tyrus said. "I used to be a person with plans: New York, London, L.A. Plays to write, films to direct. Now none of it will happen. Every day will be the same as every other one, except just a little shittier, until one day it will all—" Tyrus made a magician's *poof!* gesture.

"Well, what's the spring play gonna be?" Eileen asked. "At least you have that to look forward to."

"What does it matter?" said Tyrus. "It's all the same. It's like you fall in love for a few weeks or more. Then, after you strike the set, it's like it never happened. You're lucky if you get a card at Christmas."

"That's not true," Eileen said. "You've mattered to so many people. How long've you been teaching?"

"Fifty-two years."

"That's amazing," said Eileen. "What'd you do for your fiftieth anniversary?"

"Nothing. Who would want a fuss over something like that?"

"North Shore didn't do anything?"

"Of course not."

"Not even cupcakes? Not even a watch? A card?"

"They knew I wouldn't want that."

"But fifty years," said Eileen. "There should've been a party. There should've been cake. They should've named the Annex after you—not Trey. Just because the Newsons have money, just because they felt guilty, that shouldn't mean they get to name things so they can feel better about themselves."

"They liked the speech I gave at Trey's funeral, so they made a dona-tion. I thought it was a nice gesture."

"Even so, it should be your name there, not his."

"But I'm still alive," said Tyrus.

"Then that's more than enough reason for a party," Eileen said. "And if no one else was classy enough to throw you one, I will."

"Oh, will you?"

"Yes. Absolutely." And the more Eileen thought about it, the more she liked the idea. She could rent out some party room at Tommy Nevin's or Prairie Moon or wherever. Everyone who'd taken a class with Tyrus or acted in one of his shows would be invited. Newspapers and TV stations would cover it; maybe Franklin could write one of his long articles that nobody ever finished reading. It would be like the massive Eileenfests that she used to throw every summer where she hauled trays of food out of Houlihan's and turned her apartment into Party Central. There would be an open bar, killer music; Sammy could organize it, probably pay for it too—he had the dough. Eileen needed a job, a partner, a new purpose in life; what better way to make that happen than to throw a bash for a few hundred old acquaintances and friends to show off what she did best?

Finally, she would have a good reason to contact people. She didn't have to call as *poor Eileen whose husband just croaked* or *poor Eileen who needs a job and a fella.* No, this would be ass-kicking, stage-managing, U-Stuff-It executive Eileen who still threw the best parties with seven kinds of cheese, eight kinds of beer, and nine kinds of ham.

By now it was dusk. Sidewalks were crowded with men and women in business attire and I VOTED stickers heading home from the Metra station. Eileen walked Tyrus to his car; along the way, she grabbed his ass; she wanted him to feel wanted again, didn't want him to feel as if his life had passed, for that would mean her life was passing too.

"We're totally doing that party," she said. "I'm not gonna let you out of it."

"Whatever will be, will be," said Tyrus.

Eileen spent her drive home concocting her guest list for "Tyrusfest." She wanted every generation of Tyrus's students represented. When she got out of her car in her mom's driveway, she leaned against the hood and typed a text message to Declan: Dec-Dec, way too long since we last rapped. How's the wife? How's the kid? Save for being widowed, having no job and no money, I'm doin' GRRRRREAT! HA! Did U know Ty-Ty has been at North Shore for 50 years and those MF'ers still haven't thrown him a PAR-TAY? We're gonna throw him the biggest bash EV-UH. You're my first choice to be on Planning Committee. Are ya in or ARE YA IN? DM me!

She walked to the house and saw a note taped to her front door. Probably that asshole "I'm with Her" girl. She loved the idea of that little bitch waking up in the morning, checking her phone, and finding out

Trump had won. It probably wouldn't happen, but what if everyone in America was a lot more like Eileen than they pretended to be? What if all their thoughts were a little nastier than they let on? What if they all liked the smell of their own farts, and threw random trash in the recycling when no one was looking, and thought, *Bip*-bap, *bip*-bap, when they saw someone with a big ass waddling by, and held their breath when they walked past a homeless person, and called Homeland Security when their landscapers did a shitty job? What if they all said "I'm with her," but what they secretly meant was *Fuck you, I'm voting for Trump*?

Eileen read the note—a brief message on Century 21 letterhead: "Sorry I missed you. Lemme know when's good—Danny C."

Eileen practically had a coronary right there. She ran to the street to see if Danny was driving away. Nope. She shook her head and laughed. *Win some, lose some*, she thought; she'd voted for Trump, bumped into Ty-Ty, and had begun planning Tyrusfest, but she'd missed out on boning Danny Cirillo. After she got into the house, she texted him: Sorry I was out when you came. I'll be here all nite. Cum on over. She liked spelling it that porny way.

Eileen hadn't even taken off her shoes when Danny texted back: 8:00 okay?

It wouldn't be quite accurate to say that Eileen climaxed the moment Trump declared victory. But close enough. When Fox News called Pennsylvania, essentially giving him a lock on the presidency, Danny was already dressed, putting on his loafers, and telling Eileen he had to get home to his wife and kids, but maybe they could do this again same time next week. In fact, when Hillary was calling Trump to concede, Eileen was too spent to do anything other than lie on her rumpled bedding, assembling the Tyrusfest guest list, which was already up past 120 when she finally fell asleep. She hadn't listened to the radio or watched TV that night, and the only reason she found out what had happened in the election as early as she did was because the CNN news notification on her phone woke her up.

But no matter how excited Eileen had been to cast her vote, she barely registered the TRUMP DECLARES VICTORY IN NEW YORK CITY alert. She was far more distracted by the other message on her phone. It was from

Declan: No way would anybody catch me dead at any party for Tyrus Fucking Densmore.

Eileen stared at the message, trying to figure it out. God, people could be so self-involved, she thought. She couldn't believe anyone could hold a grudge for thirty-five years. She didn't get how anything that had happened so long ago could still matter.

Mr. Van Daan

E ileen's message inviting Declan to help plan the abomination she was calling Tyrusfest wasn't the only trigger, and it was hardly the first. Every time Declan drove past the North Shore campus or saw the unread copy of *The Diary of Anne Frank* on his son Tuan's desk, every time the song "Amanda" by Boston came on the radio, the events of spring 1982 returned to torment him.

All that wound up happening—to Declan and everyone around him—wasn't solely because of the election either, though those first dazed weeks in November had completely undermined Declan's vision of how the world was supposed to work: good deeds rewarded; villains getting their comeuppance. Nearly every day, Declan still thought of that horrible mistake Densmore tricked him into making and the confession Densmore all but forced him to write in his diary. But really, he didn't know why he kept beating himself up over what had happened when others did far worse, felt no guilt, and faced no consequences. Densmore still lorded over his Annex, treating his actors like his prisoners, and he still lived in the same lovely house and made nearly two hundred grand a year. Trump was on TV every day threatening Muslims and immigrants, and he was about to enter the White House. Declan had gotten kicked in the balls and punched in the face for mistakenly thinking someone wanted him, and where was he now? Still in his shabby Sauganash bungalow with too much clutter, not enough furniture, a wife and son who barely tolerated him, memories he would never be able to shake, and a fate he figured he would just have to endure.

The only time Declan felt free of guilt, anxiety, or self-doubt was on Thursday trivia nights at the Deacon's Daughter, a neighborhood bar on the northwest side of Chicago. Declan and his team, the Serviceable Villains, hadn't lost a match this season, but on the last trivia night before Thanksgiving, the topic was football, and neither Declan nor his teammates had been able to answer a single question in either the "Defensive Deviates" or "All-Pro Sex Offenders" categories. They were eliminated in the first round, at which point the whole fateful conversation began.

While the other teams competed to win free drinks and a fifty-dollar gift certificate to Hub's Gyros, Declan sat at the bar nursing an O'Doul's in the company of his three teammates: part-time set designer and full-time mattress salesman John Herrington, whom Declan called "John Falstaff"; John Shelley, a retired landscape architect (Declan called him "Old John of Gaunt"); and "Mistress Quickly," aka Dr. Patricia Roebling, a prim, effervescent assistant English lit professor at Northeastern Illinois. Patricia served as volunteer dramaturge and botany researcher for the site-specific productions of *Arcadia*, *A Midsummer Night's Dream*, and *The Norman Conquests* that Declan had directed at Indian Boundary Park, where he worked full-time as activities coordinator. The two Johns often told Declan that Patricia was in love with him, but Declan said Patricia was just bored and lonely; she was twenty years younger than he was, and anyway, he was married and Patricia was in a serious long-distance relationship with her grad school boyfriend, who taught classics at Oklahoma State.

Above the bar, a TV was broadcasting a rerun of *The Bumbry Show*. In the episode, "Exeunt, Pursued by a Thespian," Calvin Bumbry Dawes's son was trying to escape the advances of a drunk, lecherous theater director named "Nicol" on a trip to New York.

Some of the other people at the bar were laughing at the crude slapstick, but Patricia watched with her mouth open, hands on her cheeks— Edvard Munch by way of Macaulay Culkin. "How can people laugh at that?" she asked. "There's nothing funny about it; it's deeply, deeply disturbing."

"Oh, I don't know," said Declan. "If you lived through it and you don't want to cry, laughing's pretty much the only thing you can do."

Patricia's eyes watered. "You lived through something like that?"

"Not 'something like that'—*exactly* like that." Declan explained that he had acted in school plays with the star and creator of that series, and that he was originally supposed to go on a trip like the one the show was spoofing. "Maybe if I'd gone, I'd have my own show, and Calvin would be here tonight. But it's probably better this way," Declan said. "If Cal hadn't made it big, he might not still be on this planet. Whenever we talked about what we'd do with our lives, Cal nominated himself 'Most Likely to Die at Twenty-Seven.'"

"And what were you most likely to do?" Patricia asked.

Declan sighed. "I don't like to think about what I *was* most likely to do *before you were born*," he said. Patricia laughed giddily at this. "I prefer to think about what I'm most likely to do in the future."

"And what's that?" asked Patricia.

"Drink more O'Doul's!" John Falstaff said with a big belly laugh.

"And learn something about football, you pathetic git," said John of Gaunt.

They stayed for another round. Declan didn't care for bars, but he liked this one. He felt a little like Prince Hal in *Henry IV* here, carousing with drunks yet knowing he would eventually become king, and he tried not to remind himself that he was now probably twice Prince Hal's age. But then the bartender said he and his teammates were too loud, and some of the other teams were complaining, so they all went out to the parking lot, wished each other a happy Thanksgiving, and vowed that, come next Trivia Night, they would start another winning streak.

The two Johns got into their cars, but Patricia—as she often did—lingered.

"Did you ride your bike here again?" Declan asked.

"No." Patricia made padding, flippety-floppety gestures with her hands. "Walked."

"Then I shall squire you home."

Though Declan had known Patricia for the better part of a year, he still couldn't get a read on her. She seemed to be one of those inexplicably good people who had come to teaching literature simply because she loved it so much. When she had asked if she could join his theater company as dramaturge, he had no idea she would take the job so seriously or that she would be so good at it. She had taught him more about Shakespeare than he ever learned in college or even while performing the Bard's plays in daytime, twenty-bucks-a-show performances for school groups at the Ivanhoe theater. She had referenced Polonius to teach Declan what "mansplaining" meant, told him that Hamlet had been "virtue signaling" when he leapt into Ophelia's grave, and stunned Declan when she explained that, because of the rhythm of Shakespeare's verse, he had intended either for the character of Vaughan in *Richard III* to be pronounced "Vo-han" or for the actor playing him to speak with a stutter and call himself "V-Vaughan." Yet, no matter how kind Patricia seemed, no matter how intelligent, pretty, and poised, whenever Declan saw her outside the Deacon's Daughter, she was alone and looked as if she had just stopped crying.

She was wearing an iridescent green crushed-velvet dress, black stockings and pumps, and a black pillbox hat, as she sat with her hands in her lap while Declan drove casually, or as if he were attempting to look casual. He often had trouble telling the difference between when he was feeling an emotion or just acting it out. Which was why, though he was being truthful when he began telling Patricia about Densmore, he couldn't say whether he was relaying these stories because he needed to unburden himself or because the stories seemed to affect Patricia so deeply.

"And all this happened when he was your teacher?" Patricia asked.

"That's right," said Declan.

"How horrible."

Patricia lived on Bernard Street in a spacious Queen Anne, but she had only half of the top floor, accessible via two flights of rickety wooden back steps. Declan followed Patricia into her kitchen nook, struck by how pristine and well put together everything seemed: alphabetized cookbooks; a gleaming, dish-less sink; sponges that looked new.

Patricia filled a kettle with water. "Tea?" she asked. "Beer, wine, and Diet Coke are also possibilities." She opened the refrigerator—so well organized: Where were the half-eaten dinners covered haphazardly with cling wrap? Where were the smudged and splattered bottles of condiments? Where were the cans of cat food, the wilted produce, the pints of melted ice cream, there because someone had spaced out and forgotten to put them in the freezer?

"Tea would be great," Declan said.

She poured the tea—made with leaves, not bags; in matching China, not random NPR giveaway mugs—and they sat side by side on the sofa, cups and saucers on Patricia's glass-and-chrome table, which was topped with neat stacks of the New Yorker, Harper's, and American Theatre.

"We don't have to keep talking about your old director," Patricia said. "I'm sure it's upsetting; we can change topics."

"I don't mind," Declan said. "It's just that, at a certain point, you can't keep blaming your past for who you became—and it's not like I was totally blameless back then."

Patricia's nostrils flared. "What is that supposed to mean?"

"Honestly?" Declan asked, employing one of his signature conversational gambits: small confessions designed to avoid larger ones. "I was kind of an asshole kid. There were reasons—family stuff, a nasty divorce, pretty typical—but I was envious, I was self-involved, always looking for approval. I was a shitty boyfriend, clingy, overbearing. And if I'm being honest, I did enjoy the attention. Whenever Mr. Densmore pinched my ass, grabbed my crotch, or even slapped my face, I felt special—chosen."

"You were a child," said Patricia. "You cannot possibly be blaming yourself for your own assault."

"Assault?" Declan frowned. Could you actually call the things Densmore did assault? "I don't know," he said. "It's kind of a gray area, isn't it?"

"What you're describing is not a gray area," said Patricia. "Did you ever talk to anybody about this?"

"My wife; my son."

"What did they say?"

"Pretty much 'It happened three decades ago; get over it.'"

"What about the police?"

"And tell them what?"

"Exactly what you told me."

"Maybe I should've, but that time has passed."

"Isn't that up to the police to decide?" Patricia asked. "Do you have to make that decision for them? That's probably why that monster has gotten away with everything he has for so many years. There's always some excuse—'It's too late'; 'No one will believe me'; 'It's a gray area'; 'I'm to blame too.' It's not just about what he did to you; it's about what he might still be doing—to other kids."

Declan chuckled ruefully. "I'm not sure why you're more upset about this than I am."

Patricia looked down at her folded hands.

"Did something like this happen to you?" he asked.

"Not exactly like this."

"But kind of?"

"Yes. Kind of." Patricia said she didn't really want to talk about it, but after she moved from tea to wine, she described a snowy night in Ann Arbor when she and her boyfriend, Ezra, had gone over to his thesis adviser's house for dinner, and they'd all had too much to drink, and the adviser suggested they spend the night. Ezra had conked out upstairs, and she couldn't sleep, so she'd started reading a book about Aeschylus and Euripides on the couch in the den. Ezra's adviser had written the book, and he kept coming in, asking what she thought of it, if she wanted to discuss it, if she wanted more wine. Then, out of nowhere, he'd started pawing at her, breathing his hot wine breath in her face, telling her how beautiful she was as he ripped off her underwear.

"The worst part was that, in spite of everything he was doing, I felt embarrassed for him," said Patricia. "I just wanted him to get it over with before his wife or Ezra came in."

"Did they?"

"No. And when he was done, he kissed me and stroked my hair, like he wanted me to think it had all been romantic while I was just sitting there, shaking, mortified."

Declan took her hand. "I'm so sorry," he said.

"It's all right."

"What happened after?"

"Nothing," Patricia said. "I finished my thesis, Ezra finished his. And, whenever there was a party where the guy might show up, I made an excuse."

"Did you tell anybody?"

"I couldn't really, because . . ."

"Because . . . ?"

Patricia shook her head.

"Does your boyfriend know?"

Patricia mouthed, "No," and Declan felt both a pang of sympathy and a rush of validation: she had told no one else but him. "Why?" he asked.

"Because if I said anything, it would've jeopardized Ezra's work. He would've denied it or said we were both to blame. It was just easier to move on."

Patricia excused herself to use the bathroom. In her absence, Declan surveyed his surroundings and saw all the trappings of a woman he would have fallen in love with had he been twenty years younger or had it been twenty years earlier. The lilies she had arranged in an indigo vase—he loved the idea of a woman who bought herself flowers. Propped against a bookcase was a black musical case—a violin? A viola? He imagined she was good at playing it. He imagined her playing in string quartets. He imagined playing her the same way Rudolf Nureyev played Nastassja Kinski with a bow in *Exposed*, a movie he had seen downtown at the Fine Arts when Patricia was—*Christ!*—probably in kindergarten.

Declan had always divided his life into roles he had played: quiet child, lonely adolescent, high school star, college optimist, struggling actor, happy newlywed, mature father and family provider. He had always seemed to be on an upward trajectory, but it was hard to see the past decade as anything more than a steep downward slope. And the worst part was that he didn't see any way to rise anymore, while there was plenty further to fall. His job at Indian Boundary was tenuous, his agent hadn't called in months, and the only time anyone asked for his autograph was when he signed the checkout screen at Jewel or Whole Foods.

But at least he was healthy, employed, married. And, in some way, he couldn't help but look back and see that his life had peaked, not just in high school but at the precise moment he had walked into *Anne Frank* auditions without any doubt of which way he was headed. He imagined his seventeen-year-old self looking at this life—the cramped little house no bigger than the one he'd grown up in; the theater productions so inconsequential that even third-tier critics didn't attend—and barely recognizing the man still thinking of 1982, the year it had all started to go wrong. Chronologically, he seemed too old for a midlife crisis; emotionally, he still felt too young. What would it be like to live here— somewhere that wasn't suffused with the overpowering stench of cat litter, teenage boy, and his wife's expensive soaps and shampoos that she didn't let him use? With someone who believed in his dreams and understood his anxieties and gave him advice because she cared about him, not just because she wanted him to shut up?

Patricia came back from the bathroom daubing her eyes with a tissue. She took the armchair across from Declan. "So," she said, "will you go to the police?"

Declan considered. "I will," he said. "On one condition, though."

"What?"

"We both do it. You tell Ann Arbor what happened to you; I'll tell the police here what happened to me. We'll support each other. We'll both have someone to tell."

Patricia pulled her head back slowly, like someone sitting too close to a movie screen, trying her best to see everything at once. She shuddered, then stood, bowed her head, and made a series of circles with her hands, trying to summon strength. "All right," she said. "We'll do it."

"What'll you tell your boyfriend?" Declan asked.

Patricia smiled and sighed. "I don't know. What will you tell your wife?"

"I don't know that either." At the door, he held her in his arms and kissed her cheek. She ran her hands up and down his back. He told her she smelled like lilacs, then wished her good night.

"Goodnight, sweet prince," said Patricia, and Declan didn't know whether to feel happy she was calling him a prince or disturbed that she was quoting a line from Shakespeare spoken to someone who was already dead.

*

All else being equal, Declan would have preferred if the officer who agreed to speak with him had been white. Not that he was racist; quite the opposite, the way he saw it. He just sensed that any Black officer would find his grievances trivial, reeking of white privilege. Given all cops had to deal with—drive-bys, drug busts, gang initiation shootings—he feared they would laugh him out of their station. And yet, when he met the officer—a tall, slim, goateed bald man in a crisp white shirt, suit pants, and a solid navy-blue necktie—it wasn't as if he could request someone a little less, well, African American.

"Mr. Spengler, I'm Officer Tounslee. Sorry to keep you waiting."

Declan followed Officer Ray Tounslee Jr. into a windowless office that smelled like the fish tank his son never bothered to clean. He sat in a Band-Aid-colored metal folding chair across from Tounslee, feeling extremely uncomfortable—as if he were already guilty of something. He had always bristled at the fact that, whenever his agent had sent him out on casting calls for *Chicago P.D.*, it was for victim and suspect roles, never for a cop, but he guessed it made sense.

Officer Tounslee poured Declan a watery coffee and talked jovially about what his son and daughter had cooked for Thanksgiving. All the while, Declan sensed Tounslee sizing him up as a potential criminal, felt as though he had to preface every statement with some hackneyed cop show qualifier: "To the best of my recollection . . ."; "I had the impression that . . ."; "What I believe to be true is . . ."

Declan feared that Tounslee would mock him for coming forward three decades too late, but the unnerving thing was that the officer seemed to take him so seriously. He typed notes on an iPad, made sure names were spelled right: "That's Tyrus with an *i*? Or a *y*?"

"Does it matter that all this was more than thirty years ago?" Declan asked.

"Not necessarily," said Tounslee. "Why don't you tell me what you want to tell me, and we'll take it from there."

One memory led to the next and then another. Declan talked about the way Densmore would pinch and grab him; about the porn mags the man kept on his desk; how Tyrus would turn the pages, point to the white dicks, then the Black ones and say, "This one's Declan; this one's Calvin; this one's Trey; and here's another Calvin," until he found a particularly large dick. "That one's me," he'd say.

"This Densmore's still teaching at North Shore?" Tounslee asked.

"Last I heard."

"Let me ask you this, Mr. Spengler: Were you the only one targeted? Or were there multiple people?"

"Multiple. For all I know, he's still doing it. Should I get in contact with some of them? Would it give you more to work with if we could establish, you know, a pattern of behavior?"

"It could help," said Tounslee.

Declan rattled off costars from *West Side Story*, *The Caine Mutiny*, *Anne Frank*, and a half dozen other shows. He'd lost track of some of them, and some changed their names: Carrie Hollinger now signed her holiday cards CARRIE WEEKES; Franklin Light wrote under the name Frank Lichtenstein; and a lot of them had moved far away—for example, Calvin Dawes, Rob Rubicoff, and Fiona Grenfall.

"Fiona Who-the-what-now?" Tounslee asked.

"This girl who was in a show with me," said Declan.

Raymond laughed. "*Dah-yumn*. Man, I went with this girl named Fiona, long time back."

"Probably not the same one," Declan said.

"Oh, why's that?"

Declan tried to avoid saying the obvious, i.e., that the way the officer said "*FIE-ona*" made it sound like a Black person's name and he doubted that the Mrs. Van Daan who had lived in that fancy house by the lake would have had anything to do with a young Officer Tounslee. "Not that unusual a name," he said. "What was your Fiona like?"

"Nah, doesn't matter," Tounslee said. "We were talking about your Fiona, not mine."

Declan said he'd call Tounslee as soon as he had talked to some of his old classmates and had more information, but the officer's demeanor had changed. His responses became curt and distant. After Declan shook Tounslee's hand, he could have sworn he heard the officer mutter, "Mr. Fuckin' Van *Dah-yumn*," but he must have been imagining it.

*

When Declan got home, he shoved aside the past few days' worth of *Chicago Tribune*s and unopened mail on the dining room table, then sat with an uncapped pen and legal pad, ready to write down the names of people he could talk to about Densmore.

But where to begin: Carrie? Whenever he called her, she sounded glad to hear from him, but in a sad way—as if she were performing free services for one of her clinic's undocumented patients. She had real, pressing problems to deal with every day, and the idea of calling her to talk about high school seemed embarrassing. Calvin? He could try that old phone number but feared it no longer worked and he would have to be reminded of the fact that he had no part in Calvin's life anymore. Judith would condescend to him; Fiona wouldn't remember who he was; Amanda had disappeared, and really, thank God for that, because then he'd have to confront the fact that he'd never gotten up the guts to apologize for what had happened at the Grenfalls' house. His mind Rolodexed through his classmates and fellow actors, twirled past those who might help, those who wouldn't bother, those who wouldn't remember, all of whom would remind him that, although they knew what Densmore had done, they didn't have time to bother with it now.

That night he skipped dinner. He told Tessa and Tuan he had a work deadline, went into his study, started up his computer, and spent hours scrolling through headlines, each of which filled him with despair. It was like being in some dark sequel to *Back to the Future*: a man wakes up, finds himself in a world where Donald Trump has been elected president, then has to return to his time to warn everyone, "But, guys, *guys*! You've got to believe me!"

He clicked open Facebook. God, he hated that site. He didn't like looking at pictures of other people's vacations and happy children, and he hated those GoFundMe posts asking for money he didn't have to defray healthcare costs or to help pay for the funerals of people he hadn't realized were dead. He had told Eileen he wanted nothing to do with Tyrusfest, but he clicked on the Facebook event page anyway.

On the screen there was a banner festooned with red balloons and gold streamers, CELEBRATE GOOD TIMES, C'MON! written across them in rainbow script. The page already had seventy-two likes. I'll pop for the kegs, Sammy Doulos had posted. Carrie wrote that, with her work and family schedule, she didn't usually have time to go out but hoped everyone would have a "great time!" Tyrus himself weighed in with Shakespeare: If it were done when 'tis done, 'twere well it were done quickly.

Declan typed, not even thinking about the implications of what he was doing: Much as I feel that all of us are owed some sort of celebration, I can neither attend this event nor can I condone its existence. For nearly all four years of high school, I was abused, both mentally and physically, by Tyrus Densmore.

Declan continued to type, adding more details as he remembered them: How Tyrus had reached into boys' tights so that he could "stream-line" their bulges; how Tyrus, stepping in for the actress playing Anita in *West Side Story*, had slapped him so hard that one of the man's rings cut Declan's cheek and drew blood. Tyrus Densmore is a predator and a creep, Declan concluded. He shouldn't still be teaching and we shouldn't be cele-brating him; we should put him in prison. And if you want to help me put him there, send me a DM.

Declan clicked POST. Then he shut down his computer, resisting the urge to check every other second to see if people had said anything about it.

After his wife and son had gone up to bed, he sat on the couch in the TV room and watched a Korean ghost movie. He liked watching movies from countries as far away as possible; that way, there was less of a chance he would see an actor he knew performing in it, mockingly reminding him, *You thought this would be you but it wasn't.*

He fell asleep in his clothes. When he awoke, it was still dark outside. Too early to get up, too late to go back to sleep.

He opened Facebook. There were more than one hundred alerts on the Tyrusfest page: CARRIE WEEKES AND 86 OTHER PEOPLE REACTED TO YOUR COMMENT; JUDITH NAGORSKY AND 46 OTHER PEOPLE COMMENTED.

The words he had written returned to him like a memory of drunk misbehavior. Had he written all that? Had he really put it out into the world? Declan clicked on the page, closed his eyes, took a breath, opened them.

Almost all the reactions were smiley faces, hearts, or crying emojis. Every word of this is truth; thanks for this, Declan, it's a long time coming, Judith wrote. This is the bravest thing I've ever read. I wish I'd known about this. Crying here, wrote Carrie. Will Newson, one of Trey's brothers, who now worked as a litigator, wrote that he had heard some of these stories but had never realized their extent and wondered if Densmore had been partly to blame for his brother's depression. Check your messages; I DM'd you, he wrote.

There were comments from people Declan had never met—theater legends whose pictures he had seen in framed photographs on the Annex walls; kids who had graduated long after him, some young enough to be his children: I hear you, man; This is tragic; Please take care of yourself.

Declan didn't have time to fully read any comment before a new one appeared: another heart, another crying face, a blinking ellipsis—SOMEONE IS TYPING A COMMENT. A man named William Nicholson direct-messaged him to say that he had attended North Shore ten years after Declan graduated and had information he "might find enlightening."

Eileen also replied: Who the hell do you think you are, hijacking this post with some made-up pity fest from 35 years ago? The man is 77 years old. Get over yourself. Get a psychiatrist. And get off this page!

Declan left his house before his wife and son woke up. He drove to Caldwell Woods, where he jogged for the better part of an hour, stopping every five minutes or so to take out his phone and check Facebook to count the new likes. Then he headed to Northeastern.

Patricia was supposed to have office hours now, but she wasn't in yet, so he waited, studying what was taped to her door: Junior Year Abroad program flyers, Shakespeare and Jane Austen quotes, *New Yorker* cartoons. A few students—scruffy Asian boys in athletic wear—sat on the floor, also waiting. Declan regarded the boys smugly, wondering what they would think if they knew he had been in their professor's apartment and that the two of them spent Thursday evenings together at the Deacon's Daughter.

"Isn't Patricia coming in today?" he asked the English department secretary.

"I don't know; she didn't call in sick, but I haven't seen her," the secretary said.

Declan went back to his car. He drove from campus to Tre Kronor, where he bought coffees and maple Danish pastries. He took them to go, then went to Patricia's house. Her shades and shutters were down, and Declan didn't see any light on inside. He rapped on the door, then on the glass. He was going to write a note and leave it in her mailbox, but it was full: letters, magazines, today's *New York Times* and the one from the day before—AT CINCINNATI RALLY, TRUMP REITERATES PROMISE TO DEPORT MILLIONS. Declan knocked on the glass again, louder this time.

He took out his phone, pressed Patricia's name on his contacts list. He let the phone ring once, twice, and as he did, he heard Vivaldi: the opening stanzas of "Spring" from *The Four Seasons* playing once, twice, then again—Patricia's ringtone. He hung up. Dialed again. He heard Vivaldi once more. Either she had left her phone behind or she wasn't answering. He called again. This time when the Vivaldi ringtone stopped, he began to leave a message: "I did what we talked about, and I'd really like to talk to you."

The door opened. Patricia stood before him in a plain white T-shirt, white pajama pants with black musical staffs on them, and bare feet. No makeup or jewelry. She looked smaller and younger than she had before. There were dark shadows under her eyes. She forced a smile.

"You're the only person in the world I feel like seeing right now," Patricia said.

Declan handed her a coffee, didn't ask what was wrong, just started talking. "I did it," he said. He told her everything that had happened since he had seen her: his conversation with Officer Tounslee; his Facebook comment on Eileen's party page; the outpouring of love and concern from old friends and strangers. "It's happening," he said. "I don't even know what it is, but it's happening."

Tears streamed down Patricia's cheeks. "I'm so proud of you," she said.

"Jesus, Patricia," said Declan. "What's the matter?"

She shook her head. "Ezra."

"Who's Ezra?"

"My boyfriend. I told him what happened and what I was going to do. I told him and he broke up with me."

Declan didn't know whether he should feel excited or terrified. "I am sorry," he said. He held her close even as hot coffee sloshed on his shirt and jeans. "I am so, so sorry, Mistress Quickly; I am here for you always."

Peter Van Daan

As soon as Franklin read Declan's response to the Tyrusfest invite, he knew that this could be the start of a good story, one that might generate—God help him—clicks. He just didn't think he was the right person to do it.

Yes, in a small way, the tale of Tyrus Densmore dispensing favors, trampling boundaries, and sexually humiliating his charges in his Annex like some authoritarian thug was a variation on the tales of social justice and systemic inequality that Franklin specialized in. At the same time, though, Franklin had always avoided writing articles in which he appeared as a character. In the best journalism, the writer disappeared, showed people in their own environments, and let readers draw their own conclusions. Although he shared most of his late father's political convictions, he experienced a visceral revulsion at the man's need to put himself and his opinions at the center of every damn story he wrote. And, really, with a new administration coming to Washington, sending dog whistles to white supremacists and threatening to hunt down refugees and shut down borders, could he really justify writing about something that happened when he was fifteen?

Still, for the first time in his career, Franklin was scared. Journalists had always been an endangered species, but the business was worse than ever. He'd seen the best minds of his generation destroyed by aggregated news sites, by automated news bots, by publishing empires that had rebranded writers as "content providers," by once-proud newspaper buildings turned into ghost towns or sold off and converted to condos. Of the reporters and editors he had come up with, save for the ones who had family money or successful spouses, just about all were out of the business: they taught in J-schools; they made big money in PR, advertising, and marketing; they worked for billion-dollar corporations that peddled "branded stories" that posed as journalism. The most farsighted or the most cynical of his compatriots, depending on your point of view, had cashed in their bylines and masthead positions at the *New York Times* or the *Wall Street Journal* for consulting gigs where they took six-figure payouts to advise the elimination of the editorial positions they previously held.

When Franklin had come back to Chicago to take care of his dad in his last years, make as much sense as anyone could of his finances, organize the man's pack-rat clip files, and donate them to the Carter Woodson branch of the Chicago Public Library, he had never intended to stay. His plan had been to go to Oakland, Detroit, or Mexico City, somewhere interesting and cheap. Falling in love with Juliana Fuentes, one of his dad's home care workers, had not been part of the plan. He had vowed never to have children; his globetrotting, sleep-on-a-yoga-mat, and live-on-black-coffee-and-street-food lifestyle did not lend itself to being a decent father. He couldn't have imagined he would fall for a woman who already had a kid. He had never wanted a full-time job; he figured he could just keep writing investigative pieces for the *Atlantic* and *Harper's*, record stories for *This American Life*, edit book-length collections of his essays, and collect the occasional five-thousand-dollar honorarium for lecturing journalism students at Berkeley.

But someone had to take care of Maria Graciela and pay for her childcare while Juliana was studying for her social work degree; and after Juliana's first job was eliminated when Chicago's previous mayor, Richard M. Daley, shut down the school where she was working, someone needed a job with health insurance. The *Tomorrow* gig had sounded like the most reasonable option when he took it—an (admittedly small) office in Pilsen with an (admittedly meager) view of the elevated train tracks and an (admittedly paltry) expense account, plus a small staff of (admittedly inexperienced) research assistants whom he mentored while the rest of the editors performed the hard labor of running a once-influential alternative weekly turned digital news site during a time of increasing competition and decreasing ad dollars.

The journalism awards Franklin won didn't translate into ad money, though, and ten-thousand-word exposés, no matter how worthy, got fewer page views than five-hundred-word quick hits aggregated from articles in *The Daily Beast*, Buzzfeed, and the *Tribune*. During his seven years as investigative editor, the paper had been sold twice and had gone through three publishers; it was now led by Violet Dinh, a twenty-nine-year-old Atlanta transplant and turnaround artist who had never spent more than a year and a half at any publication.

It was a Monday. Juliana had left home early for another substitute teaching gig that would never turn into a full-time job. Franklin had dropped their younger daughter, Emma, off at daycare, then Maria Graciela at Walter Payton Prep, arriving at work just in time for the nine o'clock staff meeting.

He used to love newsrooms: the ones he had visited when his father was alive, the ones where he had interned when he was starting out—AP and UPI wire machines buzzing and clicking; typewriters clacking; reporters on phones, conducting interviews, badgering sources; heated arguments about politics in the commissary and by the vending machines. But entering the *Tomorrow* building was like walking into a war-torn city after a neutron bomb had gone off. Half the offices were empty or filled with their downsized occupants' detritus. Eerie silence predominated; cubicles were occupied by beaten-down millennials scrolling Twitter, listening to music through headphones, surreptitiously filling out job applications or updating their CVs on LinkedIn. People barely talked, just messaged each other on Slack.

Today, though, the mood in the conference room was unusually jubilant. There were platters of doughnuts, bagels, fruit salad; coffee from Intelligentsia; pitchers of fresh OJ; bottles of sparkling grape juice.

"What are we celebrating?" he asked Violet. With her black sweater set and glossy black hair, she could have passed for an Orthodox Jew in his old neighborhood had she not been the daughter of Christian pastors from Vietnam.

Violet threw an arm out, gesturing to the Big Board, the nickname Franklin had given to the mounted computer screens in every room with their constant stream of data: how many page views; how many articles shared; how many retweeted.

"We're celebrating TEN THOUSAND, BABY, YEAH!" Violet said.

The number of page views on the Big Board was at 10,037, and some young staffers, most of them members of the disproportionately robust advertising and marketing departments, were snapping photos of the screen, posing in front of it, taking selfies. Violet popped a grape juice bottle, someone said, "Hey-O," and Violet echoed that sound: "HEY-O!" She poured cups of the purple bubbly and hollered as if trying to make herself heard at a bar during Happy Hour. "They told me this shit would be IMPOSSIBLE," she said. "They said we'd never hit more than five thousand views. And this morning—look! We've DOUBLED IT, BITCHES!!!" She held her grape juice cup aloft.

"Twenty thousand by 2018!" someone shouted, and Violet downed her glass and said, "I will drink to THAT!"

Franklin didn't drink when the others drank, didn't applaud when they did. He just kept staring at the Big Board.

"Feelin' all right there, bud?" Violet asked.

Franklin nodded. "Yeah, fine."

"Not eatin'? Not drinkin'?"

"I had breakfast."

"Something botherin' you?"

"Well, yeah, actually, it is." Franklin pointed to the top stories on the screen: 10 REASONS TRUMP WILL BE A ONE-TERMER; MELANIA'S 8 BIGGEST FASHION FAILS; WHY PEOPLE ARE CALLING "LA LA LAND" A BLAH BLAH MOVIE. "None of it's original," he said. "All of it's reactive, all of it's just regurgitated from somewhere else, and no one's reading any of it for more than thirty seconds."

"Our advertisers don't count how long people spend reading a story, just whether they open it or not," Violet said.

"So," Franklin said, "it makes no difference? One hour? One second? Content is content? Who cares what people read as long as they click?"

"We're gonna have to take this conversation off-line, Frank."

Franklin left the room, once again mentally walking himself through scenarios in which he either quit or got fired. But he felt trapped: What else was he qualified to do? Work in a bookstore? How many were even left in Chicago? Teach high school? He didn't have the certificate or the money to go back to school to get it. Fix bikes? Yeah, maybe that: move to Oregon, open a bike shop. He'd do it if he wasn't married; he'd do it if he didn't have kids. He always thought he would spend his life in constant motion, and since he got married, all he'd been doing was running in place.

Violet caught up to Franklin later that morning when he was pouring himself his fourth coffee of the day in the otherwise empty cafeteria. "You don't like me very much, do you, Frank?"

"That's actually not true," Franklin said.

"Then what's your problem?" Violet asked.

"I just think you're wrong," Franklin said.

"About?"

"People. You don't give them enough credit. You don't have to—"

Violet made sarcastic air quotes. "'Dumb it all down'?"

"Yeah, something like that."

Violet sat on a table and put her feet on a chair. "Can I ask you somethin', Frank?"

"Sure."

"Have you ever looked at your stats?" Violet took a couple of pages and pie charts out of her purse and unfolded them.

Franklin made a face as if she'd just thwacked him with a broom. "Yeah, I don't need to see those," he said. "I'm not an idiot. I see what people click on; I know it's not what I write."

"You're not gettin' the whole story, though." Violet pointed to a number and said that Franklin's articles were read less than those of any other writer on the site.

"Yeah, I get it." Franklin sipped his coffee. "Read you loud and clear."

"But stay with me." Violet showed him a chart labeled TIME ON SITE. No, not many people read Franklin's stories, but when they did, they spent more time with his articles than anybody else's. "Do you know what that means?" she asked.

"Tell me."

"You're the best writer we've got, but you choose the most boring-ass topics. Get the right one, we'll be golden. What're you workin' on now?"

Franklin told her he hadn't decided what he would be writing next. He mentioned a dispute over whether a collection of skeletons at the Field Museum of Natural History should be returned to their countries of origin.

"Sounds great; I'm sure the five hundred people who read it will totally dig it," said Violet. "Work on it in your off hours and sell it to *Harper's* or *Atlas Obscura.*"

Franklin said he'd been researching modern-day redlining, how real estate agents were weaponizing Instagram to keep Black and brown people out of majority-white neighborhoods.

Violet pantomimed a yawn. "Important piece. Get an intern to do it and split the award money."

Violet registered zero enthusiasm for stories about the pollution of the Cal-Sag Channel, the gerrymandering of Chicago public school districts, the dark money that linked Chicago Cubs' ownership to the Republican National Committee, the sagas of undocumented immigrants fearful of the incoming administration in Washington.

"That's all you got?" Violet asked.

"Well, there is another thing, but I'm not sure it's a good idea for me to do it." He opened Facebook and clicked on the Tyrusfest page. "These people I knew in high school, they've got a story that's probably worth telling. I haven't looked into it too much yet, but there's a lot of chatter and whatnot."

Violet leaned over Franklin's computer and scrolled through the comments, at first skeptically but then with increasing interest. "This was your high school?" Violet asked.

Franklin nodded.

"This Densmore guy, you were in one of his shows?"

"I was, yeah."

"*Anne* fucking *Frank*?"

"Uh-huh."

She kept reading. "And Calvin Dawes was in it?"

"He was."

"And Rob Rubicoff?"

"Yeah."

"Who's written about this?"

"No one as far as I can tell. But I know everyone in the story. It would be impossible for me to be—"

Another set of sarcastic air quotes from Violet: " 'Objective'?"

"Something like that."

"Can I drop some knowledge on you, Frank?"

"Yeah?"

"Just because you don't use the word *I* in a story doesn't mean you're being 'objective.' You stop being objective the moment you choose to tell one story instead of another. Stop worrying about if you're 'objective' and tell the story people will want to read. Or else—"

" 'Or else'?"

"Or else we can get someone else."

"To write it?"

"Or else we can get someone else."

*

Franklin started researching the story using old yearbooks and alumni lists. Each source led him to more. Todd Merritt, who had been one of the first commenters on the Tyrusfest page, told Franklin about his New York trip with Densmore. At a Swedish diner, Franklin met Declan, his lawyer Will Newson, and a sprightly, nervous young woman named Patricia whose exact relationship to Declan was unclear. "It's complicated," Declan said, then looked at Patricia, and the two of them burst into sexually charged laughter.

Ray Tounslee Jr., the police officer investigating Declan's claims, was tight-lipped at first, but after he realized Franklin knew who he was and remembered him meeting Fiona after rehearsals, Tounslee clapped him on the shoulder. "*Dah-yumn!*" he said. "You're like the first white dude in this town who remembers me from back in the day."

"I wouldn't have seen you becoming a cop, Raymond," said Franklin.

"Me neither," said Ray. "But I figured it like this: if someone's gonna be hasslin' kids the way I got hassled, I'd rather it was someone like me doing it." He leaned in closer to Franklin. "You haven't managed to track down Fiona for this, have you?"

"She's hard to reach," Franklin said.

"I know it," said Tounslee. "Let me know if you do."

Franklin met Carrie in the main office of her Casa Segura neighborhood health clinic with the door shut to block out all the hubbub: English as a second language classes, job training sessions, Carrie's teenage daughter answering phones, nurse practitioners administering shots, conducting physical exams. It seemed to Franklin as if he and Carrie spoke often, but he couldn't actually remember the last time they'd been alone in a room together. Even though they now lived closer to each other than they had since high school, whenever they saw each other, their conversations got awkward quickly. During their last dinner at Carrie's house, her husband, Adrian, avoided eye contact with him for the whole meal, then started cleaning up, shutting off lights, and telling their daughter to go upstairs and finish her homework before coffee and dessert had been served.

At Casa Segura, Carrie answered Franklin's questions about Densmore in a distanced, clinical tone, as if she'd been someone else back in high school and had only a passing familiarity with what that person was like.

"You don't think being in that show made any difference in your life?" Franklin asked. "You gave your daughter the same name Anne gave her diary. You saw how Densmore treated people who were too afraid to speak up for themselves. You don't think that has anything to do with why you're running a clinic down on Howard Street and not at Northwestern or the U of C?"

"That's just a really simplistic way to think about it. There're a million different events that contribute to where you wind up; it's never just one," said Carrie. "Anyway, I was already on that path. If anything, it just made me realize it was the right one."

"But you wanted to be a pediatrician back then; you never said anything specifically about poor kids or immigrants."

Carrie shrugged. "It's just such a long time ago, Frank," she said. "And when I think about the patients who come in here, it's really hard to compare them to us or to compare who I am now to who I was then."

"You don't ever think of yourself as being a victim of trauma?" Franklin asked.

"Not like them."

Still, over the course of his interviews, Franklin began to see how universal this story was. Save for some North Shore administrators who refused to comment, everyone he talked to seemed to have a Densmore in their lives: a coach, a teacher, a camp counselor. Some version of Densmore's story had played out in just about every article Franklin had ever written. It was the story of pimps beating illegally trafficked sex workers who tried to escape brothels in mob-run suburbs; it was priests and altar boys, cult leaders and their flocks; it was the president-elect sowing divisions between white and Black, red and blue, American and foreigner.

The more Franklin researched, the sadder he felt—for everyone in this story. For Declan, so filled with nostalgia, rage, and regret; for Trey, who thought the Annex would be a refuge, but only because he could make himself believe it was safer than his home; for Eileen, still defending her teacher, unable to see who he really was and what he helped turn her into. Franklin even felt bad for Tyrus—for the boy he must once have been, full of triumphant dreams. And he felt bad for Franklin Light—that kid grieving for his mother, in love with Carrie yet somehow already knowing they would never be together in the same place at the right time. He remembered himself as a boy in Densmore's house, wearing just a T-shirt and underwear; he wondered how close he'd come to being a victim. He thought of that boy lying in bed at night, listening to his grandmother screaming in the next room, then in the daytime acting as if she were in a new world where none of the past had happened. Yet of course it had. No doubt his grandmother was dreaming of the war; only three and a half decades had passed since then, about the same amount of time that had passed between the end of high school and the start of the article he was writing.

On the day of the presidential inauguration, when Franklin got up from his desk to get another coffee, looked at the Big Board, and saw a dozen clickbait articles about Donald Trump, he thought that one of the most dangerous things about focusing exclusively on one immoral man was that it allowed smaller offenses to go unnoticed. Maybe that was why Densmore almost always directed plays about grave injustices: so his own might seem puny by comparison. Maybe we all needed a Trump in our lives to preserve the illusion of our own innocence.

*

Franklin was nearly done with his preliminary interviews when he called Densmore. He was still at his *Tomorrow* desk, long after everyone else except for the cleaning crew had gone home. Out his office window, he saw snow falling past the lights onto train tracks, rooftops, and the Harrison Park playground.

The phone picked up after the third ring. "Yes?"

"Is Tyrus Densmore available?"

"Speaking."

The man's voice sounded just as it had when Densmore had directed *Anne Frank*: the ironic flirtatiousness, the seemingly good humor that could instantly morph into malice. "Well, well," Densmore said, "who might be calling me from the *Tomorrow*?"

Apparently the man had caller ID.

"An old student of yours—Frank Lichtenstein."

"Ahh, young Mr. Van Daan," Densmore said.

"That's right."

"I've been following your career from a distance," said Densmore. "I even have one of your books on my shelf, though, truth be told, I haven't gotten around to reading it. How's life treating you? Are you still pining for your lovely Anne? You know, I always wondered what would have become of those two lovebirds had they survived. It was a gift, in a way, dying so young, before they could marry, have children, and grow sick of each other."

Franklin forced a laugh. "I'm calling you, Mr. Densmore," he said, "because there's a story I'm researching, and I'm hoping you can shed some light on it."

" 'Tyrus,' please," Densmore said.

"All right, Tyrus. Is your schedule free? Do you have some time to talk? Anywhere's fine—your home, my office, a café."

"Topic being?"

"We can go over all that when we meet. It's a little complicated to discuss over the phone."

"I have plenty of time now," said Densmore. "You know, I've heard some of your stories on that radio station where they're always begging me for money. You've grown into a thoughtful, articulate man; I'm sure you can explain what you want to talk about, and then, of course, we can find a time to meet."

Franklin swiped his phone screen and tapped his voice recorder app. "I'm going to be recording this conversation. Is that all right?"

"As you wish."

Franklin pressed RECORD. "Well," he said—his voice quivered slightly, the hand holding the phone trembled; talking to Densmore, it was hard not to feel like he was fifteen again. "I've been spending a lot of time on social media; what do you think of Facebook, Instagram, Twitter, and all that crap?" Try to model the mindset of the person you're interviewing, his dad had taught him; never start with yes-or-no questions.

"I rarely indulge," Densmore said. "Why trouble myself with a fake world when so many problems need to be solved in the real one?"

Clearly, a lie: Franklin had seen Densmore on the Tyrustest page; only after Declan commented had the man deactivated his account. "What led you to that conclusion?" asked Franklin.

"Well, just look at our new president and his fake stories," Densmore said. "I like my fantasies onstage and my reality in the life I lead. I have no desire to spend time in a place where people can assert anything without proof."

"What particular assertions do you have in mind?" asked Franklin.

"I won't dignify them by repeating them," Densmore said. "If you want me to talk about something specific, go ahead and ask."

"Right," said Franklin, "I've been talking with some old students of yours—Declan Spengler, for example."

Densmore snorted. "Actors. They do have such a talent for self-mythology, don't they?"

"So you have an idea of what he's been saying?"

"Refresh my memory."

"Well, Declan has talked about some things you did, and a lot of people have corroborated it: groping, pornography, getting kids drunk."

Densmore inhaled deeply; it sounded like he was dragging on a cigarette. "You don't believe these fantasies, do you?"

"I've interviewed twenty-five people so far. It's hard to believe they're all lying about being molested."

Densmore seized on the word. "Molested? You're calling me a 'molester'?"

"A lot of people have used that word."

"Molested?" Densmore took another deep breath or drag. "Are you accusing me too? Did I 'molest' you as well?"

"Well, I certainly remember some inappropriate remarks you made while you were fitting me for a Peter Van Daan costume."

"And what else do you recall?" Densmore asked. "Or is that it? A costume fitting, some dumb jokes thirty-odd years ago and a lot of baseless accusations from people with axes to grind on social media? Did you speak to anyone at North Shore? Has anybody ever accused me of anything in fifty-two years?" He cackled and imitated a girl in *The Crucible*: "'*I saw Tyrus Densmore with the devil! I saw Tyrus Densmore with the devil!*'

"I am sorry," Densmore said, "that people's lives didn't measure up to their dreams. I know what that can be like, and it is a bitch. I am sorry that I may have given people credit for being more talented than they turned out to be; I'm sure that sucks for them. But let's not rewrite history. I know the people making these accusations. I know about the parents who abused them or, worse, ignored them. I know about their philandering fathers, their suicidal mothers. But my accusers—they're not innocent either. I know the secrets they kept, the drugs they abused. I know about the anonymous fucking they did in Calvary Cemetery, what they did for money in phone booths outside Dyche Stadium; I know about the girls they got drunk and tried to rape. I gave them something to believe in. And now, for them to turn around thirty years later, forty years later, and blame me—it's all a bit rich, isn't it?"

"So," said Franklin, "you never touched anyone."

"What? Of course I touched people. Every director 'touches people.' Grow up; you're better than this. Do you need your job so badly that you have to resort to this trash? I had high hopes for you, I respected your father, I lied for you so you wouldn't get busted for living in Chicago, and this is my thanks?" He hung up.

Franklin put his phone back in his pocket. Outside, it was dark and snow was still falling past the amber lights onto the fields, the playground, and the tennis courts. When he left his office, the newsroom was empty. Violet's office was dark. The Big Board was down to five thousand views. It listed the top twenty stories, and Franklin hadn't written even one of them.

*

Two days after the conversation with Densmore, Franklin was trudging northwest on Milwaukee Avenue toward home with a loaf of bread and a bag of groceries when his phone vibrated. He took it out, and looked at the display: UNKNOWN CALLER.

"Hello?"

"Young Mr. Van Daan?"

"Oh, how are you, Tyrus?"

Tyrus's tone was smoother than it had been during their previous conversation. Tyrus had once said he'd turned down an offer to be a classical music presenter on WFMT, and although most of Tyrus's stories sounded like self-aggrandizing bullshit, this one had the ring of truth to it; he sounded like he could be introducing operas or announcing sales on prosciutto at Convito Italiano.

"Allow me to apologize," said Tyrus. "You caught me at a bad time on the day you called. It was my son's birthday, and ever since he took his life, that day sends me into dark, dark places."

"I'm sorry about that," Franklin said. "Is there something you want to talk about now?"

"There is. But you said face-to-face would be better, and I believe you're right. I'd like to set the record straight, so you can tell a story that's more complete, more nuanced. Would Friday evening at my house work for you?"

"I can make it work," Franklin said.

That Friday, Franklin felt anxious. He didn't know what he possibly had to fear from a septuagenarian drama teacher, but Franklin sensed a threatening undertone to Densmore's invitation. Before he left work, he wrote Densmore's name and address in big letters on a legal pad and laid that pad atop his keyboard. He texted the name and address to both his wife and eldest daughter, so that, on the off chance he didn't come home, they'd know where to start looking.

When he got to Densmore's house, the driveway was full. Four vehicles were in it; two were police cars. A third squad car was stalled on the streets, hazard lights flashing.

Suicide? It would have fit Densmore's taste for drama, would have put an end to all the stories that were circulating. But Densmore was outside. He was standing on the sidewalk in the snow, in a black overcoat with the collar turned up and a black hat that looked like something he might have worn to the opera. He looked older, of course he did, but not as much as Franklin would have expected. It was almost as if, when Densmore had directed *Anne Frank*, he'd been too young for the role he was playing and had only recently grown into it.

"No, it's all right," Densmore was telling a pair of police officers. "I don't want to press charges now that I understand the situation. I just want to make sure he gets the help he needs." Poking the ground with his walking stick, Densmore moved past the officers and greeted Franklin with a handshake and an apologetic smile. "Your timing is either dreadful or impeccable; I can't decide." One of his basement windows had been smashed and there was a big muddy circle on the lawn as if someone had gotten wrestled to the ground there.

"Someone broke into your house?" Franklin asked.

"Evidently." Tyrus pursed his lips as if he had been acting friendly on reflex but now remembered who Franklin was and why he was there.

"You were at home?"

"Upstairs. Drawing a bath."

"And you heard the glass shattering?"

"Not the glass, a bang. I was terrified, as you might imagine. My testicles shrank to peanuts from their normal walnut size. But once the police got here, my scrotal sack loosened. It all would be funny if it wasn't so sad."

"Do you know who broke into your house?" Franklin asked.

"Yes, and so do you," Tyrus said.

Across the street, lights were on in upstairs windows. People were peeping out. A kid was standing on a lawn, passing a snowball from one gloved hand to another, squinting at Densmore's house. Franklin approached the double-parked squad car.

From the back seat, Declan looked up slowly. Then, seeing Franklin, he looked down fast before Officer Ray Tounslee drove off. Red lights streaked west through the accelerating sleet.

*

"Do you know what Declan was looking for?" The two men, Franklin and Tyrus, were standing in the den where they had met three and a half decades earlier. In 1982, Franklin had been wearing a T-shirt and underpants. Today, both men wore coats. Tyrus stood on an armchair, duct-taping a black trash bag to his broken window. Glass was strewn about the carpet.

"It's all so pathetic that I don't even know if I want to say," said Densmore. "I know he came here to hurt me; even so, I can't help but pity him."

"Wanted to hurt you?"

"Hurt me while protecting himself, yes."

"What was he looking for?"

"Can't you guess?" Tyrus stepped down from the chair, carefully avoiding the glass on the carpet. He gestured to the wall of bound notebooks on his shelves.

"The character diaries," Franklin said. He remembered finding the assignment odd—how Densmore required each cast member to keep a detailed journal to develop their characters, the more personal the better. And if it wasn't personal enough, he'd keep needling you until it was.

"Why would Declan want diaries?" Franklin asked. "What's so important in them?"

"Perhaps there's a story in there he doesn't want people to know." Tyrus reached for a diary, then stopped. "What does it matter?" he said. "Here's the truth. And you can quote me on this all you want. I don't claim to be innocent. No one in the world is. Have I been the kindest, most understanding teacher? I never wanted to be. Have I made some vulgar jokes and said some things I would like to take back? Naturally. But if people are going to exaggerate stories, recontextualize them, or just plain make them up, I won't let that go unanswered. If they want to tell tall tales about me, I'll tell true stories about them."

"But the students who wrote those diaries were children," Franklin said.

"Oh, please," said Densmore, "don't give me a lot of bosh about the sanctity of childhood. Half were old enough to vote or join the army. I despise this society; everyone wants it both ways, to be treated like children or adults depending on what suits their purposes. And if you publish a lot of libelous nonsense from dissatisfied adults claiming to have been mistreated children, my life won't be the one ruined. I have my house, my savings, my job, and, more than that, I have my sense of self. And no amount of shoddy, clickbait 'journalism' can take that away from me. Now, if you'll excuse me, I have to go to Home Depot to buy a new window, and maybe with a little luck I'll find someone I can suck off in the men's room. That's a joke, by the way. I like to tell jokes, sometimes in very poor taste. And if you want to burn me at the stake for that, go ahead and try. Good luck with your 'story.'"

*

Declan was waiting for Franklin when he got home. He was standing in front of Franklin's town house door, puffy black coat and gray knit hat speckled with snow and ice. "How you doin', Frank?"

Franklin tensed. "Yeah, what's up?"

Declan breathed into his hands to warm them, then nodded toward Franklin's door. "Can we go inside? Talk a little?"

"No, we can't," Franklin said. "I'm late; my family's waiting for me to start dinner."

Declan's eyes were bloodshot and his voice was hoarse. "Okay, I'll wait in my car. When'll you be ready to talk?"

"You're not hearing me," Franklin said. "You can't just wait around. This is my home. I'm off-duty. How'd you even get this address?"

Declan's eyes registered wounded fury. "Do you have any idea what I've been through?"

"I think I have a vague idea, but I'm done for the day. You can call me at the office or on my cell in the morning. We'll set up a time."

"An *appointment*? What did Tyrus tell you?"

"I'm not gonna get into that."

Something was off about Declan; he exuded desperation and entitlement, as if he hadn't prepared for the possibility that Franklin wouldn't do what he said, and now wasn't sure what he might do. "Did he show you something?" Declan asked. "Did he talk to you about character diaries? Those are private; you can't publish what's in them. How far are you along in our story?"

"This is not 'our' story," Franklin said. "If you have more to tell me, great, but whether or not I use it is up to me. If you want to talk, I'll listen, but only after we've set a time. And don't come to my house without an invitation. Ever."

*

"So, what's going on?" Franklin asked Declan at Chiqueolatte early the next morning. The two men were at a window table that looked out onto the gray, traffic-snarled avenue. Franklin drank black coffee; Declan, chamomile tea.

Declan eyed Franklin's phone. "Is that on?"

"Not yet."

"Can we make this off the record?"

Franklin grimaced. "Off the record" was okay once in a while with certain key sources, but not with people who got cold feet when they realized they didn't get to control the narrative. "I'm not a big fan of 'off the record,'" he said. "Only when lives are at stake."

"And you don't think I qualify, I suppose," said Declan. "Well, okay. If I can't say what I need to say off the record, I'll have to withdraw my cooperation."

" 'Withdraw your cooperation'? I don't even know what that means."

"It means pull all my quotes."

"That's not how this works," Franklin said. "You don't get to say things, then take them back. What's this about? The diaries?"

Declan stared at Franklin's phone again.

"It's not on," said Franklin. "Is this about the diaries? Is that why you broke in?"

"I didn't break in; I was set up. He lured me there—Tyrus."

Franklin opened his voice recorder app.

"And I'm not gonna talk about that either," said Declan.

"What's in the diaries?"

"Not now," said Declan. "Later maybe. After I've had time to think it all through. But for now, we're gonna have to kill the story."

"That's not on the table."

"Fuck," said Declan. "I didn't have to talk to you. I could've brought this story to anyone else. I talked to you because we have a history and I trusted you. Patricia was right: never trust a reporter, even if you were friends."

"We were never friends," Franklin said. "We were in a play together once and we didn't even like each other."

"You're still holding a grudge? After all this time? That's what this is about?"

"I have no clue what you're talking about, man."

"Frank," Declan said, "I know you might still have hard feelings because of the whole Carrie thing, but you're gonna need to get past that. We're all married now; we're all adults."

"Listen." Franklin spoke quietly but firmly. "This may be difficult for you to understand, but this story really doesn't have anything to do with you. It's never about specific people; it's about what their stories represent, what they mean, why they matter. I know I've written stories that have changed specific people's lives, and that's not always a good thing. That's something I live with every day. But every story I write, I hope in some small way it can help make the world a better, safer place. That's the idea, anyway. I don't know what will happen after I publish this story, but what I *hope* is that it will help more people come forward, and they can tell their stories. Maybe it will force someone like Tyrus to think before he does something, so there won't be more stories like this to tell."

Declan sipped his tea, then fiercely licked his lips. "How many times have you delivered that self-righteous little soliloquy, Frank?"

Franklin cocked his head and inhaled sharply.

"Do me a favor," Declan said. "If you're gonna fuck me over, do it with a little honesty. Don't give me a speech telling me you're gonna fuck up my marriage, my family, and my relationships, and tell me to feel grateful. Don't pretend it's because you wanna do the right thing. You and I both know that if Carrie or anyone you actually cared about asked you to keep something quiet, you'd do it in a heartbeat, but since you've got a problem with me, you'll do whatever the hell you want."

"Okay"—Franklin pressed RECORD—"we're on the record now; I need to know what you're talking about."

"I have nothing more to say." Declan put on his jacket and hat and walked out of the café. He took one more sip of tea, then slammed his takeaway cup into the trash.

Riding the el south to his office, Franklin took out his laptop and checked Facebook to see if Declan had posted anything new, but he had deactivated his account and all his posts were gone.

*

The story took a solid week to write. Franklin worked on it not just at his desk in his office; he wrote on the subway to and from work and at night after the house was clean and Juliana and the kids had gone to bed. Editing the piece took another day and a half—rearranging sections, trimming quotes, removing first-person narrative when he found it indulgent, putting it back when he decided that getting rid of it had been dishonest.

Putting the article into the *Tomorrow*'s content management system took nearly another day. When he had first arrived here, a team of deputies would have done it for him; now they were all working temp jobs in the gig economy, so he did it himself: cropping pictures; hyperlinking to audio files; choosing and styling pull quotes; writing headlines that would work on the site and on Facebook; scheduling Twitter posts, identifying "influencers" to tweet at.

When he was finally done with all that, he moved his cursor over the PUBLISH button. One click of the trackpad would put it out in the world. So anticlimactic. Just one tap of his index finger. It seemed unjust in a way: out of proportion that something could create such an impact but arrive with no sound any louder than a finger touching a keyboard. *Tap*—and there it would be on-screen in Densmore's home, and in Declan's too. You could do it from an office, from the subway, from your phone, anywhere you had a decent connection.

He tapped his trackpad and, just like that, his story was published, and there was no taking it back. He got up and put on his coat. He walked out through the empty news pen and then he shut off the rest of the lights.

Mr. Kraler

"Did you read it, Dawes?"

"Yo, did I read what?"

"Your email."

"No, motherfucker. No, I never read my motherfuckin' *email*. All I get is ads for dick extensions, boner pills, and come-ons from Nigerian princes offering me less money than I make in a year."

"*Huhuhuhunh*. Read your email, Dawes. I'll wait."

Snow was flurrying past the window, and Calvin felt his mind once again cueing up the Rod Serling *Twilight Zone* voice-over: *Here is Calvin Bumbry Dawes, sitting in his plush-ass condo smack dab in the middle of New York Titty, on the fifteenth floor of the Harlem Langston with a view of Frederick Douglass Boulevard, and beyond, the snow-dusted trees of Morningside Park and the bell tower of the Cathedral of St. John the Divine . . . Consider the case of one Calvin Dawes, here in his white silk pajama bottoms and monogrammed smoking jacket, because, when he was little and watched old movies on Channel 9, rich dong-pullers like David Niven always wore smoking jackets . . . This is Calvin Dawes, with so many credits on IMDb.com that they don't fit on one screen . . . Meet Calvin Dawes, who once cracked the* Billboard *Hot 100 charts with a crossover hip-hop comedy album called "The Lyin' Bitch in the Wardrobe" . . . This is Mr. Calvin Bumbry Dawes, putting aside a recently polished-off plate of tofu scramble and vegan sausage because eating meat is all kinds of fucked-up if you think too much about it . . . Here is Calvin Dawes with a new show and a development deal with Netflix and a soon-to-debut one-man stand-up show called* The Empty Chair *based on an upcoming six-night residency at the Beacon Theatre—none of which he really needs to do, he sure doesn't need the dough, but whenever he isn't working, his mind latches on to dark, dark thoughts . . . Yes, here is Calvin Bumbry Dawes, talking on his goddamn phone to Todd Merritt . . .*

"Fine, Merritt; fine, motherfucker. Get off my ass. Lemme read the goddamn thing."

"I'll wait," Todd said.

Calvin had cut off just about all contacts with his youth, had set foot in his hometown only a handful of times in the past thirty-some years—stepfather's funeral; mother's retirement party; half sister's confirmation; a photo shoot; some bullshit career expo he'd been talked into—and he had little memory of any of those times, since trips back "home" always sent him into such a maelstrom of anxiety that he was usually trashed the entire time. Even if he didn't drink anymore and now weighed in at a svelte 245—even if he lived in a hotel where he was a part owner and had instructed the staff to refuse him alcohol if he ever asked—whenever he crossed the Evanston border at Howard Street, his imaginary AA partner would be like, "Fuck it, man; let's get some hooch."

Todd was the exception, and he didn't really count because they'd met in New York and had never hung out together anywhere else. But even Todd had fallen out of touch recently.

"Did you find it?" Todd asked.

"Yeah, man, I found that shit." Calvin opened the link Todd had sent him, and read Frank Lichtenstein's byline and the headline: THREE AND A HALF DECADES LATER, MEMORIES OF ABUSE LINGER. He skimmed the opening paragraph. "Okay," Calvin said. "I think I get the gist."

"Read the whole thing."

"Yep, reading now." Calvin put down the phone and went to the john to take a shit. He wasn't going to read the entire article, just wanted enough time to pass so it would seem as if he had. He had gotten wind of the fact that a story about Densmore was in the works. Franklin had tweeted at him and sent him a bunch of emails—Calvin vaguely remembered the wiry, do-gooding Jewish kid trying to get up on Anne Frank—but he hadn't gotten back to him. Ditto for Declan, whom he'd avoided ever since he'd gotten his first major guest spot on a TV show ("Lucius" on *Hill Street Blues*), after which Declan had started leaving him presumptuous messages implying they'd been better friends than they were. Nor had he followed up on a call from Officer Tounslee of the EPD, because what good would any of that do? Had "T.D." been a disgusting lech? No shit. Why relive all that? You survived hell, you got out, you didn't go back for a guided tour.

"So," asked Todd, "have you read it?"

"Yeah, more or less."

"And?"

"And, well, tell me something I don't know, motherfucker."

"We've got to do something about it."

"About what?"

"You didn't read it, Dawes; I'm quoted in it."

"So what, man? You're quoted in *Variety* and *Backstage* every other fuckin' day."

"Did you actually see what Densmore said?"

"A bit, yeah."

"He got real specific—about heroin, about Calvary Cemetery, about Dyche Stadium. Find that part; read it."

Calvin scrolled down until he found the paragraph Todd meant: "If they want to tell tall tales about me, I'll tell true stories about them."

"Yeah, I get it," Calvin said. "So?"

"He was talking about me," said Todd. "It was a threat."

"Threat to do what? Motherfucker's gotta be, like, two hundred years old."

"One of the things he said—he was quoting my character diary practically word for word. There's a lot in there I haven't told anybody, not even you."

"Okay, yeah, that's fucked-up bringing that shit back up. Granted. But people say all kinds of fucked-up jive. That's the world we're living in. You think you got problems? *Please, honky.* You know what a problem is? Try going into a shop called Big and Tall and still not finding anything your size. Try getting charged for two seats whenever you fly Jet Blue. You know what? Try getting half the accolades of Forest Whitaker even though you're the same damn size. You wanna talk about problems? Try getting shaken down for an autograph in Indianapolis because some dumbass cracker thinks you're Refrigerator Perry; try auditioning for a John Hughes flick and learning your character's name is 'Fat Black Winston'; try meeting Bruce Springsteen and having him ask, 'Hey, y'all play saxophone?' Then come back and tell me your problems, skinny white man. Why does this even matter? You got your Tony Awards, your Obies, house in Cape May, all that shit."

"That's exactly it," said Todd. "This remarkable career, and the first thing that'll come up when you google me will be what Tyrus said. When you read my obituary, that'll be the first line."

"It's a little early to start worrying about your obituary, my man."

Todd didn't say anything.

"Hey, wait—what's goin' on?" Calvin asked.

"I'm sick," said Todd.

"Aww, fuck. Like how sick?"

Todd took a halting breath.

"Shit," Calvin said. "Bad?"

"Yeah. Bad."

It was funny in a morbid sort of way: you grew up thinking you were immortal, but then you spent your early adulthood paranoid that anything could take you out; you practiced safe-ish sex so you wouldn't get AIDS, religiously checked your lymph nodes to make sure you didn't have meningitis, ducked out of the way of secondhand smoke so you wouldn't get lung cancer. Then you made it past forty and you started thinking you were immortal again. It was funny to think that things could still kill you.

"Like that kind of sick?" asked Calvin.

"Not even. I wish," Todd said. "At least that would be manageable."

"What is it?"

"It's bone cancer. Same thing as when I was a kid. They told me back then my chances of surviving five years: less than ten percent. That's why I was such a train wreck at North Shore. And I wrote about all of it in my diary, every messed-up thing I did. Tyrus kept nagging me: 'More personal; dig deeper.' I thought he was trying to help, but it was like he was getting me to write an insurance policy so he'd always have something to use against me. I wrote everything and gave it to him; I thought I'd be gone soon enough, and at least there'd be some record I was here. I'd be dead, but in the diary on his bookshelf I'd live on. Somehow I survived, though—more than forty years cancer-free. Then, out of nowhere, I notice I'm getting tired more. And not the tired I'm used to; the tired I remember from back then. Like even lifting your head takes so much effort you'd rather not bother."

"What'd you do?"

"Ignored it, like an idiot. Then one day I pass out right on the steps at Broadway-Lafayette. Cut my head, eleven stitches. And when I wake up and finally get my bearings, I'm not in the emergency room; I'm in the oncology ward. And it's like I've always been there—you know, never left. And the last four decades or whatever of good health? It feels like something I just dreamed up back in Children's Memorial. Except my parents are gone, and the only ones left are me and my sister, and we haven't spoken since my mom's funeral. Did I tell you what she said to me there?"

"What?"

" 'Your lifestyle killed her.' "

"Man, that's some bullshit."

"I know. And that's why it's so fucked: Densmore bringing all this back up, threatening to tell more. Because he knows what I went through. He read every word of those diaries. Then, the New York trip, he pulls that shit on me, knowing how vulnerable I was. Even now, he feels no remorse. He'll tell everything everyone ever told him in confidence, and he doesn't care. He is still there; he is still fucking with people, and someone has to make it stop."

Calvin fumbled for his next question: "Is there any . . . ?"

"Cure?" Todd asked. "Hope?"

"I guess," said Calvin.

"No. After they started using those words—'palliative,' 'hospice care'—I'm like, 'Don't say anything else.' How much time do I have?

I don't want to know. I've got one show opening in April; maybe I'll make that one. I've got two more in the fall; I probably won't make those."

Calvin assayed some mollifying bullshit, told Todd he had to focus on things that would make a real impact. "Go knit yourself a Pussyhat, man," he said. "Donate a million bucks to Amnesty International. Do something that matters."

"That's what I'm saying, Dawes," Todd said. "Little things like this are what actually matter, because they have bigger implications. I don't like indeterminate endings, you know that—not in theater, not in real life. I believe in people getting what they deserve. I love the classics: you sleep with your mom, you blind yourself; you kill the king, someone kills you. That's why I got so pissed at John Patrick Shanley, opening night of *Doubt*. I screamed at him, people were watching: 'Which is it, John? Did he diddle those kids or not? Which? Fuck your ambiguity.' Look at Shakespeare; his best plays are the ones where you know it's comedy or tragedy. Nobody ever does *Measure for Measure* or *Cymbeline* because no one knows what the fuck they are.

"Here's the thing," Todd continued. "I'm gonna be dead soon. And I don't want to hear anything about miracles. And after I'm gone, I want people to remember me for what I did and who I was, not what Tyrus said about me. And I want Tyrus remembered for who he really was. It's like those Nazi war criminals getting tracked down sixty, seventy years later. You think it's too late? Bullshit. You're a criminal in Act I, you get punished in Act II. You lead a good life, you get celebrated in Act II and you get a beautiful funeral and a fitting epitaph. That's justice."

Epitaph? Calvin didn't like to think about that shit. If there was some life after death, he'd be so overjoyed that the last thing he'd worry about was what people were saying about him in his old life. Calvin thought of epitaphs he might want: LASTED WAY PAST 27, SO THERE'S THAT; STILL COLLECTING RESIDUALS, BITCHES; I'LL BE RIGHT BACK AFTER THIS WORD FROM OUR SPONSOR . . .

"Okay," Calvin told Todd. "But what do you think I can do about all that?"

"Go public," said Todd.

"With what?"

"Tell your story. If you tell people about Tyrus—what he did, who he was, what he tried to do to you—that's what people will remember; they'll listen to you."

Calvin started to object, but he knew Todd was right. People did listen to him, no matter what random shit he said. He'd go on Twitter, say, "I had some toast for breakfast," and five thousand of his followers would like his post and another five thousand would tell him what they had for breakfast, as if he gave a shit. If you wanted to criticize some article or call someone out, there were dozens of Calvin GIFs you could do it with: Calvin shaking his head; Calvin rolling his eyes; Calvin flipping the bird, pointing at his dick, doing some wigged-out dance.

"I don't know, man," Calvin said.

"Calvin . . . ," Todd began, but didn't finish, because they both knew what he meant: Calvin owed him this much, owed him far more, could have asked him to do anything and Calvin would have had to say yes.

"Lemme think about it," said Calvin.

"Don't take too long," Todd said. "I mean that."

Calvin lay on his sofa and looked out at the snow; it was falling down harder. On the one hand, given all that Todd had done for Calvin—jump-starting his career, setting him up in New York, not so much saving Calvin Dumbry Dawes's life as killing off the old C.B.D. and replacing him with a new, super-stock model—he had to go along.

But, man, he hated the idea of coming off like some tragic figure, sharing his story with Oprah: *You get a tragic backstory, she gets a tragic backstory, every motherfucker in the room gets a tragic backstory.* They'd say he was in denial when he told them no, he wasn't angry about what happened, that he found it funny and that's how he coped. Even the worst things cracked him up: when his doctor had told him he had to watch his diet because he had a hole in his heart, he'd laughed; the image just seemed funny to him.

Early critics of *The Bumbry Show* marveled at Calvin's bravery, the way he crossed the line in creating a series that was, as he had pitched it, an NC-17 *Cosby Show* with all the good parts Cosby cut out: Dad inadvertently prescribing Viagra to his patients and walking in on a waiting room full of dudes with raging boners; his daughter getting kicked out of school for bringing her parents' *Joy of Sex* book to show-and-tell, then being unable to unstick the pages. He wasn't trying to be daring, wasn't trying to tell his life story, just trying to write what he thought was funny. Yes, he'd written an episode inspired by his trip to New York with Densmore, but he hated the idea of people parsing it for what was and wasn't real.

Calvin finished his tea. Kids in down coats and knit hats were trailing sleds across Frederick Douglass Boulevard; garbage trucks rumbled by, dirty orange shovels scraping the street, spreading salt. Todd was probably watching the snow too. What would it be like to watch everything, knowing it might be the last time? That tree in the planter down there—you'd never see it bud or bloom again; the snow—that might be the last time you'd see it fall. That gray sky? You'd see it go dark but never back to blue. Like being locked in a dark annex, hiding from the soldiers outside, knowing you might never get out.

Fine, fuck it. He went to his desk, powered up his computer, and opened Twitter. If he ever wanted to waste a morning and an afternoon, here was a hell of a good place to do it: 374 notifications; 525 direct messages; a bunch of bullshit about "witch hunts," "illegal leaks," and some cracker named Jeff Sessions, who looked like he had a sphincter where a mouth should have been, talking about sealing up America's southern border.

What's happening? Twitter asked him.

Calvin typed: Listen up and check this shit out, y'all. He copied and pasted the link to Franklin's article. He tweeted it out.

Instantly, ten people liked his post.

He wrote a second post: Goddamn it! Read the thing before you like that shit, muthafuckas! They liked that one too.

He started a third post. Once he started writing, it was hard to stop—like drinking in high school when he'd keep throwing back rum and Cokes until he was too drunk to stand or the bottle was empty.

Okay, pull up a chair, let's hot tub time machine it back to 1982, mofos, he wrote. I'm a 17-year-old drama homo at North Shore Magnet.

He spellchecked his post, tweeted it, wrote another:

My home life's shit, so are my grades. Only 4 things keep my morbid, self-destructive ass alive.

Post 5: 1) Old movies on Channel 9; 2) Ronrico Rum; 3) Richard Pryor albums; 4) the Theater Annex at North Shore High.

He was up to 125 likes now. He kept tweeting.

The Annex is run by a twisted, vampire-looking motherfucker: Tyrus Densmore.

Brother takes an interest in kids—not like Father Flanagan, more like Father Jerry Sandusky.

Dude's up in everyone else's business, but he keeps outta mine. My mouth's too big, and so's everything else about me.

But that shit changes when I get cast in—y'all gonna think I'm making shit up but you can check it: Diary of Anne Muthafuckin' Frank.

Next post—a GIF of a bug-eyed Scatman Crothers at his piano playing "Jeepers Creepers" in *The Cheap Detective*.

Calvin tweetstormed all he remembered about Densmore, about *Anne Frank* and the "New York trip." His followers and retweeters responded with kind words, sympathetic GIFs. He kept typing—his first meeting with Todd; Todd's warning about Tyrus; that scene in the hotel room.

But Densmore was only part of the story, Calvin wrote. The man hadn't been some isolated creep skeezing his way through the Annex, just the first creep Calvin had met, the one who had prepared him for a rogue's gallery of perverts who rode roughshod through his industry. Tyrus wasn't even close to the worst pervert Calvin had met; he was more like a "starter pervert."

So, let's name names, muthafuckas! Calvin wrote that he felt thankful he had met Densmore when he had been so young because the man had hardened him, made him view everyone as a potential predator. If he hadn't met Ty, God knew how he would have reacted at the wrap party for a TV movie about televangelists Jimmy and Tammy Faye Bakker: he'd felt a hand in his waistband, and, in front of everyone, he'd asked, "Uh, Mr. Spacey, are you missing a hand? 'Cause I think one of yours is in my pants."

Densmore had done Calvin the favor of making him believe the worst about anybody, even his childhood heroes, so that when he was on the set of *Ghost Dad*, shooting the shit about how hard it was for him to find a partner, and Bill Cosby said Calvin just needed to slip some pills into a date's drink, Calvin was the only one who suspected Cos wasn't joking.

As Calvin continued to tweet, he didn't particularly care if anyone but Todd was reading his posts, so he didn't think about whether his hundred-odd tweets would matter. Not until late in the afternoon, when he took the elevator down to the lobby, did he sense that something in the outside world had already started to change.

Maxwell, the hotel concierge, always insisted on calling Calvin "Mr. Dawes," even after Calvin had told him to stop calling him "Mr.," unless he wanted a foot up his ass. Today he smiled, said, "Nice to see you, Cal," and Calvin had to check himself in a lobby mirror to make sure he hadn't lost fifty pounds overnight.

Maeve was working the front desk in her black, long-sleeved turtle-neck that covered most of her tattoos. He asked if there was any mail for him. She handed him some magazines, then gave him the sort of smile that actresses were paid big money to give Jason Bourne and Ethan Hunt. "Thank you, Calvin, truly," she said.

It was still snowing, but Calvin had an hour and a half before *Empty Chair* tech rehearsal, so he decided to walk—give himself something to tell his doctor next time she asked if he'd been exercising. "Shit, yeah, woman—I walked all the way from the Langston to the Beacon!"

Black leather bag over a shoulder, black knit cap pulled down over his ears as if he were a Russian sailor on a clandestine mission, he stopped at the corner fruit stand, where he put down a dollar for his daily snack: two bananas and an apple. Alpon, the proprietor, clapped Calvin on the arm. "You are speaking good truth to power, my friend," he said.

As he crossed 110th Street, he felt his phone vibrate. He looked at the display—Todd.

"Hey, man, what's up?"

Todd didn't speak, just laughed lasciviously—"*Huhuhuhuhuhuhuh.*"

"I said 'What's up?' freak," said Calvin.

"I just asked you to tell your story," Todd said. "I didn't tell you to go break the internet."

"Yeah, I don't know about any of that 'breaking the internet' shit. I guess I got carried away."

"Maybe a little bit." Todd laughed again, then stopped. "Seriously, thank you."

"No problem." Calvin felt uneasy with the sincere tone the conversation was taking; it reminded him too much of the cheesy, moralistic closing moments of the sitcoms he'd grown up with, which was why he had always ended *Bumbry Show* episodes on irreverent notes—a daughter yelling "Suck my dick" at her grandmother; a son cutting short a serious talk with his dad, then heading up to his room to crank up Cypress Hill, fire up a bowl, and jerk off. "So," he asked Todd. "You'll be okay to see my show, right?"

"Wouldn't miss it," Todd said.

"Opening night—gonna put your ass in the motherfuckin' front row."

"Center seat?"

"You know it, brother."

Calvin walked south along Central Park. The snow was pristine, only a few boot prints in it. In the pond, ducks paddled in fast circles. On just about any other day, Calvin could take this walk without a single person greeting him. Today he felt like an army hero. He got thumbs-ups, handshakes, hugs. Nannies introduced him to their charges. A German tourist in a Stars-and-Stripes USA hat beamed when she saw him: "Oh my *Gott*," she cried. "I just *retweeeted* you."

So many people were stopping him that he had to flag down a taxi. When the cab stopped at a light at the corner of Eighty-Sixth and Amsterdam Avenue, the driver rapped on the glass partition.

"You are Mr. Calvin Dawes?" The driver held up his cell phone and showed Calvin its screen. "Do you know that you are trending on Twitter?"

Calvin glanced at the screen: #MuslimBan was the top trending topic; #CalvinDawes was number two. All over the nation, he was being tweeted and retweeted, he was being aggregated on Vulture and Vox, analyzed on Jezebel and the *Advocate* website. Opinionators were opinionating about him on Medium. The *Tomorrow* article he had linked to was open on the screen of Professor Judith Nagorsky in her Northwestern University office; it had been bookmarked by Dr. Carrie Hollinger at

Casa Segura; Asya Loh started crying when she was halfway through, and decided she couldn't read the rest; Eileen Muldoon had sent the article along with an urgent text to Tyrus Densmore, who invited her over for coffee and a chat. At the offices of the *Tomorrow*, where Franklin had gone expecting to discuss the terms of his severance, the number on the Big Board had shot up past twenty thousand and Violet was offering him a promotion and a raise. In his Washington, D.C., office, Rob Rubicoff was reading the article and chuckling, and when his executive assistant asked what was so funny, he said the arc of history was bending toward justice. And the moment after Calvin stepped out of his cab on Amsterdam, then pushed opened the doors to the Beacon's back entrance, the entire crew stopped reading their phones and burst into applause.

*

On opening night for *The Empty Chair*, Calvin stood backstage at the Beacon awaiting his cue. The idea for the show went back to the very beginning of his career when he'd been juggling bit parts in small films with occasional work for a catering company that liked employing someone his size because it discouraged party guests from eating too much. On nights he wasn't working, he played open mikes and show-cases at comedy clubs where he was paid in free drink (singular) or a cut of the door if he could bring in more than fifty people. Most nights, half the seats were empty and the other half were occupied by comatose drunks so far gone that Calvin would pitch his routine to one of the empty chairs. "If I can get a chair to laugh," he liked to say, "I'll be the best damn comic who ever lived."

In the late 1980s, when his career started taking off with a recurring role on *A Different World* and his first spot on *The Tonight Show* (when David Steinberg was guest hosting, but still), he was starting to sell out clubs in New York and L.A. He would set aside one ticket and leave it at the box office for someone he knew would never show up. He'd gotten the idea from the honky who coached the Houston Oilers and always left a ticket for Elvis.

It started out as a gimmick: he'd leave a ticket for Richard Pryor or Eddie Murphy, knowing full well they wouldn't come. But after he started getting cast in bigger roles, appearing on the covers of *Jet*, *TV Guide*, and *Entertainment Weekly*, playing Luther Abercrombie opposite Charlie Sheen in the cop buddy movie *Abercrombie and Bitch*, selling out college towns and old movie palaces, he still liked looking out and seeing at least one empty seat. The seat kept him honest, reminded him that, no matter how successful he was getting, something would always be missing. He would leave a ticket for his dad, who hadn't talked to him since he was twelve; he'd leave one for his mom, who was occupied with her grandchildren and never visited or called.

But now that he was at what seemed to be the peak of his career—full houses wherever he went, people retweeting whatever he wrote—it seemed self-indulgent to say something was still missing. And if sometimes he felt the return of his old friend darkness, the gloom that made him feel as if he had nothing at all and long to curl up under the covers with a bottle of rum; if sometimes he thought of his mom and how far away she was; if sometimes he wished for a true love, the comfort that couldn't be found at the hands of some high-dollar sex worker—if sometimes all that kept him from throwing himself off the George Washington Bridge was the fear of being written off as some clown-crying-on-the-inside cliché—the truth was that he really did have everything he needed. The show was called *The Empty Chair*, but there would be no empty seats.

The opening music went up—the theme to the climactic scene of *The Good, the Bad and the Ugly*: "The Ecstasy of Gold." Calvin stood in the wings, rocked on his heels, shadowboxed, his preshow workout: left to the gut, right to the jaw. The stage lights went down. A roar from the crowd—straight up: not applause, not a gasp, a legitimate roar. Someone leaned in close to him: "You're on, Calvin."

He walked, nearly danced, as the cameras and lights followed him. He pumped his fist to the music, the spotlight pooled center stage, and he stepped into the light. He held his hand high; the crowd went quiet. In that moment it seemed like he could do anything—even run for president. Someone had to take on Trump in 2020; why not him? Put him on as Oprah's running mate; no ticket would be bigger, not even twin reincarnations of William Howard Taft.

"The name of the show, motherfuckers, is *The Empty Chair*." A baby follow spot burst on and swept across the faces of all the people in the theater for the sold-out show. But then it lingered front row center where one seat was empty. The light moved on as Calvin kept staring at that empty chair.

He stood in the spotlight, silent. His eyes burned, hot tears exploded inside them. He swallowed hard. *Oh, shit, oh, shit*, he thought. He wished he could stop the show—*Hey, hold on, guys; I'll be back in an hour or two.* He wanted to take out his phone—*Hey, Todd, man, you on your way? Everything all right?* But the show had its own motion and all he could do was roll with it. And besides, he had a pretty good idea what that empty seat meant.

When the show was over, he skipped the party, told the guys backstage to make up some excuse—"Calvin has the shits." He got into an SUV, asked his driver to take him to Todd's apartment, and—after the doorman there said an ambulance had left two hours earlier—told his driver to take him to Weill Cornell.

Visiting hours were over at the hospital, but he was Calvin Bumbry Dawes, so rules didn't apply. Only family members were allowed in the ward where Todd was being treated, but he was Calvin Bumbry Dawes, so they let him go right up.

"Aww, fuck, man." Calvin started crying the moment he walked into Todd's room, "Aww, fuck fuck, fuck." Todd was under a white sheet, eyes closed, tube in his mouth, a thin layer of gray-and-white stubble on his face, a machine helping him breathe. A bandage was wrapped around his head. He looked like an old man. Someone should have at least given him a shave. Calvin put a hand on Todd's shoulder, kissed his cheek.

Snow fell fast upon the East River, on the empty trams gliding to and from Roosevelt Island. Along FDR Drive, cabs and buses, wipers going, crept through the slush. Calvin could feel it again—that dull ache, that gathering darkness. He hoped someone had been with Todd when it had happened, whatever it was. He couldn't stand to think that Todd might have been alone. The idea that Todd had collapsed when he was on his way to the Beacon to see Calvin was too much to bear.

He felt under the sheet for Todd's hand. It was warm; at least there was that. He sat there holding Todd's hand. Man, he wasn't down with this death-and-dying shit.

He looked up and saw a woman in a pale blue uniform standing in the doorway. Calvin cleared his throat and blinked away the tears. "It's okay," he told the nurse, his voice catching. "I was just leaving."

"That's all right, Mr. Dawes." She reached into a pocket and pulled out a pen and a pad. "I know this might not be the best time, but what you've been writing—it's meant a lot to me." She gestured to Todd. "And I know it's meant a lot to him too."

"He talked to you about that?" Calvin asked.

"It's the only thing he wanted to talk about," said the nurse.

Calvin signed his autograph and gave the nurse a hug, and as he walked out to the elevators and down to the lobby, then out and into the snow—a few sprays of blood on it—he thought of how so much could change in such a brief time. One moment you could be on a stage, pumping your fist as a sold-out crowd gave you a standing O; the next, you could be heading home alone from a hospital where the best friend you'd ever had was dying.

But at least he had told the story Todd wanted him to; at least now it was out in the world.

Mrs. Frank

When she got the panicked call from the high school informing her that Tyrus Densmore had resigned his position with no advance notice and asking if she would consider stepping in to direct the school's spring play, Judith knew she had to say yes, no matter how many commitments she had already made. And she knew which show she had to choose, no matter how many heinous memories that choice might trigger.

But as she toted her RED ORCHID THEATRE shoulder bag full of clipboards, pens, stapled scripts, and audition forms and entered the Trey Newson Memorial Theater Annex at North Shore Magnet for the first time in the twenty-first century, she was surprised to discover how unfamiliar the place actually seemed.

The entirety of the Annex, reeking of Sammy Doulos's weed in her memory, smelled like floral air freshener. The classrooms seemed to be in the wrong places, the girls' bathroom was twice as large as she remembered, and, in the common room, there weren't any vending machines stocked with stale candy bars, flat soda, and off-brand fruit juice; just a coffeemaker, a well-stocked mini-fridge, a sink, and a microwave. In the hallways, there were no longer any framed photos of old productions—no Judith with silver hair, playing Mrs. Gibbs in *Our Town*; no

Judith as Edith Frank in a ratty overcoat with a construction paper yellow star; no physical evidence whatsoever of the years she had spent here save for the bronze plaque dedicated to Charles "Trey" Newson, which spoke of someone who didn't sound much like the Trey she had known: 1965–1992: HERE IN THE ANNEX, HE FOUND THE LOVE OF FRIENDS AND A SENSE OF HOME.

But it was a Saturday, so no one was around to tell her how much had truly changed. Maybe everything was the same as it had always been, and it only looked different to her because her life had changed so dramatically.

If, back in high school, you had asked Judith what her life would be like when she was in her early fifties, she would have guessed something like this: after her mother had died—either from an actual act of suicide or a suicidal lifestyle—Judith would have left the Chicago area for good. She would have been dreeing her weird in New York, living paycheck to paycheck while running a downtown theater company that showcased women playwrights. Heartbroken that Fiona had left America for Canada before her junior year had even ended, she would be a clinical depressive, listening to Joni Mitchell's *Blue* on an eternal loop, only sporadically able to rouse herself from a fetal position in her funky Alphabet City loft full of stray cats and rescue dogs. Her father and evil stepmom would be retired and living on some vile Miami estate, sending her checks that she would refuse to cash no matter how much she needed the money.

Except for the dogs and cats, Judith had been wrong about it all. Her mother, indestructible as a Warner Bros. cartoon character, was as healthy as Judith could remember her being, so much so that, after Judith's stepmom had divorced her dad—presumably because he'd shtupped another secretary—Judith's parents had reconciled and were now living together downtown in a Michigan Avenue condo as if neither the infidelities nor the divorce nor the psychotic episodes had ever happened. Whenever Judith visited her parents with her wife, Lourdes, and their children, Winnie and Hazel, she had the sense that Herb and Estelle Nagorsky were conspiring to make her feel like the heroine of some dystopian sci-fi show: "*No, you don't understand; they're not really like that!*"

Evanston would have been the last place she would have imagined herself, yet this was where she had researched her dissertation on the children's theater pioneer Winifred Ward and her partner, Hazel Easton, and it was where she was now an associate professor at Northwestern, a sought-after director at theaters and summer festivals throughout the Midwest and now—the latest bullet point on her CV—adapter and director of North Shore's spring production: *The Diary of Anne Frank*, or, as Judith was calling it, *Anne Frank AF.* She was setting the damn thing right here in 2017 with the Franks and Van Daans as mixed-race immigrant families hiding out from American authorities.

Judith was taking as inspiration something she'd heard that poseur dipshit Bono say when he'd introduced "Helter Skelter" at a U2 concert at Soldier Field: "Charles Manson stole this song from the Beatles; we're stealin' it back." Her version of the play would steal Anne Frank's story back from that 1982 production and its aftermath, which, the way she saw it, had changed all their lives. *Anne Frank* was why Carrie had found her calling and why Declan still couldn't find his. *Anne Frank* was where Mr. Densmore taught Rob and Eileen what they could get away with, and it was where Franklin had seen a future in writing stories that held people like them accountable. *Anne Frank* was why Calvin, Amanda, and Fiona had never wanted to come back to this town, and it was why Judith was trying to find a way to give people a reason to stay.

In the case of Trey, well, it was pointless to guess how much *Anne Frank* contributed to the way he wound up—skinnier, jumpier, more anxious each time he had tracked Judith down and asked her for money, always apologizing and promising he'd pay her back someday, and if he didn't, she could hire his brother to sue him—but maybe if the Annex had been more like the place she saw now and less like the one she remembered, *Anne Frank* could have saved him.

The show had made Judith into the director and professor she was by teaching her exactly what not to do. You didn't mock, order, and terrorize; you listened and tried to understand. You didn't imprison people; you offered them an escape. You didn't show people who they feared they were; you showed them who they could be. The idea of her *Anne Frank* was to let the audience and the actors see the Anne in themselves, not the potential Nazi in everyone else. And that's why she was setting the play here and now: not just to score political points about the terrifying new order—Anne Franks sleeping under Mylar blankets at the border; Anne Franks drinking poisoned water in Flint, Michigan; Anne Franks hiding from drone strikes or dying of hunger or risking their lives to board rickety, overcrowded boats heading for the West—but to remind people there was time to save the Franks and Van Daans out there right now.

Judith arranged the scenes and audition forms on a hallway table, then went to make herself a surprisingly good pot of coffee, and by the time she came back, the first actors had already arrived. "Okay, people," she said. "Let's get to it."

*

Running *AF* auditions was tough work—a lot tougher than Judith's usual gigs. Casting a high school show wasn't necessarily about picking the most talented performers or the ones who claimed to have the most experience; it was about finding the actor who needed the role most and assembling a cast that reflected the school's diversity. Over the course of a wearying morning and afternoon, she auditioned tall and short Annes, blonde and brunette Annes; Black, white, and brown Annes; a dozen bright, perky Annes; and a dozen even brighter and perkier Annes. She'd seen a herky-jerky Anne who seemed to be hopped up on goofballs, and an insufferably precocious boy who said it was unfair that only girls were being considered: Wouldn't casting a boy as "Andy Frank" make the production "more inclusive?"

She consulted her call sheet: "Kitty Weekes?"

Judith hadn't had lunch, and she was starting to feel delirious; all the names on her sheet were blurring together. She had had more than her fill of being informed that, in spite of everything, people were good at heart, when a girl wearing a black hoodie and carrying a grimy CASA SEGURA tote bag slouched into the theater, hands shoved deep into the pockets of her baggy jeans; she had long, dangling, dirty-blonde hair that she didn't bother tossing out of her eyes.

"Hi, Kitty, I'm Dr. Nagorsky. You can sit or stand, whichever makes you most comfortable."

"Standing's fine," the girl said.

Judith looked at the call sheet again. "And you're . . . seventeen?"

"Uh-huh."

"You're a senior here?"

"For the time being."

"What's that like these days?"

"It has its positive and negative aspects."

"I can imagine; I went here."

"Yeah, I'm aware of that."

"Right," Judith said. "So you're on your way to college. Where?"

"U of C. Probably I'll transfer out after first semester, though."

"Where to?"

"Not sure yet. Columbia, maybe? Stanford? McGill?"

"Pretty far away."

"Uh, that's the general idea."

"I get it, believe me." Judith studied Kitty's form. There was a space for auditioning actors to list previous acting experience. Kitty had left it blank.

"You've never acted before?"

"No. I've wanted to, but the director here—my mom warned me about him."

"Tyrus Densmore? What'd she say?"

"Just to steer clear."

"Well, anyway, he's gone now."

Kitty limply pumped her fists in the air with mock enthusiasm. "Woo-hoo," she said. "Was he really that bad?"

"Worse, probably. Whatever your dream was, he found a way to crush it," Judith said. "So that's why you're auditioning? Because you haven't had the chance before?"

"Yeah. Plus, I like your idea: *Anne Frank* in 2017. It seems pretty on point."

"You know the show?"

"The book. My mom read it to me when I was little. She told me I was too young, but I kinda made her do it."

Judith smiled, remembering herself as a kid, always reading the most depressing stories, listening to the saddest songs, hoping they would make her life seem cheerful by comparison. "What'll you be auditioning with?"

"It's kind of an original thing." Kitty reached into her pocket. She pulled out a crumpled sheet of paper and unfolded it.

"Whenever you're ready, child." Judith called people "child" now, felt oddly comfortable doing it.

Kitty kept one hand in her hoodie pocket; with the other she held the paper, but it seemed more prop than script—she barely looked at it as she spoke: "When I heard my dad's phone vibrate, I knew the text on it wasn't my business, but I looked anyway."

Obviously, Kitty's monologue was autobiographical: anyone who walked in and read a speech off a sheet of paper or phone screen and said they were auditioning with an "original" piece was invariably reciting something they had written themselves and, more often than not, recounted in therapy. What intrigued Judith was that she saw no separation between the girl who had walked into the Annex and the one now onstage relating a tale in which she learned her dad was cheating on her mom by inadvertently picking up his phone and seeing his texts. During any audition, there was usually a clear transition between person and performer: now they were acting; now they weren't. To blur that line so effortlessly was a rare talent—or evidence of a rare pain. The girl's monologue had nothing to do with Anne Frank's story, yet the feelings of confinement and the need to break free seemed so intense that her words resonated more than those in all the scripted monologues the other auditioning actors had recited. Kitty spoke for less than two minutes, yet in that time Judith had the impression she'd met the girl before, understood exactly what she was going through.

"Tonight, when I get home, I should probably say something to my mom or dad, but I probably won't. I don't wanna hurt my dad, and my mom would probably be happier not knowing. Anyway, I'm outta there soon enough." The only reason Judith knew the monologue was over was because the girl stopped speaking, not because anything changed in her manner.

Judith handed Kitty a short scene, one where Mrs. Frank and her daughter argue about whether she's been spending too much time with Peter.

Kitty didn't take the pages right away. "You want me to read for Anne?" she asked. "I'm not really seeing that."

"How do you mean?"

"Well, look at me." Kitty made a sour face. "This is what Anne Frank's supposed to be like?"

"Why not?"

"You know: all that optimism, all that pirouetting. It's like the exact opposite of me."

"Why don't we just try and see how it goes," Judith said. And although the girl was right—Anne was rarely this somber or sardonic—when they read together, Judith had the same uncanny sensation: she understood this girl, knew her. Somewhere, they had acted this scene together before.

"See what I mean?" Kitty said after they were done. "I mean, I get that it's acting, that it's about pretending to be someone you're not. But that line—'In spite of everything, I still believe people are really good at heart'?—how can I say that without sounding, excuse me, without sounding like I'm full of shit?"

"That's the point, though." Judith took off her reading glasses. "You should feel like it sounds full of shit. You read the newspapers, you watch TV, you see what's going on in the country: your home isn't what you thought it was when you were younger; of course you can't believe people are good at heart. But in *here*"—she tapped the pages of her script—"and in *here*"—she pointed the script at the stage—"you can try to create a place where people will believe that it could be true. What if the play created the best possible versions of every character onstage and everybody who watches can see the best in themselves and everyone else?" Judith invited Kitty to sit beside her. "I was in this show—thirty-however-many years ago."

"I know."

"We all came into it at a time in our lives when we were dreaming of everything we might do one day, but the director beat those dreams out of us, and some of us still haven't gotten them back. We acted this story, and, at the end of it, most of us were done believing in anything. It amazes me that some of us got beyond that, that nearly all of us are still here. I don't want to pretend that Anne was all that different from the way we were. I don't want her to be some naïve saint who comes in thinking people are good, then goes out thinking the exact same thing. I don't believe that any more than you do. I want her to have doubts, real doubts—like the ones you have, the ones I had—but, by the end, she comes to believe in the people around her and in the power of telling them her story. Having people listen is what gives her hope. I don't know if that's the way the story is supposed to be told, but that's the way I want to tell it, because I've seen it done by someone who couldn't see the hope or beauty in any story, and I didn't like how it turned out."

Kitty scratched the back of her neck. "Yeah," she said. "I asked my mom what being in this show was like, but she didn't want to talk about it. I said, 'How come you never did any shows after this one?' She was just like, 'I was focusing on other things.'"

"You keep mentioning your mom as if I'm supposed to know who she is," Judith said.

" 'Cause you do," said Kitty. "Or you did."

Judith shook her head.

"Caroline Weekes. Hollinger when you knew her," said Kitty. "Carrie. Hollinger."

Judith lost any pretense of directorial objectivity and teacherly distance. "Fuck me running," she said, then covered her mouth, laughed, and apologized. She could see it now. The hair was lighter; the girl had to be a half foot taller than Carrie had been, her voice was nowhere near as sweet, and this girl had a tough, cynical, and knowing streak Carrie had never had. But Judith knew the face, and she remembered playing mother to a girl who looked like this, trying in vain to shelter her from the doom that lay just outside the Annex, all the while knowing a different sort of doom was inside it too.

It made an odd sort of sense that Carrie would have a daughter like Kitty—so disillusioned when she realized the world was nothing like the one her mother had tried to make for her. Whereas Judith—Judith who had taken first aid classes to learn how to apply a tourniquet to her mother's wrists—was the one with the just-about-perfect marriage and the fabulous kids who still made her believe that anything was possible: that no matter how dark the world might seem, eventually you could see all that was still good in it, if you were lucky enough to survive. Judith knew what had given her this strength and hope. It wasn't anything she'd seen at home or in the Annex but what she'd found outside it—love, luck, faith in herself, and one night in a theater when she had watched a Kabuki version of *Macbeth*, a show so unlike the script it was based on but one that captured its spirit and made her believe that, in spite of everything, you could still create beauty in the world.

Judith knew she wasn't supposed to—knew this just wasn't done anymore—but she couldn't help herself. She opened her arms and held Kitty close. And as she embraced this girl, she felt that she was not only Dr. Judith Nagorsky holding the daughter of someone she had known long ago; she was Edith Frank holding the daughter who had always run from her.

"Rehearsals start next week," she said.

Mr. Dussel

Tyrus Densmore studied himself in his full-length bedroom mirror, admiring the view of this man for the last time as he finished dressing to attend Tyrusfest and the opening night performance of *Anne Frank AF*. He knew a party held in his honor was some sort of sick joke. But he'd always liked sick jokes. And he couldn't resist seeing what sort of misguided production Judith Nagorsky had slapped together in his absence, he was sure it would be some sort of sick joke too.

How did the man look? Better than you'd think. There were lines and creases on his face, but those he hadn't addressed with concealer gave him character. He was ten pounds lighter than he had been in his prime, and his face had a dusty pallor to it—perhaps the result of the pescatarian diet his physicians insisted he follow. Getting around had become more of a challenge; soon he'd probably need a decent cane instead of the piece of shit he'd filched from the North Shore prop room and used primarily as an affectation. But how many men this old looked this good? How many commanded so many second glances at the Lyric Opera bar? How many still drove? How many lived by themselves—without some caretaker wishing them dead or robbing them blind? He read the obituaries routinely with the icy confidence of an exiled king, marking the downfalls of former enemies while he awaited his return to power. Todd Merritt was gone; Tyrus Densmore would be coming back.

Those who hadn't seen him since he'd delivered his two-sentence letter of resignation to the superintendent, then driven out of the North Shore faculty lot for the final time, were probably thinking he'd been defeated and was living out his pathetic final days in shame. They had little idea of his memory for slights and disobedience, his capacity for revenge, and the patience he had to see it through. All those who doubted him, all those who'd spoken out against him, would soon learn how stupid they were to underestimate him.

Declan had been first to come forward, so he was first to fall. Tyrus thought he'd given the man ample warning of what would happen if he talked to anyone about his absurd accusations. On Facebook, posing as "William Nicholson," Tyrus had urged Declan to break into his house and steal his old diary in which he'd confessed to assaulting Amanda Wehner, along with the photos Eileen had given Tyrus of a pale, scrawny Declan fumbling atop that sad girl and getting exactly what he deserved.

Declan hadn't for a moment guessed that "William Nicholson" had been a figment of Tyrus's imagination, a name derived so easily from Tyrus's acting hero Nicol Williamson that it was as if Tyrus had affixed a giant, illuminated sign to his chest: C'EST MOI!

"Mr. Densmore will be out of town that evening and his alarm is broken; now's your chance," William Nicholson had written. And right on cue, Declan had smashed a downstairs window, tripped the alarm, then all but run into the arms of the cops. That should have been enough to silence Declan forever, but alas, not. Franklin's article had been published in the *Tomorrow* with Declan's quotes all over it, so Tyrus had sent copies of Declan's diary entries and Eileen's photographs to Declan's wife, his son, his silly little girlfriend, Patricia, and Frank Lichtenstein.

He would have liked to have seen Declan's face when he realized what he had set into motion. But that was one of the most beautiful yet vexing things about drama: you never got to see everything. And some of the most important moments in theater—Lady Macbeth killing herself; the Franks and Van Daans leaving the Annex at gunpoint; Shelly Levene breaking into his office and stealing the Glengarry leads; Declan

Spengler's relationships falling apart—happened offstage and were left to your imagination.

Tyrus didn't regret that he was probably ruining Declan's life, nor did he feel particularly proud, only satisfied that justice was being done. He didn't know who would be next; Calvin Dawes and Franklin were the most obvious choices. Trey Newson had been a kind, lost boy, but the rest of his family was another story. Eventually, though, he would take care of all of them. He knew their secrets and their weaknesses, so there was no question of whether he would succeed; it was only a matter of time.

Tyrus checked his dresser drawers, made sure they were empty. The boxes were already downstairs in the living room, carefully labeled and stacked. He picked up the first of the suitcases, lugged it to the hallway at the top of the stairs. Then he went back for the next. After Susan had died, he had removed all evidence of her infirmities: the stair lift, the three-pronged canes, the walkers. He briefly felt sorry that he'd had the Stair-Glide taken away. It would have helped with the luggage, but that was okay: when he got to New York, he would have to rely on himself.

There had been a time—not long ago, actually—when he had perceived the future as one long moment of waiting to die. Even though he had spent so much of his life anticipating Tom's death, when the call had come from the night nurse, he felt as if someone had clubbed him in the gut—not just once but again and again and again. He would drink himself to sleep, then wake up in the middle of the night gasping for air. By then Susan was pretty far gone: How many times did she forget their son had finally succeeded in hanging himself, and how many times did Tyrus have to remind her and watch her face dissolve all over again? All that kept him going were the classes he taught at the high school and the plays he directed there, each darker than the next. How he had gotten the administration to agree to a season of shows by Edward Bond, Sarah Kane, and Tracy Letts, he had no idea. No doubt they were afraid of him and knew he was grieving and eager to die.

But he did not fade away the way he thought he would. He had read and seen so many stories about husbands and wives—together for decades, then dying within hours of each other; yet, after his wife died, his strength returned in subtle ways. He stopped waking up at night; he started going out again, seeing theater, flirting at bars. He returned to directing the plays he'd always loved: *A View from the Bridge*, *To Kill a Mockingbird*—classic dramas about justice with lots of good parts for strapping young men and a few cute girls to keep the boys interested.

Still, even before people had started airing their old grievances, he knew he was living on borrowed time. The culture was changing. People hated their new government and what it was doing, but they felt powerless to change it, so they lashed out at easier enemies. You couldn't stop the president, but you could try to stop Tyrus.

He could have occupied the next months or years by defending his good name, but that seemed a rather dull pastime: challenging accusations all day long, admitting he had done this, asserting he hadn't done that, pointing out that what he had done was nothing compared to what sports coaches and other "inspirational leaders" did every day. How many times would he have to listen to sanctimonious hypocrites berate him for behaving in a way that had been perfectly acceptable at the time? What had he done? Had he driven drunk off a bridge at Chappaquiddick and left his girlfriend to drown? Was he separating parents from their children and locking them all up? He had given his actors hope, a purpose; if he was guilty of anything, it was caring too much for them. He was so weary of the cliché of innocent youth, of people pretending that adulthood was a real thing and not just an artificial construct, as if the word *teenager* wasn't just something someone made up. Did any adult remember what it was really like to be a teenager? Had they ever listened to teenagers' conversations or read their diaries?

He had always liked the separation between theater and reality—had sought out his career for that very reason—but so often he wished that real life could be more like the stage. A play was life compressed into a few hours at most. You played a role for some weeks; if you were lucky and the play was a hit, maybe you'd do it for a year. But then it was over: you tore down the set, brought the costumes back to the shop, lugged the marked-up scripts to the recycling center, then onto the next character. Yet, in life, you played the same role assigned to you on the day you were born, and this was called a good, respectable existence. For too long he had been Tyrus Densmore, lord of the Annex, flawed hero, misunderstood villain, star in a tiny, insular universe. To stick around awaiting the reckoning was to admit he had reached his tragedy's final act and from now on would be only a minor character in other people's dramas. But he refused to accept that his story was nearing its finale. At worst, this was the end of Act II, which would set the stage for an astounding Act III reveal.

Tyrus checked the wallet app on his phone, made sure the ticket and boarding pass were there. He put the phone back in his suit jacket. He would be on the last flight to LaGuardia, where he would become William Nicholson, seventy-seven-year-old first-time actor. How remarkable it would seem for there to be a novice actor of his age—mind still sharp, legs in reasonable working order, talents undiminished.

William Nicholson would arrive fresh in New York with the enthusiasm of a recent Juilliard grad but the experience of a three-time Oscar nominee. Days after his arrival, he would check out of his hotel, get an apartment, an agent. He would hire a videographer to produce his actor's reel, an engineer to record his voice-overs. He would show up at open calls at six A.M., charm every actor there. He would frequent industry bars, buy drinks for youngsters who would view him as a delightful oddity—this handsome old duffer with dreams of making it on Broadway. They'd take him under their wing. He would amass stage credits, get guest spots on cop shows and sitcoms where he'd dispense grandfatherly advice. He'd amaze his younger counterparts with his stamina. And if none of that worked out, he would rent a theater, hire actors and a publicist, produce his favorite plays, and perform nude scenes in each of them.

Tyrus checked his phone. Soon the car would be here. The driver would help him with his bags and boxes. They'd drive to the UPS store and send the boxes to the storage unit he'd rented in Queens. Then on to North Shore, where a ticket for *AF* would be waiting for William Nicholson. He'd watch the show and leave either at intermission or the moment the lights went out at the end of Act II. He despised curtain calls; the only one who did it right was Nijinsky, who didn't bow, just mimed masturbating, which was all curtain calls were good for. His driver would speed him to Tyrusfest, where, one last time, he'd play the role of Tyrus: drink too much, tell filthy jokes, cup someone's balls, wouldn't care if little Frankie Lichtenstein or any reporter saw him. Then he'd excuse himself, say he needed to make a quick call and that he'd be right back to offer a toast.

By the time they realized he wasn't coming back, he'd be at O'Hare. They'd call him; his phone would be dead. He'd never answer it again. The next time they'd see him would be onstage, on TV, or on the big screen. They'd check the credits, look for his name, but they wouldn't find it—and then they'd wonder: Were William Nicholson and Tyrus Densmore different people, or were they one and the same? Eventually, someone would figure it out, but by then it wouldn't matter. He would be part of the inner circle, where each protected his own—that sordid world of casting couches, sex rings, and underage massages. His secrets were nowhere near as scandalous as those of other show people; keeping them would be easy. As a performer and director, he was an unparalleled professional; when it came to depravity, he was strictly amateur.

Suitcase in one hand, walking stick in the other, he took the first step down. He felt strangely unbalanced. Too much weight on one side, not enough on the other. He gripped the stick harder, placed the tip on the step below. He hefted the suitcase and heard a crack—so subtle he didn't immediately understand, and by time the meaning registered, there was another snap, then a crunch. The stick splintered underneath him and he fell face-first. The suitcase fell out of his hands, fell faster than he did, slid down to the floor as his face slammed into the marble stairs, a spark of pain igniting first in his chin, then his skull, radiating throughout his entire body.

It occurred to him—not in any logical sense but in a fragmentary way—that he was falling inelegantly, so unlike any way he had fallen onstage: clutching his chest then tumbling to the ground as Tybalt in *Romeo and Juliet*; arms thrown back as the final blow was thrust home into Cyrano. As he fell, he sensed that every part of his body was in the wrong place—legs above, head below. When he looked upward, all he saw was a juddering, pale brown water splotch on the white ceiling, tiny dots of colored light floating upon it.

He still held the walking stick—the top third of it, anyway. He tried pushing it into a step, then the wall—useless. He flung it behind him. Sweat poured down his cheeks. He wiped it away with the back of his hand and saw it was blood. He felt dizzy, the ceiling spun, the pain so intense he couldn't pinpoint exactly where he'd been hurt. He tried to right himself, pushed his hands down hard, but they didn't work the way they were supposed to. He thought he might inch downward, but something was wrong with his legs. Blood kept spilling—onto the stairs, his hands, his cheeks. It filled his mouth. He spat it out, a big red spray on the white wall.

A horn honked outside—maybe the driver. He made as if to call out, but too much blood was in his mouth. He spat again, made a gurgling noise, then his mouth was full again and he had to spit once more, as if he were drowning in blood. He reached into his pockets for his phone with the one hand that seemed to still work. Both pockets were empty; the phone must have fallen out. He could hear it vibrating a short distance away. He thrust out his arms; one hit the banister, the other grazed the wall, but he could barely move as he feebly gargled out another bloody yell. His thoughts back-and-forthed between the profound and the mundane. He wondered how much his house would sell for, he wondered how his life might have been different had his son been healthy; and he wondered if, when he managed to stand, he would be able to get to the theater on time.

He held a distended hand up to his face: blood was smeared over the palm and fingertips. He was conscious of the theatricality of the gesture, yet did it anyway. He didn't doubt that he could find a way out; he would not die here; he understood how death worked: you fell to the ground, you moaned, your eyes fluttered, the stage went dark, but then the lights came back up. He would look back at this moment with a wry smile, tell the story to his new admirers in New York—the time he cheated death. Yet, his breaths were wheezy, his vision blurred, and he felt moved to write something on the wall in his blood, something that would make this moment seem important, not just pathetic. He could draw a swastika, make them think some Nazi had thrown him down the stairs; he could write someone's name—Declan, maybe, or Calvin or Franklin; fuck with them one more time. He could apologize for everything, or he could write that he'd done everything he'd been accused of and more, and he didn't regret any of it.

He spat again; the blood on the wall was darker this time. Everything looked dimmer, as if a bulb had blown. He had to keep trying to get to the bottom of the stairs, get to the phone. First, though, he'd write something on the wall, the word he loved to say more than any other. He heard the word in his mind before he started to trace it out with a finger; he imagined himself raising his hand high, then making a tight fist as he fiercely whispered: *"Blackout!"*

*

The party at Prairie Moon had been going for a half hour when Eileen decided to check up on Tyrus. It would have been completely in character for him to show up late, but she didn't like that his phone number was no longer in service. And besides, everything about Tyrusfest without Tyrus seemed lonely and lame—the WELCOME TO TYRUSFEST! banner and blue-and-white bunting; the gold and pink streamers; the bar; the buffet; the DJ table where "Eileen's Kick-Ass Playlist" was currently fading from "I'm Still Standing" to "I Will Survive."

The only people Eileen knew here were ones she couldn't stand. Declan was pacing the room, hands in the pockets of his salt-stained black overcoat. What was he doing here? Hadn't he said he would never come? Some of Tyrus's colleagues from the high school were on the scene, even though she was sure they would have fired Ty-Ty if he hadn't resigned. Franklin, all 145 pounds of weaseliness, was circulating, digging for dirt. She wanted to go all Sonny Corleone on him—call out, "Hey, c'mere," then spit on him, break his phone, and tell him to keep away from her fuckin' family. But Tyrus had told her not to turn anyone away—he had his own plans for all of them—so when Franklin tried to make phony small talk, she just told him she didn't speak to the "fake news media" and walked away.

The rest of the crowd consisted of theater-y people whom Eileen didn't recognize and didn't care to know: heavyset women and gay guys who weren't even cute or well dressed; kids who looked like they were just out of college, here only for the open bar and free snacks. And there was only so long she could talk to Sammy, watch him pump the air in front of his crotch and say "*Pfft, pfft, pfft*" and then show off pictures of his Maserati and his gorgeous kids and his hot Black wife.

"I'm gonna head to Ty-Ty's. Maybe he needs a ride," Eileen told Sammy.

Sammy leered at Eileen. "*Pfft, pfft, pfft,*" he said.

In her car, Eileen tried Tyrus again, got the out-of-service message, steered into traffic, and followed the path to the house she had visited so many times before. He always seemed annoyed to see her, but that was his charm. Tonight, when he opened the door, he would glare and ask why she was checking up on him, and she would say it was because Irish whores always made house calls, and he would laugh and let her hug him.

Tyrus's car wasn't in his driveway; his garage doors were shut, but there was a lot of light on in his hallway and front room. She rang his doorbell. When no one answered, she knocked. She texted Sammy: Ty there yet?

Nope, Sammy texted back. But the strippers are!

Eileen leaned hard on the doorbell, cupped her hands, looked in the door's window. There was a dark red splatter on the wall, a black shoe on the stairs that seemed attached to an ankle. She slapped the door with her palm, pressed the doorbell again. "Ty-Ty! Tice-A-Roni! Come on, it's Tyrusfest time!" She fumbled in her bag, got out her keys. So often they had joked about it. "I'll see you on Thanksgiving," she'd say. "You're not invited," Tyrus would respond. "I've got the key," she'd tell him. "I'm changing the locks," he'd say.

Eileen opened the door and started to yell "Tyrus!" but she couldn't even finish saying his name before she saw his body. It looked fake, like a scarecrow stuffed into a black overcoat, black shoes, gray socks. She wouldn't have thought it was real if it hadn't been for all the blood: splattered and smeared on the wall, where it looked like someone had started writing a *B*; dripping from the pale, gray hand frozen in the act of reaching for a suitcase. Why all these suitcases? Why so many boxes? The bottom part of a splintered walking stick lay in a puddle of blood. Her stomach heaved. Her hands and feet felt cold. "Tyrus!" Her voice trembled; her body shook. She didn't want to check for a pulse, didn't want to know for sure he was dead. "Ty-Ty!" She could see only the side of his face—so pale, as if whatever had made Tyrus had already bled out of him. She tried yanking him down the rest of the stairs, could barely budge him. She called 911. The dispatcher had an accent. "Christ," she said, "do you even speak English?"

She paced as she waited for the paramedics. She couldn't stay in the hallway with all the blood. There was no furniture in the living room; there were shelves in the den but nothing in them. She wanted a drink, but there was no more liquor cart, no more wine rack; the refrigerator and freezer were empty.

Sirens were approaching. An ambulance, two squad cars, and a fire truck drove up. Scarcely two minutes had passed since she had made the call, and she couldn't help but think how efficient the fire department was when it didn't matter. When Tim had collapsed in his office and she had called, it had taken fifteen minutes for those bastards to get there.

Across the street, she could see faces in windows, gawking. Disgusting. She rubbed her hands together, trying to warm them while she answered the police officers' questions and the paramedics went about their business with rote efficiency. They didn't even perform CPR. Two fire-fighters rolled a gurney to the front door and brought it inside.

An officer—TOUNSLEE on his nameplate—led her to the kitchen. No, she told him, she wasn't the wife, wasn't the daughter, just a friend. "It was supposed to be his night," she said. "It was supposed to be a party, not a wake." Tounslee gave her a Kleenex. She wiped her eyes and blew her nose. "It's their fault," she said.

"Whose?" Tounslee asked.

"Everybody's." She could picture the whole crowd at Tyrusfest: eating Ty-Ty's food, drinking Ty-Ty's champagne, tucking ten-dollar bills into the G-strings of Ty-Ty's strippers, none of them caring whether he showed up or not.

Eileen asked if she could ride along to the hospital in the ambulance or one of the officers' cars, but Tounslee said no, that was against protocol, although probably that was just bullshit: if she were some blonde, big-titted bimbo, he would have totally said yes. So she drove behind them, wishing all the while she had somebody, anybody, to call or talk to.

Her phone buzzed: Sammy. "What's the holdup?" he asked.

"The holdup? The holdup is he's fucking dead. Tell everyone to go home. I'm on my way to the hospital now." She hung up, didn't answer when Sammy called back, just followed the squad cars, wondering why they were so slow. Maybe because they were trying to revive him, more probably because there was no reason to rush.

God, she hated this place, she thought as she entered the emergency ward: lights too bright, sounds too loud, phones ringing, people babbling, babies crying, gurney wheels rolling, the clunk of a Coke can in the pop machine. It was hard not to think about the fact that everyone else here had a purpose; they had jobs, responsibilities. They had to greet people, talk on phones, type on their keyboards, mop floors, give directions, answer questions. Well, not everyone answered questions: when she asked the Mexican or Puerto Rican or whatever girl at reception about Tyrus, the girl said she couldn't tell Eileen anything; she wasn't family. That was such bullshit. Like being related to someone made you matter more. Like being someone's sister or daughter had ever done her any favors.

"Family?" she asked. "What does that even mean?" Maybe she should have said she was family. She could have been Tyrus's daughter, some niece. How would they even know? Maybe she should have said she was his second wife. Maybe she should have been his wife for real. Maybe she should have offered to marry Tyrus after Susan died; she preferred men twenty-five years younger to twenty-five years older, but that wouldn't have been the worst idea. She would have made him wear a rubber, maybe two at the same time, but she would have been there and he wouldn't have fallen. Or she could have saved him.

"What'm I supposed to do?" she asked. "Wait 'til his name's in the obituaries?"

"I'm sorry," the receptionist said. "I know this is hard."

"You don't know; don't pretend you do." Eileen walked toward the automatic doors. Pinned to a bulletin board was a flyer for Casa Segura in English and Spanish. WORRIED ABOUT YOUR IMMIGRATION STATUS? WE OFFER FREE JOB TRAINING, ESL CLASSES, AND ANONYMOUS MEDICAL CARE. That was so fucked-up: Where was Eileen's free medical care and job training? She was on a Cobra plan that cost more than $800 a month; she'd shelled out $750 for three career-coaching sessions with some pimply dumbass who was younger than Danny Cirillo and nowhere near as hot.

She got in her car, started it up. It was making more noise than usual, as if trying to clear its throat. The red CHECK ENGINE light was on, but all that meant was that the car was trying to convince her to spend another grand she didn't have—not while she was still unemployed and her mother was still at home. She drove fast, blasting the music her mother always told her to shut off, hoping the louder the music and the faster she drove, the better chance she'd have to obliterate every image assaulting her brain: Tyrus so gray; the blood on his hands, on the wall.

She drove past houses where she'd trick-or-treated, houses where she'd partied too hard, houses where everyone she had known was dead or gone. She passed the sites of razed restaurants where she'd waitressed, where she'd gone on dates with men, every one of whom was dead, married, or gross.

Outside Prairie Moon, she stopped the car. People were moving around inside, dancing. Someone, maybe Sammy, had his hands in the air and was swaying them this way then that. Had he not heard what she'd told him? She wanted to go right in, turn the lights up all the way, pull the cord out of the sound system, throw the food in the trash, tell everyone Tyrusfest was canceled and she'd see them all at the cemetery.

Instead, Eileen drove on. How many days would have to pass before the pain lifted? Would it ever? Did any of the people responsible for the state she was in have the slightest idea of what they had done? Declan, who had made those awful accusations? Franklin, who had printed them? Calvin, who had broadcast them to the world? The high school that had forced him out? If Tyrus had still had a job, that's where he would have been: in the Annex, alive, not dead in a house full of boxes and suitcases.

She passed the high school, then circled the block around it. On the marquee, ANNE FRANK AF, DIRECTED BY DR. JUDITH NAGORSKY. TICKETS $20. ALL PROCEEDS TO BENEFIT CASA SEGURA. Oh, fuck that. Not a word about Tyrus, as if he'd already been replaced and they'd forgotten him. Maybe she should go in and tell somebody what happened, she thought; maybe she should make some kind of announcement at intermission; maybe she should tell people where they shove their "proceeds."

She couldn't find a space in the lot, so she parked on Emerson Street and walked across the athletic field to the front doors.

No one was at the security desk; the hallways were empty. She walked past glass cases stuffed with trophies won by generations of students she had no connection to. Walls were full of photos of beaming National Honor Society members; half of them had names she couldn't pronounce. She took the stairs up to the Annex. She remembered running to get there on time, arms full of props. Now, when she reached the theater door, she had to stop and catch her breath.

She quietly opened the door, followed the glow tape to the nearest aisle. She stood at the back and looked out at the set: the Franks' secret Annex. What the fuck was this supposed to be? There was the tiny kitchen and dining room, the wooden stairs that led up to the bedrooms. But everything else was wrong. The cyclorama didn't look like Amsterdam; it looked like Texas and it had graffiti all over it. Half the actors weren't white. Anne's dad was Black, her mom was wearing some hijab sort of thing, and the girl who was supposed to be Miep was Japanese or Chinese. For a split second she was happy Tyrus wasn't alive to see this, because it probably would have killed him.

She walked out of the theater. There was still a pay phone in the hallway. She used to call her dad from that phone if rehearsal was running late. "Find a nice boy to drive you home," he'd tell her. Once, she'd checked the phone's change dispenser and found two crumpled twenty-dollar bills in it. She couldn't believe her luck, started to take the bills, until she realized Sammy must have been using the phone as a drug drop, so she left the money there.

Could this phone still be a drug drop? Hell, she could use some drugs right now. She'd never done one, not even a joint—and all for what? Here she was, fifty-two years old, no job, no husband, living with her mom, planning parties for people who died before she could make the first toast. And meanwhile, her brothers had wives and houses and children in Santa Clara and Scottsdale; and meanwhile, Tim's Pantsuit Mafia widow and her children owned the house that she thought would be hers; and meanwhile, Declan was married with a kid and Judith was married with two kids and Carrie was married with a kid and Franklin was married with two kids and Calvin was famous and rich as shit and Rob was married with kids *and* famous and rich as shit. Who would remember her? She had been there for Tyrus; who would be there for her?

Beyond that wall there was an auditorium full of people, all of whom had paid twenty dollars to get in, and where would all their "proceeds" be going? Not to the school, not to the neighborhood, certainly not to her. No, they would be going to people who took everything and contributed nothing.

Or maybe it didn't have to work that way.

Eileen knew that what she was about to do couldn't right every wrong, but she had to do it. And although she knew some people would think she was doing something insensitive, twisted, or severely fucked-up, she also knew that it was, in fact, justice. Did people really think they could just pretend the past hadn't happened? That the fifty years Tyrus taught here didn't matter? That you could just erase her life, her story, and replace her with new people who hadn't paid any of the dues she and her family had? She felt a calmness and clarity as she picked up the phone, punched in the numbers, and waited for someone to answer. In her mind, over and over, she said the phrase that still soothed her: *Fuck you, I voted for Trump. Fuck you, I voted for Trump.*

"Hello," she said. "I'd like to report a place that's sheltering illegal immigrant gangbangers. Yes, I'm standing outside and I can see them going in there right now. They have guns, they have knives. Yeah, you've gotta come quick; it's on Howard Street and it's called Casa Segura."

*

Ray Tounslee Jr.'s shift should have been over by now. The news trucks, ambulances, and squads were already gone. And although the police tape was still over the front door, nothing was really keeping Ray from taking it down. What had happened was obvious: an old man had fallen down the stairs, then lay there bleeding until he had died. In his own little world, he may have been a big man, but outside it, he looked the same as anyone else. Some people had wanted the man dead, no doubt— some people would have liked to see him in jail or court—but as far as justice was concerned, this would have to do. One thing Ray had always known about Lady Justice: her bitch ass never showed up on time.

Ray stood in the empty front room; all that remained of Tyrus Densmore were the suitcases, the boxes, the blood, and two parts of a cheap, broken old cane. When Ray was starting out at the police academy in Maywood, people told him he'd get used to it—the violence, the bodies. But there had never been that much to get used to. Nearly thirty years on the force, and you could almost count the number of bodies he'd seen on two hands and a foot: half in car crashes, one in a murder-suicide, and the rest in situations like this—a friend or neighbor knocking on a door, getting no answer, calling 911 and saying, "He isn't picking up his phone; I'm worried something might've happened."

Even on the big, bad streets of Evanston, he had spent most of his time handing out parking and speeding tickets and chasing down drunk drivers who'd I-bond themselves out before the night was through. He'd break up fights on el platforms, bum-rush panhandlers out of Dunkin Donuts, show up too late at domestic disturbances where wives didn't want to press charges and husbands said it was just a misunderstanding. Some of the other E-town officers—young bucks looking to make a reputation, older law-and-order types who liked to pretend they were at a big-city department—seemed to see more action than he did; they boasted of "stiffs" down at the morgue, "floaters" they'd pulled from the lake. But his approach to living on this side of the law had been more or less the same as the one he'd taken when he'd been on the other side of it: if you tried to stay out of trouble, ninety-nine times out of a hundred, you could.

Ray may have gone into this career with high-minded ideals of changing the way justice was meted out, making sure all people were treated equally. But at the end of the day, it was just another job, one with security and a good health plan. His mom had worked as a receptionist in City Hall, his dad had painted houses; his big sister coached volleyball. He wasn't sure if being a cop was any more demanding or useful than what they had done with their lives. His daughter was an undergrad at Syracuse; his son was in business school at Indiana; both were happy to hear from him whenever he called, but they didn't need him anymore. He could have retired two years ago, got his full pension, would do it now if he had something he wanted to do instead. He didn't need to be in this house; if someone had been waiting for him at home, he would have gone.

The boxes were in the living room—a dozen of them, six stacks two-high, sealed shut with packing tape, and addressed to Tyrus Densmore at a storage facility in Queens. He took out his tactical knife, slit open a box.

Manila file folders were arranged alphabetically with names and dates printed immaculately in black ink. He picked one out at random. Inside was a notebook with a pale orange cover; in the right-hand corner, the name of the student and a date: CELESTE BONILLA, SEPTEMBER–OCTOBER, 1977. At the center of the cover, the name of the show and the character Celeste had played: OUR TOWN, EMILY.

Ray opened the notebook: "October, 14, 1977: This will probably be the hardest part I'll ever have to play. Emily is so much like me. That's what makes it hard." Ray turned to another page: "Mr. D asked me and Kirk to come over to his house on Saturday so we can practice the kiss. I said we don't really need to because it's not like George and Emily would have had privacy in Grover's Corners anyway." Then a page toward the end of the journal: "I cried all through dinner last night. My dad asked what was wrong and I couldn't explain."

Almost every journal was achingly personal, something no one should have ever read, let alone demand someone write. Trey Newson said he feared his dad and brothers would murder him if they learned his girl-friend didn't exist; Judith Nagorsky wrote of coming home to find her living room window broken and her mother bloody and shivering on the couch; Todd Merritt wrote that he was spending his nights trying to "fuck away the cancer"; Amanda Wehner wrote that she was thinking of killing herself—"Powerfully written. More like this, please,"Densmore commented.

And almost as heartbreaking as any of this pain, depression, and self-doubt were the entries written by kids who thought they would have amounted to more. They had won none of the awards they imagined, never run for the political offices they claimed they would win, never ended up with the partners they thought they would.

The FIONA GRENFALL folder was one of the thinnest. On a white label on her notebook cover, she had printed her name and the one character she had played: MRS. VAN DAAN.

Ray was not a nostalgic man; you couldn't be if you wanted to do this job right. He didn't cut people breaks on DWIs because he'd gone to school or played semipro baseball with them, didn't return calls from his late wife's family when they asked him to "wipe their records clean," however that was supposed to work. But the moment he started to read Fiona's first entry, he felt transported back to a world it seemed he had only glimpsed: sunrises on Loyola Beach and long drives in a fresh-smelling car with leather seats and, thumping from the speakers, what-ever crazy-ass music Fiona listened to; a world that had shattered so suddenly one night so many years ago that, until this moment, Ray had not even felt sure it had actually existed.

"I am looking so forward to playing Mrs. Van Daan," Fiona had written. "Such a welcome relief to pretend to be someone well past her prime, who isn't being ogled and fussed over the whole time."

Ray sat on the floor reading Fiona's diary in the glow of the single naked bulb that lit up the gray walls, the buffed floors, the storage boxes atop it. He sought to be dispassionate, reading out of what he pretended was professional interest, but once he got to an entry midway through the diary, he couldn't anymore: "Crikey! I believe I have fallen in love."

It shouldn't have mattered. Thirty-five years later, who cared that a girl he had briefly dated, a fleeting relationship that led to a night more frightening than any he had ever experienced on the police force, had loved him? Was she even the same person she had been back then? Was he?

Still, for just a moment or two, Ray allowed himself to bask in the memory of someone he must have been in some other lifetime. He remembered walks by the lake, block parties in Rogers Park, long drives to Promontory Point.

But Ray knew how this story ended, and he went on reading with mounting dread.

"I thought I was born with the Midas touch," Fiona had written. "Turns out everything I touch turns to shit."

She had written of the tears she had shed after Ray got out of her car, knowing she might never see him again. She had thrown a party to distract herself, but that had turned to shit too: the "Guardian Angel" naked on the bed, that awful young man with a bloody nose, writhing with his hands between his legs. "That's what I do to people. I make teachers contemplate suicide when I reject them, make lovely young men get into fights and end up in police stations, pretend I don't realize when people love me, that I don't understand why I make them cry.

"I'm through with it all," she had concluded. "From here on in, I shall lead a solitary life. If I were appropriately credentialed, I would become a nun. Alas, I am not. So I'll spend my life in libraries and laboratories. I'll live in some impossibly remote landscape where I'll surround myself with animals, for though they may love me, they will never fall *in love* with me."

Ray held the notebook, pondering: *What if it hadn't happened the way that it had? What if he hadn't seen* Anne Frank *that particular night?* It was a useless line of thought, one he associated with the chumps he arrested. *What if they hadn't had that one last beer? What if they had just kept walking?*

Of course, he wouldn't have traded in the life he had led. He had loved his wife, had never really considered whether he had loved Fiona all those years ago, because, until now, it had never crossed his mind that she had loved him.

He walked out of the house and slipped under the police tape. It was a clear evening now, quiet. If this really were some "impossibly remote landscape," no doubt you would have been able to see every star. He looked briefly up at the starless sky, then stopped at the sound of something rustling.

His hand went down to his weapon. He held it as he strolled toward a bare sycamore tree. A man was leaning against it.

"Mr. Spengler," Ray said. "There's nothing for you here. Don't you think it's time you went home?"

Ray probably should have stayed longer, just to make sure Declan actually got back in his car and drove off. But there was a lot of chatter on Ray's radio. Something was happening down on Howard Street.

Anne Frank

C arrie had turned off her phone, so she didn't get the calls and texts
when they first started coming in from the clinic. Tonight she was
seeing her daughter in *Anne Frank AF*, and for once she wasn't worrying
about work. Kitty was right, Adrian too, even as combative as he could
be on the topic: for one evening, her patients and co-workers could get
along without her. What was the point of having people work for you
if you didn't let them do their jobs? With the hours she kept, she would
be lucky if she didn't wind up in a clinic herself.

In front of the high school, a WGN news truck was parked in a loading
zone and a reporter was interviewing one of about a dozen protesters
incensed because *AF* featured a multiracial cast and was apparently using
Anne Frank to criticize U.S. immigration policy. A rabbi held a small
prayer book; a kid, maybe fifteen, wearing a dark suit, a red tie, and an
American flag lapel pin, carried a handmade sign: IT'S A JEWISH THING;
YOU WOULDN'T UNDERSTAND.

"Clueless bastards," Adrian Weekes muttered to his wife.

Carrie tugged him into the school by the sleeve of his leather coat.
"Come on."

"Seriously," Adrian said. "Someone's gotta talk some sense into these
morons' heads."

"They have the right to protest," said Carrie.

"Yeah, they do." Adrian said. "And if they don't see the connection between what's happening now and what happened then, it's my right to call them a bunch of ignorant, xenophobic zealots who should be the first we load onto boxcars. You know, the best thing about *Hillary* losing the election?"—Adrian said "Hillary" like a swear word, uttered it with the same dripping contempt with which he said "neoliberal," "women's march," "Zionism," or "9/11"—"at least now all this bullshit is out in the open. There's no doubt anymore who the good and bad guys are."

When they got up to the Annex, Carrie found her place at the back of the line of students, parents, and faculty waiting to get into the theater, then noticed that Adrian wasn't standing beside her. He was leaning against the closed door of a classroom, fiddling with his phone. She walked over to him. "Didn't we say no phones tonight?" she asked.

"We said no phones for you; I'm not addicted to mine," said Adrian. "I just gotta deal with this last-minute bullshitty client thing. Go in; I'll catch up."

Carrie often found it strange, the way Adrian seemed to have little to do with his days, then suddenly after dinner and on weekends he would sneak away to field calls for Feng Over Function, his interior design business. But whenever she asked why his clients couldn't call during normal work hours, he'd get defensive and say she didn't understand how his job worked and he could just as easily ask why she worked twelve-hour days and never took vacations. Then Kitty would plead with them to stop arguing, so Carrie would just let it go. During the first years of their life together, Adrian had been so charming, thoughtful, and romantic that she figured marriage would be the one area in her life where she wouldn't have to work hard. Oh, well—at least he was still sweet to Kitty.

The thought that he might be having an affair did briefly enter her mind from time to time. But she couldn't understand how people with careers and families had the time for infidelity. Leave aside the question of the immorality of the act or the casual cruelty of it; she couldn't fathom the logistics. Like, where did affairs even happen—and how? And if her worst fears were right and she confronted him, where would that lead? Arguments, therapy, couples counseling, lawyers. The whole thing sounded so emotionally draining and time-consuming that she couldn't bear to think about it.

She excuse me'd and thank you'd her way into her row, unable to remember the last time she'd been in a theater. It wasn't so much that she felt immune or indifferent to art as much as she never allowed herself the time or space to stop and experience it: Kitty often said that the only song her mother knew was the theme to *All Things Considered*. There had been a time when Carrie went to movies and concerts with Adrian and Kitty, but the two of them got so annoyed with her checking her phone or leaving midway through that she let them just go on their own.

Carrie hadn't been in this particular auditorium for more than thirty years, but whatever had happened during that long-ago time when she was more or less the same age Kitty was now didn't occupy her thoughts for long. When you had so many things to think about—patient histories, management challenges, fundraising drives—it was easy to put off other unpleasant topics. Like the fact that Tyrus Densmore had taught here for more than three decades after she'd graduated and, no matter how many parents' associations and community boards Carrie had sat on, she'd never said a word about him. Like the fact that soon Kitty would be leaving home for college, and then it would just be her, Adrian, and the dog at home, and what would they have to talk about then?

Carrie was busily trying to shove that particular line of thought into the compartment where she relegated other topics she preferred to avoid when she saw a woman walking toward her, wearing a series of wraps, leggings, a black YOUR FUTURE IS FEMALE; MY PRESENT ALREADY IS T-shirt and pointy, paint-splattered, black shit-kicker boots that peeked out from underneath skirts and slips; there were so many layers, it was difficult to figure out exactly what her outfit was and what function each article of clothing was performing. The woman's jet-black hair, only a few tinselly strands of silver in it, was bunched atop her head in a loose bun held in place by chopsticks.

"If it isn't my sweet little Anne!" Judith said.

"Mom!" Carrie laughed, and the two women embraced.

As teenagers, they had always felt a little frightened around each other: to Carrie, Judith had been the epitome of bohemian cool and experience;

to Judith, Carrie had been a paragon of virtue and intelligence that she could never match. But now that they were adults and mothers of teenage girls, conversation was effortless, joyful, particularly for Carrie, who by now had pretty much forfeited the luxury of friendships.

"I can't wait for you to see your girl up there; she's a natural," Judith said, and Carrie knew this was probably true. In her youth, she had excelled at everything she tried, but only because she was so scared of failing that she spent as many hours as was necessary to make sure she succeeded. Whereas somehow Kitty was able to do all Carrie ever could plus more while watching *Black Mirror,* playing *Minecraft* on her phone, and sleeping until noon on weekends.

"Are your girls here tonight?" Carrie asked. Judith pointed them out, and there seemed to be an enviable effortlessness to them too: a pair of funky kids with dyed hair, wearing vintage dresses, bright, patterned tights, and sneakers, whispering to each other and giggling.

They made plans for after the show: Judith and her wife and kids were going out with the cast for pizza, and Carrie said of course she and Adrian would love to join.

"I'd say we should all go to Yesterday's like we used to, but Yesterday's closed down," Judith said. "How's that for symbolism?"

Carrie laughed freely. She kept smiling when she saw Adrian looking peeved as he entered their row, but her smile started to feel forced, as if she were trying to convince both Judith and herself that she could feel as relaxed when he was around as when he was elsewhere. Adrian gave Judith a perfunctory handshake but didn't say much, so Carrie talked up his business until it became obvious to her and probably to Judith that she was talking only to compensate for Adrian's negative energy. She wanted so much for others to see all the potential in the creative, unpretentious, and surprisingly shy man she was spending her life with, and felt disappointed when they didn't. If only Adrian could feng shui himself as easily as he could an office space.

Judith told Carrie it had been good to catch up, but the show was about to start and she was going up to the lighting booth to watch. "Your wife's a wonderful woman," she told Adrian. "You're lucky to have her."

"Everyone is," said Adrian.

At the back of the stage, the cyclorama faded into view, suggesting the wall the president wanted to build on the United States' southern border—black with red-white-and-blue graffiti spray-painted on it: AMERICA FIRST; COPS LIVES MATTER; MAKE AMERICA GREAT AGAIN. Over the PA system, the sounds of ambulances and helicopters were interspersed with bursts of speeches and radio broadcasts: Hitler at the Berlin Sportpalast; Mussolini declaring war on France and Great Britain; Trump on the campaign trail: "*Get 'em outta here; get 'em the hell outta here.*" Speeches, sirens, and bootsteps crescendoed; then the image on the cyclorama shifted, and everything looked the same but in German: MACH DEUTSCHLAND WIEDER GROSSARTIG.

Otto Frank and Miep Gies entered. He was a big kid in navy-blue slacks and a light-blue short-sleeved bus driver shirt with a CHICAGO TRANSIT AUTHORITY patch on one sleeve; she wore tight jeans, Converse sneakers, and a red Chicago Blackhawks jersey with GIES and the uniform number 1943 on it. She pulled the jersey over her head and he unbuttoned his shirt; they tossed them onto the floor with the rest of the clothes, then picked up their outfits—Mr. Frank, a white shirt and frayed dark suit jacket; Miep, a dowdy, loose-fitting gray dress. More actors entered, shedding street clothes then donning costumes, seeming to inhabit both present and past.

For Carrie, watching the actors enter and change was a little like watching a dream—not that she tended to remember her dreams. She was seeing something happening now and long ago, she knew these people and yet they were strangers, the story they were about to tell was unfamiliar yet one she knew by heart.

Could it be that Franklin was right after all? she wondered as the houselights dimmed. When he had suggested she had chosen her career because of what she had seen in the Annex, she told him he was being simplistic and presumptuous, but now she wasn't so sure. Why else did the angry voices spewing hate through the auditorium speakers fuse in her mind with the sound of Tyrus Densmore in this Annex—mocking, threatening, humiliating? And why else did the fear, anger, and weary resignation she saw on the faces of the actors as they took their places remind her of those same emotions she'd seen in her fellow actors on the last night they'd performed this play? And why did everyone up onstage remind her of someone she had cared for—a patient she had treated, a grieving family member she had tried to comfort, someone she wanted to speak up for because she remembered a time when she couldn't?

In fact, the only person who didn't seem entirely familiar was her own daughter.

Kitty was last to enter. A baby spotlight shone on her, sitting in her bed, writing in a diary as if she had been there all this while, as if she were always there—watching, writing.

"Things went well for us. Then the war came."

Carrie had been keeping herself together fairly well, but the moment she heard her daughter's voice, she shivered and started to sob. She had almost forgotten what crying felt like. Whenever she felt herself about to cry for someone she read about or saw in a movie, she reminded herself of all the patients she encountered every day, and if she cried for them, she would never be able to stop. She had learned to be stoic, to keep her eyes dry, her face immobile when patients told her of seeing friends murdered, families ripped apart, parents dying of diseases that should have been eradicated years ago.

But as she watched Kitty—twirling in a skirt, admiring herself in a mirror, fighting with Mrs. Van Daan over that stupid coat—she wept as she hadn't since she was a child. For she now understood that the way Kitty seemed up onstage—trapped, frightened, trying to hide her pain from her parents—must have been the way she felt at home sometimes, trying to make her mother believe that everything was all right so she could go off and save the world.

So much of the Kitty up onstage seemed truer than the one she knew—the angry outbursts, the impassioned sighs, the emotions Kitty felt but never let her see—the same way Carrie had kept her inner life secret from her own parents until that first semester at Stanford when her father visited her and saw how skinny she had gotten. "Do you get eight hours of sleep?" he asked shortly before he drove her to the health center. "You mean in a week?" Carrie asked.

Onstage, Mrs. Frank sent her husband to comfort Anne—*"It's you she wants!"*—then collapsed in tears.

Carrie could understand the pain Anne's mother felt—being so close to someone yet having no clue what they were feeling or thinking, knowing you might never be able to help. Any day the Nazis might break down your door and you'd never know any more than you did now; any day your daughter would leave home and you'd never have more answers than you already did.

She watched Anne up in the annex with Peter—Kitty with a boy half a foot shorter than her.

"Did you change your mind, the way I changed my mind about you?"

"Well—you'll see."

How often had Carrie and Franklin rehearsed that scene—backstage; in Franklin's family's apartment after she'd broken up with Declan; in the basement of Beth Shalom; up in her bedroom with her father tapping on the door every ten minutes: Did they want snacks? Something to drink? "No, Dad; no, it's fine, thanks." Carrie had come to think she understood Anne and Peter so well that, during the few months she and Franklin dated—before her father took her and the family to California for a year; before she went to Stanford and Franklin had gone off to Columbia; before she had served in the Peace Corps in Cameroon; before Carrie had come to believe that they would never wind up in the same place—she felt as if the spirits of Peter and Anne could live on within them. And after she had abandoned that dream, she thought their spirits could live on in Kitty in a perfect world she'd create for her, one built on trust and love.

When she learned that Kitty had been cast as Anne, she thought she might have actually succeeded. But now, watching her daughter—those mournful silences as eloquent as any words she spoke—she knew she was wrong. Who even was this girl? Was it too late for them to be as close as they once had been?

Anne and Peter leaned in as if to kiss, but they stopped before their lips touched. Two police officers in riot gear were pointing automatic weapons at them. Downstairs, the Franks and Van Daans had their hands in the air—Gestapo agents in black coats and boots were waiting.

Anne began to give her final speech, but she was soon drowned out by marching boots, by gunshots and sirens, by voices crackling over walkie-talkies. The actors onstage froze. They looked straight out at the audience. The stage lights burst on bright.

Carrie remembered the final moments of the *Anne Frank* she had starred in, how Densmore had made the characters' lives seem so utterly hopeless, as if they were locked inside a tragedy they would never escape. How trapped she had felt on the stage that last night—Densmore judging her, Declan watching her. When she first knew Declan, he had seemed like such a creative, vulnerable, funny, romantic kid until he became tortured, needy, and insecure—always having to touch her, always demanding reassurance. Back then, she had thought only how annoying all that was; she had been too young to step back and ask where Declan had learned to act that way and who had taught him. Yet the answer must have been somewhere in the back of her mind all along, there with all the other abuses she hadn't allowed herself to think about until Declan started talking about them and Franklin wrote about them for the *Tomorrow*. Why else had Carrie told her daughter that, of all the dangerous places in the world, this was the one where she wasn't allowed to go?

Still, in the image Judith had created—the Franks, the Van Daans, and the rest of the cast staring into the eyes of the audience as if they were all part of one family—there was a beauty and a sense of connection, of characters reaching out across time so that you could almost begin to feel the words that Anne turned around to spray-paint in phosphorescent white on the cyclorama: IN SPITE OF EVERYTHING, I STILL BELIEVE . . .

The lights dimmed slowly, and there was silence. Soon only the words remained, glowing in the dark.

The auditorium stayed that way—quiet and black—for a long time. And in that silence Carrie vowed that she would be more straightforward, more honest—would make sure that, no matter how busy she was, her daughter would come first. She started to wipe her tears—no, she thought as she stood to applaud while Adrian headed for the exit; no, she'd leave them there. Pretending she hadn't been crying was just another sort of lie.

But after the show, when Kitty walked out the backstage door into the Annex hallway with the rest of the cast, and Carrie ran to her, Kitty didn't seem to register her mother's tears. The fact that her mother had stayed for the whole show seemed even more confusing than the fact that she'd apparently been crying. "Why're you still here?" Kitty asked.

"Shouldn't I be?" asked Carrie.

"You haven't checked your phone?"

"No. It's been off the whole time. What's going on?"

"Check your phone," said Kitty.

"Whatever it is can wait. Dad and I are going out with you and the cast and Judith and the kids."

"Yeah, I don't think that's gonna be happening," Kitty said. "Check. Your. Phone."

Carried turned on her phone and looked at the display. "Oh, Jesus."

Kitty smiled, a blend of "Sorry" and "Told you so."

"How did you hear about this?" Carrie asked.

"From the news," said Kitty. "I got an alert."

Carrie looked at her daughter through new tears. "I'm sorry, Kit." She walked to the stairwell and scrolled through her alerts—eight missed calls and half a dozen texts, all from the clinic:

Carrie, can you give us a call over here? Don't mean to bug you on your night off.

Then: Hey, call us when you get this. This is seriously messed up.

And later: We need you down here, C.

The second-to-last message: R u ok?

Finally: ?

She called her voice mail. The messages were tough to hear—too many people walking by, chattering. She faced the wall, pressed her phone tight over one ear, the palm of her hand over the other. She could still make out only half of what was being said, and there were too many pronouns to understand completely: "They're here." "We're gonna have to get outta here." "Call us when you get this."

Kitty was still in the hallway, laughing with Judith's daughters. She looked happy in a way she rarely did at home. Carrie walked over to her. "I've gotta go," she said. "We'll have to do this some other time. Have you seen Dad?"

"Nope."

"When you see him, tell him I had to leave. You can explain why. I'll catch a Lyft or something and see you at home. I'm so sorry, Kit."

"It's fine, Mom. Obviously."

Carrie rushed downstairs, then outside. Adrian was standing by the car turnaround, talking to someone in a van. Carrie turned her back to him and called the clinic. Straight to voice mail. She called her office manager's direct number. Straight to voice mail too. She texted the managers' group chat—Be there in 20 minutes—then called for a car.

Adrian walked back toward the school entrance carrying a big bouquet of red, white, and pink roses. Carrie caught up to him as he was about to open the main door. "Why aren't you upstairs with the rest of them?" he asked.

"Something happened at the clinic," she said. "I'm not sure what. Someone called in a complaint to Homeland Security, there was a raid; it sounds like a nightmare. I called a car. They're all still going out. You should go with them. I'll be home when I can."

Adrian didn't seem to be processing. "What happened at the clinic?"

"It got raided," said Carrie.

Adrian's lips curled upward, the beginnings of a smile. It lasted for only a second. He stopped the moment he noticed Carrie noticing him doing it, but Carrie remained stuck in time, frozen at that smile.

"What?" Adrian asked.

Something told Carrie not to say what she was about to say. But then she thought: *Honest, straightforward, say what's on your mind.* "Did you?" she asked.

"Did I what?" Adrian was charming when you agreed with him, but when you challenged him or seemed to doubt his version of events, his face took on a belligerent, doltish aspect. "*Did I what?*"

"Call?"

"What call? Who?"

"The clinic."

"What?" Adrian had never been violent—he just got surly and snide—but you could tell when he wanted to hit someone or something, and that was almost as bad. "You think I would seriously do something like that?"

"I don't know what you would or wouldn't do anymore, Adrian. I have no idea what goes on in your mind. I have no idea what you do when I'm at work."

"Yeah, well, I could say the same thing about you."

"That's not remotely fair. This night was supposed to be about Kitty, and every time I turn around, you're off making some surreptitious phone call."

"Oh," said Adrian, eyes big and sarcastically earnest. "Do you wanna know who I was on the phone with?"

Carrie's phone vibrated. She checked her display: YOUR DRIVER, ZADIG, IS ALMOST HERE. GET READY TO MEET HIM.

"I happened to be talking to the florist, making sure Kitty's bouquet would get here. Which is something"—Adrian brandished the flowers—"that you, who thinks you're the only one who cares about your daughter, didn't think of."

Carrie's car pulled up. "You don't bring roses to a fucking Holocaust play!" she shouted. She got in the car, then slammed the door. She considered texting Adrian to apologize, but if she was being totally honest now, she wasn't all that sure she was sorry.

The car drove east, then turned north on Ridge, heading past the university facilities building that stood on the site of the old Tinkertoy factory. The driver had a French-language news station on; the announcer spoke too fast in an accent Carrie had trouble deciphering. She thought she heard the word "clinic." "What's he talking about?" Carrie asked.

"*La politique.*" The driver told her that the Haitian president was in Miami, reassuring immigrants in Little Haiti that they wouldn't lose their temporary protected status. It was a different story than the one Carrie thought it was, but still part of the same story. What was happening to America? Carrie barely recognized it. All the sights out her window were familiar—streets where she'd learned to drive, places where she'd taken Kitty to parties and soccer games, the nursing home where she'd visited her grandmother, and then her mother—but every day all the stories she heard insisted she was living in a world unlike the one she thought she knew. In spite of everything, she didn't know what she believed about this country anymore.

Casa Segura was on Howard Street across from the site of the old Wisdom Bridge Theatre. The clinic had been fashioned out of three adjoining storefronts that had once been a convenience store, a travel agency, and a pet groomer. As Carrie got out of the car, everything looked both right and wrong at the same time. On days the clinic was open, it was a bustle of activity: nurses and doctors coming in for their shifts, families arriving in groups, cars running their engines outside, neighborhood kids Scotch-taping posters for church carnivals in the window, thumbtacking them to the community bulletin board. On closed days, it was desolate: drawn blinds, locked grate over the door, kids or old people peering in, trying to see if anyone was there.

Today, the lights were bright, but nothing seemed to be going on. Whatever had happened was already done. Carrie keyed in the entry code and opened the door. No one at the front desk or waiting on the benches; no one in the classrooms or examination rooms. At the reception desk, there was a pad of paper on a clipboard—phone numbers and scrawled signatures; they stopped abruptly at eight forty-five P.M. Cheery signs on the walls printed in half a dozen languages seemed sad and ironic: WE WELCOME REFUGEES HERE.

"Dr. Caroline."

"Inez, what happened?"

A stout nurse in gray scrubs, her hair long and black with little puffs of white in it, ran to Carrie. Usually, Carrie shook hands with her colleagues. Tonight, she and Inez embraced.

"What happened?" Carrie asked.

"It was insanity," said Inez. "Mayhem. Everything."

"What?"

"All at once it happened. We had so many people here, I don't know why so many people. The line, it went onto the sidewalk; maybe because the weather's been better. Then out of nowhere—"

"The raid," said Carrie.

"*Precisamente.*"

Inez held Carrie's hands as she described what had happened—a seemingly normal evening interrupted by armed men in black vests, helmets, and military gear blocking entrances and exits, forcing their way into rooms, flashing emergency warrants, questioning people, rifling through papers. *Why were they here?* They'd gotten a call. *A call from whom?* They couldn't say. *What about a lawyer?* They could sort that all out downtown: "*Come on, let's get moving, we're wasting time.*"

"Where's everyone now?" Carrie asked.

"The processing center. Congress Street."

"I'll head down. Can you close up?"

"Not yet, Dr. Caroline," said Inez. "We have another problem to deal with first."

Inez shut off lights until only the emergency halogens were on. She cocked her head towards the hallway, beckoning Carrie to follow. Past the empty rooms, a door was marked DANGER. ELECTRICAL. NO ADMITTANCE. Inez opened the door, revealing a small windowless room: white walls, concrete floor, fuse box, computer server, a slatted grate where a window might have been, warm air wheezing in from outside—the scent of fried food and something that smelled like suntan oil. There were two pale orange plastic chairs; sitting on one with her feet up on the other was a girl about Kitty's age with frizzy black hair and frosted blonde tips. She wore tight, faded jeans, red socks, and a dark blue denim jacket over a pink T-shirt—on it, a photograph of some pop star Carrie didn't know.

"How long've you been here?" Carrie asked the girl, whose eyes flitted from side to side as if she weren't used to focusing on anything stationary. She mumbled something to Inez, who said something back.

"Not long," Inez told Carrie. "After everyone was gone, I opened the door and found her in here. She looks at me; she asks, 'Is it safe now?' What do I say to her? 'Is it safe now?' Will it ever be? Who can say?"

The girl's name was Eleonora Acevedo. She came from Guatemala, Inez said, then told Carrie her story: the family sugarcane farm that went bust after a rival family burnt it down; the move to Guatemala City, where her brothers got caught up with a rough crowd; the dad who gave her money to go to America, where she could stay with cousins in Urbana, Illinois. The girl had taken a bus to the Suchiate River, then waded across into Mexico, caught rides that got her from Tapachula to the border, then a raft across the Rio Grande. Dogs had chased her through tall grass until she got to a highway. Hitchhiking, walking, sleeping wherever she could, she had found her way to Illinois, where she worked for nearly a year cleaning hotel rooms until her cousins told her that America was different now: having her live with them had become too much of a risk; maybe she should go to Chicago and apply for asylum there.

"This is only the second night she's been in the city. She can't stay here all night. She needs a place. Can you think of somewhere?" Inez asked. "I wish I could do it. But my mother, she always needs help, and so many people are there, going in, going out, and I don't know who half of them are. Do you know some place? Somebody? At least until we find her a lawyer?"

The answer was obvious. So was its rejoinder. The answer should have been that Carrie herself could do it. Wasn't that exactly what the play she'd seen tonight should have told her to do? Wasn't that the exact sort of answer she had been taught to give even before *Anne Frank* back in high school, when she was tutoring Hebrew school kids? Wasn't that the philosophy she had based her entire career on?: Welcome the stranger, ask no questions. Wasn't that why she had spent those years in Cameroon? Wasn't that why she had taken a year off med school to volunteer for the Red Cross—why she had quit her job at Rush-Presbyterian to found Casa Segura with fifty thousand dollars of her own money that she still hadn't told Adrian about because she knew he'd flip out? Of course she should tell Inez and Eleonora yes.

But of course she couldn't. Because she couldn't rule out the possibility that Adrian had made that call tonight. And even though he denied it, she could no longer say for sure that her husband hadn't become that sort of person or that his anger at being accused wouldn't turn him into one.

"I think I know someone who might be able to help." Carrie stepped out into the dark reception area and took out her phone. She looked out onto Howard Street. A police car was parked across the way.

"Yeah, hey, what's going on?" Franklin asked. The phone connection was bad. There was crackling in the background, something that sounded like sirens, then a gust—wind, maybe.

"Frank?"

"Carrie? I can barely hear you. Where are you?"

"The clinic."

"Can I call you right back?"

"Can you make it *really* right back?"

"One minute."

Carrie held her phone in her palm. She turned the ring volume all the way up, briefly worrying that Franklin wouldn't call back, but he was the only person she knew who was as reliable as she was: a minute meant a minute, no more.

"Hey, what's up?" Franklin's voice was softer on the phone now but clearer; it sounded like he was in a car.

"Where are you?"

"You probably wouldn't believe me if I told you."

"Where?"

"In front of Tyrus Densmore's house. He's dead, and someone tried to set his place on fire."

*

Franklin entered Casa Segura in a flurry, a dead ringer for his rumpled father: shaggy hair bouncing, collar of his slate-colored shirt askew, old paint splatters on his blue jeans and boots. He kissed Carrie lightly on the lips.

"You smell like smoke," Carrie said.

"Yeah. Sorry about that." He told her about Densmore, the accident, and then the fire.

"Do they know who set it?" Carrie asked.

Franklin didn't say anything.

"Do they think it might have been—" She stopped, unable to bring herself to say Declan's name.

"It's kinda looking that way," said Franklin.

"That poor, tortured soul." She took a deep breath. "I don't think I have room in my brain to think about that now. C'mon." She took Franklin's hand and led him to the electrical room where Inez was sitting with Eleonora.

"He is your husband?" Eleonora asked.

"No," said Carrie. "Just a good, good friend."

"We better get going," Franklin said. "I doubt anyone'll come back here tonight, but why risk it?" He spoke to Eleonora slowly and clearly in both English and Spanish. "I'm a journalist," he said. "And I might write about you and what happened tonight. That okay?"

Eleonora nodded. The idea seemed to perk her up, as if talking to an American reporter was something like being a movie star.

"We can take my car," Franklin said.

"I just need to help finish up here first," said Carrie.

Franklin held up a hand. "Five minutes?"

"At most."

Carrie helped Inez close up and turn on the alarms, then met Franklin and Eleonora in his Toyota. During the intervening time, it seemed as though Eleonora had recounted her entire autobiography. Franklin had always had that effect on people—made you feel not only that your story mattered but that by talking to him it would matter more.

They drove to a Bakers Square and sat in a booth where Franklin ordered cheesecake and black coffee; Eleonora, a Coke, fries, and a cheeseburger; Carrie, just jasmine tea.

"You can take it easy," Franklin told Eleonora. "Odds are you'll be okay for now. This is a 'sanctuary city,' and they're not gonna track everyone down even if they want to. You got forty million undocu-menteds in the country and more in Chicago than anyplace outside New York or L.A. Most people here, everyday people, they're on your side, and when they hear what happened tonight, there'll be an outcry like you wouldn't believe." He handed her a small black notebook and a pen. "If anything ever comes to mind, anything you think I should know, you can write it in here."

"You really think you can write about this?" Carrie asked Franklin.

"Don't you think I should?"

"Will they let you?" The last time Carrie and Franklin had talked about his job, he seemed desperate: his stories didn't get enough clicks, but he couldn't live with himself when he tried to write stories that did.

"Nah, my boss told me I'm 'golden' now," Franklin said. "Ever since Cal tweeted that story I wrote about Densmore, I keep getting more and more followers. A million people follow me on Twitter and Instagram, and I can't even figure out how Instagram works or what I'm supposed to use it for. I just got a raise." He took out his iPad and scrolled to a page on it. "You know all about the sanctuary movement, right?"

"Sure." Carrie knew that a few of her clinic's patients were staying in church basements and rectories while they waited for asylum hearings. She didn't know many details, though. Part of the point of the way her clinic operated was that they asked only for as much information as they needed, didn't check IDs, didn't know anyone's story unless someone wanted to tell it.

Franklin swiped his iPad screen. On it was a list of names, places, phone numbers, and email addresses. "It's a whole network," he said. "Like a new underground railroad. Priests, rabbis, imams, people like you and me, they're opening their doors, talking in coded group chats, burner phones, all that whatnot. Half the people on this list, I'd trust 'em with my kids, probably trust 'em as much as you or me."

Carrie scanned the list. Halfway down, she felt a warm rush of recognition—the same lovely feeling she got when she saw someone she'd missed for a long time.

"I forgot he's still there," Carrie said.

*

The framed news clippings and photos on the wall of Jeremy Horvath's study in Beth Shalom narrated the rabbi's history: Horvath, hands locked with those of other protesters behind a NO NUKES banner; Horvath shaking hands with Senator Tom Hayden; Horvath at a Season for Concern candlelight AIDS vigil; Horvath at a fundraiser, embracing state senator Barack Obama; Horvath with a group of pastors touring the wreckage in Gaza; Horvath and his husband holding hands as they walked down the steps of the U.S. Capitol.

At Beth Shalom, Horvath had always been the cool rabbi, the one nearly all the girls had crushes on, the one who spoke with a hot New York accent, drove a Dune Buggy, talked about the years he'd spent on a kibbutz, and, at school assemblies, interspersed "Maoz Tzur" and "Ocho Candelas" with songs by Carole King and Jackson Browne.

Now Horvath's silver beard was perfectly coiffed, his silver hair expensively groomed. With his deep-red collarless shirt with silver buttons, tight black jeans with silver snaps, boots with silver buckles, and small silver hoop earring, he suggested more hip Spanish priest than veteran suburban rabbi as he set about converting his study into living quarters for Eleonora. He drew the drapes, pulled the couch into a bed, wiped the refrigerator and two-burner stove. He led Eleonora into the sanctuary, dark save for the orange Eternal Light that had been flickering over the pulpit three and a half decades ago when Carrie had first brought Franklin here. "You can pray to any God you want," Horvath told Eleonora. "This is a safe space."

They stayed for nearly an hour, discussing how long Eleonora could stay, how Carrie and Franklin could come by to take her shopping or go outside with her when she felt like taking a walk, how Horvath could raise money for her from his congregation. But Carrie's mind kept returning to those words the rabbi had spoken in the sanctuary: "a safe space." The phrase and concept seemed so easy to grasp yet harder and harder to find. When she was a child, her house had seemed safe—even when her sister had a fit or her mother berated her. But then, sometime in high school, maybe because she was past the age where she ignored the arguments her parents had behind closed doors, maybe because she had felt herself growing older and seen her mother and father growing old, she felt safest elsewhere—in the Annex until Declan and Mr. Densmore had ruined it; with Franklin at his home or in this place until they went their separate ways; with Adrian and Kitty in the house her parents had bought for them—until she came to believe that anyplace that felt safe wouldn't feel that way for long. Like the Annex where the Franks and Van Daans lived until the Nazis arrived. Like the theater tonight after the final blackout until the lights came back up. Like America until she realized it wasn't the place she thought it had been and maybe never was. The idea for Casa Segura had been that it would be safe too.

She held in her tears when she was in the synagogue, but the moment after she left Eleonora with the rabbi and got into Franklin's car, she lost it. It was a dry night, but she squinted as if the windshield were spattered with rain. She told Franklin everything: about her arguments with Adrian; her suspicions that maybe he was seeing someone else; her fears that she had neglected her daughter, and that Kitty was happiest when she wasn't at home. She told him about the play, the calls, the texts; about the moment she got to the clinic and knew there was no such thing as a safe place.

"You know I'm here for you anytime," Franklin told her.

"That's not a place," she said.

Franklin held her hand as he drove, interlaced his fingers with hers but didn't say anything. It was an odd, familiar ballet the two of them had started performing years earlier when one or the other was with a new partner, or both were: they would hold hands but wouldn't acknowledge they were doing it, kiss without looking the other directly in the eye, stop without either telling the other they needed to stop, as if both of them sensed that remaining silent would confine their feelings to a different realm, one more closely aligned with a world they dreamed as opposed to the one in which they lived. Once you talked about it, it wouldn't be safe anymore.

The porch lights were on when they got back to Carrie's house, but the driveway was empty and the only lights on in the house were the ones she'd turned on before she and Adrian left. Adrian hadn't come home; maybe he was still out with Kitty, Judith, and the rest of them. She hoped they were having a good time.

"Do you want to come in for a bit?" Carrie asked. "I have to check in with everyone downtown and walk the dog, but no one's home and it's quiet. Coffee or something? Have you had dinner?"

She liked the idea that helping Eleonora would give her and Franklin a reason to talk and spend more time together. It felt a little like fulfilling the promise of the roles they'd once played. Ty Densmore was gone; the Franks and the Van Daans were dead. The world was full of new Anne Franks. If Anne and Peter had survived, wouldn't they have devoted their lives to people in situations like theirs?

Franklin took a long time before he answered. "I'd really like to, but I should probably get back," he said. "A lot happened tonight. I gotta write it all down and get it posted to the site while it's still fresh. Let's talk tomorrow."

"Okay." Carrie kissed him. "Tomorrow."

She got out of the car. Franklin waited until he saw she was safely inside. Then he drove home to write while Carrie turned on the lights in her kitchen, where there was only a dog to greet her.

Margo Frank

It was the op-ed that changed her mind. Up until Asya Loh read the essay Rob Rubicoff published in the *New York Times*, she had been phenomenally successful at staying as far away as possible from her hometown and the life she had led there. On family road trips with her husband and kids, she had driven around Illinois; she vetoed any plane trip if there was a transfer at O'Hare. Asya didn't even like riding on planes that flew over Chicago. On the few occasions she did, she imagined doomsday scenarios: the plane losing power, making an emergency landing; she would have to rush the cockpit like Mikhail Baryshnikov in *White Nights*, a movie she had watched five zillion times with Laurence when they'd first started going out. Whenever she and Laurence got lost or missed a highway exit, they quoted that scene: "*Vhat do you mean? Ve are landink in Russia?!*"

Asya had just returned from her morning dog walk down to the creek. Laurence was already awake and dressed, wearing the olive-green cardigan she'd bought him last Christmas. He was sitting on the back deck beneath the hummingbird feeder, sighing as he read the newspaper.

Asya unleashed the dogs and poured food into their bowls. "What're you reading, pal?"

"God, this Rubicoff guy." Laurence retied his ponytail. "He was the creep from your high school with the bad acne and the Mercedes and so forth, right?"

"Yep, you got it." It was always stunning to Asya, the way Laurence applied the same attention to detail to her life as he did to his lectures on cinema. He only had to see a movie once to recount its entire plot and quote dialogue from it. The same was true for her past, which he referenced as if it had been a film they'd seen together and he'd paid more attention to: "The obituary for this teacher guy—he's the pederast who wore those turtlenecks and directed you in *Anne Frank*?" Or: "The fellow who wrote this story about this Guatemalan girl hiding in Chicago—he left those messages you didn't return, right?" And: "That crazy cult they're doing a documentary on—that was the one your mother was in for a few years, wasn't it?"

It was oddly comforting, the way Laurence spoke of her past as if all that had happened to her meant no more or less than if it had happened to a character in a movie.

Asya sat beside Laurence, took his newspaper, and scanned the essay Rob had written. She felt a brief tightening in her chest, but she had seen his name in the news often enough that it was no longer surprising. Rob had done everything in his life that Asya might have expected short of ending up in a white-collar penitentiary. He'd gone from Carleton to Georgetown Law, dropped out and gone to business school. After that, his career was, to Asya, a haphazard series of articles Laurence gave her and she glanced at, of talk show appearances that Laurence called her in to watch and she walked away from, of books with provocative titles displayed prominently on the tables she tended to avoid when she was at Barnes & Noble: *The Case for World War IV*; *Why Torture Works*; *The Myth of Campus Rape*.

This piece challenged the unwritten rule against arresting undocumented immigrants in houses of worship. The sanctuary movement was "blasphemous and ludicrous" and "made a mockery of faith itself," wrote Rob, identified as "executive director of DC Consulting and a former speechwriter for George W. Bush." He name-checked the case of

Eleonora Acevedo, awaiting a hearing on her asylum case while holed up in the synagogue he went to as a kid.

"Enough is enough," Rob wrote. "What we need here are 'shock and awe' tactics. Let's move in coordinated fashion on any place of worship suspected of sheltering illegals. Will there be bad press? Of course. But the results will be worth it: Illegal immigrants will no longer see America as their 'safe space.'"

Asya felt triggered. But it wasn't quite a "This Is the Guy Who Abused Me Back in High School" triggering as much as it was a "This Is One of the Millions of Guys on This Planet Who Hold Appalling Views" triggering, an all-too-familiar "Here's a Rich White Guy Getting a Platform for Writing Something Triggering" triggering.

She handed back Laurence's newspaper. "I'm not even sure why I read that whole thing," she said. "He's just some gross troll. It's not like he's got the power to do what he's talking about anyway."

"If only." Laurence refolded the newspaper so that the front page was visible and flicked a finger at an article: LONGTIME WASHINGTON INSIDER TIPPED FOR IMMIGRATION CZAR POST. There was a color picture of Rob in a suit and tie, looking a little paunchier than Amanda remembered, but the smug smile was the same.

Most days, she drove Laurence to campus and they drank tea together in his office before her first sessions, but today she didn't suggest it; she felt as though she might vomit. "Fuck, I don't have time to talk about this now, Laurie," she said. "I've gotta get to the studio; I don't wanna be late."

She thought the ache in her gut would go away, but it stayed there for days. Normally, she could roll with whatever was troubling her; she'd brood about the world's injustices, but only for a short time, because there were physical therapy sessions to lead, yoga or hip-hop classes to teach, dogs to walk, laundry to do, a grandson to babysit. This time the thoughts were as relentless as they had been after one of her inconclusive biopsy diagnoses during the previous year's cancer scare; they pursued her whether she was asleep or awake. She imagined people trapped inside churches, huddled together as ICE agents kicked down their doors, Rob bossing them around, telling them how to do it.

Images and memories strobed before her, a mixture of past and premonition. A girl alone with family, friends, and a boy she longed to kiss, then boot steps just outside their door: Was that something that happened to her sister in a show, something that would happen again in the future, or something that just happened over and over? A girl, dazed and dizzy, waking up to a hand between her legs, a flash burst in her eyes as she punched and kicked. Had that happened, would it happen, or was it just always happening? A girl alone in an empty sanctuary, her face illuminated by the dim orange glow of the Eternal Light—was that face from a photograph in an article she read or from a memory of the Annex?

The visions haunted her on her walks with her dogs and without them; in her classes and sessions where she'd lose track of time; at the Citgo station where she tried to fill up a tank that already had plenty of gas in it; in bed with Laurence, who touched her and said something felt different and asked if anything was wrong. "No," she told him, "just the state of the world," and Laurence smiled and said, "Ahh, well, if it's only *that*."

One night she woke up screaming, screamed until Laurence held her and she remembered she was safe. The dream hadn't been one of the recurring nightmares she'd had since she was a child: alone in a room full of mannequin heads spinning round and round, and each time they came full circle, there was a different face. And it wasn't one of her other nightmares that was so literal it wasn't worth bothering to interpret: lying on a stage, unable to move, while Rob and Declan marched toward her in storm troopers' uniforms.

In this dream, her children were little again. She was holding their hands and walking them down to the creek. But when she got to the water, she noticed her hands were empty. Misha and Ginger weren't there; they were across the water, staring back at her—not angrily or pleadingly, just wondering why she was on the other side. Then the water began to rise. When it was up to her waist, she screamed.

The dream could have signified anything. Or nothing at all. But when she told Laurence about it and he asked her what she thought it meant, she said that the children made her think of people she could save, if only she could cross the water before it drowned her. And what was the water? asked Laurence. The past, she said, a barrier that would grow harder to overcome the longer she waited.

"Are you sure you want to dredge all this back up?" Laurence asked as he lay beside her.

"I think I have to try," said Asya.

The next morning Laurence walked the dogs, and Asya took a long walk by herself. She went to the creek, called the main number for the Department of Justice in Washington, and found herself tangled in the branches of a phone tree: "If you know your party's extension, please enter it now."

Asya didn't have a clue who she should talk to, so she hung up. She took a breath. Felt dizzy. She walked to a tree stump, sat on it, listened to the ripple of the creek. She scrolled through the missed calls on her phone. The call she was looking for had come in months ago, but she recognized the number—it was the only one with a Chicago area code.

"Hello?"

She forced herself not to hang up. She thought of kids in detention centers. Of Anne and Peter freezing at the sound of Nazi boots. Of Rob undressing her, then leaving her alone until Declan became an unwitting accomplice in his cruel plot. You couldn't give power to a guy like Rob; people had to know what kind of person he was.

"Frank Lichtenstein?"

"Yeah, who's this?"

She said her name, and he seemed to already know why she was calling. "Oh, hey, Asya, good to hear your voice," he said, then: "Lemme close the door here and get some privacy so we can have a conversation."

Franklin tried small talk, didn't get very far with it; she thought he sounded kind of smarmy. "Wow, been a long time hasn't it?" he said. "You takin' good care of yourself?"

"Yeah, I'm good."

"You got kids?"

"Two. They're adults, but yeah."

"Two's a good number. And you're still chillin' in Colorado, right?"

"Yeah. Colorado."

"Beautiful part of the country. You ever talk to anyone from, you know, back in the day?"

"I don't."

"Hey, I actually saw Carrie just this morning."

"Carrie, yeah, she was a nice kid."

"Do you want me to tell her you said hey?"

"Nah, that's all right."

"She's got a daughter who's starting up at U of C."

"Nice."

"She's having some problems. Marriage can be harsh, man. It's not really a natural state."

"Yeah. It doesn't work out for everybody."

"So," Franklin said, "I'm gonna record our conversation so I can remember everything we talk about without writing it all down, okay?"

There was a breeze, and it was cool enough for Asya to wonder if she should have worn a sweater, but the phone was hot against her ear. "Wait, you wanna record this?"

"Just so I can be accurate."

"Hold on," said Asya. "Are you gonna use my name? I just called because I wanted to say some things about Rob that I think are important if they're really serious about him getting this job, but if you're gonna quote me, no way can you use my name. I have children; I have a grandson. They don't know anything about this."

Franklin sounded smooth, unconcerned. "Yeah, well, why don't we do it this way? I tell most people I never do interviews off the record, but since we know each other—"

"I don't really remember you, honestly," Asya said.

"That's fine," said Franklin. "We can record, then later we can decide where, if anywhere, we go from there."

"But no name," Asya said.

"No name for now," said Franklin.

"No name," Asya said.

"Okay, so tell me what you wanna tell me."

Asya started slowly, but Franklin drew her out—not by what he said as much as by his silences, which she felt she had to fill before saying, "That's off the record," or "That part's *really* off the record."

"Does that mean the other stuff's on the record?" Franklin asked.

"No," she said. "It's all off the record."

When she spoke of her old life, it seemed more depressing than she had thought it was while she was living it: coming back to her dad's condo and finding no one home every night; forging her mother's signature on permission slips; a little girl in her tap class telling her, "When I grow up, I wanna be just like you," and her thinking, *No, kid; no, really, you don't.* Although she had tried to put all this out of her mind for three and a half decades, apparently it was just below the surface: her dad with his waitresses; the baggies of weed on the coffee table beside used Kleenexes and stubbed-out cigarettes; her mom in California with her hairy boyfriends; the long afternoons at Baba Asya's house, listening to her tell stories about surviving the famine, until Baba Asya wasn't there anymore. She talked of walking from car to car on the Howard–Englewood el line—waiting for the end to come so at least she'd know where she was.

"And then Rob . . . ," said Asya. "Off the record."

"For now," said Franklin.

"Yeah, for now."

"He was your boyfriend for a while?"

"Kinda sorta."

"You loved him?"

Asya spat out a laugh. "Fuck no."

"But you had to like him at least a bit, no?"

"I don't even know that," said Asya. "I mean, I guess, maybe. But it's almost like the point was I was waiting for someone to step in and tell me to stop all the shit I was doing, just to prove to myself that there wasn't any person who'd do that—that I was really on my own."

"I wish I knew you better then," said Franklin.

No response.

"Okay," Franklin said. "Tell me about Rob."

Asya stared past the trees to the mountains. Way out there, it looked like a warm summer day, but here she could see her breath. "You have to understand something," she said. "I'm a very private person. I'm private about who I am now, and I'm private about who I was then. I don't want this to become something that takes over my whole life. That's why I'm so serious about not using my name."

Franklin sighed.

"What?"

"You know," Franklin said. "I don't know if I should even tell you this, and if you wanna hang up after I say what I wanna say, I'd totally get it. But look—we can do this however you want: quotes, no quotes, names, no names, pseudonyms, whatever kinda whatnot you decide. It won't matter. There's no privacy anymore; that's all been shot to hell. Everything catches up, whatever you did; if you were a Nazi criminal or just someone who made a mistake when you were a kid, it all comes back. When we were at North Shore, people were always like, 'This'll go on your permanent record.' No one realized that'd turn out to be a thing. As soon as I publish anything you say—even if Rob doesn't come after you, and he probably will—people'll try to figure out who you are, doxx you, all that kinda whatnot. Chances are they'll do it too. I found your number, and I'm only one guy, and I don't have anywhere near the resources they'll bring."

"So here's what I think we should do," said Franklin. "Are you there?"

"Yeah. I'm here."

"'There's really only one way to tell your story and to have it make any impact. And that's on the record. With real names. I can fly you out to Chicago. You can tell me everything exactly how you want so no one else'll tell it for you. We'll do pictures, and your story will be out in the open. Or, you can tell me to fuck off and just hang up right now." He waited for her to say something.

"Hello?" he said.

"No fuckin' way am I flying to Chicago," said Asya.

She looked out at Colorado: mountaintops haloed by clouds, sunlight on green water. She let the cool air fill her lungs. She held it in for a moment or two, then let it out. If she had been born here, it might not have meant as much, but Colorado would always feel like freedom to her. No matter what happened, she would have this view, one that all the Franks, Van Daans, and Acevedos in the world might never be lucky enough to have.

"No," she said. "If that's really how we have to do it, you'll have to come here."

*

She decided she would do the interview right in the sunken living room of her house. Originally, she had suggested a coffee shop off US 36 where no one she knew would overhear. But in the end she decided Franklin was right: anyone would be able to figure out who she was, so she might as well act as if they already did.

Franklin said there would be pictures, so she dressed for the interview: a gray RESIST T-shirt with a fist on it, worn over a black sweatshirt; a pair of silver wind chime earrings she had bought on a Hopi reservation during a road trip with the family when her kids were little. She made tea and egg salad sandwiches, turned on jazz on KCPR. Laurence had offered to cancel his lecture and join her for the interview, but she didn't want to worry about him worrying about her, so she told him she'd call if she needed him. Ditto for Misha and Ginger, who had their own lives and didn't need to be bothered.

A silver rental car pulled into the driveway. Asya stepped out onto the front stoop and surveyed her garden. Her dad, the onetime hippie who lately had gone full-on Trump, had told her it was too wild the last time he visited. But Asya liked it this way: goldenrod and cornflowers hiding in the tall grass, black raspberries growing here and there, pints and pints if you knew where to look.

Franklin wore wrinkled jeans, an untucked black T-shirt, and boots, a military green messenger bag over a shoulder. He looked awkwardly concerned, like someone paying a condolence call to a stranger. He loped toward Asya, arms open as if he'd been planning to give her a hug, which seemed pretty clueless to her. She held out a hand: "I'm Mrs. Loh," she said. He shook her hand firmly: "Frank Lichtenstein."

"I thought you said there'd be a photographer."

Franklin tilted his head as if to comment sardonically about the state of his industry. He waved a cell phone at her. "That's me," he said. "I'm a one-stop shop."

Just about everyone else who visited Asya got a tour of her house, but Franklin had to ask, and even when they got to the rooms, she stood with Franklin outside them, like a museum guide making sure tourists didn't go beyond the red rope.

"You know," Franklin said, inspecting the books in the study, "back in high school, I was a little scared of you."

"You were supposed to be."

"Yeah, you were pretty badass. Those concert jerseys, that beret, and that Guardian Angels jacket. Was that for real? Or were you just knocking around with all that?"

"I never did things that weren't for real," she said.

"You wanted to protect people."

"I guess."

Franklin laughed lightly. "Old habits."

They sat down at the living room table. Asya poured tea, and Franklin helped himself to a sandwich.

"The only reason I'm even talking to you is because maybe it could help somebody if people find out who this guy really is," said Asya.

"You're talking about Rob?"

"Uh-huh."

"Tell me what it was like being with him back then."

"Well, if I'm being honest, it was actually pretty fun at first," Asya said. "It was sort of liberating, being around a total asshole—especially when you thought you were kind of an asshole too. Both of us—we had a lot of the same anger, things that pissed us off."

"Like what?"

"Parents, mostly. We both wanted to get out, go anywhere, leave them behind. We talked about that all the time."

"Not a lot of love talk?"

"Fuck no, we never talked about love, only maybe to make fun of it. Love was bullshit; love was for suckers. People who said they loved you, we were like, 'Fuck them.' People who loved you died; people who loved you left you with your dad because they loved some guy in California more; people who loved you banged their waitresses and didn't even notice if you were in the room or not. I mean, I didn't want to love anyone, and Rob didn't seem like he could. I thought that meant he wasn't good at any emotion, which would've been fine with me. But I was wrong, I guess. He was really good at hate."

"Who did he hate?"

"You mean other than me?"

"Okay, yeah."

"Who did he not? His brother, his dad, Densmore."

"Who probably deserved it," said Franklin.

"But it wasn't about that," Asya said. "There wasn't any righteousness to it, no matter what he said. It was just about winning. He liked setting traps, seeing who he could catch. Then he set another one, and he caught me in it."

Franklin checked the voice recorder to make sure it was still running. He unzipped his bag, pulled out a manila envelope. "I think I should show you these," he said. The name FRANKLIN LIGHT was written across the envelope in neat black letters. "But I wanna warn you before you look."

Asya took the envelope, peered briefly inside, and saw there were photographs in it. "It's okay," she said. "I think I have a pretty good idea what's in here. I still remember the flashes." She glanced at the outside of the envelope. "No return address."

"Densmore's handwriting, though. They came in the mail a couple days before he died."

"Where'd he get 'em from? That Eileen chick?"

"Why her?"

"Who else? I remember going down the stairs, some Prince song playing, and there's Eileen doing the bump, camera bouncing against her hip."

"Yeah, her and Densmore seemed to have stayed pretty tight."

"Man, I'm so fuckin' glad I got outta there." Asya took out the photographs, went through them one by one: an unmade bed in an otherwise tidy room. A small girl lying naked—face toward the camera, eyes closed. A boy with his shirt pulled up, slacks pulled down. At first, she couldn't see the boy's face, just the back of his head and his mussed-up hair, but of course she knew who it was.

She proceeded through the photos: the girl kicking the boy; the boy crying in pain; the boy on the floor. Then, one final image, this one in color: Rob at the Grenfalls' poker table, dealing cards and chewing on a cigar. But that wasn't a photograph; it was a memory: the last thing she recalled seeing before she left Fiona Grenfall's house, ignoring Carrie calling after her as she walked back to an empty apartment, put on her GUARDIAN ANGELS jacket, and left to begin Asya's life.

She handed the photos back to Franklin. "I don't need to see them any more," she said. "I remember all of it." She could picture the house in Skokie, she told him. She remembered waiting in the car with Eileen for Rob to come back with the coke. And then the house by the lake: iron gates; chandeliers; people dancing; grown-up guests in cocktail dresses and suits; polished marble floors and stairs; the rooms—so many of them. It was nobody's idea of a prison, but that's how she thought of it. She remembered Eileen giving her a drink, then dancing away with her camera; she remembered Rob leading her upstairs, the steps swirling, the carpet like sand under her feet, then Rob pushing her down on the bed; she remembered waking up naked as if no time had passed but seeing herself as if from outside rather than from within.

"Fucking assholes," she said.

"Who specifically?" asked Franklin.

"Rob, Eileen, Densmore . . ."

"And Declan."

"I'm not sure Declan had much to do with anything," Asya said. "I think Rob was pissed and wanted to get back at me. Declan was just a mixed-up kid."

"We all were."

Franklin took a breath. His eyes were red. He looked out the window and watched the bluebirds. He shut off his phone's recorder. "Shit, I don't know, maybe you're right," he said.

"About what?"

Franklin rubbed his forehead. "This," he said. "Maybe it won't accomplish anything. Maybe it'll just fuck up your life and everyone else'll just go on to the next thing. People's attention spans, they're just so short now. One day there's some huge scandal; three days later it's like, 'Did that even happen?' First they talk about kicking out Muslims; then it's trans soldiers; then it's another Black kid getting shot. Something can happen, worst thing you ever imagined; you leave town for a week, you come back, and no one even talks about it. Everything just keeps moving right along—tap tap, click click."

Asya shrugged. "I hear you," she said. "If this were just about me, I'd let the whole thing go. I don't need any of this in my life. I don't want to have anything to do with who I was back then. That's why I have the life I do: I keep my past in the past. But I saw the article you wrote about the girl, and I saw the pictures of her."

"Eleonora?"

"Yeah. It's not the past for her. You can see the trauma that's still there, and I haven't forgotten what that felt like. I managed to save myself—well, good for me—but what difference does that make if Rob or whoever goes after someone else and I don't try to save them? I'm willing to put it all out there; I just want you to promise me something."

"Sure."

"Whatever you do with this story, whatever happens with it, this is the last time we talk, you and me. I don't want to hear from you ever again, or anybody from back then. Don't give anyone my email, my number, none of that. Nothing personal, but can you promise that?"

"Yeah," said Franklin. "Okay."

"All right," Asya said. "Now turn that recorder back on."

Mr. Frank

At Ronald Reagan Airport, another scrum of reporters was waiting for Robert Rubicoff, founder and president of DC (Damage Control) Consulting. While he joined the check-in line, they hollered the same questions they'd been asking him for the past week.

"Mr. Rubicoff, how're you feeling about the prospects for your nomination?"

"Reasonably well, thanks."

"Have you heard anything from the administration about the confirmation timetable?"

"Just what I read in the papers—same as you."

"Are you concerned that anything you said or wrote in the past might come back to haunt you?"

"Everything comes back to haunt you, you'll make sure of that. That's your job."

"Where're you flying to today, Mr. Rubicoff?"

"Why? You wanna come with?" Rob smirked. "Sorry, guys, you're gonna have to give me a little space and find something better to do with your time, or else people here'll start thinking I'm a celebrity."

At the departure gate, Rob called his wife and told her he'd let her know when he had landed in Chicago. Then he sent a text to

Franklin: Looking forward to chatting about old and new times. See ya at the New Apt, buddy.

Ever since news had broken about Rob's appointment to serve as deputy secretary of the Department of Homeland Security in charge of immigration policy, he knew the shit would be hitting the fan. He just hadn't known which particular variety of shit it would be. He had prepared to do battle with any number of old adversaries from the *Carletonian*, who, basing their allegations solely on rumor and innuendo, published an article blaming the Conservative Union, which he led, for the destruction of a cardboard shanty village built to protest their college's investments in South Africa. He had considered that someone might unearth photos of the blackface Halloween party at Georgetown where he'd dressed up as Jesse Jackson in a rainbow Afro wig during the year he'd been in law school before deciding the legal profession was for suckers. He had been all but certain someone would question him about his time at Wharton when he had written a paper calling for the abolition of the minimum wage and the legalization of sweatshops. The email from Franklin asking him to comment on accusations that he'd spiked Amanda's drink at a party where she'd been assaulted had come completely out of the blue. In the past thirty-five years he hadn't heard a peep from or about Amanda. But he shouldn't have been surprised: as he had advised George W. Bush, Tony Hayward, Robert Mugabe, and Crown Prince Abdullah, "Prepare for the attack from the enemy you don't anticipate."

Be safe, Rhonda texted him.

Always. Rob shut off his phone, looked up at the mounted televisions, and caught a glimpse of himself telling reporters nothing of substance before the broadcast cut away to an ad for antidepressants. People said TV put fifteen pounds on you, but the opposite seemed to be true for him—maybe because whenever he spoke, he imagined himself to be a much larger man.

When the announcement came, inviting first-class passengers and platinum card holders to board the aircraft, he could see people around him almost but not quite recognizing him, asking themselves the same question: *Is that the guy who was just on TV or just another fifty-something dude who looks like that?* He waved the ticket on his phone at the gate attendant, then boarded the plane to O'Hare.

He had reserved a room for two nights at the Standard Club downtown. If he had his choice, he would have spent his entire time in the city, never set foot in the suburbs where he was raised. But he had one trip to make just outside the city limits.

*

In Chicago, Rob rented a Thunderbird and drove south on the Kennedy Expressway, conducting phone interviews with Al Jazeera and National Palestinian Radio or whatever the local public radio station was called these days. He liked talking to the liberal media, liked playing the role of the affable conservative who brushed away challenges with a distant chuckle. He gently corrected their out-of-date stats about illegal immigration, laughed when they misquoted him, then directed them to the actual citations, and when they talked about what his proposals might mean for people like "Eleonora Acevedo," he pronounced her name better than they did.

White liberals like his interviewers were an endless source of entertainment for him. He liked confusing them by leading a more stereotypically woke lifestyle than they claimed to. No self-respecting critic could keep a straight face and call him a fascist, a xenophobe, or a racist when they knew that his wife, Rhonda, an attorney, had graduated from a historically Black college, that his eldest son, Boris, had started his school's gay-straight alliance, and his daughter, Alex, posted selfies from every antigovernment protest since Trump had taken office. He understood the liberal mindset and how to mess with it because he'd grown up in that milieu and was well acquainted with its hypocrisies. The moment he had taken a job working for George W. Bush, his supposedly open-minded parents had stopped speaking to him and still hadn't even acknowledged their grandchildren, even though every single one of his parents' friends was white and rich, and the only Black person he'd ever seen them talk to was the lady who used to clean their house. And the only time he ever heard from his brother, chief muckety-muck of the environmental action whatever-it-was, was when the self-righteous piece of shit flamed him on Twitter. Republicans had their own sets of problems: plenty were idiots, self-promoters, and sleazebags who made him want to shower right after he'd shaken their hands, but at least they didn't try to pretend they were saving humanity.

Traffic was heavy on the Kennedy, but cars were moving fast. It was strange to think that of everyone on this highway—cabbies and limo drivers squiring healthcare and telecommunications CEOs from O'Hare downtown; moms taking their kids to hockey practice; traveling sales-people listening to sports talk shows; ambulance drivers racing gunshot victims to the nearest trauma center—he was probably the only one about to change history. Not in some amorphous way but in a very specific one. And what excited him most, what made him beat his palms hard against the steering wheel in time with the Isley Brothers' tune that Lin Brehmer was playing on WXRT, was not the changes themselves but the fact that he could make them. What had it been like for the builders of this city—the Daniel Burnhams, the Louis Sullivans, the Helmut Jahns, whose architecture he could see up ahead—to look upon their work and realize they had changed their world?

He exited the highway at Nagle, then headed east, driving past a world that never really changed. Oh, some of the businesses were different, sure. The Jewish steak house where his father treated elderly relatives to prime rib and double-baked potatoes, the Italian restaurant where waiters sang "Happy Birthday" as if it were an aria and arias as if they were "Happy Birthday," the amusement park he had referred to as the "dirty Kiddieland," the movie theater where he'd felt up Amanda during *Stripes* and gotten a hand job from Eileen during *Tron*—those were all gone, but the insignificance of the buildings that had replaced them was the same.

Rob pulled into the U-Stuff-It Storage Solutions lot. On either side of the low, flat brick building that looked like the world's grimmest motel were businesses that had recently gone under: a flattened restau-rant encircled by fence and barbed wire; a suite of abandoned offices. Stenciled on their windows were names that sounded like fronts for sex trafficking operations: EXECUTIVE STRATEGIES, INC.; DESTINY ENTERTAIN-MENT PARTNERS; AMBASSADOR TRAVEL HOSTS.

At U-Stuff-It, just about all the outside lockers were padlocked. Two Asian men, maybe a father and son, were hauling bushels of rice and boxes of pots and pans into the back of a van; a white man Rob's age was wrestling a couch into an SUV; everything about this place reeked of divorce, bankruptcy, and petty crime.

Rob's locker was inside on the second floor, near the end of a dim, windowless hallway that smelled like the new interior of a cheap car. Every so often he had thought he might take the items from his past that he hadn't thrown out and bring them home. But he liked the separation, liked that his current life remained unsullied by his suburban Chicago history. He spun the combination on his locker, pulled down hard, opened the hasp, rolled up the door, and found—nothing.

He thumbed up the brightness of his phone flashlight, swept the thin beam of light over the locker's concrete walls and floor. A white envelope was taped to the back wall. He crouched to walk into the locker and snatched the envelope. His name was on it in a handwriting he recognized.

He left the storage door open and took the envelope into the hall. A girl—about his youngest son Sasha's age—was holding her mother's hand as she walked happily past him; maybe Mom had finally paid off the back rent; maybe the woman had kicked her Oxycontin addiction and they could finally take their stuff back home. He didn't know what their story was, but he was sure it was depressing.

He unsealed the envelope, breathed in a faint scent of stale, sweet perfume, and fished out a letter: "Don't worry. I've got it. Call me." The note was signed MIEP GIES.

*

Rob asked Eileen to meet him for breakfast at the club. He didn't want to meet her at the house where she was still living with her mom, didn't want to take the chance of running into old neighbors who would wonder what he might be planning. He didn't like the idea of visiting Eileen on her own turf, wanted to believe he had not only transcended his past but that it no longer existed. He couldn't grasp that people he had grown up with still lived here, that they took care of elderly parents, ran their families' auto parts stores, sent their kids to North Shore, and thought that made them better than families whose kids attended Evanston, New Trier, Niles, or Glenbrook, as if all those places weren't full of shit. The thought that he, a fifty-two-year-old man, could drive ten miles north and meet the same woman in the same house where he'd brought her to orgasm while the rest of her family was downstairs watching *Trapper John, M.D.* revolted him. Ty Densmore was dead; Declan was awaiting trial for setting fire to the man's house. All that made sense. The confounding part was that some people and buildings were still standing.

In previous years, when he had spoken on the phone to Eileen, he kept his tone casual but distant—like a star athlete forced to do community service at a home for the aged. During college he had seen her on breaks, occasionally allowed himself to be lured into old, appalling habits, but he had barely seen her since then. After she met Tim Donovan, she didn't call anymore, just sent cards—one on Rob's birthday, another around Christmas. No actual content in them, just photos of her and Tim, and sign-offs in red ink: YOUR LOVE FOREVER, EILEEN or SLOPPILY, SWEATILY YOURS, EILEEN accompanied by smiley faces, hearts, and HA!

Before breakfast, he went to Walgreens and purchased a box of condoms—size extra large. Not because he needed the roominess per se but because he liked the looks on the faces of drugstore workers when they unlocked the case for him and he pointed out what he wanted. "Gonna be gettin' it ON, my man!" the manager said.

In the Standard Club dining room, Rob's table looked out over Plymouth Court. The bright sunshine did little to mitigate the cheerless view of this part of the Loop, which seemed always cast in the shadows of skyscrapers, office buildings, and elevated train tracks. The scene inside was just as drab: tables topped with white cloths and good silverware, populated mostly by posses of men—dark-suited lawyers and finance bros who looked as close as you could get to goyish Washington, D.C., in Chicago's oldest Jewish professional club. Some men at the other tables offered nods of solidarity; maybe they recognized him and agreed with his politics; maybe they hoped he agreed with theirs; maybe they had no idea who he was, just looked at him and thought they saw their own reflections. The difference was that his job was in the capital and theirs was in Chicago, and things that happened here just didn't matter as much.

Eileen pranced into the dining room toting Rob's old leather briefcase. She wore tight blue jeans, heels, a billowy, low-cut, tangerine-colored top, and a haze of L'Air du Temps perfume.

"Sorry I'm late." Eileen hugged him, then flopped down on the seat opposite his. "If I told you what kept me, it'd take at least three hours, and I'm sure you don't have that kind of time, Robbo." She put the briefcase on the floor.

"You look good," Rob said. It was true: as a teenager, Eileen looked like a young Julia Child. However, when you got to be Rob's age, a middle-aged Eileen Muldoon forced you to acknowledge that, for a while, Julia Child had actually been pretty damn MILFy.

Eileen did most of the talking. She dropped names of people Rob didn't know, didn't wait for him to ask who they were. "Mary" was a nightmare—so demanding on her bad days but even more so on her good ones. "Danny" was another problem: he kept saying he wanted to leave his wife, but now it was time for him to either shit or get off the pot.

"Who did you tell him you were seeing this morning?" Rob asked.

"An old boyfriend. He gets so jealous; it's hysterical."

It amazed and amused him, the behaviors social protocol required. He was bigger than Eileen, worked out three times a week at the gym, played softball on Saturdays at Maury Wills Field. Nothing was keeping him from reaching under the table and just grabbing his briefcase.

Instead, he drank his coffee, nibbled his English muffin, watched Eileen scarf down her scrambled eggs and bacon, and chuckled as she reminisced about the locations of some of their most sordid teenage hijinks: the top of the tower at Lighthouse Beach; the slot car track at Tom Thumb Hobby & Crafts; the men's room at the Mill Run Theatre during a Peaches & Herb concert. He briefly worried she was speaking too loud, that some reporter at the next table might be secretly recording them. But hardly any journalist he knew could afford this club's fees; the few who could came from family money and would have been on his side. So he relaxed and laughed along with her. "You're right," he said.

"After that night we broke into Fritz That's It!, I never looked at salad bars in quite the same way, and I still never order ranch dressing."

Eileen laughed so hard, she choked on her cranberry juice.

"So," Rob said, "there's one thing we haven't discussed yet."

"Yup"—Eileen cast her eyes down toward the briefcase—"the elephant between my legs."

"Well," Rob said, "maybe we could start discussing it now."

"Maybe somewhere a little more private?"

"My room's upstairs."

"Shall we, Mr. Rubicoff?"

Rob had not been unfaithful to his wife, at least not since he and Rhonda had had children. And those instances when he had strayed in the early years of their marriage had been one-offs, so trivial they barely constituted infidelity—a hooker one of Silvio Berlusconi's minions sent to his hotel room as a thank-you gift for helping the Italian prime minister develop an American media strategy; a Steve Forbes staffer who was a fan of his writing and followed him into the john at CPAC. The main reason he hadn't told Rhonda was because speaking of what had happened would have made it seem more important than it actually was. And he had used a rubber both times. He did somewhat regret that he would have to keep this encounter secret from his wife and children, but what happened between him and Eileen would be over in an hour or two, whereas what he would do after he was confirmed for his job would last for generations.

"Whoa, plush as hell, Robbie-Rob." Eileen took a seat on the sofa by the window in Rob's room and kept the briefcase by her side. Rob's condom packs were on his pillows like thin mints.

"Want to use the bathroom? Freshen up?" Rob asked. "It's a good shower—really strong pressure."

"No," Eileen said with a laugh. "I'm okay."

"Then I will."

Rob took his time in the shower, used the shampoos and exfoliating soaps, and made sure not to empty all of them, since pilfered hotel bathroom products were his son Sasha's favorite gifts when he returned home from business trips. He turned the water as hot as it could go and the room steamed up.

When he walked out, he stepped through the fog like a hot chick in a 1980s music video, then advanced toward the bed in his open white robe, halfway erect dong poking out as if he were some beloved liberal icon for whom this behavior was standard operating procedure.

Rob pulled down the covers, got in bed, and took a condom pack off his pillow. "Shall I roll my own?" he asked.

Eileen was still dressed and she hadn't moved. The briefcase was in her lap; atop it, a typed document. She looked at Rob without enthusiasm, and when she spoke to him she sounded less like a horny Miep Gies and more like the former executive vice president of U-Stuff-It Storage Solutions. "Oh, so tempting," she said. "But things've gotten so complicated. I don't want to complicate them any more. And I've kinda gotten used to younger guys and, no offense, Robby, even in your prime, I'm not sure you could've kept up. I'm sorry if I gave the wrong impression."

"No, that's fine. Better, actually." Rob sat up stupidly in bed, unsure whether to get dressed or stay as he was. "Then why'd you want to come up?"

Eileen held up her papers. "For this," she said.

"What's that?"

"A contract."

It looked like something she had copied and pasted from the internet, a purportedly legal document sold to fools who ordered garbage for $19.95 from the Home Shopping Network, hicks who waved flags at rallies supporting the politicians he worked for but were too dumb to remember to show up on Election Day. He skimmed the document. "But what would you do?" he asked.

"It's up to you, Rob-Rob," Eileen said. "I'm not particular."

What she wanted was not the pile of cash he was prepared to part with, not the vigorous cunnilingus he would have performed upon request. All she wanted was for him to help her get a job. "I've been following your career for so long," she said. "And I'm not getting any younger. I need someone to give me a shot. I banked everything on

Tim and the storage business, and all I've got to show for it is debt, an old mom I can't take care of and who doesn't even like me, and a house we won't be able to afford. No one wants to hire me for anything; my references suck. The only call I've gotten in the past year was from T.J. Maxx—cosmetics section, part-time."

"For once, I'd love to do something I really believe in," Eileen said, "where I don't have to say I'm sorry just because I'm white and my grandparents came here legally and spoke English. Single, middle-aged white ladies—our lives matter too."

"What happens if I don't help out?" Rob asked.

"Do we really have to go there, Rob-Rob? You know how hard I work; you know how organized I am, how loyal. Frankie Lichtenstein keeps calling me and I haven't told that manipulative little douche a thing."

"What about your mom?"

"What about her?"

"How would she manage without you?"

"Oh, Ms. Mary does just fine for herself when I'm not around. And maybe my brothers could pick up some slack for once."

"And your boyfriend?"

"I deserve a lot better than some third-string, two-timing real estate guy, don't you think?"

Rob could have said many things. He could have said he wouldn't be in charge of hiring his staff, but that would be, at best, half true. He could have said Eileen wasn't qualified, but Washington was full of unqualified nepotistic hires. Eileen had been a B– student taking "regular" classes in high school and had barely been able to hack SIU; sure, he could find her a job in Washington. He took a pen from the night table, signed both copies of the contract, and handed one to Eileen. "Thanks so much," she said. "This'll be so fun. Like being back in high school, the old cast together again."

Rob nodded, though he knew Eileen was wrong about that. He was a man of his word, and he would help her find a job in D.C., but that didn't mean he'd see her every day, or even any day. He didn't need her meeting Rhonda and the kids, insinuating herself into their lives, coming around on weekends, bringing Betty Crocker meat loaf, asking if there was anything good on TV. He could install her in some office as far away from him as possible, find her a gig with the sleaziest horndog on Capitol Hill or some rabid right-wing closet case in need of a beard, let her become that guy's problem.

Eileen handed Rob the briefcase, kissed him on the cheek, then reached under the covers, laughed, and gave his dong a friendly yank.

"Good to see you again, old pal," she said, then made for the door.

Rob waited to hear the elevator doors open and close. He turned the combination—6969—and flipped open the briefcase. Yes, all these years later, they were still here.

*

Decades of character diaries written by the drama students of North Shore Magnet had been destroyed in the fire at Ty Densmore's house. All that remained were the pages that a few posterity-obsessed or forward-thinking students like Rob and Eileen had xeroxed and kept for themselves.

Rob's entries were just as he remembered them: a largely truthful yet slightly altered history of the time he spent as Anne and Margo's father. Every day was chronicled: how he struggled to get Otto Frank's accent right, the way Judith harangued him about needing to find the "emotional core" of his character; Trey's unfortunate departure; Declan's unfortunate return.

And then, his final night in *Anne Frank*: he had driven with Eileen and Amanda to the party at Fiona's house. Amanda had kept bugging him to get drugs, but he refused. She started drinking as soon as they got to Fiona's. He'd had enough of her act, then went off to play poker. He'd been playing for maybe a half hour when he heard a commotion, then Judith and Fiona talking about some wasted girl upstairs. He'd stepped away from the game and saw Amanda stumbling down the staircase, looking pretty out of it. He figured she was just in one of her crap moods. Sometime later he saw Declan leaving the party, clutching a big wad of bloody Kleenexes to his face. Maybe he should have put two and two together, but it was better he hadn't. If he had known that Declan had tried to assault Amanda, he might have lost control, kicked the guy's ass, and had his admission to Carleton rescinded. He'd thought Declan was a good dude, but sometimes it was hard to tell what people were like when they didn't think they were being watched. "I still don't entirely believe it. I just wish I'd stayed with Amanda so she didn't have to fight that creep off on her own," he wrote.

Miep Gies's character diary corroborated Rob's narrative: "I feel bad for Declan. He's a great actor and he's always been nice to me," Eileen wrote. "But he deserved a lot worse than what Amanda did to him."

Rob read through the diary entries one final time. Taken separately, they might not have meant all that much. Together, they dismantled whatever Amanda might have said about him and anything Franklin might have been preparing to write. He put the papers back in the briefcase, then he got dressed to meet Franklin.

*

At the bar of the New Apartment Lounge on East Seventy-Fifth Street on Chicago's South Side, Rob sat on a stool next to Franklin. People might have thought Rob had chosen the venue because it wasn't the sort of joint where anyone would care about their conversation, and there was some truth to that. Others might have thought he had picked the New Apartment because he liked meeting white liberals in places that made them feel uncomfortable; there was some truth to that too. But the main reason was that he just liked the place: the drinks were cheap, the vibe was low-key, and even on jam session nights when anyone could get up and play, the jazz was top-notch.

Rob and Franklin showed each other pictures of their wives and kids—the middle-aged man's version of measuring dicks. Franklin somehow managed to drop the name "Carrie" five times into their conversation, almost like he wanted Rob to ask about the status of their relationship. How small would your life have to be to still care about high school girlfriends? Rob wondered. Maybe that was all you could think about if you found yourself living in the same town where you'd grown up. He briefly imagined Peter Van Daan having actually survived the war, then many years later meeting up with an old friend who asks what he's been up to.

You know how it is, Peter tells him. *Texting a lot with Anne, going out with her for coffee and whatnot.*

Rob put his briefcase on the bar and raised his eyebrows in a self-consciously conspiratorial fashion.

"I guess we're getting to the part of the conversation where you ask if we can talk off the record," Franklin said.

Rob laughed. "Is that how it usually works?"

"Pretty much," Franklin said. "We shoot the shit for a while, then right when we're about to get to the important part, it's like, 'Let's go off the record.'"

"And people honor that?"

"That's kind of how the game's played."

"We play it differently in Washington," said Rob. "When you say something's off the record there, that means you're getting to the stuff you actually want people to know. If you really want something 'off the record,' you just don't say it."

"So, this whole conversation," Franklin said, "you're on the record for all of it."

Rob took out his phone, placed it on the bar, and swiped the voice recorder app. "I am if you are," he said. "We can work it like this: you ask me questions, I ask you questions. You ask me about Amanda, I ask you about Carrie. It sounds like you're seeing quite a bit of her. What do your wife and kids think about that? Have you talked to them about it?" Rob's finger hovered over the RECORD button.

"Okay." Franklin took his phone and put it back in his pocket. Then Rob put his phone away too. "Okay," Franklin said. "Let's just talk for a bit first and see where this goes."

"Fine." Rob took a slug of whiskey. "Now that that's out of the way, why don't I summarize the story I think you're planning to write."

"Shoot," said Franklin.

"All right, stop me when I get something wrong. In the spring of 1982, when I was seventeen and you were, what, fifteen?"

"Yeah."

"We acted together in *Anne Frank*. After the last performance, but before the cast party, I drove to a house in Skokie because Amanda wanted me to get some cocaine. But when I was there, I didn't get the coke; I got some kind of knockout drug. How'm I doing so far?"

"Keep talking," said Franklin.

"All right, so we hit the party and I slip Amanda the drink with the drug in it."

"Or you get Eileen to do it."

"Sure, why not. I take Amanda upstairs to the bedroom. She's still wondering where the coke is, but she's getting woozy, and when she's out cold, I strip her naked and leave her there so Declan can assault her."

"I've got that figured a little different," Franklin said. "I see you trying to set up Densmore—I remember you asking people for dirt about him for some article you said you wanted to write—but he outsmarts you and sets up Declan."

"Which sounds exactly like something that twisted fuck would've tried. Is that what Amanda says happened?"

"I want to know what *you* say happened."

"It doesn't really matter what I *say*, Frank. If I were you, I'd be more curious to hear what I *said*." Rob opened the briefcase, took out the diary pages, and gave them to Franklin. "Take your time reading them," he said. "I'm not in a hurry, and my handwriting was always shit."

Franklin read the pages, holding them close to his face, and Rob turned to the little stage at the back of the bar. About eight or nine musicians were up there, playing "Body and Soul." Rob always wished that he had the talent for music; his kids could play, but he never had the gift or the patience. Sometimes he told himself that his ability to write speeches and manipulate people was its own art, but he knew it wasn't the same thing.

Franklin handed back the pages. "Those are from your character diary?"

"They are," said Rob. "I can airdrop you PDFs if you need them; Eileen's too."

Franklin whistled, impressed. "Interesting. You got any other stuff you wrote back then so I can see how it compares?" he asked.

"Like what?" Rob smiled. "You wanna read my creative writing assignments? My term paper on *Old Man and the Sea*?"

"Or anything, really." There was a pause; Franklin let the music fill it. "You just don't strike me as a very nostalgic guy, Rob."

"That's absolutely right."

"I'd be willing to bet," said Franklin, "that from your time in high school, this is just about the only thing you kept."

"Point being?"

"Point being that the only reason anyone would keep anything that long is if they know they're guilty of something and they'll need something to back up whatever story they want to tell instead of what actually happened."

Rob raised his glass respectfully, then drank. He liked when he could spar with someone on his intellectual level; he'd choose to drink with a smart adversary over a dumb ally any time. When he first decided he wanted to marry Rhonda, it wasn't because she was hot or because she had good manners; it was because she was the first woman he'd met who could beat him in chess. "Okay, so then what?" he asked Franklin.

"How do you mean?"

"Let's say you publish what Amanda said happened and then what I said happened. The only people who really know are me, Amanda, Eileen, Declan, and Densmore. Densmore's dead, Amanda was wasted, Declan's a nutjob, Eileen backs me up, and it all took place more than thirty years ago. Not much of a story; not one that'll change anything."

"Maybe not yet."

"You were there that night, Frank; what did you see? What do you remember? Anything? Did you see Amanda that night? Did you talk to her? Did she tell you anything? Or were you occupied with other things? Carrie, maybe?"

Franklin didn't say anything.

"Go ahead, publish the story; I can't stop you. I'm sure other people will jump on it. Ten percent of America will believe you, ten percent will believe me, and the other eighty percent won't give a shit because they've got their own lives to worry about and they don't trust anything anybody says. Nothing gets accomplished. Amanda or whatever her name is now gets dragged into the mud. I have to answer some uncomfortable questions from my wife and my kids; that sucks for me, but I know how to navigate shit like that, so nothing changes. It's not like any of this keeps me from getting the job or doing what I plan to do. And even if it did, they'll go with some other guy who'll do pretty much the same thing—except you won't have any history with him and he won't offer you any kind of deal."

Franklin laughed. "You're offering to cut me a deal?"

"I might be."

"Buying me out?"

"Nah. I mean, look how you dress; you're not in it for the paycheck."

"Then what?"

"You take a lot of interest in your subjects, Frank; they really matter to you."

"Nothing unusual about that."

"I wouldn't be so sure. You take a lot more time and care than a lot of writers do: the Densmore piece, the one with the girl in the shul. If I don't get in and someone else does, I'm not gonna be able to help you with that."

"But I spike the story and you will? That's what you're saying?"

"I know things," said Rob. "In that position, I'll have access to information and resources you might find useful."

"You're actually serious?"

"I am."

"You're saying you'd help me."

"Could be."

"Like when a certain policy might be going into place or some action is about to be taken, you could—what? Alert me? Is that the idea?"

"That's the general outline, yes."

"And you'd do that if I killed a story?"

"It doesn't have to be that transactional, Frank. If you prefer, we could call it an act of friendship. Politics aside, I always kinda liked you, or maybe I just thought Declan was sort of a dick and I liked that you made his life hell without even trying."

Franklin looked into space. He seemed to be having trouble finding the right words. "Do you really believe in anything you're doing, Rob?" he asked. "Or is it all just a game to you?"

"You know, it's possible to answer yes to both questions," said Rob.

Onstage, the musicians were playing "I'll Get By (As Long as I Have You)." The sax player wasn't much to look at. She wore a dumpy black sweatshirt with a sequined silver crown on it, but her playing was so good, it didn't matter. You never knew which note she'd hit or how loud or how long she might play it. Rob wished people could be as unpredictable as music; it would make life more interesting.

"I'm gonna have to take a little time to think this through," Franklin said.

"Of course," said Rob. "You have my cell, my email."

Rob knew Franklin wouldn't give him an answer right away, but after he offered his hand and Franklin shook it, he figured he had all the answer he needed. "You wanna stick around for a bit, man?" he asked. "Listen to the rest of the set? Order another round?"

"I'd like to but I gotta head back," said Franklin. "I guess for now I should wish you good luck with the new job."

"Yeah, good luck to you too, man. We'll be in touch."

Franklin started tapping on his phone before he was even halfway to the door. He should have been texting his wife to tell her he'd be home soon, Rob thought; he should have been texting Amanda What's-her-name to tell her what Rob had proposed; he should have been texting that girl in the shul or that sanctimonious rabbi keeping watch over her. But Rob was willing to bet all that tapping was Franklin texting Carrie, who would tell him what to do. She'd always been smart, and she'd know that killing the story was the only right answer.

Rob ordered another drink. Soon he'd be on a plane heading home for Washington, and everything would fall into place. For now, though, he would savor his privacy, sit back, sip his whiskey, and listen to the jazz.

*

The New Apartment was a three A.M. bar, and Rob stayed past last call when the only people left were the hard-core alcoholics and the musicians who were packing up their instruments. He tipped the bartender a twenty, shook hands with the sax player, gave her his card, then headed outside.

The sky above was black, but when he looked east on Seventy-Fifth Street, he could see just the slightest hints of gray in it. He got into his car and started it. He took out his phone, placed it in the dock, and checked the screen. A news alert was on it: WILL A DECADES-OLD ABUSE ALLE-GATION AND A HISTORY OF MANIPULATION DERAIL RUBICOFF'S NOMINATION?

Rob clicked on the link and saw Franklin's byline. He felt a momentary twinge of rage as he recalled Franklin tapping on his phone on his way out of the bar, but then he looked in his rearview mirror, checked himself, and smiled.

Mrs. Van Daan

R abbi Jeremy Horvath was preparing a sermon in the study where Eleonora Acevedo had lived since the spring when he heard a loud, insistent pounding coming from the front of the synagogue. And although he had been anticipating the disturbance and knew what it meant, he kept writing. His sermon's subject was Jakiw Palij, the last surviving Nazi collaborator in America; an effort was underway to deport him. If the plan went through, it would be the first time the United States had deported a suspected Nazi war criminal since John Demjanjuk, who had died in Germany in 2012, appeal still pending.

More knocking. The rabbi ignored it.

For the first time in his life, Horvath wrote, the country would be free of the Nazis he'd grown up fearing. The Days of Awe were approaching; it was a time that traditionally filled him with pride and hope—pride for all he had accomplished in the previous year; hope for all he might do in the next. Yet, here in his seventieth year on this planet, that optimism eluded him. Each battle he had won was always replaced by a newer, tougher one. His parents had fled Europe. They came as refugees to America, where they fought Irish, Polish, and Italian kids who called them sheenies and kikes; they voted for Stevenson, Kennedy, and Johnson, hoping the next generation of immigrants would have it easier. Horvath traveled with them to New York, where they rallied for Soviet Jewish immigrants—so many of whom, three decades later, voted for a man who was now trying to reverse just about everything he and his parents had fought for.

The last Nazi might soon be gone, but that didn't mean the struggle was over.

The knocking persisted.

Horvath put down his pen. He stood, then walked down the dim corridor until he reached the front doors and pushed hard on the panic bar to open them. "Isn't this a bit much?" he asked.

Noyes Street was blocked off with sawhorses. Squad cars were parked on either end of the block, red and blue lights blinking, twirling. A half dozen vans were stalled in the loading zone, cargo doors open. Men in boots, helmets, and thick black vests with ICE and POLICE printed in big white letters on the front and back held weapons against their chests as if they were patrolling a war zone.

A thick-necked officer in a tight navy-blue suit held an iPad and clipboard. "Rabbi Horvath?"

The rabbi nodded. "What can I do for you?"

"My name's Eugene Roche." The officer was a clean-cut, law-and-order type who exuded painstaking literal-mindedness. He showed the rabbi his ID and the document attached to his clipboard: a deportation order for Eleonora Acevedo. "Will you allow us to pass and enter, Rabbi, so we can execute our orders?"

The rabbi shook his head and sighed. "This is a house of worship, Officer Roche," he said. "Everyone's welcome. But it's a holy place, and"—he gestured to his head—"anyone who comes in has to wear a kippah."

Roche shouted instructions to his team, then turned back to Horvath. "You got any exits here other than this one and the one in back?"

"Only the two."

"Nothing in the basement?"

"No, the stairs just lead right back up here."

"And Miss Acevedo, is she awake?"

"How would I know?"

"The study's where?"

The rabbi gestured down the hall. He stopped at the bin of kippahs, picked up a satiny white one, and handed it to the officer, who placed it on his head. The other agents entered, donned kippahs, then followed the rabbi.

"How many people you got with you?" Rabbi Horvath asked.

"Eighteen."

"And afterward you're goin' where?"

"That's not really your concern, Rabbi."

"Eleonora, does she get a lawyer?"

"That's not really your concern either."

" 'Not my concern.' When my congregants ask what happened to her or where she is, what do you suggest I say? That it's not any of their fuckin' concern?"

"I don't appreciate the language."

"Sorry, man." The rabbi didn't like Holocaust analogies, yet as the agents followed him to his study, the comparison seemed unavoidable. He thought he had written the last line of his sermon, but he might have a bit more to say.

"Do we need a key to the door?" Roche asked.

"No. Should be open."

The officer rapped on the study door. "Miss Acevedo?" He banged louder. "Still asleep?"

"Like I said before, man, how would I know?"

"Step to the side, Rabbi." Roche shoved open the door. His eyes flitted past the bookshelves, the desk with its lamp still on, the legal pad and pen, the couch with afghans draped over it. "Where is she?"

"Eleonora?" asked the rabbi. "I got no idea."

"She in the building?"

"Nope. She just took all her stuff and went."

"When?"

"I haven't the slightest idea."

"To go where?"

"I don't know that either. She's gone; she packed her stuff. I specifically told her that if she decided to leave, she shouldn't tell me where she was going, so when I said I didn't know, I wouldn't be lying. Go on, look around all you want."

The agents fanned out. They stormed into the classrooms, threw open closet doors, went into bathrooms, checked stalls, made their way through the dark sanctuary in the blinking orange glow of the Eternal Light. "Is there a way to get some more light on in here?" someone asked. They snaked from one pew to the next, put up seats, swept flashlights underneath them, spoke into the mics on their shoulders: "No, nothing." "No, there's nothing here." "Nobody." The agents scuffed the carpet with their boots.

"If you'd listened when I told you she was gone, I could've saved you a whole lot of trouble, man," the rabbi said.

"I'm gonna have to ask you to come along with me," said Roche, "answer some questions."

"Which questions?"

"We'll get to that." He led the rabbi to the front door.

Outside, dawn was starting to break; red and blue lights were still flashing in the glow of a purple-black sky as the rabbi stepped toward a white van. On its side, the seal of an eagle and the words DEPARTMENT OF HOMELAND SECURITY.

"Morning services start in an hour and a half," Rabbi Horvath said. "Will I be back in time?"

"I don't see why not," said the officer. "But that's gonna be up to you."

*

Eleonora was sitting next to Carrie in the back of Ray Tounslee's Ford Intrepid. Ray was driving, and Franklin was in the passenger seat as Earth, Wind & Fire played loud on Ray's stereo. Ray had told Franklin he should wait to publish his article until they'd gotten Eleonora safely away, but Franklin said that wasn't an option. He had the whole story more or less ready to go before he'd met with Rob, and waiting would have meant giving Rob the opportunity to get out in front and discredit it. Plus, Franklin said that delaying a story to serve his own personal agenda felt dishonest. So Ray said, "Fine, you wanna be a hero? Let's be heroes." Franklin called Carrie; Ray called the rabbi and told him to wake Eleonora. And now here they were on I-94 bound for Canada, with three legitimate passports and a passport for Eleonora that actually belonged to Franklin's eldest daughter, who looked enough like this girl at a glance that they hoped no one would ask any questions.

Ray had struck up a friendship with Rabbi Horvath and Eleonora while he was at the synagogue to monitor the protests that had been spreading throughout the city and suburbs. Each time Ray talked with the girl, she spoke better English, needed Horvath and Franklin less and less to translate. The first few times Ray had seen her at Beth Shalom, she had offered little more than hesitant "Thank yous" and "That's nice of yous," and it was easy to lose sight of just how deeply her ordeal was affecting her. Now that she had the English words to express her feelings, Ray could tell exactly how scared she was: Other cars on the highway—were they following her? Tollbooth workers, travelers at rest stops—did they recognize her? Police officers at the side of the road—would they arrest her? Everything seemed to bring back memories of the things she had seen back home that she was now able to describe: the charred half-naked body of a boy in her family's sugarcane fields; her oldest brother the last time she'd seen him—in a white T-shirt with a hole ripped through it, dark red and getting darker; the back of a bus where she'd hidden while boys no older than her roved the aisle, guns on their belts and in their hands, shooting as people cried out in anguish.

"Almost there; buckle up, y'all." Ray stood in traffic, inching his car toward the Ambassador Bridge. While Carrie texted her daughter and Franklin texted his wife, Ray tried to defuse the tension by teaching Eleonora about American culture courtesy of the stereo: "This is Earth, Wind & Fire; this is the dope shit"; "This is Post Malone; it's bullshit."

"Come on, don't worry; getting through this'll be easy," Ray told Eleonora, but, really, what did he know? He had no stamps in his passport; the farthest he'd ever traveled from Evanston was Disneyland with his wife and kids. He'd kept these plans secret from his son and daughter because he knew they would have tried to talk him out of it, would have parroted back the same lecture he'd given them their whole lives: keep a low profile, do what you're told, don't take unnecessary risks, remember who you are and what you look like, doesn't matter what the truth is, what matters is what they'll choose to believe.

A banner was stretched across the bridge—a Canadian flag and the Stars and Stripes; between them, in big black letters, UNITED WE STAND. Customs officials in black uniforms and baseball caps strolled between cars, peered in windows, took passports, driver's licenses, and customs declarations, opened trunks and examined what was inside.

The border agent looked barely old enough to drive. He stepped out of his booth. Ray took off his sunglasses and handed over the passports. The agent studied them, then leaned into the car. "Mr. Tounslee?"

"Yep."

"Dr. Hollinger?"

"Yes."

"Mr. Lichtenstein?"

"Uh-huh."

"Miss Lichtenstein?"

No answer.

Eleonora was staring out her window as if she had already forgotten what her name was supposed to be.

"*Miss Lichtenstein?*"

Carrie poked her and the agent took a closer look at Eleonora's passport.

Ray called out. "Hey, man," he said. "If you want, you can run a twenty-nine on all of us. But they're all gonna come up as 'None.'"

"You some kind of cop?" the agent asked.

Ray nodded. "Sergeant." He pulled out his ID, handed it over.

The agent took the ID, looked it over. "Shouldn't you be thinking about retiring soon, Sergeant?"

"I would if I could figure out something else to do with my life."

The kid laughed. "I sure hear that," he said. "You married?"

"Widowed."

"Real sorry about that. Kids?"

"Grown. 'Bout your age."

"You all on some kind of business?"

"Vacation," said Ray. "Meeting up with a pal we haven't seen since high school."

The agent nodded toward Eleonora, who was focused on the bridge and all the water beneath it. "Doesn't she talk?" he asked.

"Talks plenty when she wants to."

"What's she got to be so upset about?"

Ray laughed. "You wanna spend the last days of your summer vacation with your folks and their old school pals?"

"Yeah, I hear that." The agent gave back the passports. "You have a good day, now, Sergeant. And you find yourself a hobby. Keep safe."

Ray saluted the agent, hit the gas, and rolled on into Ontario with the stereo blasting the O'Jays, "Now That We Found Love"—all the while wondering if it had always been as easy for people to lie to him as it was for him to lie at the border. The trick, it turned out, wasn't to make anyone believe you were innocent; it was to make them believe you were one of them so they wouldn't care if you were guilty. Maybe if he'd known that when he was seventeen, everything could have turned out differently. After he had slammed Trey Newson to the ground, he could've told the cops to run a "29" on him; they would have asked if his dad was a cop, and he would've said, "Yeah, Chicago PD, brother," and they would've let him go.

He took a deep breath and let it out: "*Dah-yumn.*"

Eleonora had done her best to hold back her tears at the border; now they flowed. "It's all right," Ray said. "The worst of the bullshit is over. All we gotta do from here on in is drive, eat, and sleep. You got nothing but possibilities in front of you. Ms. Grenfall will get you all set up; you can stay with her as long as you need. You'll go to school. You'll make friends. No one'll send you back. What do you wanna do?"

"I've been trying not to think about that," Eleonora said. "Every time I dream of something, it doesn't come true—unless it's a nightmare; those wind up happening."

"No nightmares anymore," said Ray. "Just the good stuff."

They had hoped to make it to Ottawa before they turned in for the night, but once rain started needling down, Ray could barely keep awake.

He could have let Carrie or Franklin drive, but they weren't on his insurance, and the last thing he needed was for cops to pull them over, run the license plates, and check their IDs again.

The woman working the front desk of the Best Western asked how many rooms they needed. Ray asked for four, but Franklin said three would be fine: "Carrie and I can share."

Ray looked the two of them up and down, started to say something, then stopped. "Okaaay, then," he told the woman at the desk. "Make it three rooms."

Eleonora held up two fingers.

"You don't want your own room either?" Ray asked. "All right, you take the bed; I'll take the damn floor."

Eleonora pecked Ray on the cheek as if he were a kindly grandfather. He had a hard time seeing himself that way, but he had to get used to the idea that others did. "Come on, now, let's get some shut-eye," he said. "I'll call up Ms. Grenfall, let her know we're on our way."

When he got to the room, he called Fiona, and when she didn't answer, he left a message on her voice mail. "We're still making real good time," he said. "We'll be there Friday between noon and one, just like you said. Looking forward to seeing you, serious."

*

Anne Frank and Peter Van Daan had showered. Anne Frank had called her daughter to make sure she was okay, and Peter Van Daan had called his wife to say he had arrived safely at the motel with Ray and the girl. Anne Frank and Peter Van Daan then walked down the hall to check on Eleonora and Ray and found Eleonora sitting up in bed, writing in her notebook and watching a reality show, while Ray was crashed out on the carpet, snoring.

Anne and Peter were now in their room wearing what passed for pajamas: him, a white T-shirt and plaid boxers; her, a maroon U of C T-shirt and black yoga pants. They were sitting in the two armchairs in front of the beige curtain they had drawn across the windows.

For a while Anne and Peter avoided discussing the fact that the two of them were alone in a motel room and that Anne no longer lived with her husband and Peter's wife was with the kids visiting family in San Diego. Instead, Anne and Peter discussed the coming day: the drive to New Glasgow; how long they might stay. They asked after each other's children: Kitty had found an apartment and roommates in Hyde Park; Maria Graciela had one year left of high school; Emma, a year of pre-K.

"You hear from Declan at all?" he asked.

"A little," she said. "He sends me letters. I haven't answered. It's like, what would I say? I'm sure he's lonely and I can't imagine what he's going through, but I wouldn't want to give the wrong impression, particularly given the situation with Adrian, or lack thereof. Have you heard from Amanda?"

"Asya?"

"Yeah."

"No, I made her a promise. She'll be hearing from more than enough people without hearing from me, and if she wants to get in contact, she knows how."

For the first time in as long as they could remember, Anne Frank and Peter Van Daan were together and had no other place they needed to be. For now, Casa Segura would have to remain closed. Peter's wife and daughters wouldn't be back home until Labor Day, and as far as his job was concerned, Violet didn't give a damn if he set foot in the *Tomorrow* building again as long as he kept writing stories that topped the Big Board.

The only problem was that the man and woman getting ready for bed weren't really Anne Frank and Peter Van Daan. Anne and Peter were dead. Peter had died in Mauthausen, Anne in Bergen-Belsen, and Carrie and Franklin were just two people who had pretended to be them long ago and couldn't help thinking that having played those roles should matter.

They often returned to the topic: What if Anne and Peter had survived? Would they have wound up together? Both knew but never admitted they were really talking about themselves. If she hadn't left North Shore for her final year of high school, if she hadn't gone to college in California and he hadn't gone in New York, if she hadn't been in Africa while he had lived in Central America, if he hadn't been in

Chicago while she had been in Ithaca, if they both hadn't married other people after running out of hope that they would ever be together, what would have happened?

"Well, here we are," he said.

"Yep, here we are," she said.

He held her hand. She didn't take hers back. He leaned in closer; she remained still. He pressed his lips to hers. He closed his eyes; hers stayed open. "What?" he asked.

"I don't know," she said.

They kissed. She pulled back, still holding his hand. "What?" he asked again.

"Isn't it too late?" she asked.

"As long as we're alive, nothing's ever too late," he said.

"You have a wife," she said.

"Technically, you still have a husband," he said.

"You have two daughters," she said.

"You have one," he said. "And anyway, kids are resilient. The best lesson to teach them is to be true to their feelings, live their lives honestly."

"Is this honesty?" she asked. "I've been trying to live honestly; is this what it's like?"

"It feels honest to me."

Another kiss, longer this time. She stopped. He sighed. "What?"

"What happens after?" she asked.

"I don't have an answer; that's kind of the point."

They found their way to the bed and got under the covers. "It's been a long time," he said.

"It has," she said.

"Nothing has to happen," he said.

"No. It doesn't."

He brushed her hair away from her face, wiped the tear from her eye.

"How do I look?" she asked.

"Older and the same," he said.

"Same with you," she said.

"I love you, Carrie," he said. "I always have."

"But what does that mean?" she asked.

"Only that."

What happened between them—the way they undressed, drew themselves to each other, gasped as they felt the pressure of each other's bodies until they couldn't say for sure where one ended and the other began—happened as it nearly always did: in darkness, without words. But afterward, inevitably, the silence had to be broken; inevitably, their eyes grew accustomed to the night.

They lay in bed for a long time, side by side, hand in hand, gazing not at each other but up at the broken wooden fan, at the stained, bulging ceiling tiles. "I've never been able to focus on the present, you know that," she said. "That's kind of my curse. I always think, 'What'll happen tomorrow?' and then 'What'll happen the day after that?' I can never let myself think about how happy I am at any moment, only how happy I might be later or how sad or angry I might make someone else feel."

"Yeah, I've never wanted to live that way," he said. "I'm happiest when I don't know what's gonna happen, when I'm not thinking about consequences—when it's all, like, 'Follow your instinct, figure it all out later.' People get hurt; they do. That's gonna happen regardless. Every time you win something, someone else loses. Maybe tomorrow will come, maybe it won't; you can't count on it. One morning I was a kid and my mom was there for me. She made me breakfast, kissed me on the cheek; that afternoon she was gone. That can happen to any of us any time."

Carrie looked up. "You still think she's up there, watching?"

"Sometimes I think she is."

"What do you think she's thinking?"

"I think she understands."

"I'm just not sure that's a way I can live," she said. "Like, what's the point of being with someone today if you're not sure they'll be with you the next day? Maybe that's why we can never really be together."

"Maybe that's why we have to be," he said.

"What do you think they would've done?" she asked.

"Who?"

"Anne and Peter," she said. "I always think of what would have happened if they got out. I think of them finding an apartment together, finishing school, coming to America, starting a family, becoming grand-parents, great-grandparents. But maybe they would've just wound up with different people, and that would've been that."

"I don't know," he said. "The point is, none of it happened. There's no happily ever after when you look close enough at any story. There's happy for a moment, but only if you freeze it in time. It all keeps moving. Anne and Peter, their tragedy wasn't that they didn't get to be together; it's that they didn't get the chance to choose to be apart. They didn't get to fall out of love, to follow their dreams and see them shattered; didn't get the chance to marry the wrong people, realize they'd made a mistake, then try to fix it while they still were young enough to do something about it, to get back together even when they thought it might be too late."

He held her as they kissed, but this time he could feel her elsewhere. He may have been right there in that moment, but she couldn't help imagining the morning and the next night, couldn't help thinking about other people's futures that were none of her business, but that didn't make them matter any less. She imagined Franklin packing his things and leaving his family's house; she imagined the talk he would have with his wife and kids about how everyone had to be honest and follow their hearts. She tried to imagine the conversation she'd have with Kitty, and she couldn't decide which would be worse: Kitty feeling devastated or Kitty not caring at all. She thought of Eleonora in the room down the hall, her and every other kid she had seen at Casa Segura: How much would any of them have given for some harmony? Who cared how real it was?

Franklin kept his arm around Carrie as she turned away. "It's late," he said. "We'll have more than enough time to talk all this through. This conversation isn't over yet; we can keep having it. There's time." He said good night and told her he loved her again. He held her closer when she said she loved him too. But when he awoke in the morning, she was gone. And even though he wasn't shocked to see that Carrie had taken her suitcase and hadn't left a note or even sent a text, he started to cry the moment he saw the one thing she had left behind: *The Baron in the Trees*, the book Franklin had loaned her on their first night together more than thirty years ago.

He showered and dressed. He wheeled his suitcase to the lobby, where Eleonora and Ray were already sitting near the breakfast buffet. Franklin asked if they had seen Carrie and they told him they hadn't. At the front desk, he asked if she had left a note and the clerk said no. He wiped his eyes with his sleeve, not knowing whether he should call her or not, try to follow her or not, head back to Chicago or keep going with Ray and Eleonora. He took only a small bit of comfort in the fact that his world still seemed to be made up of infinite choices, of decisions that might or might not be right, of stories that could end any number of ways—of chances that Peter Van Daan and Anne Frank had never had.

*

Fiona had listened to Ray's most recent message three times, but she hadn't returned it: "We'll be there Friday between noon and one, just like you said. Looking forward to seeing you, serious." She liked how he sounded, always had, probably too much. She didn't know exactly how many people he was bringing with him or how long any of them might stay, but it didn't matter: he could have brought a whole village. She certainly had the space—plenty of room at the inn, she thought.

It had all gotten to be a joke with her, hadn't it? Some empty catch-phrase she had been uttering in one form or another ever since she'd been a girl. When Fiona was growing up, she was convinced that her parents were spies, not "diplomats," as they claimed, and she still wasn't sure she was wrong. Everywhere they lived seemed far more opulent than should have been the case for career foreign service workers. There were always vacation homes that Fiona would offer up as sanctuary for friends, colleagues, random acquaintances, and polite strangers.

In primary school in Hong Kong, when everyone was obsessed with extraterrestrial life, she told her classmates about the home in the Cotswolds: "If Mars invades, we can all go there." During secondary school, the fear was World War III—the U.S. and Soviets vaporizing Europe. If there was a nuclear winter, she told her friends and their teacher, Lloyd Crowder, her parents still had the house in Kenya; it had such a lovely garden. During her brief time in the preposterously posh home in Evanston, she fantasized that she had been alive during the

Second World War: imagine how many families she could have hidden in a place like that.

Fiona made similar offers at college and graduate school, at the universities where she taught, the laboratories where she worked, and at the Canadian Broadcasting Corporation, where she produced *Endangered!*, her lovely, grim documentary series that had started with black rhinos and had now worked its way to human beings. She dangled the possibility of shelter after Chernobyl, after 9/11, after the bombings in London and the murders in the supermarkets and nightclubs of Paris: *If the fallout spreads over Western Europe, if Al Qaeda detonates a dirty bomb, if some evil bastard starts shooting, if hurricanes wipe away everything you own, call me or just stop by; I have a place.*

And yet, until she got the call from Ray—darling Ray with his wife long gone and his two children grown; sad, sad Ray, whose life she thought she had ruined just like she had ruined the lives of everyone who made the mistake of getting close to her; reliable, middle-aged Ray whom she longed to see almost as much as she desperately wanted to avoid—she had done none of that. She had done little with her life other than "raise awareness," a phrase that, to her, translated roughly to "doing fuck-all." She had raised awareness in classrooms about the rising temperatures of the world's oceans; she had raised awareness about the plight of those daft polar bears and Siberian tigers. But really, what had Fiona Bloody Grenfall done other than donate money and give lofty speeches while she polluted the countryside and depleted the ozone layer with her punch-red Jaguar and its criminally poor gas mileage and shitty air conditioner? How many people had she ever really helped?

In her professional life, she may have been a champion of the environment, but when it came to personal relationships, she was a one-woman aerosol spray can, a human defoliant stripping bare the lives of friends and lovers. She often imagined describing herself in the same cheeky, portentous tone she used while reading voice-over scripts: *The Fiona Grenfall attracts her mates with salty, irreverent love calls and gaudy sartorial displays, but do not be fooled by this cunning creature's alluring exterior: the Grenfall is as deadly as any viper.*

Fiona couldn't help but believe there was a sign in the fact that, just a few short months before that yam-hued, pussy-grabbing Neanderthal was elected to the presidency of the once-free world, her annual trip to visit her parents was delayed because a tropical storm, one that had actually been named Fiona, was churning across the Atlantic. Tropical Storm Fiona had lost just about all its strength before it made landfall. Would that Fiona Grenfall could have said the same for herself. There should have been a separate classification for her just as there were ancient terms of venery for other creatures—a murder of crows, a parliament of owls, a massacre of Grenfalls.

Was she exaggerating? Hardly. She was a woman of science, and the evidence was overwhelming. People seemed to suffer in direct proportion to their proximity to her. She had nearly led Lloyd to suicide; she had almost gotten a poor girl raped; she had broken Judith's heart; she had all but put Ray in the back of a squad car herself. The pattern had continued into her twenties—leading addicts further into their addictions, turning optimists into cynics, robbing dreamers of all their ambitions.

In her thirties, when she was lecturing at Oxford, she had seen a therapist. Most relationships ended poorly, he told her, most lives were fraught with misery; for her to see herself as the cause of any of that was delusional, narcissistic. She had been willing to accept this assessment until six months into their sessions when the therapist told her that he wanted to discontinue her treatment because he had fallen in love with her. She never saw him again.

For a while she thought she could sate her desire for companionship and her talent for destruction by getting involved only with out-and-out bastards. But she was an unreliable judge of character and the bastards she shagged—incels at academic conferences; wiry sociopaths she met in mosh pits; oil company executives; whaleship captains—turned out to be relatively decent human beings who, after she was done with them, became even bigger bastards than she had imagined them to be.

She couldn't stand the idea of hurting Ray again even if she knew it was presumptuous to think he still might fancy her. How had he tracked her down? "Damn, woman, I'm a cop," he'd told her. She had kept up with no one from Evanston, or any other place she had left. The only stage she had trod upon after the Annex was at Wembley Arena, where Prince picked her out of his audience to dance with him; then, after she laughed and told him she couldn't believe how short he was, the Artist Formerly Known as Her Hero angrily shouted, "Git off the stage!" and booted her back into the anonymity of the crowd.

Fiona checked her upstairs and downstairs one more time, searched for any stray bits of dirt, lint, fuzz, but of course there were none. She couldn't help herself: style and cleanliness were her nervous tics. Her mind craved order. She couldn't set a table with a napkin or spoon askew; every meal she served had to be color-coordinated like a bloody Mondrian.

No matter. Come tomorrow, Ray would arrive with his guests between noon and one. They would find the doors unlocked. Lights would be on in the hallway, the dining room, and the main staircase. They would find a refrigerator and freezer full of food, fresh sheets on the beds, towels in the bathrooms. She was leaving them the names of immigration attorneys, neighbors to call in an emergency, lists of restaurants, directions to the Atlantic Superstore, printouts about the nearby high schools, and an ATM card with twenty thousand American dollars on it; she was sure the girl could use it. Once Ray had left, she could work with the girl to help find her a more permanent living situation. Or the girl could just live there however long she wanted: Why not?

Fiona's note was on the dining room table: "I'm so sorry I'll not be able to meet you; I'd been looking so forward to it. But, sad to say, work beckons. For the time being, I'll be at my flat in Halifax—closer to the studio, closer to work. Don't worry about the money; it's the very least I can do."

Fiona would have very much liked to see Ray, the girl too, and the others. Generally, she adored people, which was why she hated having to keep her distance from them. She felt the same sort of regret about being a human being on planet Earth in the twenty-first century: she loved the world even though she knew she was part of the species ruining it. She was glad to be without husband, children, encumbrances of any sort. In theory, she wouldn't have minded having a daughter if she could keep her from the bastards of the world, wouldn't have minded a son if she could have kept him from being a bastard, wouldn't have minded bringing any child into a world that didn't seem intent on destroying itself.

The luggage was already in the trunk of her car. She slipped into her sandals, grabbed the keys from the hook. She opened the door and stepped outside. The air was so fresh, you could almost make believe you weren't standing upon the surface of a doomed planet.

She got in the driver's seat. She put on her sunglasses, opened the windows, lowered the top. She turned the ignition key and was pleased to hear the engine roar to life. It bloody well should have, it was expensive enough; it bloody well didn't half the time, it was a fucking Jaguar, wasn't it?

She shifted into drive, spun the car into a smooth one-eighty, pressed on the gas, then slammed down hard on the brakes. "What the bloody hell?" At the end of the driveway, a black Ford Intrepid was blocking her path.

A man was leaning against the hood of his car. His head was shaved clean and he had a salt-and-pepper goatee. He looked lean and muscular but wore the outfit of a middle-aged American dad—black polo shirt, khaki cargo pants, loafers, an expensive-looking watch, sunglasses up on his head. Stepping out of the car was a girl in a plain white blouse, black tights, and a black skirt, all of which looked like they had been picked out by a man who knew nothing about clothes and was just trying his best not to make a mistake.

At that moment Fiona could have done many things. She could have made a bloody run for it. She could have gunned the engine until these intruders got out of her way. She could have pulled the car onto the lawn, bumpity-bumped down the hill, and driven over the embankment, hoping she wouldn't shoot the suspension all to hell.

Instead, she turned off the engine and got out of her car. "You're a little on the bloody early side, aren't you, Officer Tounslee?" she said.

"Yeah, sorry about that," said Ray. "I just had a notion that if we showed up when you told us to, you'd be gone, and I kinda wanted to see you before that."

"Guilty as charged, officer," she said. "What made you think that?"

"Whenever someone's too specific about when they want you to be somewhere, chances are they're making plans to be someplace else," he said.

"Well, that's my life story, isn't it: the more I plan something, the more likely I am to fuck it up. At any rate, it is good to see you." She kissed his cheek.

"Good to see you too."

Christ—how she longed to fling away all her fears and regrets, to throw her arms around him, to say she was sorry one more time for what had happened in the past. Instead, she took Eleonora in her arms and pressed her close. "You're so very welcome," she said. "We'll do our best to make sure you'll be safe so you can start your new life here."

"Thank you, Ms. Grenfall," Eleonora said.

"And there'll be none of that 'Ms. Grenfall' shit," said Fiona. "There's absolutely no need to thank anyone—really, this is the only decent thing to do." And as she said those words—"the only decent thing to do"—she gasped, remembering Otto Frank welcoming the Van Daans to the Annex: *It's the only decent thing to do.*

"Is something wrong?" Eleonora asked.

"No," Fiona said. "I'm just remembering what someone said to me once when I was—how old are you, Eleonora?"

"Seventeen."

"Right. Seventeen." Fiona looked to Ray. "Do you remember seventeen, Officer Tounslee?"

"I remember the parts I like remembering," said Ray.

Eleonora was only an inch or two shorter than Fiona, but she looked smaller than Fiona had imagined she would be, smaller and more delicate. When she thought of herself at that age—telling her parents she'd be studying at the library, then sneaking out to the cinema with Lloyd; plunking a jug of wine into the trunk of her car, driving to Howard Street, then lying in just her knickers under a blanket on the beach with Ray as they watched the sun rise over the lake; strutting across the Annex stage as Mrs. Van Daan—she pictured someone nearly the same age as she was now. But the truth was that she had been hardly more than a child, hadn't she? In *Anne Frank*, she had worn the sort of dowdy clothes she still felt too young to wear; on her face, she had drawn the lines that had started to appear only a few years ago; she had sprayed the gray in her hair that she somehow had managed to avoid. They all thought they had been so bloody clever, but they had merely been playing at being adults, hadn't they—living in a world where men like Lloyd Crowder and Tyrus Densmore made them think they were grown up to take advantage of the fact that they were really still just children. How many years had she spent feeling awful for what she had done when she had taken barely a moment to register what had been done to her—to all of them?

She had thought she had known so much of the world, or at least Lloyd had fooled her into thinking she did. How much more of that world had Eleonora seen by now? She remembered pleading with Lloyd back in England—no, no, everything would be all right, wouldn't it, don't throw yourself off a building, don't take those pills, life was worth living, wasn't it? She remembered tapping the back window of a squad car, the blank expression on Ray's face as he got out of her car for the last time. She remembered the Annex—that place where they acted out roles in a play, having no idea they were rehearsing what their lives would be like, all those little dramas returning for unwanted encores, this time performed with the backdrop gone and the stage ripped out from underneath them. She thought of the families they had played—hidden away in their Annex, fighting each other because there was no way to fight the bloody Nazis. She thought of the story she had read about Eleonora escaping to America. She imagined the girl hiding in a temple, then riding away from the country she thought would protect her. They were all survivors, weren't they? Anne Frank had said that what had been done couldn't be undone, but the point was to make sure it never happened again. The poor girl had been wrong, though, hadn't she? It just kept happening, over and over again.

Fiona didn't cry easily. She was almost morally opposed to sentimental or maudlin displays. And yet, as she studied the face of this dark-eyed, dark-haired girl, as she looked at Ray, imagining the boy he had been, as she thought about how young she was when she lost him, the sobs rushed forth.

She held Eleonora, and Ray put his arms around the both of them. She laughed, but the laughter felt like crying too. She tossed her head back and looked up at the sky. It was clear and blue, but her eyes were so full of tears that the sky was filled with tiny rainbows.

Elsewhere—not all that far away, really—the first sections of a wall were being erected on the United States' southern border. Elsewhere, a good deal farther away, there was a crack in an ice shelf in Antarctica and a chunk the size of New York City would soon break loose. Elsewhere, neo-Nazis were converging on the campus of the University of Virginia in Charlottesville. Elsewhere, Declan was in a courtroom hallway, starting letters to Patricia that he kept ripping up; Carrie was on a train back to Chicago with her phone switched off while Franklin, who had just gotten back home, was pacing his floor, leaving messages for Carrie until her mailbox was full; Rob was holding an impromptu press conference, brandishing pages from a diary and saying that the woman who had accused him of planning her assault had always been troubled and he hoped she'd get the care she needed; Asya was in a car with Laurence, driving out of town while journalists staked out her home; Jeremy Horvath was in his study, rewriting his sermon; Judith and her wife, Lourdes, were flying a kite with their daughters at Lunt Avenue Beach; Eileen was in her childhood bedroom with the door closed, ignoring her mother's shouts while she scrolled through ads for apartments in Washington, D.C.; Calvin was pouring liquor down his toilet as he tried to stop thinking about the last time he saw Todd; Mr. and Mrs. Charles Newson were holding hands and standing silently over their son Trey's grave.

Elsewhere, three bird species had already gone extinct this very year; wildfires were blazing in California; floods were pouring down in Asia; a hurricane was ravaging the Carolinas; and in a school somewhere in America, a girl was getting ready to play Anne Frank and feeling sad that it would be over so soon. But in front of a nineteenth-century farmhouse in New Glasgow at the edge of North America, on a windless, late-summer day, a woman, a man she had known long ago, and a girl she had just met were standing beneath the brilliant blue sky, knowing they might have no hope to change anyone's future but their own, and for now that would have to be enough.

Soon there would be time to talk about everything that had happened—both to them and the world they were living in—and to discuss how they would proceed from here. But, for now, there were practicalities to attend to, weren't there? The man and the girl had been on the road for some time; no doubt they were hungry, no doubt they could use something to drink, no doubt they needed to shower and change and find a place to put their car.

Fiona cleared her throat. She wiped her cheeks, then her eyes. She took both Eleonora and Ray by the hand and led them up the path toward home.

"Come on, then," she said.

ACKNOWLEDGMENTS

The seed for this novel was planted a number of years back at a bar in L.A. during a conversation with two old friends I'd acted alongside when we were kids. Although I don't remember all the details of our exchange, the thing that has stuck with me is the enduring power of friendship and its ability to mitigate even the darkest memories. In that spirit, I'd like to acknowledge all those I've met along the way whose generosity and kindness have contributed to the creation of this novel.

A huge thank you to Anjali Singh, whose keen intelligence and menschiness led me to my hilarious and indefatigable agent, Stéphanie Abou, who in turn led me to this novel's brilliant, eagle-eyed editor, Elizabeth Ellis.

I remain forever indebted to Lali Morris, my first director, who taught me to love art and collaboration, and who continues to inspire me to this very day; to Cindy Spiegel, for her genius, her counsel, and her friendship; and to Marly Rusoff, one of the greatest champions a writer could have.

Thanks to the friends who managed to keep me sane during the writing and editing process—Paul Creamer, for the stories, the phone calls, and the texts; Kate Mattson, for her enduring discernment of Whiches; Jerome Kramer, for being the most astute reader I've ever known; and Robin Chaplik for maintaining the same decency and humor that she had when I first met her back in the '80s.

Thanks to the members of my pod—my wife, Beate, and my daughters, Nora and Solveig, and our dog, Oscar—for facing everything 2020 and 2021 threw at them with love, patience, and grace. And to Julie B. and Sylvie Langer for always being there during those difficult months.

Thanks for reasons too numerous to catalog here to Joan Afton, Dan Beers, John Cody, Pam Cytrynbaum, Pat Dunne, Sean Dwyer, Gina Fattore, John Fink, Dan Friedman, Jennifer Gilmore, Anna Goldenberg,

Julianne Hausler, Sanja Karabegovic, Kristin Kloberdanz, Jim Lash, Mike Lenehan, Ellen Mason, Doug Matejka, Charlie Meyerson, Jordan Moss, June Newberry, Tina Pohlman, Adrianne and Steven Roderick, Wendy Salinger, Liza Schoenfein, Jeff and Sila Shaman, Alison True, Anya Ulinich, and Talya Zax.

And thanks to Barbara Darko, Daniel Loedel, and everyone at Bloomsbury for welcoming me to a new home, and to Jodi Rudoren, Irene Katz Connelly, Rachel Fishman Feddersen, Mira Fox, PJ Grisar, and the *Forward* for their support.

This novel was written and edited on the B, C, 1, 2, and 3 train lines, and at Cafe Amrita, Demitasse Coffee & Tea, Dulceria, M.A.C.C., Montroussier, Tre Kronor, and various park benches and picnic tables in and around Central Park. Thanks to everyone there for creating a cyclorama of sorts that helped me to imagine this novel.

A NOTE ON THE AUTHOR

ADAM LANGER is a journalist, an editor, a podcast producer, and the author of a memoir and five novels, including *The Washington Story*, *Ellington Boulevard*, *The Thieves of Manhattan*, *The Salinger Contract*, and the internationally bestselling novel *Crossing California*, which was described in the *Chicago Tribune* by James Atlas as "the most vivid novel about Chicago since Saul Bellow's *Herzog* and the most ambitious debut set in Chicago since Philip Roth's *Letting Go*." Formerly an executive editor at *Book* magazine and a frequent contributor to the *New York Times*, he currently serves as executive editor at the *Forward*.